Romantic Suspense

Danger. Passion. Drama.

Montana Abduction Rescue
Jodie Bailey

Showdown In The Rockies
Kathleen Tailer

MILLS & BOON

Jodie Bailey is acknowledged as the author of this work

MONTANA ABDUCTION RESCUE
© 2024 by Harlequin Enterprises ULC
Philippine Copyright 2024
Australian Copyright 2024
New Zealand Copyright 2024

First Published 2024
First Australian Paperback Edition 2024
ISBN 978 1 038 91748 5

SHOWDOWN IN THE ROCKIES
© 2024 by Kathleen Tailer
Philippine Copyright 2024
Australian Copyright 2024
New Zealand Copyright 2024

First Published 2024
First Australian Paperback Edition 2024
ISBN 978 1 038 91748 5

MIX
Paper | Supporting
responsible forestry
FSC® C001695

Published by
Harlequin Mills & Boon
An imprint of Harlequin Enterprises (Australia) Pty Limited
(ABN 47 001 180 918), a subsidiary of HarperCollins
Publishers Australia Pty Limited
(ABN 36 009 913 517)
Level 19, 201 Elizabeth Street
SYDNEY NSW 2000 AUSTRALIA

Cover art used by arrangement with Harlequin Books S.A.. All rights reserved.

Printed and bound in Australia by McPherson's Printing Group

Montana Abduction Rescue

Jodie Bailey

MILLS & BOON

Jodie Bailey writes novels about freedom and the heroes who fight for it. Her novel *Crossfire* won a 2015 RT Reviewers' Choice Best Book Award. She is convinced a camping trip to the beach with her family, a good cup of coffee and a great book can cure all ills. Jodie lives in North Carolina with her husband, her daughter and two dogs.

Visit the Author Profile page
at millsandboon.com.au for more titles.

Thine eyes did see my substance,
yet being unperfect; and in thy book all my members
were written, which in continuance were fashioned,
when as yet there was none of them.
—*Psalm* 139:16

DEDICATION

To Carole, Jessica, Laura, Lissa, and Shannon...

For the prayers and the brainstorms and the food
and most definitely the laughter.

Also, did I mention the food?

I love you, ladies!
Here's to many more years of all of the above!

Chapter One

He should have known this was a trap.

Ian Carpenter sped down a winding back road near Glacier National Park, pushing his old reliable pickup to the limits of its capabilities as he raced to save himself from his pursuers.

What was happening? The threat to his life had ended three months earlier when Ronnie Thornton died in prison, the last member of a crime family whose threats had driven Ian to take refuge in witness protection. It should have been safe for him to return to his hometown.

It wasn't.

Behind him, a sleek sedan kept pace, toying with him. The driver raced up on his bumper then backed off before charging again. Likely, he was searching for the right place to clip Ian's pickup and spin him off the mountain.

He had to get off the road and to good cover before that happened or they barreled into a populated area and put others at risk. Glacierville, Montana, rested peacefully in the valley, and the last thing he wanted was to see an innocent family caught up in this wild chase, the victims of whoever was running him down.

Gripping the steering wheel, Ian took a curve at a speed that made his palms sweat. Only his prior training with the Peak County Sheriff's Department kept the truck from hurtling off the mountain.

His pursuer misjudged the curve. The back end of the car slipped to the outside.

Ian didn't slow to watch. He pressed the gas pedal to the floor, trying to reach the one place where he might be safe and help could potentially find him.

There.

The turnoff snuck up on him, and he wrenched the wheel, tearing through brush and past trees onto an old logging road that wound deep into the woods. He winced as branches screeched along the paint of his restored Ford pickup. When he'd first gone into hiding, the vehicle had been his outlet, the physical labor of repairs a way to block his fears and regrets from drowning him.

Best not to worry about a paint job when his life was on the line.

A large metal gate appeared in the center of the road. Ian slammed on the brakes and fish-tailed to a stop just short of the barrier.

This was new.

Guess he was on foot from here.

Grabbing his pistol from a custom pocket on the side of the seat, he shoved the door open and raced into the underbrush. Ian barreled down the rocky hillside toward the densest part of the forest, where a creek cut a ditch at the base of Calham Mountain, about seven miles outside of Glacierville.

When he reached thick underbrush and deep shadows, he pulled his phone from his pocket and surveyed the area, trying to orient himself.

From the logging road above, the sound of gravel under braking tires skittered across his nerves.

He'd gained a lead, but not much.

Heart racing, he opened a new text then typed the number he'd long ago committed to memory. There was no one else who could get him out of whatever this was. 911. At our old place. Outsider

Typing out his old code name nearly knocked

him back two years, but any emotion was drowned by adrenaline and urgency.

He sent the text along with a prayer that Meadow Ames would see it and come immediately.

Not that God had time for his prayers, but it was worth a try.

When he'd been undercover with a multiagency human-trafficking task force led by the US Marshals, Meadow had been his handler. If he ever needed her to back him up, it was now.

Otherwise, he was as good as dead.

Pocketing the phone, he listened. Judging from what sounded like wild elephants crashing through the brush above, there were at least two people in pursuit.

Who were they? This had to be about something other than the undercover op that had taken down the Thornton family's human-trafficking ring. Ronnie, the patriarch, had died awaiting trial in prison three months earlier. His son and their most trusted bodyguard had been killed in an explosion during a takedown gone wrong on the day Ronnie was arrested.

After Ronnie had hired an assassin who'd almost succeeded, Ian had been moved into witness protection, where he'd spent the better part of eighteen months in Texas living as Zeke Donner. With Ronnie dead, he'd been cleared to return to the area, though he'd been hesitant to do so.

Only his cousin's call for help had dragged him back.

Either some unknown foe wanted him dead, or he'd stumbled onto a greater mystery.

Well, he wasn't waiting to find out. Carefully, he crept toward the stream and the footbridge above it. He'd met Meadow there often when he had intel to pass along on the op. He would conceal himself in the underbrush to wait for her and any backup she brought with her.

Hopefully, she'd muster an army.

At the edge of the clearing, Ian stopped and scanned for a good place to hunker down. It would have to be far enough from the water to keep his pursuers from stumbling upon him but close enough for Ian to see Meadow when she arrived. He kept moving, careful not to break branches or disturb leaves.

Behind him and to the left, the sound of movement stopped.

Ian froze. Their stillness would make it easier for anyone listening to hear his movement.

"Hey, Deputy!" The shout rang through the evergreens and echoed off the slope.

Ian's breath caught in his throat. They knew he'd been a Peak County sheriff's deputy.

This wasn't some random act.

He shrank into the underbrush, hardly daring to breathe until his pursuers moved. They were only a few hundred yards away and would easily spot him if he tried to maneuver while they were hunting.

"You aren't getting away from us, traitor!"

Traitor?

Wait. That voice. It was familiar.

Sweat sheened his skin. It couldn't be. Silas Thornton was dead. DNA had identified his body in the rubble of a warehouse after a catastrophic explosion. There was no way he was stalking Ian through the Montana wilds.

Ian inched to the right, angling to see up the slope. Several hundred yards uphill, a woman crossed a narrow clearing, moving parallel to Ian's position.

Recognition jolted through him. Desiree "Des" Phelps had been Ronnie and Silas's chief muscle and their most trusted enforcer. Although built like a ballet dancer, she had the strength of a lion. A seriously angry lion.

Realization burned hot in his veins. They'd been played. After the task force had arrested Ronnie and rounded up his underlings, they'd surrounded a warehouse in Missoula to apprehend Silas and Des. The team tossed several flash-bangs into the building, and one had ignited a fuel tank. Two bodies inside were incinerated, but DNA from two teeth and a toe had identified them as Des and Silas.

Clearly, the pair had sacrificed their own body parts in order to avoid prison, and now they were hot on his trail.

As they began to stalk the underbrush again, Ian eased along as well, keeping to the thick vegetation along the creek as he moved away from them.

An animal startled in the bushes nearby, racing up the slope.

A gunshot cracked through the trees, and three more followed, slicing through the air only feet from his position and sending panic through his system at the remembered piercing of a bullet that had nearly ended his life.

This was it. He was done.

Defenseless.

Paralyzed by fear.

Closing his eyes, Ian waited for death.

★ ★ ★

"This was a colossal waste of time." Deputy US Marshal Meadow Ames sat back in her chair and reached over her head, trying to stretch the tension from her shoulders. She'd been holed up in a conference room at the Glacierville, Montana, police department all day, hunched over computer files and physical files, studying the murder of Henry Mulder until her neck ached and her eyes burned.

Across the table, Elk Valley, Wyoming, police officer Rocco Manelli dragged his hands down his face. He looked as exhausted as Meadow felt. Like Meadow, Rocky was a member of the Mountain Country K-9 Unit, composed of law enforcement officials from across several Rocky Mountain states. "I've chased suspects for miles on foot and not been this exhausted." At his feet, his K-9 partner, a chocolate Lab who specialized in accelerant detection, yawned. Rocco grinned. "Even Cocoa has had enough."

"At least Cocoa is awake." At Meadow's feet, her partner, a vizsla trained in tracking and search and rescue, snored lightly. "Grace zonked out an hour ago." People often mistook Grace for a Weimaraner, although that breed was typically gray while her K-9 partner had a gorgeous rusty coat.

Shutting the laptop the Glacierville PD had provided so they could access the department's electronic files, Rocco gave her a rueful look. "I'm with you. This was a bust."

They'd spent the day digging through evidence and interviews in the homicide case of Henry Mulder, who'd been killed a few months prior by a serial murderer dubbed the Rocky Mountain Killer that Meadow and Rocco's interagency K-9 unit was hunting.

Ten years earlier, the killer's first three victims were found in a barn in Rocco's hometown of Elk Valley, Wyoming, on Valentine's Day. All were in their late teens and early twenties, and all were shot in the chest. They were graduates of Elk Valley High School and members of the now disbanded Young Ranchers Club.

A decade later, the killer was active again. Five months earlier, Henry Mulder had been killed in Glacierville, while Peter Windham had been murdered in Colorado. More recently, Luke Randall had been killed in Idaho. Like the first three victims, they were each shot in the chest and found in a barn. They, too, were EVHS grads and former YRC members.

There was a chilling difference in the latest three killings, however. Stabbed into the new victims was the same typed note: *They got what they deserved. More to come across the Rockies. And I'm saving the best for last.*

In response to the murders, FBI Supervisory Special Agent Chase Rawlston had been tasked with heading the Mountain Country K-9 Unit. Fifteen K-9 officers from various federal, state and local agencies were working together to hunt down the killer before he could strike again.

Combing through the files in Glacierville had led to nothing but a literal pain in Meadow's neck. Neither she nor Rocco had taken a break since lunch, when they'd dashed to a café up the street for sandwiches then out to their SUVs to feed the K-9s and to check their phones, which the police department didn't allow inside rooms with evidence after a leak of confidential information several years before. Meadow longed for sunlight and a muscle-stretching run, even though the July weather was unusually warm.

They retrieved their weapons from locked

storage, turned in the borrowed laptops and files, then headed into late-afternoon sunlight.

Rocco slid sunglasses onto his face. "You headed to your house?"

While the MCKU was investigating, home base was the Elk Valley Chateau Hotel in Elk Valley, where the first murders had occurred. That HQ was almost fourteen hours away, so they'd been authorized to stay in Glacierville while they dug into the Mulder homicide.

Because Meadow's home was only about thirty minutes from Glacierville, on the road to Missoula, she'd opened it up to members of the unit who were in the area, setting up a space in the guest room for the team members and their K-9 partners. "I am. You heading that way or going somewhere else first?"

Rocco glanced at his watch and then at the sky, where dark clouds were piling up on the western horizon. "I think I'll drive around and admire the scenery, mull over what we read today and what we saw at the crime scene yesterday. Give me a chance to clear my head. Might stop and eat at the farm-to-table place you told me about. All you ever have when somebody bunks at your house is cereal."

"You're the only one on the team who complains, food snob, but I understand wanting to take in the scenery. Just keep an eye on the weather." The mountains around Glacier National Park offered the kind of spectacular views that helped clear her head after a long day of dealing with murder and mayhem. It was one of the reasons she'd accepted the position with the US Marshals office in Missoula, where she'd been based before taking the temporary assignment with the MCKU. "I'll likely be asleep by the time you show up, but you know where the key's hidden. We've got to be up and rolling early since Chase wants a seven a.m. video conference with us all."

"Yes, Mom." Rocco headed for his SUV with Cocoa at his heels. "See you later."

Meadow clicked the button to open the rear of her vehicle, where Grace's custom kennel was located. The SUV had been outfitted with everything from a built-in water bowl to automatic windows and an alarm should the air-conditioning ever shut off while Grace was inside.

The K-9 bounded into the vehicle and settled in as Meadow filled the water bowl then shut the door.

Rocco was backing out when Meadow

climbed into her vehicle. She grabbed her cell phone from the locked glove box and glanced at the screen.

The temperature warning flashed angry red. *Great.* Meadow slipped the phone into its holder, positioned in front of an air vent, and cranked the AC. While it didn't often crack ninety degrees in Glacierville, the day had been unusually warm, and her car had been closed up for longer than normal. She rolled out of town and headed for home, waiting for the phone to cool down and power up.

She peeked at Grace in the rearview then pointed the car south. "You ready for one more night at home?" They'd wrap up odds and ends tomorrow and head back to Elk Valley the next day. It might be a while before she saw home again. The one plant she'd managed to keep alive had given up hope, but she'd watered it the night before and would water it again tonight. It had come back from worse neglect. "So, home, girl?"

Grace tilted her head as though she understood, then found a chew toy and busied herself with it. Grace's training had taught her that inside the vehicle was an off-duty space. Vizslas were known for chewing, and Grace was a champion at destruction if she didn't have something to keep her busy.

Meadow's shoulders had just begun to relax when her phone lit up and pinged repeatedly. She pulled into the parking lot of a coffee shop and popped the device free, flicking the screen to see if she'd missed many calls and emails. She doubted it, given that the team knew to call the police department if an emergency came up while their cell phones were out of reach.

She grimaced at the number of notifications. In the distance, the dark clouds continued to build. If she wanted to beat the coming storm, she'd need to get moving. "I'll try to make this quick, Grace."

The K-9 didn't seem to care. She and her chew toy were perfectly content.

Meadow opened the texts first, since the most urgent messages would be there.

Her fingers froze. Three notifications down was a number she didn't recognize, though the sender was clear.

Outsider.

She'd never expected to see that code name again. It swirled hot and cold around her heart.

Forget the rest of her messages, Ian's 911 took

precedence. She slammed the phone into its cradle, jammed the SUV into Drive and roared out of the parking lot, headed for the mountains between Glacierville and Cattle Bend. Ian wanted to meet in their "old place," where they'd exchanged intel when he was undercover. That meant he was twenty minutes away, in Calham Nature Preserve.

She prayed the entire drive. There was no way to know what the threat was or how long Ian had been in the area.

She gripped the wheel tighter, ignoring the burn behind her heart. There was also no way to know why Ian hadn't reached out when Ronnie Thornton had died and the threat to Ian's life had ended.

He'd remained distant and silent while Meadow had pieced together the heart Ian could never know he'd broken. Despite the fact that he'd repeatedly talked about his aversion to dating and marriage, she'd managed to fall hard for the law enforcement officer with the light brown hair and deep blue eyes. There was something broken about him, something that her own heart had connected with. In the end, she'd wound up shattered when he went into WITSEC, and that pain was only magnified when the threat to his life ended and he didn't reach out.

Until now...when he needed help.

She roared into the parking lot at the trail-head, unsure if she was relieved or disturbed to see no other vehicles. At the rear of the SUV, she pulled her badge over her head and shoved it into her pocket, then removed the MCKU patches from Grace's harness. She had no idea what she was getting into, and sometimes it was safer not to be immediately identified as law enforcement.

She slung a small backpack over her shoulders, checked her sidearm, then plunged down the path toward the creek, where they used to meet when Ian was undercover and she was his handler. It was the one place he'd felt truly safe when they were working together on the human-trafficking task force, the one place they'd felt free to openly talk about everything from the case to their personal lives.

Where they'd become friends.

And where her feelings had grown deeper as time passed, while his had stayed firmly in friend territory.

Right now was the wrong time to be leading with her heart. Besides, she'd put her feelings for Ian on ice when he'd disappeared into WITSEC.

As Meadow neared the creek, she stepped off the trail to follow a narrow footpath that disappeared beneath the bridge.

No one was near.

Motioning for Grace to sit, Meadow listened, wary of calling Ian's name. Without knowing the nature of the threat, her options were limited. Calling out could put them in jeopardy.

If she had something of Ian's for Grace to sniff, she could set her partner onto his trail. Unfortunately, all she had was memories.

Thunder rumbled in the distance, and wind tangled the treetops.

She clucked to Grace, who trotted beside her as she inspected the clearing. Up the hill, someone had clearly walked through the underbrush.

Ian? Or someone else?

She carefully followed the trail, eyeing the ground and the bushes until…

A cell phone.

It felt as though her heart stopped for several beats as she knelt and inspected the phone, then flipped it over. It must have fallen from a pocket, landing on its corner. The screen was shattered, and the device appeared unusable.

It either belonged to Ian, or to whoever had threatened him.

She'd take her chances.

She collected the phone, let Grace scent it, then gave her partner a moment to pick up a trail.

Nose to the ground, Grace sniffed in a small circle, then took off parallel to the creek, following a barely there path through the underbrush. After pausing to regain the scent, she headed off again with Meadow at her heels.

With a jerk on her leash, Grace pulled toward the creek then stopped, looking up and down the bank. No scent.

Whoever they'd been trailing had crossed about two hundred yards up from the bridge, where the underbrush was thick. Where were they heading now? Were they friend or foe?

She led Grace through the water and toward a thick stand of brush about halfway up the hill.

She headed into the deepening shadows and paused to scan the sky. The clouds were thickening and—

Something rustled in the trees behind her.

A hand clamped over her mouth.

Chapter Two

Ian grunted as Meadow's elbow drove back into his ribs.

She spun, gun in hand, and aimed at his center mass before he could process what had happened. Beside her, a red dog that looked like an oversize hound took an attack position, growling low.

Yep. He'd forgotten how quick she was, and his recovery from a near panic attack had him at a disadvantage. He held his hands out to his sides, ribs aching. "It's me."

Eyes wide, she lowered her weapon, sliding it into her hip holster reflexively. "What's going on?" She reached toward him, hand hovering near his shoulder as though she wasn't sure he was real. "What's the danger?"

Ian took his first deep breath in what felt like days. "We need to get to shelter first. I've been hiding for an hour, and I'm not sure where they are." He dipped his chin toward the dog. "Can you call off the bodyguard?"

One hand motion reset the dog's demeanor. The animal sat, gaze on Meadow, waiting for the next command.

Ian watched as well. Meadow Ames was everything Ian had tried to forget. Her dark hair was up in a ponytail, which made her blue eyes even more haunting than his dreams remembered.

Ian shook away the thought. There was no time for a reunion, not with armed assailants stalking the woods. "Two shooters with pistols out here. Not sure where they went, but I know they're after me specifically." He could save the shocking revelation of who was stalking him for later. It was too much to get into when he wasn't sure how Silas and Des were alive. "How far away are you parked?"

The sky shook with thunder, and raindrops dotted the ground. Hopefully the noise would cover their escape.

Meadow turned, leading the way toward the creek. "I'm at the parking lot at the trailhead, so it's at least a half mile to—"

Up the hill to the left, the underbrush

crashed. A cascade of rocks rolled down the slope and splashed into the creek.

Meadow whirled and ducked into the brush, dragging Ian down with one hand and the dog down with the other.

They crouched in the thicket, both listening. Even the dog's floppy ears were raised slightly. The animal lifted its nose and sniffed the air, still watching Meadow.

This was no ordinary dog. If he had to guess, he'd say Meadow had transferred to a K-9 unit, though her clothing and the dog's vest were nondescript, making it impossible to identify who she was affiliated with.

About a hundred yards away, something big moved through the brush, too close for comfort.

Meadow drew her sidearm.

Ian did the same.

The dog sat at attention.

"Hey, traitor!" The male voice rang through the trees, echoing off the mountain. It came from above and behind, not from where the initial rustlings were. "You can't stay out here all night. Might be better to take your chances with us than with whatever nature wants to throw at you."

It was clear neither Silas nor Des knew exactly where they were hiding, but the pair was closing in.

Ian and Meadow huddled deeper into the brush. At least it was summer and the foliage was thick. If it was winter, he'd already be dead.

Fat raindrops smashed cool against Ian's skin. The waning day and dark clouds left deep shadows. Still, if either of their assailants got too close, Ian and Meadow would be easy to spot.

To the left, the rustling drew nearer.

The dog growled low in her throat, a deep rumble that carried through the forest stillness.

The rustling stopped.

An explosion of sound flurried to the left and a woman—Des—yelled. "Bear! Get out!" Branches rattled and rocks rolled and bounced down the hill.

Overhead, thunder crashed and the sky opened up. A torrent of water seemed to fall all at once, the rain drowning out the sound of the fleeing assailants.

But not loudly enough to drown out a stream of expletives screamed from above. "We aren't leaving, Deputy! We know you're here!"

Despite the shouted threat, Des and Silas

bolted, shadows in the rain, heading toward the logging road.

Meadow shoved her bangs out of her face. "What now? They aren't wrong about wild animals roaming around, and I also don't like the idea of trailing those two when we have no idea where they'll take cover."

Neither did he, and he had a better idea anyway. He'd been heading for shelter when Meadow had found him. "If you trust me, I know a place we can lie low until the storm passes and we can get some backup in here and get out. I'd say we're less than a mile from it."

"Sounds good to me. Lead the way."

The rain had already soaked them to the bone, and mud was rapidly making the ground more difficult to traverse. They made their way to the creek and crossed, hurrying along the thin open area at the bank as the rushing water greedily accepted the rain. At least the deluge would wipe away any trace of their path. Hopefully, it would keep up until they reached safety.

What felt like hours later, Ian gently slid vines and overgrowth to the side of a metal door built into the slope and flipped the dials on an all-weather padlock. He ushered Meadow into an old bunker then dragged the vegetation back over the opening and shut the door, shoving a huge bar into place to bolt it from the inside and hanging the padlock from a hook beside it.

The cavernous space was pitch-black and eerily silent after the roar of the rain. The air was stale and musty, but it was breathable. The ventilation fan had died long ago, but enough air leaked through the system to keep them alive.

A soft rustle, then a beam of light cut through the inky darkness as Meadow shone a flashlight. "Is this one of the old World War II bunkers?" She illuminated the ceiling, walls and floor of the space, which was about fifteen feet wide and thirty feet deep. Carved out of what was once a cave, the bunker had been built to provide shelter in case of attack during one of the most terrifying times in world history.

Ian reached for his cell phone, but it was no longer in his pocket. He turned a slow circle. Maybe he'd dropped it in—

Meadow held out her hand, his cell phone in her palm. "I found it in the brush. It's how Grace tracked you, but I'm pretty sure it's a brick now."

He inspected the device then tossed it onto a metal table. How was he going to get in touch with his cousin if his phone was toast?

That was a worry for later. He'd have to survive if he wanted to find out what had frightened Brooke. "Shine your light to the back wall." Ian strode deeper into the space, following her illuminated path, and opened a metal cabinet anchored to the rear wall. He dug out a small oil hurricane lantern and waterproof matches, quickly lighting the lamp to dispel the darkness.

Meadow moved her thumbs over her phone's screen, then grimaced. "I've got zero signal in here."

"I normally get a bar or two, but the rain must be hindering the signal."

"Maybe." Meadow looked around the room. "How did you know this was here?"

Sliding the lantern to the center of the table, Ian glanced around the space he'd hoped to never see again. "Remember how, when I was undercover, I told you I had a place to go where no one could find me?" He held out his hands and turned slowly as if showing off a brand new vacation home. "Here we are. Chateau Carpenter, the envy of billionaires the world around."

Meadow sniffed what sounded like a short laugh, then let the dog off of the leash so she could explore the space. Sliding a backpack from her shoulders, she surveyed the room. "You stocked this place?"

"A few canned goods. A few sets of clothes. A go bag. Just enough to get by for a few days if I ever had to get out quick." He jerked a thumb toward a second metal door in the back wall. "There's a smaller room back there where I stashed my gear. You can go in there and change into something dry. The clothes will definitely be too big for you, but it's better than sitting around and freezing in wet jeans."

"I keep clothes in my backpack." She eyed him as though she was about to say something more...or as though she couldn't believe she was actually standing in his presence.

"Yes?" They'd always been honest with each other in the past. It had been a requirement if he wanted to survive his time undercover. He nearly hadn't, but that wasn't her fault. She'd done all she could to protect him. If she was thinking things now, he wanted to hear them.

"Just getting adjusted to seeing you."

Ian sucked in air through his teeth. As he had settled into his new life in Texas, carving out a space where he was comfortable and safe in more ways than one, his colleagues had been left in the dark. His disappearance into WIT-

SEC and his decision not to return when the threat was over had likely gone unnoticed by his blood family, but Meadow...

She'd definitely noticed.

He'd considered reaching out, but it was better for both of them if he kept his distance. They'd parted as friends. She didn't need to know she'd haunted his dreams.

And he didn't need to entertain any illusions there could ever be something between them. Once she knew him well, she'd realize he wasn't worth the effort, and he couldn't handle that kind of heartbreak. There had been more than enough abandonment in his life.

Still, he owed her an apology.

Before he could speak, she called to the K-9, who trotted to her side. Meadow walked into the back room, shutting the door behind them.

The past hour had been a shock for both of them. Neither of them had awakened assuming the day would end with them together in an abandoned bunker after shots were fired.

Shots fired. At him. A nightmare he'd never wanted to relive. Terror had paralyzed him flat to the ground in the brush, almost costing him his life.

It had taken long minutes for the panic attack

to subside, long minutes in which Des or Silas could have found him and ended him.

Yet they hadn't.

Ian went to the exterior door and checked the bolt, his jaw tight. It was almost enough to make him believe God actually cared.

Almost. But not quite. People liked to talk about God being a Father, but fathers and mothers were unreliable and cruel. He wanted no more of that. God. The Creator was easy to believe in. Jesus and salvation? Sure. That was for the whole world. But a God who cared specifically and personally about him?

Nah. Nobody cared that much about him, no matter what the guys who'd led chapels on the rodeo circuit had said.

No matter that Meadow Ames had once made him imagine, for only a moment, that someone might.

Texting her was a mistake. He should have handled this himself.

He should have told her to bring reinforcements.

He should have done a lot of things.

But he hadn't, and now, not only was his life on the line, but he'd dragged Meadow right alongside him into danger.

★ ★ ★

The backup hiking pants and athletic shirt she kept in her day pack had saved her more than once. Ruefully, she inspected a few scratches on her arms before pulling her sleeves down over them. Given the terrain they'd crossed, she was grateful there were only a couple of small cuts.

Well, what was done was done. She hung her clothes on hooks along the wall. They wouldn't dry completely in this damp, enclosed space, but they might be less soaked by the time she crammed them into her pack again.

By the light of her flashlight, she surveyed the room. The space hollowed out of the mountain was an arch covered by corrugated aluminum and supported by thick metal poles. While the outer room held built-in shelves and a metal table and chairs, this one had metal bunks built into the wall. Ian had tossed a couple of blankets and some clothes in vacuum-sealed bags onto the bed frames. Otherwise, the room was empty.

She glanced at her phone. Still no signal. If she could reach Rocco for backup, she'd feel a whole lot better. There was no telling how long he'd wander around before he figured out she was "missing" and tracked her vehicle.

Until then, she and Ian were on their own.

With no way of knowing who was taking potshots at Ian or where they were, leaving this safe haven would be foolish.

She pulled the band from her ponytail, squeezed out the water and tied her hair back again.

Her hand stopped halfway through the motion.

The person in the woods had called Ian *traitor. Deputy.* Her eyebrows drew together. Either someone from his past had spotted him, or someone connected to the Thornton family knew he'd returned to the area.

But anyone from the op who'd want him dead was dead themselves.

And why was Ian in the area in the first place?

She shoved her phone into a pocket on her pants and headed to the outer room.

Ian had pulled the light jacket off and was inspecting his hands, which bore scratches of their own. He looked up when she came in. "Feel better?"

"I do." She was more concerned about him. Ian had nearly been killed over a year and a half ago when Ronnie Thornton managed to pull some strings from prison. Being pursued by gun-toting assailants today had to have taken its toll. "Did they shoot at you?"

He studied his hands carefully in the thin light, his expression tense. "They shot at a rabbit I spooked out of the bushes." His voice was strained.

Meadow waited, but he offered nothing more. Plenty of people who'd suffered the kind of pain and recovery he'd endured had lingering PTSD. Had he frozen in the woods? Panicked?

He'd taken a bullet to the torso and lost his spleen shortly after their investigation concluded, courtesy of one of Ronnie's henchmen, prompting federal authorities to offer him protection until the trial and beyond. Sitting vigil in the waiting room of the hospital while Ian fought for his life wasn't a memory Meadow cherished.

It wasn't one she wanted to think about now either. "Something wrong with your hand?"

"Got a splinter in my palm. It'll work itself out."

"Let me see." She pulled a chair around and sat in front of him. "You have a first aid kit, I assume?"

He jerked his head toward the table, where a small plastic box rested.

Opening it up, Meadow donned gloves and retrieved tweezers and ointment. She took his hand. Even through the gloves, his skin was warm.

Focusing on the splinter instead of the man, she cleared her throat. "You pack a thorough first aid kit."

"I was a medic in the army before I was a deputy." He flinched as she dug the tweezers in.

Yet another little tidbit she hadn't known about the man she'd once cared about and maybe even…

No. That was the past. She'd never told him her feelings. He'd repeatedly spoken of his aversion to dating and marriage, of how he planned to live life as a bachelor. His family trauma ran deep, so Meadow had worked hard to guard her heart against any growing feelings. Obviously, his own heart had been as cold as he'd always said, or he'd have reached out to her after Ronnie died. As much as touching him sent a *zing* through her veins, she needed to focus on now. Developing or growing feelings for a man who would never return them would only lead to heartache.

Meadow worked quickly, removing the splinter and applying ointment. Pulling off the gloves inside out, she dropped them on the lid of the kit. "All done."

"Thanks." Stiffly, Ian stood and walked away, shutting the door to the rear room behind him. When he came back, he was dressed in a black hooded sweatshirt and sweatpants. He sat at the table and repacked the first aid kit. "You have questions." He glanced at her and almost smiled, the shadows of the lantern flickering across his face. "I can tell because your personality right now is…" He ran his hand palm-down through the air, as though she'd flatlined. "I know you. You're louder and more take-charge than this."

Meadow rested her hands on the cold metal table. "I don't even know where to start." The question burning her throat was the last one she'd ask. *With Ronnie dead, you were free to come out of hiding. Why didn't you reach out?*

The only conclusion was that he hadn't stayed away because of his safety, but because of her.

They'd been acquaintances before his undercover mission and had grown into friends during it. The least he could have done would have been to let her know he was safe and well when the threat went away.

Except, perhaps the threat hadn't died. "Who

was stalking around in the woods? They called you *Deputy. Traitor.* Somebody from your past? Before the Thornton op drove you into hiding?"

"If only." Ian shook his head. "It was Silas and Des."

Meadow sat back hard against the chair. *Impossible.* "Silas and Des are dead. There's DNA to prove it."

"We had teeth and a toe. Not hard to sacrifice those if you're desperate to evade capture. It's possible the explosion that we thought killed them wasn't an accidental detonation but was part of an escape plan Silas and Des had set up from the start. After all, they led us to that warehouse. They controlled the chase. Maybe we followed them where they wanted, and we believed what they wanted us to believe. Maybe they've been lying low, waiting for me to return."

If she didn't sound like herself, neither did he. Ian had always had a swagger about him, a brash recklessness that rode the edge of dangerous. It was one of the reasons she'd suggested him for the undercover op.

Now he was subdued. Quiet.

For the first time, she took a good look at

him. During the op, he'd worn a beard and had kept his hair long. He must have gone for the clean-shaven look in his new life. He currently sported a five-o'clock shadow, and his brown hair was shorter, tousled on top where he'd hand-dried it after their dash through the rain.

But his eyes... They were still a striking blue, although stress had carved lines at the corners that weren't there before. The story of his difficulties undercover and his dance with death were etched there.

She wanted to comfort the friend he'd been, but after over a year and a half of zero communication, he was an odd combination of confidant and stranger. She wasn't sure what to do with that, so she sat with her hands clasped on the cold metal, trying to digest what was happening. "Are you sure it was them?"

"I saw them both, plain as could be." He pushed away from the table and stood, pacing to the wall. Running his hand down the back of his hair, he stared at a shelf containing several large plastic boxes. "I should have been more careful."

"Careful of what? Who would have suspected that two dead people would come after you?" How had this happened? DNA from teeth and a toe had indicated Ronnie Thornton's son and second-in-command had died in that explosion along with his enforcer. So many questions. Either someone involved with the investigation was dirty or...

She shuddered to think much further, although Ian had hinted at it earlier. Silas had been identified by a toe recovered at the scene. Des by two teeth. The explosion had been so violent that very little else remained. It was possible they'd...

She shuddered at the idea someone would mutilate themselves in order to avoid arrest. But when it was life in prison versus life without a toe? She wouldn't put it past either of them. "So what really happened in that warehouse?"

Ian shrugged. "Who knows? Like I said, it could have been a fallback plan all along. They led us to that warehouse, so it could have been an elaborate setup."

"But how did they find you?"

"I have no idea. I thought it was safe to come back, at least for a few days."

Even though he'd stayed away initially. "Why come back now?" *Without telling me?*

"My cousin Brooke reached out. She thinks a friend is in trouble and asked me to poke around before she reaches out to the authorities in case she's wrong."

"Your cousin?" Meadow purposely infused her voice with confusion. In the hospital, while he was medicated and out of his head with pain, he'd told her awful stories about his family. But when he'd been fully awake, he'd shown no recollection of revealing his secrets. She'd pretended ignorance until the day he'd vanished. Out of respect for his privacy, she'd maintain the pretense now. "You always told me, told everyone, that you don't have any living relatives."

"Aside from my cousin, there are none who want to claim me and none I want to claim." He cleared his throat and resumed his seat. "I always kept in touch with one cousin. Brooke. She's twelve years younger than me, just turned nineteen. Always looked up to me for some reason." He stared at the table, tapping his finger on the corner of the first aid kit. "When I walked away and joined the army, she was the only one who wrote. The only one who cared. She was just a kid, but she made the effort and never stopped."

Meadow didn't know how to respond to his obvious pain.

Ian finally met her gaze, his expression almost tortured. "When Ronnie died, I reached out to her. Told her I was alive and was staying in Texas, where I was working with a vet to rehab horses for the rodeo circuit. I liked it there. I had friends. It was a new start, away from here and from the family who'd hurt me." His gaze flicked away from her and then back. "I should have told her to talk to the cops about her friend. I shouldn't have come back."

"You didn't know about Silas and—"

"Still. I should have been more careful. And now I've dragged you into it." His eyebrows drew together. "I never should have called you. It put you in the line of fire and—"

"Never apologize for asking for help." This time, she dared to touch him. Reaching across the table, she rested her hand on his. "I once promised to be by your side until the end, and it's not over yet, so here I—"

The door rattled and something crashed against it.

They both rose, and Grace leaped up, growling low at the door. Meadow hissed a command that caused her partner to sit, then reached for her pistol as a muffled voice drifted through the metal barrier.

"If you're in there, Deputy, you're not coming out alive."

Chapter Three

Ian clamped down on angry words he never said anymore. He might not be sure God actually cared about him, but he did recognize his need to respect the Almighty's rules. He'd given up a lot of things the year before when he'd started going to chapel on the rodeo circuit, but his mouth had proven the toughest thing to tame, especially under stress.

Right now, *stress* was all he had.

Something pounded against the door. "You should know by now we won't give up."

Meadow and Ian whipped toward each other. They were at the disadvantage in this game. Des and Silas knew they were somewhere in the vicinity, though they might be guessing about their presence in the bunker. Meadow and Ian had no intel, no way of reaching the outside world. Ian had backed them into a corner.

Worse, he'd backed *Meadow* into a corner.

Given his background in law enforcement, getting them into this predicament was inexcusable.

She grabbed his wrist and whispered, "This is not your fault."

Ian tightened his grip on his pistol and balled his other fist, tugging from her grasp. That was debatable, but not at the moment.

Together, by some unspoken signal, they crept to the door. The voices outside were muffled but audible, discussing their strategy.

"You can't be sure he's in there." Des's voice was smooth as silk, a slight Creole Louisiana accent threading through the words.

"Where else would he be?" As much as Silas looked like he'd swaggered straight out of a *Sopranos* episode, his accent was all Lower Alabama. He cultivated a look and persona designed to make people underestimate him, but he was deviously intelligent. If he was ever seen bumbling around, it was to throw his prey off balance. "Know what? I'm not hanging around out here too long waiting on him to show himself. It's getting dark, and I don't have a rifle on me to handle bear. Or other big game."

There was no response. Likely, Des was close to the door, listening for movement. The dim lantern light didn't reach that far, but any noise above breathing would likely pass through the minuscule gaps around the metal door.

Never had Ian heard his own breaths so clearly. He tried to keep them shallow. A few feet away, Meadow did the same. She looked at him, gun low and at the ready. He'd trusted her with his life before, and here he was doing it again.

Only this time, hers was in his hands as well.

"We'll come back tomorrow," Des finally said. If they were leaving, that would give Meadow and him time to— "But we're sealing off the door in case he's really in there."

Meadow met his eye and winced.

Des was crafty. Silas had always been the business-minded one while Des was the tactical one. Outside, metal screeched on metal. A former New Orleans cop, Des still carried handcuffs as her quick way of restraining anyone who got in her way. Likely, she'd threaded those cuffs through the holes for the padlock to lock the entrance.

Someone pounded on the door. Silas's voice followed. "See you in the morning, traitor."

The sounds of movement faded, and Ian's shoulders sagged.

With two fingers, Meadow motioned for him to follow. She walked through the bunker and into the back room, as far as they could get from the door. "Thoughts?"

"We're stuck in here until they come back."

"*If* they come back." She stared toward the main entry, her face a mask of determination. "They weren't certain we're here. Pretty sure all of the blustering was a test to see if we'd react." She checked her phone then shoved it into her pocket, clearly frustrated with the lack of signal. "Plan?"

"They can't get in here without some serious power tools. This place was designed to withstand a bomb blast. It might be old, but it's solid. I made sure when I first set it up as a refuge. We've got enough food and water for a week. We won't run out of oxygen because the air…"

Air.

Their ticket to an escape. "I know how to get out of here, but we'll have to wait until dark." Ian pointed to a wall-mounted fan near the top bunk, less than two feet square. "You aren't claustrophobic are you?"

"Nope." She followed the line of his finger. "Ventilation system?"

"It leads to the outside, and hopefully the

opening hasn't been buried by a rock slide. The fact we're breathing says it's at least partially open." Hopefully it was also hidden enough to keep Silas and Des from finding it. If either of them thought long and hard, they'd realize the shaft existed. If they didn't already know, they'd definitely figure it out by morning.

Meadow was already climbing the bunk, her partner sitting patiently to the side. "Screwdriver?"

"Will a knife work?" He passed his pocketknife to her. She opened it and made quick work of removing the fan. "Kill the lantern. We don't need light leaking out."

Ian obeyed, then felt his way back in the pitch-dark that hung heavy in the bunker. Near Meadow, the inky blackness was softer, though he wouldn't call it light.

After a moment, Meadow's flashlight lit and she descended from the bunk. "It's open, though I can't see the end. There's light coming from somewhere. As soon as it's dark, I'll make my way out and pray they aren't standing there waiting."

"No doubt." It was their only shot, or he wouldn't send her through alone. Given the width of his shoulders, he'd never be able to make the crawl without getting wedged into place.

That and, though he'd never admit it, small spaces weren't his favorite.

Meadow brushed past him and went into the main room. The lantern lit shortly after. "Now, we wait."

When Ian followed, she had already retaken her seat at the table. "Should be full dark in a little less than an hour. I'll have to orient myself once I get through and pray I'm not coming out on the side of a sheer rock face."

True. He sat across from her. "Hungry? I could at least play host. There's some canned ravioli around here."

She smiled. "Childhood favorite?"

Definitely not. There were very few things he wanted to carry forward from his childhood, and he certainly didn't want to talk about his past. Instead, he jerked his chin toward the K-9 resting on a blanket in the corner. "What's up with your new partner?"

"Her name's Grace." Her voice stretched as she looked over her shoulder at the dog, who raised her head at the sound of her name. "After your op, I asked to become a K-9 handler again. That's what I did before I joined the task force that you were on. I was feeling a little…lost, so I reached out to one of my mentors from when I was first in, Sully Briggs. He reminded me how much I loved having a K-9 partner. I'm on the fugitive task force now, when I'm not working with the Mountain Country K-9 Unit to catch the Rocky Mountain Killer. Grace is a tracker, which is a good thing, or else I might not have found you." She turned to face him. "Tell me how you wound up in the woods today."

"Not much to tell." If anyone but Brooke had asked him to return, he'd have ignored the request. "My cousin works at one of the diners in Cattle Bend while she's going to community college. I'm supposed to meet with her in the morning, but I thought I'd cruise by and check on her before then. I'd just parked on the street in front of the diner when this Charger came up and basically aimed right at me. I didn't know who it was at first, just took off with them in pursuit. It wasn't until I was in the underbrush that I saw them and figured it out. How they knew I was coming into town, I have no idea. It could have been sheer coincidence they spotted me, but I don't know."

He'd thought it was safe to return. He'd been wrong.

"It's odd, for sure." Meadow twirled her phone on the table. She often fidgeted when she was thinking through a problem, a quirk he remembered from working with her. He'd always thought it was cute, though Meadow was too tough to be labeled *cute*. "With Ronnie dead, you're no longer considered a protected witness, but your identity and location remain classified as long as you wish. Maybe they lay low, gambling you'd come back home once you believed you were safe?"

"Maybe, but I don't consider this home."

"They don't know that." She looked up, seeming to try to make sense of his statement, but then her gaze shifted. "There's something else it could be." Meadow laid her palm on his busted phone. Her forehead creased. "I'm working on a serial-killer case out of Elk Valley, Wyoming, but one of the murders happened in Glacierville. We were at the PD going over files, and I heard some of the officers talking about how several young people have gone missing over the past four months in the surrounding counties. All late teens or early twenties. Beyond being concerned for their safety, I didn't give it much tactical thought, but—"

"But that's the age group the Thorntons targeted when they were operational as human traffickers." Ian planted his elbow on the table and rubbed the bridge of his nose. "Silas and Des must be starting the operation again. We're close enough to Missoula that they may have assets here that weren't seized in the initial investigation." He felt sick to his stomach, and it had nothing to do with hunger. "They're rebuilding their 'inventory.'" How many young men and women would fall prey to people who treated them as merchandise to be auctioned off to the highest bidder?

This shouldn't be happening. "We shut them down." The words ground out through clinched teeth. He'd been undercover for months and had nearly died bringing the Thornton syndicate to justice. The idea they were back, preying on the vulnerable...

He shoved away from the table and paced the room, feeling caged. "We have to get out of here. We've got to alert local law enforcement and our old task force—"

"Right now we have to be patient." Meadow's demeanor was calm, but her eyes were determined.

He knew that look, and he hated it. She was prepared for patient waiting.

Ian wanted to take action. To charge out and apprehend Silas and Des before they could continue an operation that would leave behind a horrifying path of physical and emotional destruction.

Meadow crouched on the top bunk, the metal cold against her knee, and shoved her head into the pitch-black darkness of the air-shaft. She didn't dare use her flashlight. If Silas and Des were skulking nearby, light would draw them like moths, and they'd be waiting with guns drawn when she emerged.

She closed her eyes and breathed deeply. There were more immediate concerns, however.

Spiders. Snakes. Creepy-crawly critters.

Literally anything could be lurking in the metal tube that offered their only route to escape, and she'd be crawling along the unfamiliar passage blind. Small spaces didn't bother her, but unseen spiders?

She swallowed against her gag reflex. *Lord, help me.*

Flight instinct made every muscle in her body rebel against the darkness. She didn't look back at Ian, who was keeping Grace occupied. If she did, she'd morph into a full-blown, feather-covered chicken. One step back would mean zero steps forward.

And she had to move forward.

It had been a long wait for full darkness, plenty of time for her mind to weave monster spider webs. The sooner she plunged in to face whatever dwelled in the dark, the sooner she'd be out in open air.

With one more prayer that definitely wouldn't be her last, she hefted herself into the narrow space and stretched out on her belly. A barely there breeze brushed her skin, raising the hair on her arms. She reached out her hands, exploring the damp, cold metal ahead of her.

A bulbous *something* scraped beneath her fingertips.

Meadow gasped, whacking her head against the metal roof. *Ew. Ew. Ew.*

I don't want to do this. The refrain looped through her thoughts. A shaky breath and a prayer forced a reset on the mantra. *I can do this.*

If she didn't, they were dead. Silas and Des could return with dozens of thugs. Their best chance at survival was flight.

But…spiders…

Terror squeezed her lungs. She slid her fingers over the bump and found a series of them. Rounded metal rivets ran across the floor where the metal had been pieced together. Okay, so she knew what those were.

Somehow, the evidence that the bumps were all man-made loosened the vise around her lungs.

"You okay?" Ian's whisper wafted to her.

"Good." She kept her answer short, not certain how far the metal tube would carry sound. On grit and prayer, she inched forward, farther from the light and deeper into the unknown.

Meadow closed her eyes, seeking a sense of control. She had no way to judge how far she'd traveled or how far she had to go. Without gravity holding her to the floor, she wouldn't have been sure which way was up or forward. Her mind swirled, disoriented.

The barely moving air tickled her arms, mimicking a thousand spiders' feet.

Meadow gagged on fear.

Her jaw convulsed, knocking her teeth together. She wanted to dig her fingernails into her arms and scratch until the sensation went away.

Only the small tactical part of her mind kept her moving forward, and it was shrinking rapidly.

A damp puff of air carried the scent of rain. Had she reached the end?

Her eyes popped open, but there was only darkness.

Focus on the fresh air.

She set her face into the increasing breeze, fighting for inches. Maybe—

Something brushed her face.

Meadow squeaked a swallowed scream and dug her teeth into her lower lip. Staccato breaths burned her nose. She actually whimpered.

Whimpered.

Gulping air, she swiped at her face. A sticky cobweb clung to her fingers.

Oh, let it be an old cobweb and not an active web.

A thousand minuscule spider legs skittered across her skin.

Real? Or imagined?

She shuddered. Her breaths came faster. *There's no way there are thousands of spiders in here.*

Or is there?

Meadow puffed air through pursed lips, trying to focus on anything else. Blue skies. Warm blankets. Training with Grace.

If only she knew where the end of this narrow shaft was.

The urge to stop and bury her face in her arms was real, but if she did, she'd never move again.

Sweeping her hands in front of her, Meadow pulled forward.

The cobwebs became more prevalent. Her heart rate picked up with each wispy, sticky contact.

Nausea built in her body with every move. She'd never had a panic attack before, but there was always a first time.

The air shifted, cooled. The breeze stiffened. The scent of rain grew stronger.

Meadow opened her eyes. The darkness seemed different somehow. Softer? She still couldn't see her hand in front of her face.

Except…

Meadow waved her hand and a slight shadow moved.

Relief weakened her muscles until they shook. The end had to be near. There was no other way she was getting out without losing her mind.

A square of lighter darkness appeared.

The grate. Meadow pulled like she never had before, heedless of what might lie between her and freedom. She no longer cared. She just wanted out.

Her fingertips scraped metal grate, and she laced her fingers through it to move herself closer with a final burst of strength, holding her face inches from the opening, terrified to press her cheek against it for fear of a rogue spider's retaliation.

Freedom was eight metal screws away. *Lord, don't let this thing be rusted shut.*

She was not going backward down that metal tube of terror.

As her eyes adjusted to the dim light, she listened. Rain still fell, though it was a gentle shower now. The wind tousled the trees.

Only the sounds of nature reached her ears.

That didn't mean Silas and Des weren't lurking nearby.

As much as she'd hated the ventilation shaft, she'd reached the most dangerous part of her journey.

Every inch of her wanted to bash her way out, but removing the screws would take calm and steady hands. Ian had sent her forward with his pocketknife, so she felt for the screws and prayed the small screwdriver tool would hold up to the strain.

Swiping sweat from her palms onto her sleeve, Meadow took a deep breath and went to work. It felt like hours, but a few minutes later, she eased the last screw from its place and jerked the metal grate away from the opening. It scraped with a sound that had to be heard for miles.

Gently, she eased it against the wall beside her and slipped forward, sweeping vines away from the opening as she scanned the area. The light seemed so bright outside, though the moon and stars were obscured by clouds. The shaft's opening was in the side of a steep hill, about three feet up from the level ground below. High enough to avoid flooding, low enough for her to exit headfirst without hurting herself.

Meadow wanted to launch herself from her prison, but she waited, listening for movement that might indicate either Silas or Des had found the grate and were lying in wait.

There was no evidence of another human, though they could be hiding. If only she had Grace, who was a rock star at alerting to the presence of others.

Wriggling out of the shaft, Meadow extended her hands and caught herself on the ground, where she rolled onto her back and lay still, staring up at the clouds, which glowed dimly in the lights from nearby towns. Rain dotted her face, and she reveled in fresh air and freedom. She breathed mountain air for long moments before she finally felt strength in her bones...along with a sheepish blush over her spider scare.

She'd never confess that to anyone.

Carefully, using the soft glow from the clouds to guide her, she felt her way down the hill toward the bunker's door, wishing for her flashlight but wary of giving away her position if someone was tracking her. Neither Des nor Silas were the outdoorsy type, so she was hopeful the rain and the threat of wild forest animals had kept them away.

At the bottom of the hill, she crouched, listening. Other than the rainfall, the breeze in the trees and a few small rustles of night creatures in motion, no sound came to her.

Wary that a bullet could slam into her back at any moment, she pulled her handcuff keys from the pocket she'd stashed them in, crept to the entrance and used the universal key to unlock Des's cuffs. She knocked three times lightly, paused, then knocked twice, Ian's signal to open the door.

The bolt slid back with a screech before the door eased open and Ian peeked out.

Meadow ducked through, and Grace was at

her side immediately, licking her hand in greeting as she waited for a command. Meadow gave her a quick ear scratch, but her focus was on Ian. They couldn't waste time talking. "I think it's clear, but we should get moving. I don't trust them not to come back now that the storm has passed. Silas was never a patient one. If he suspects you're in here, he won't wait until morning to be sure."

Ian turned toward the table then stopped to study her in the lamplight. "You okay?"

"Just ready to move." She walked past him to gather her pack and Grace's things.

He swiped at her shoulder as she walked by.

Meadow froze. "Why?" She had suspicions, but boy, they'd better be wrong.

"No reason. We should get moving."

Ignoring the fear that powered through her, Meadow kept walking. The spider he'd swiped from her shoulder was the least of her worries.

Outside that door, the enemy could be waiting, and she needed to focus less on skittering critters and more on flying bullets.

Chapter Four

After extinguishing the lantern, Ian grabbed his things and followed Meadow.

At the door, she stopped and held a hand out to keep Ian from proceeding.

The last thing he wanted to do was wait. All he wanted was safety and security for her and her partner...and for himself. Those long minutes alone had brought too many opportunities for past pain and fear to play games with his head.

He never wanted a bullet to pierce his flesh again, yet here he was, tensed against that very thing.

Still, he knew better than to rush forward. "Did you hear something?"

"No." Meadow clipped a leash to her K-9's harness. "But Grace is trained to track, and she'll alert if she catches anyone's scent. There's a pretty stiff breeze, so they'd have to be upwind of us, but it's something. At least the wind is blowing from the direction of the parking lot where my SUV is and the logging road where your truck is."

"They're almost definitely watching my truck."

"Which is why we're heading for my vehicle first." She eased the door open and exited with Grace. "Hopefully, they haven't realized you're not alone."

At a soft command from Meadow, Grace lifted her head and sniffed the air, seeming to scan in all directions before she returned her attention to Meadow to watch for her next command.

Even Ian knew that was good news.

Meadow exhaled slowly. "We're clear, at least in the direction we want to go. I can't promise they aren't somewhere downwind, but we'll take it slow. No flashlights. Keep quiet in case those two are roaming around looking for an opportunity."

The scar in his abdomen ached, though the sensation was all in his head. He'd spent a year and a half with his muscles tight, waiting for the slam of another bullet. None of that tension compared to the adrenaline-fueled pain of walking in almost total darkness through the woods with assailants on the hunt. He kept one eye on Grace, who constantly sniffed the air and the ground, and the other on where his next footfall would land.

He tried to keep his steps light as they crept along the creek bank, where it was easier to walk but they were slightly more exposed. All around, the woods and the creek talked, obscuring the sounds of anyone who might be sneaking up on them.

Every muscle in his body ached, reminders of a day that had nearly destroyed him.

Two days after Ronnie Thornton was led out of the courtroom where Ian's testimony had sealed his fate, the criminal had dished out his revenge. When Ian opened the door to his SUV at the sheriff's department to go on his first regular patrol after being undercover, a man had stepped from a vehicle on the street and opened fire.

Most of the bullets thwacked into Ian's SUV. One grazed his hip. The other scorched into his abdomen, slicing through his spleen before exiting out his back.

The pain hadn't hit instantly. Sheer adrenaline and training had driven Ian to return fire along with several other deputies in the lot at the time. But the world had suddenly dimmed and spun, and the last memory he had was dropping to his knees and looking down to see nothing but red. So much red…

Ian shook his shoulders to throw off the memory that still made his side ache and his head spin. Instead, he focused on keeping pace with Meadow, on the scent of rain-washed forest and the sounds of the night. All the things he'd missed in his new life in West Texas, where the air was dry and the land was parched.

Yes, he'd missed Meadow Ames. He'd denied it to himself for all of the months he'd been out of pocket, convincing himself he was happy working with the horses from the rodeo circuit and getting back in touch with the veterinarian dreams he'd had as a child.

But at night, when he laid his head down, no amount of sleep could make him forget her. It was unbelievably unprofessional to fall for your handler, and yet…he almost had.

That was the main reason he'd kept his distance after word came that Ronnie had been murdered, the victim of a homemade knife to the abdomen after he crossed the wrong man in prison. At the time, it had appeared the major players in the Thornton organization were dead, the minions in jail or scattered, and the threat to Ian's life was over.

He'd opted to remain in Texas with the new name of Zeke Donner and the new life he'd settled into, even if it fit like a shirt that was a size too small. It was safer for both himself and Meadow if he stayed in place and left her to live her life as she pleased.

Eventually, he'd move on, too.

Then the call had come from Brooke. His cousin was the one person in his family who'd ever shown him affection or had cared whether he came or went. Sure, she was the youngest, but she was also the one who'd reached out when everything went wrong. She'd never blamed him for the accident that took her brother's life. Even though she was a child at the time, she'd been aware of Dean's addictions and failures. It was the rest of the family who'd vilified Ian and shoved him out…first for not making sure Dean didn't have keys the night he died and, second, for going into law enforcement, the profession that threatened their livelihood the most. They'd shut him out completely.

Not that life had ever been easy. The addictions and dysfunctions that led his mother and

her sister to make money by any means necessary meant he'd never known what love and
safety looked like. In fact, he'd met the wrong
end of his mother's fists on more than one occasion, always refusing to fight back.

There was no way he would ever saddle a
woman with the kind of baggage he carried or
the deficiencies in his emotions. He was cold
inside. That trait had made him a methodical
law enforcement officer and perfect for the undercover job that had almost ended his life. It
did not make him a good candidate for building a future or a family.

Though with Meadow... In the same way
her name brought the image of grassy fields
dotted with spring flowers, she'd once brought
warmth to his heart.

The unfamiliar feeling had scorched his soul
and left him in exquisite pain. Leaving her behind had been the right thing to do. If he'd
had any other option today, he wouldn't have
called her, but his life had depended on her
once again.

And she'd thrown caution to the wind to
protect him...once again.

"You still good back there?" Meadow's soft
whisper slammed the door on his thoughts. She

glanced over her shoulder, the movement more visible now that his eyes had adjusted to the night.

He swallowed words that didn't need to be spoken. "Good."

They trudged up a slope now, having passed under the footbridge without him even noticing, and were headed toward the parking lot. Hopefully, no one was watching her vehicle. Ian was cold and still damp, even though he'd changed clothes. He was starving for more than a can of cold ravioli. And he desperately needed to find a place where Meadow Ames wasn't, before she fanned the embers in his heart to flame.

As they neared the parking area, Meadow slowed.

Ian fought the urge to move between her and whatever danger might lie ahead.

That would earn him a swift reprimand, he was certain. While he was a competent, highly trained law enforcement officer, Meadow's training and expertise with the US Marshals far exceeded his. She could run circles around him, but that didn't stop him from wanting to protect her.

Clearly, his heart was already in the danger zone.

The idea of what she might do if he suggested

she couldn't take care of herself almost made him smile. It was the very reason he'd bitten his tongue in the bunker when she'd hefted herself into the ventilation shaft. She was afraid of spiders and all things creepy-crawly, but her bravery knew no bounds. It was one of the many things he admired about her.

They huddled in the underbrush at the edge of the gravel parking area with Grace between them. The dog sat, nose in the air, sniffing the breeze.

Meadow gave the K-9 a whispered command that Ian couldn't quite make out, and Grace instantly lay down, her paws straight out and her nose pointed ahead, ears perked.

Meadow looked over her partner's head and directly at Ian, her expression grim.

He didn't need to be trained with K-9s to understand what he was seeing. Grace was alerting.

Someone was nearby.

They waited silently in the bushes for what felt like hours.

Ian scanned the sky. A break in the clouds could spell disaster if the half-moon shone through. While it would allow them to see anyone searching for them, it would make them sitting ducks for sure.

The darkness at the wood line on the other side of the parking lot lit up, and it took all Ian had not to duck.

A face illuminated in the glow of a cell phone. As dim as she had her phone, Des still couldn't avoid being lit by the screen as she likely texted Silas, who was probably guarding Ian's truck.

They truly were trapped.

Meadow tapped his arm and pointed down the hill toward the creek.

Smart thinking. If they moved while she was staring at the screen or before her eyes adjusted to the darkness again, then they could avoid being seen. They trekked to the creek, crossed at the narrow spot where he'd hidden before and traversed about half a mile up the other side of the hill before they stopped behind a large boulder.

Meadow crouched behind the rock, shielding her phone with her hands. "I've finally got a signal, and I'm alerting backup. Otherwise, we're never getting out." Her fingers moved swiftly across the screen as she sent a text, then opened a map.

"You know, we could circle back and take

Des into custody." It should have occurred to him sooner.

"These guys are out for blood. Des isn't the type to let herself be spotted by accident. It could have been a trap. I don't like going in without intel when they could have their own backup waiting in the wings. Even if members of my team showed up, I'd be leery of attempting a takedown in the dark without knowing who else is out there."

True. But boy, did his feet itch to head back and put an end to this assault sooner rather than later. As long as Silas and Des were prowling around, he was in danger, and so was everyone he cared about.

Ian studied Meadow's phone screen upside down, then pointed to something in the corner. "There. There's another logging road."

"It's two miles away in the dark."

"We've got no other choice." Behind them lay a known route with an almost certain fire-fight at the end. Before them lay the unknown.

Either way, they were walking into danger.

It felt like they'd been walking for hours.

A thousand imaginary spiders still tiptoed across her skin. No matter how much she rubbed her arms, Meadow couldn't shake the sensation. Until she got into a well-lit place, had a shower, and changed into clothes not coated in cobwebs and dirt, there was no way she'd feel free of that ventilation shaft.

The mountain air was chilled and damp from the earlier rainfall. If they dared to stop, she'd pull her thin rain jacket on for the insulation, but with death prowling around searching for them, a pause could spell disaster.

They'd made their way up the hill, away from the creek, following a narrow trail while stepping carefully to avoid injuries. According to the map, the trail should lead to the logging road, or at least in its general direction. Meadow kept one eye on the ground vaguely illuminated by the half-moon that played peekaboo between the clouds, and one eye on Grace to see if her partner alerted to any odd scents.

So far, the K-9 seemed more interested in sniffing the ground than the air, so they were likely safe. She glanced at the phone screen only on rare occasions in an attempt to maintain cover and night vision. The alerts were shut off to prevent even the buzz of a silent alert from giving away their location. They were headed in the right direction, but discerning how much ground they'd covered was difficult given the uneven terrain and their irregular pace.

From a few steps behind, tension radiated off of Ian. He'd been silent since they set out. There was no doubt he was constantly scanning the area. He hadn't relaxed since they left the bunker.

His stress fed hers, and she needed to do something before the imaginary spiders and Ian's tension crawled through her skin.

When the trail widened, Meadow commanded Grace to heel, then slowed to allow Ian to step beside her. "We must be getting close. There's been more foot traffic through here. It's made a clearer trail."

"Yep."

Ian tended to be a take-charge guy. They'd butted heads a few times on his op, when she'd given direction and he'd wanted to do things his way. While he'd ultimately followed orders, sometimes it had been a pain to get him there. For him to be silently following along now meant he was lost in his head. "What's going on with you?"

He didn't slow his pace but kept moving along with her, looking right and left, up and down. His surveillance never stopped. "Ready to get out of here."

"And?"

"And what?"

The sounds of night creatures filtered between them. In the distance, two owls called to each other, the almost human cry sending a shudder through her bones.

Ian flinched, but his steps didn't stutter.

It wasn't like him to be skittish. He'd been a solid rock on his undercover op, never shying away from danger. Nothing scared him. Even the day he'd been shot, he'd taken down the man who—

The day he'd been shot.

That had to be the problem. The bullet that had torn through Ian's abdomen had come perilously close to ending his life. Having another gunshot in his vicinity today had definitely played on old fears. "You can still feel it hitting you, can't you?"

For the first time, Ian missed a step. He stumbled sideways, bumping her shoulder before he regained his footing. They walked in silence for so long, she was certain he was going to ignore the question.

They split around a tree in the center of the

trail. When they rejoined one another, Ian finally spoke. "I didn't feel it hit." He sniffed and sped up slightly, as though he could outrun the past. "How did you know?"

"I'm an investigator. I made a deduction based on what I know about your personality and about your demeanor tonight."

She was several feet in front of him before she realized he'd stopped walking. When she turned, she was slightly higher up the trail, putting them eye to eye. In the thin, milky moonlight, his face was a blue shadow, but that didn't keep her from seeing he was looking right at her, studying her as though he was trying to solve a puzzle.

Even two years later, the pull toward him was real. The one she'd managed to shove aside and forget existed.

Until today.

His eyes narrowed as though he couldn't quite make out the words on a book's page. "You always did seem to know what I was thinking." The words were so quiet, he likely hadn't meant to say them out loud.

"Your expressions were always an open book. Anybody could read you." When he'd first gone undercover, she'd worried the Thorntons would see right through him, but he'd managed to convince them he was willing and able to be on their payroll.

He chuckled and almost smiled, then stepped around her and started to walk again. "No. Just you."

Was that true? Did she really know him better than anyone else?

Meadow remained behind Ian, letting him take point. He seemed to relax with her watching the rear.

He still trusted her to protect his blind spots.

So why hadn't he trusted her enough to reach out when Ronnie Thornton died?

She started to ask, then shoved the question aside. Trudging through the forest in the dark on a blind run for their lives wasn't the time to rehash the past or to air her emotional grievances.

They walked for what could have been ten minutes or an hour before Ian stopped and crouched on the trail, leaving room for her to join him. "Look."

She took a knee, and Grace obediently sat at her hip.

About ten yards up the trail, the light was different, as though the sky above opened up and allowed the moon full access.

It had to be the logging road. They'd hit straight on the clearing where she'd told Rocco to meet them.

The forest around them was completely silent. The night creatures had stilled.

Someone was nearby.

Lord, let it be Rocco.

Des and Silas were smart. They could read a map as well as she could. It was possible they'd called in backup to cover all potential escape routes.

"Think we've got bad company?" Ian's whisper sounded like a shout in the stillness.

She considered all of the scenarios. "Possibly, but I doubt it. If they had more manpower, they'd have had someone sitting on the bunker's entrance. There are a lot of logging and forestry service roads out here. There's no way they have enough people to cover them all." *Hopefully.* "Shield me while I see if Rocco has texted."

Meadow bent low to the ground beside Grace, letting the dog's body block the light.

Ian hunched protectively over her, completing a triangle that would hopefully shield the dim light of her phone from potential prying eyes. She gripped the device, focusing on the task at hand and trying to ignore how close Ian was. Closer than he'd ever been, she was sure.

What in the world was wrong with her? They were in danger. She certainly shouldn't be noticing how Ian's breath was warm on her cheek or that he somehow still smelled like soap and leather, even after the day he'd had.

She flicked the screen and a notification appeared.

Rocco. Nine minutes earlier.

Just arrived. All clear.

Meadow wanted to sink to the ground in relief. "He's here."

Ian's exhale swept across the base of her ponytail, flickering tendrils across her neck. "What are we waiting for?"

Meadow shook off the sensation of his presence. "Nothing." She let him move first because if she lifted her head, they'd be face-to-face. Frankly, in her relief, she might do something incredibly foolish.

She needed sleep. Lots of sleep, because her tactical brain was rapidly checking out in favor of her hidden guilty-pleasure heart that liked rom-coms and sappy romance novels.

She ought to read more spy stories, clearly.

It took a moment for Ian to move, but he stood slowly, turning toward the trail.

He knew better than to offer her a hand up. She'd broken him of that habit early on. She was capable of taking care of herself.

Though she knew Rocco was near, she eased around Ian and drew her sidearm, making a clicking sound against her teeth to draw Grace to her side.

With her partner at heel, she crept forward, scanning the trees and the pine-needle-covered road as they approached.

At the edge of the clearing, the hulk of an SUV silently waited.

Rocco.

They were out of the woods…

But the threat to Ian's life had just begun.

Chapter Five

"Welcome to Casa de Ames." Meadow opened the door to the small home about half an hour outside of Glacierville and ushered Grace inside, mimicking Ian's earlier grandiose pronouncement.

The K-9 bolted through the living area and straight for the open kitchen at the back of the house, diving headfirst into a massive water bowl.

Rocco's K-9, a chocolate Lab named Cocoa, scrambled across the hardwood toward Grace as soon as Rocco released her.

Ian chuckled. He'd seen horses behave similarly after long rehab sessions. Only hydration and home mattered.

Meadow dropped her gear onto a bench by the door, and Rocco did the same before he headed for the fridge. He tossed a bottle of water to Meadow then turned to Ian. "Want something?"

Ian nodded and caught the bottle Rocco threw to him, but something ugly crawled through his stomach. Officer Rocco Manelli was awfully comfortable in Meadow's home. So was his K-9 partner.

Draining her water bottle as she walked, Meadow crossed the living room, headed for a hallway on the opposite side of the house. "I'm going to clean up. You guys are on your own." She disappeared, and seconds later, a door shut.

"What was that about?" Rocco pulled two dog bowls from the pantry and fed the K-9s.

Yeah, he was definitely too comfortable. "What was what about?"

"Meadow running off before she even looks after Grace? It's not like her."

So, Ian knew something about Meadow that Rocco didn't. *Interesting.* "She's deathly afraid of spiders, but she doesn't think I know. I flicked one off of her shoulder after she came out of the ventilation shaft. I'm guessing she's been feeling them all over her since she made her way out."

"Spiders, huh? She's been hiding that little phobia from all of us." Rocco finished feeding the animals and refilled their water bowls. He poured a glass of juice, then poked around in the fridge. The man was constant motion. "You hungry?"

Ian didn't feel this at ease in his own apartment, let alone in someone else's home. It was clear Rocco was familiar with the place and comfortable taking whatever he needed. Was he here often? Were he and Meadow...a couple?

The thought curled his lip, slithering a thread of dislike for Rocco through him.

But Ian had no claim on Meadow, and this man had saved their lives. Whatever he was feeling had to be exhaustion or an adrenaline crash. Nothing more. He needed a redirect and fast.

Food should do the trick. "I could eat." Ian walked to the island that separated the living room from the kitchen. "Thanks for putting yourself in harm's way to get us out of there."

"It's what we do." Rocco shrugged and slammed the fridge door, then opened the freezer. "Meadow is the worst grocery shopper in the world. The only thing she has is frozen food. Pizza good?"

Actually, frozen pizza sounded like a gourmet meal. "At this point, I'll eat whatever you find. Canned ravioli didn't hold me."

"Been there, done that." Rocco tossed three

frozen pizzas onto the counter and started the oven, then pulled plates from the pantry. "Near-death experiences tend to amp up the appetite."

Nodding slowly, Ian surveyed the room, trying not to think about Meadow cuddling on the couch with or, worse, kissing Rocco. So what if they were dating? Good for both of them if they were. Rocco seemed like a good guy, and Ian wasn't the man Meadow needed.

Though it hadn't stopped him in the past from wishing he could be. And it didn't stop green sludge from running through his veins now.

Seeking distraction, he scanned Meadow's home. The hardwood floors were dark, and scattered colorful rugs broke up the space. There was no dining room table, just the huge island with comfy stools where he currently sat. The walls were a soft gray, making the space feel cool and comfortable. The living area held a brick fireplace painted white and a nap-worthy blue couch with a matching love seat and side chairs. It was immaculate, the result of a trait he'd come to recognize in Meadow.

"Meadow's got a guest room, and she's also got a twin bed in her office. We'll crash here tonight and make a game plan in the morning."

Rocco leaned against the counter by the stove and crossed his arms over his chest. "Any idea how these two seemed to come back from the dead to target you?"

"I'm sorry." Rocco knew way too much about Meadow's home life, and Ian couldn't focus on anything else. Either exhaustion or shock had worn away his filter. "Are you and Meadow dating?"

Rocco's arms fell to his sides, and he almost sputtered like an old Saturday-morning cartoon character.

Meadow's laugh sounded from behind Ian. "You're kidding, right? Me and Rocco?"

Ian didn't dare turn toward her. He could feel the back of his neck flaming. The red was probably spreading to his face, too. He should have kept his mouth shut.

"Hang on, hang on." Rocco walked to the island and leaned forward to watch Meadow as she walked into the kitchen. "You scoff like I'm not a serious catch." He held out his hands and turned a slow circle. "I've got it all. Brains, beauty—"

"An ego the size of the state of Wyoming." The sarcasm dripped from Meadow's words. She shoved Rocco aside and walked into the kitchen, then poured a glass of juice. She'd changed into leggings and an oversize black sweatshirt that said Yes, I'm Cold. Her damp hair hung to her shoulders, and her cheeks were slightly red from either the heat of the shower or the scrubbing she'd given them.

Time to change the subject. "Did you rinse all of the spiders off?"

She pointed a finger at Ian. "Shut your sound, pal. I'd rather forget that trek through Arachnophobia Land ever happened. It was all sunshine and rainbows as far as my memory is concerned." She pulled out the stool at the end of the counter and arched an eyebrow at him. "And *why* would you think I was dating *Rocco*?"

"You say my name like it's an ugly word." Rocco looked up from shoving pizza in the oven. "Once again, I have to ask why the idea is so repulsive."

"Dude, we'd be *Rocco* and *Meadow*. That's way too much greeting-card rhyme for me." With a heavy sigh, Meadow rolled her eyes and pivoted to face Ian. "So…why?"

He knew he looked like a deer caught in the headlights. He could feel his eyes widen. He was too tired and drained to come up with a quip. "I guess…" He guzzled his water and set the bottle on the counter. "It seems like he spends a lot of time here, so I assumed…" That sounded so juvenile. Totally like a middle-school boy. They were both going to crack up laughing at his expense.

Instead, Meadow nodded, her face growing serious. "That's because he *is* here a lot."

"In a professional capacity." Rocco threw a stack of napkins onto the island between Meadow and Ian. "Most of the team is. We're investigating a multistate serial-killer case, and one of our crime scenes is in Glacierville."

"The team bunks here if they need an overnight. It's more comfortable than a hotel, I hope." Meadow grinned. "But it probably does look weird to an *outsider*." She smirked.

Outsider. He'd used the code name in his text to her earlier, and she was letting him know she remembered.

"I heard that tone. Outsider?" Rocco rested his elbows on the island and leaned toward them, his dark eyes sparking with mischief. "What's that about?"

Meadow chuckled. "Your story, Carpenter."

It was. And it was better than talking about how he'd believed Rocco was comfortable at Meadow's house for all the wrong reasons. "It was the code name for the operation I was undercover on, the one that got me into this mess today." They needed to discuss what had happened, but Rocco had been right earlier. Food and rest came first so they could attack the situation later with clear heads. "That's it."

"That's so not *it*." Now that she was definitely spider-free, Meadow's true personality was shining through. The touch of mischief that often sparked when she was tired and her guard was down had flared to life.

"We don't have to tell this part." Because, yeah, he needed more embarrassment.

Rocco's eyebrow arched, and he leaned even closer, as though he had a secret to share. "I feel like we do."

"Oh, we do." Meadow sipped her juice. "The joint task force wanted someone to go under with the Thorntons in Missoula, and we tapped Ian, who was a deputy sheriff for Peak County but unlikely to be recognized in Missoula. His first meeting with our team was a working lunch at my office, and he—"

"And I managed to hit the table and knock over four of the six drinks sitting there. Meadow's fell right into her lap." He was taking charge of this story before she could embellish it. "For some reason, she thought it was cute to call me *Soda* after that."

Rocco's brows knit together. "And *Soda* led to *Outsider* because... Oh." He nodded and backed away from the counter, standing tall. "The book we all had to read in school. *The Outsiders*. One of the brothers is named—"

"Soda." Meadow laughed. "As a code name for an op, *Outsider* sounded a lot better than *Soda*."

Lacing his fingers behind his head, Ian leaned back in his chair. "And a legend was born."

"In your own mind." Meadow popped him in the ribs and stood. "So anyway, that's how Ian got his code name, and that's why Rocco knows my house so well. Any more questions?"

Yeah, he had more, especially if talking would distract him from the way he shivered when she touched him. "If Rocco is a cop from Elk Valley—" a fact he'd dropped on the ride to Meadow's house "—and you're still with the Marshals out of Missoula, this unit you're in must be interesting. Can you talk about it?"

Meadow looked at Rocco, and they seemed to have a silent conversation before coming to a decision as the oven timer went off. She waited for the beeps to stop. "We can tell you a big chunk about it, but strap in… It's a wild one."

Meadow watched while Rocco sliced the square pizzas into quarters. It was no surprise Ian had wondered about a relationship between them. Most of the team ran around her house like they owned the place since they spent so much time investigating in Glacierville.

She didn't want to think about the way Ian had asked the question, as though he had a vested interest in the answer. He'd almost seemed…jealous? Not in a creeptastic way, but in a way that warmed her heart.

Ian had always been attractive, with his carefully tousled light-brown hair and blue eyes that saw straight into her thoughts. They'd connected when they'd worked together and had built a friendship. Outside of the op, what would a relationship have looked like? If they'd met at the grocery store, would the same *click* have happened?

Things had certainly *clicked* for her. At some point in their off-the-grid meetings and in the aftermath of his near-death experience, she'd fallen hard for him.

Because of past family issues, it was a feeling he would never reciprocate, so she'd buried the emotion, layering on dirt after he vanished into WITSEC.

Clearly, she hadn't buried it deep enough. Even though he'd shut all doors on any sort of romantic future together, his failure to reach out after Ronnie died cut.

His reappearance today created a storm in her head and her heart.

Having him in her home made her wonder how it would have been simply to have dinner together. Watch TV together. Be normal people who had a chance at—

"You know I hate this." Rocco slid a plate onto the bar in front of Meadow and another in front of Ian. "I'm basically serving you guys ketchup on cardboard. Not my style."

"It's the most delicious cardboard I ever tasted." Meadow shut down her musings, taking a huge bite from her square of pepperoni. She refused to wince when cheese scorched the roof of her mouth. She wouldn't give Rocco the pleasure.

"It's been so long since you ate lunch, you'd probably eat actual cardboard right now."

"Put enough peanut butter on it, and we'll see." Meadow shrugged and sipped fruit juice, letting it ease the burn before she swallowed. "Next time you're around, I'll have fresh tomatoes and herbs and whatever it is you need to make homemade gnocchi or sourdough bread or whatever." She poured on the sarcasm. "We all know you're the resident food hero."

"Don't you forget it." Rocco made a face at his pizza before he bit into it then washed it down with juice.

Ian watched with amusement as he chewed.

Probably he deserved an explanation. "Rocco was partially raised by his grandmother in Italy. He's the world's greatest chef, in case you were wondering."

"Second greatest. My grandma Luna is the tops." With a jerk of his chin, Rocco addressed Ian. "You hang around long enough, I'll make you a *salsa di pomodoro alla napoletana* that will change your life."

"He's not kidding." Just thinking about it made Meadow's mouth water, but she couldn't resist one more dig. "He really does think he can turn you into a different person with his superior cooking skills."

"'Superior cooking skills.'" Rocco mimicked her like a little brother needling his sister, his voice high-pitched and whiny, then looked at

Ian and morphed into a professional. "So, the case we're working."

Ian nodded. "I'm all ears."

Debating how much she should say, Meadow put down her slice of pizza and dusted off her hands. "Ten years ago, three young men, late teens to early twenties, were killed on Valentine's Day. Their bodies were found in barns in Elk Valley, Wyoming."

"Mmm." Ian swallowed and swiped at his mouth with a napkin. "I remember that. They were all popped in the chest at point-blank range. The guys were all love-'em-and-leave-'em types, so the suspect pool was deep, and nobody was ever caught. They were all in some club together."

"You've done your homework." His jaw tight, Rocco tossed his napkin onto his plate, covering his pizza as though he'd lost his appetite. "The Young Ranchers Club. It was disbanded after the murders. The trail went cold, but nobody in Elk Valley has ever forgotten."

Meadow bit her lip. The case was personal to Rocco. He'd grown up in Elk Valley, and his father had investigated the murders, never giving up until he'd passed away a little over a year ago. Rocco had made it his personal

mission to find the killer, and when new de-
velopments necessitated the formation of the
Mountain Country K-9 Unit, he'd been one
of the first deputized.

"Y'all are looking into that again?" Ian
turned to Meadow. "Is this about the homicide you're investigating here that's linked to
Elk Valley?"

"Yes." He'd remembered her comment in
the bunker? *Impressive.* "Five months ago, on
Valentine's Day, two bodies were found, one in
Glacierville and one near Denver. Both shot in
the chest with the same gun as the Elk Valley
murders, and both found in barns. Both from
Elk Valley. Both former members of the YRC."

"But this time there was a difference." Rocco
shoved his plate aside and gripped the edges of
the counter. "Only the Glacierville victim was
a romancer. The other, Peter Windham, was a
model citizen, great guy, professing Christian
who walked the walk. The killer left notes on
both of them. Typed, stabbed into their chests
with a knife."

"The notes said, 'They got what they de-
served. More to come across the Rockies. And
I'm saving the best for last.'" The words chilled
Meadow, especially since they'd already failed

to save a sixth victim. "There was a third recent murder in Sagebrush, Idaho, a couple of months ago. Same MO, also a guy from Elk Valley's YRC."

Ian laid his napkin on his empty plate and slid it to the side, settling back to talk with a look in his eye that said he was ready to strategize. "Any link between the victims besides the YRC?"

"A dance." Rocco gathered the plates and stacked them. "All of them were at a dance about a month before the first killings. All of them but our good-guy victim participated in humiliating a young lady named Naomi."

"She a suspect?"

"She's been cleared." It had seemed to be a slam dunk, until Naomi's alibis checked out. "Even more concerning, the real killer is taunting us. He stole a therapy dog of ours, Cowgirl, and keeps making contact with our team leader, sending pictures, making vague threats. He's toying with us." Cowgirl was pregnant, which they knew from the killer's photos, and her puppies were due any day. The whole team was knotted up, watching the murderer use the dog to play mind games with them.

Rocco pounded the counter with his palm,

rattling the dishes. Both Meadow and Ian jumped. "It's sick. The sooner we catch him, the better." Jerking the plates from the counter, he headed for the sink and flicked the water on, his back to them.

Ian moved to speak, but Meadow laid a hand on his arm with a quick shake of her head. It was time to change the subject. Rocco needed a minute to deal with his personal feelings about the investigation. "I think the more pressing thing to worry about is that Silas and Des are still alive and how they found you."

"And what to do about Brooke." Ian stood and quickly filled in Rocco on the little he knew about his cousin's situation. "Whatever is going on, she's scared. I can't reach out to her with my phone busted. I never memorized her number." Something seemed to steal his next words. "I'm supposed to meet her first thing in the morning at the diner where she works, which means I'll need a vehicle."

"Des and Silas are looking for yours. We'll have it towed and put into storage so nothing happens to it."

"Same with yours, M. If they were watching it, they suspect it's connected to Ian. I can give you a ride." Rocco settled the last plate into the dish drainer, seeming to have calmed down. "Where does she work?"

Ian's gaze flicked between Meadow and Rocco as though he was making a decision.

She knew what it was because it was the same one she was coming to. They'd worked together before, knew how each other operated, had an unspoken language. "I've got it. I can run him into town to get a rental, and then we can both shadow him to the diner."

"Sounds like a plan." Drying his hands, Rocco called to Cocoa. "I think step one is we all get some rest. This day's gone on long enough."

She couldn't agree more. "Rocco, everything's set up as usual in the guest room. I've got a twin bed in the office, Ian." As tall as he was, his feet would likely hang out of the blankets most of the night, but he'd be okay.

After Rocco disappeared up the hallway and Meadow killed the lights, Ian followed her to his room with Grace at his heels. "No problem. It's light-years better than the bunker or the bushes."

Meadow flipped on the light as she walked into the room, then stepped aside and gestured as though the space was a grand hotel.

A twin bed, ready for guests, stood beneath a window on one wall. An L-shaped desk and two tall bookcases took up most of the remaining space.

Grace took a seat in the doorway, her head tilted. The K-9 knew it was bedtime, so she had to be wondering why they were in the office.

Ian looked down at her. "She's quite a partner. Very polite."

"Of course she is, but watch this." Meadow's eyes gleamed as she made eye contact with the K-9. "Grace, greet."

Immediately, Grace leaped up and pounced on Ian as though he was her new best friend. She licked his face and pawed at his chest.

Ian laughed, exactly as she'd hoped he would.

"Grace, down." The K-9 obediently sat at Meadow's side.

Ian brushed off his shirt. "Awesome, but why?"

"It's a trick my mentor, Sully, taught me. I can use it to make her seem like a regular old dog, who's a little disobedient, if someone gets suspicious." She'd worked closely with Sullivan "Sully" Briggs back in the day, and he'd taught her several tips and tricks he'd picked up over the years. He was a well-respected K-9 officer with the US Marshals Service and had recently consulted on the RMK investigation.

Meadow swept her hand around the room, weariness cutting her amusement short. "You should be comfortable here. Breakfast is served when Rocco gets up and makes it." There wasn't anything in the fridge, but no doubt he'd be at the grocery story before dawn.

Ian walked to the desk and flicked the dried leaves of a potted plant near the window. "You keep a dead plant around?"

Meadow leaned against the doorframe. "That plant refuses to die. I watered it yesterday. In a day or so, it'll look like it was never neglected."

"If you say so."

"When my grandmother passed away, someone gave the plant to our family. Weirdly, no matter how long I forget about it, if I give it water, up it pops." She shrugged, slightly embarrassed. "It kind of makes me feel like she's still around, since it keeps coming back. I'll be sad if it ever officially kicks the bucket." It was silly, getting attached to a plant she rarely cared for, but it brought her comfort.

"I understand." Ian leaned against the desk. "Thanks for coming to the rescue today and for helping me out tomorrow. I know you're in the middle—"

From behind her closed bedroom door, something crashed. Glass shattered. The house alarm blared.

Meadow whirled toward the hall as Grace stood at attention, and Ian stepped up beside her, ready for battle.

Chapter Six

There was no way Silas and Des had tracked them to Meadow's house...was there?

How?

Ian watched Meadow nod grimly to Rocco, who waited in the doorway of the guest room across the hall.

She texted something on her phone, then pocketed the device and spoke a quick command to Grace. The K-9 lay down under the desk but remained alert, watching Meadow. Without a word, she went to a safe on the bottom shelf of the nearest bookcase, opened it, and slipped a magazine into her Glock. She looked at him as she stood. "I know you're armed, but don't fire unless you have to. Stay here, as hard as that's going to be for you. I've reached out to Glacierville PD for backup."

Understood. Given that he wasn't officially in law enforcement, he could only act in self-defense.

He crouched near the door as she shut off the lights then stepped into the hall and whispered to Rocco before she moved toward her room.

Rocco went to the front of the house. After several beeps, the alarm shut off.

It took a moment for Ian's eyes to adjust. Light filtered through the blinds, likely from an outdoor light in the backyard.

The house was eerily silent, as though even the walls held their breath.

Ian exhaled slowly, his fingers tight around the pistol's grip. Since the shooting, he hated touching the thing, hated the memory of the last time he'd fired a weapon. While he carried it for protection, he hadn't pulled the trigger since that horrible day.

Meadow appeared in the doorway, a dim shadow in the milky light. "I'm going into my room. Rocco's got the living room and kitchen. Back me up."

This was risky. Anyone could be in her room. His heart hammered as he followed her to the bedroom door, taking up a position on one side as she pressed her back to the wall on the other.

With a quick nod, Meadow slowly turned the knob then pushed the door open, drawing back against the wall as though she expected bullets to fly.

Cold sweat broke out on Ian's skin.

There was only silence, so loud it almost deafened him.

Ian peeked around the doorframe. The bathroom light was on, and it illuminated the room. No one was inside. A window next to the bed was broken, but the hole wasn't large enough for a person to climb through.

The busted glass was either meant to draw them toward someone waiting outside to open fire when they appeared, or it was a diversion to distract them from the real attack.

"I've got movement at the back!" Rocco's shout from the kitchen was overlaid by a simultaneous gunshot and shattered glass.

Diversion.

Rocco's voice came again. "I'm fine. Shooter's taking potshots from the rear."

Meadow moved to run up the hall, but Ian sliced the air with his hand to keep her in place. He slid along the wall into the guest room at an angle to her door then returned with a bed pillow, which he tossed into the air in front of her door.

A gunshot shattered the silence.

Ian and Meadow both jerked back against the wall.

Opening the door had given whoever was at the window a clear shot down the hallway.

They were trapped on either side of the door. Moving farther up the hall would put them straight into the shooter's line of sight. Ian was next to the guest room, but there was no way for Meadow to go anywhere without landing in the shooter's sights.

They were trapped, and Rocco was on his own.

His heart pounded. His head roared. Bullets were flying, and he could be hit. Meadow could be hit.

They were trapped.

Trapped.

Unless…

He looked across the hall at Meadow and kept his voice low. There was one way out, but it was all on him. "I can get out the guest room window." If he did, he would be in the front yard and could flank either the shooter at her window or the one toying with Rocco.

Assuming there were only two shooters…

The action might cost him everything. Could

he physically force himself out the window when someone was firing on them?

Meadow stared at him, clearly evaluating his plan.

Come on, Meadow. Make it quick. There was no time to wait for backup to arrive, so they had to move, and the longer she waited, the more time his brain had to remember bullets were flying. Already, his muscles were threatening to give out.

Finally, she nodded. "Okay. But I'm praying. Hard."

He tightened his jaw. She could pray all she wanted. God wasn't concerned about Ian Carpenter.

Slipping into the guest room, Ian shut the door behind him to minimize any potential backlighting that might give away his position. He made his way to the window that faced the driveway and peered out from the side of the blinds.

One step at a time. One breath at a time. He could do this. He had to. Otherwise, they were trapped in a giant kill box.

It was also dark. The light from the backyard and the half-moon above cast shadows into the front yard, providing vague illumination.

Nothing seemed to be moving in front of the house, but there were too many places to hide. The trees offered cover. The vehicles offered cover. Des or Silas could move from position to position with little chance of being seen due to the deep shadows, and there was no guarantee only the two of them were lying in wait. There could be any number of potential attackers biding their time, waiting for a kill shot.

He could be gunned down before he even made it out the window.

He forced himself to breathe slowly. *One step at a time.*

Another shot cracked from the backyard, and Rocco fired back, the retort loud in the silence. "I've got one pinned behind the shed."

So they knew the position of one person out of a potentially limitless number of assailants.

Too many unknowns. Too many variables.

Yet they couldn't sit here waiting for a deadly assault. They had to be proactive.

Ian had to move.

One step at a time.

Every instinct said to curl into a ball beneath the window, yet Meadow's prayers must have been working because he somehow found the strength to keep moving. Standing to the side of the window, he wrapped the cord for the blinds around his fingers and slowly pulled.

His muscles tensed against a potential gunshot.

There was only silence.

Exposing his arm, he unlatched the window and raised it as gently as he could. It squeaked then moved easily, probably new windows from the obvious remodeling that had been done to the house.

Still no gunfire.

Either no one was watching or they were waiting for him to give them a clear shot.

A clear shot. His body went rigid. Ian pressed his spine to the wall and breathed in through his nose then out through his mouth. He rested his hand on the scar on his abdomen, phantom pain rushing through him. He could still feel the warmth of blood running between his fingers…could still see the flood of red.

The initial shot hadn't been the traumatic part. The aftermath had nearly done him in. The physical bullet to his body had been like a metaphorical bullet to his mind, leaving behind scars of vulnerability and anxiety he'd managed to wrestle to the ground…

Until today.

He exhaled through pursed lips. Meadow needed him. He was the only one in a position to save her and Rocco and their K-9 partners. Although he'd sincerely hoped never to be in a situation where a bullet could slam into him again, here he was. *Lord, help me.*

The prayer was unbidden, and with it came a fragment of scripture he'd heard at the rodeo chapel one Sunday. Something about God numbering his days and knowing what each of them would look like.

Even the day he was shot.

Even today.

God knew. Ian didn't. Was that comfort or not?

A few more deep breaths. A few more frantic prayers. Finally, his body agreed to move.

Braced for a shot, he stepped in front of the window. He slipped his right leg over the sill, holding his pistol tightly in his right hand as he steadied himself on the window frame with his left.

He had never been more vulnerable in his entire life. He hoped he'd never be this vulnerable again.

Something splintered the siding near his head. A gunshot cracked.

Fear rushed over him like a tsunami. He dove into the room and dropped beneath the window, his back to the wall. His ears roared. His heart pounded. His muscles turned to water.

Death was coming for him.

He couldn't do this.

"Ian! Status!"

Meadow's shout was a slap to his cheek. She was still trapped in the hall. He was still her only hope.

And he'd failed.

Wait. Instinct overrode fear. If the person who'd been waiting at Meadow's window was busy dealing with him, then… "Meadow! Move!" Hopefully she'd get the message that she was clear, at least for a few seconds.

A bullet hit the window, shattering glass that rained down on Ian.

Meadow's footsteps pounded up the hall. Her shadowed figure raced past the door, headed to help Rocco.

While Ian cowered.

"I've got the back. You take the front!" Rocco opened a barrage of fire.

"Got it!" Meadow responded.

Ian needed to cover Meadow, but fear rushed in, quickening his breath, robbing his muscles, scrambling his thoughts. He couldn't move. Couldn't think. Couldn't defend himself.

Couldn't protect anyone.

Sirens wailed in the distance, coming closer at a quick pace.

An unintelligible shout came from the backyard. In the woods by the house, something crashed through the brush, moving away.

Silas and Des were running instead of finishing the job of killing him.

He was too spent to pursue them. Shame burned his conscience. He'd failed.

From the rear of the house, Rocco's voice shouted, "Police! Stop and drop to your knees!"

Engines roared into the driveway, sirens blaring and lights reflecting off the walls.

On instinct, Ian slid the pistol across the floor away from him, sapping the last of his strength. There was no need to be mistaken for one of the bad guys and to come under friendly fire.

No, he had a feeling there was more fire about to rain down on him, and his back was covered in a huge, flashing target.

How had they been found?

Meadow slumped in a chair in the very Glacierville PD conference room she and Rocco had spent the previous day in. While it had been perfect for their investigative research, it had not functioned well as a place to bunk for the night. Sleep had been scarce; adrenaline and questions had chased her every time she closed her eyes. Silas and Des had managed to find her home, had known Ian was there. How? She couldn't solve that riddle. A whispered conversation with Rocco in the wee hours of the morning proved he had no answers either.

For a couple of hours, she'd managed to cat-nap on the floor under the table while Ian and Rocco tried to catch sleep in a couple of the chairs that lined the back wall of the room.

She'd slept under worse conditions, but after the relentless assault of the previous after-noon and evening, even a week in a luxury spa wouldn't provide enough rest.

It wasn't quite seven in the morning, and she was already tired of this room. Other than a quick outing with Grace a few minutes earlier, it felt like she'd spent her entire life hemmed in by these four beige walls. Somebody had better call with news soon, or she was liable to go out hunting the Thornton crew solo just to put an end to this Groundhog Day.

At her feet, Grace snorted and shifted, then settled back to sleep.

Meadow had never felt more jealous of another living creature in her life.

Since everyone had awakened starving for food, Ian had disappeared up the hall in search of a vending machine while Rocco had taken Cocoa outside for a short walk.

The night before, they'd opted to return to Glacierville for refuge at the PD while they plotted their next move. Meadow had exchanged several texts and calls with the leader of the Mountain Country K-9 Unit, Chase Rawlston, who was working to locate a safe house for them.

He couldn't find one soon enough.

Meadow had considered packing up the crew and heading back to Elk Valley, where the task force was headquartered, but it was fourteen hours away, and Ian would never leave without making contact with his cousin.

What she really wanted was her bed and some sleep, but her house was a crime scene, and with Des and Silas having evaded capture, her home was a no-go for the foreseeable future. There had to be a place where—

A pack of peanut-butter crackers landed on the table, dropped from above.

She looked up to find Ian standing behind her. "Breakfast is served. It was the best I could do on short notice. Turns out they don't serve omelets in vending machines."

"Ugh. I'll settle for peasant rations, then." She grinned as he sat a can of soda beside the crackers then rounded the table to sit across from her. It felt good to smile. It seemed like forever, which was roughly the length of this day, since she'd had a moment of levity.

It was also good to see Ian smile. He'd apologized repeatedly for "failing" her, but she'd argued each time. He'd drawn fire. Had cleared the way for her to move. That was bravery, not failure.

She opted to let that observation slide for the time being. "Chief Connor told me he'd try to bring in some hot chow with him, so we have something to look forward to."

"If I remember right, he's a fan of Clancy's, and they make a mean bacon, egg and cheese biscuit." Ian slid a pack of crackers and a drink toward the end of the table for Rocco, then tore the plastic from his own makeshift breakfast. "We're still in a holding pattern?"

"Until I hear back from our task force leader, yeah. He's got Glacierville PD and Cattle Bend PD and the Peak County sheriff on the hunt for the Thorntons and searching for a safe house for us. Hopefully, they'll come up with something soon. I reached out to my home office in Missoula, but we've got nothing right now. You know of anything?" This was Ian's old stomping grounds. He'd been a deputy for Peak County before going undercover on the joint task force. It had been risky, but he was a guy who'd kept to himself and had few ties in the immediate area, so the undercover persona had worked.

Until Ronnie Thornton had Ian shot in retaliation.

Meadow used one finger to spin the orange crackers on the table. "I know it wasn't easy for you to put yourself in the line of fire tonight. Thanks." She couldn't help reassuring him again. She'd felt helpless, trapped in the hallway while Rocco and Ian put themselves in harm's way. Useless and helpless, two feelings she hated most. She didn't want Ian feeling that way.

Frankly, she'd also been terrified, especially when she'd heard the shot as Ian was leaving the house. She couldn't imagine his level of bravery, given that he knew what it felt like to have a bullet almost wipe him out of existence.

Ian picked up a cracker and studied it in the overhead light. "I don't want to talk about it anymore." He popped the cracker into his mouth and offered a dazzling smile that didn't reach his eyes. "So, which is better, cardboard pizza or vending machine crackers?"

He was trying to avoid his emotions. "Ian—"

"You're joking, right?" Rocco walked in and dropped into a chair at the head of the table as Cocoa settled at his feet. "Neither is real food, though I'm grateful to whichever one of you brought these in."

Meadow took a slow sip of soda, wishing Rocco had waited to return. She knew a deflection when she heard one, and Ian was a mirror bouncing his true emotions into space. If Rocco hadn't stepped in, she'd have called him on it. While she might take the liberty of digging deeper when it was just the two of them, she'd never risk embarrassing him in front of a fellow law enforcement officer.

Rocco cracked open his can of soda, took a long sip, then reached down and hefted his backpack off of the floor. "We have a video call in five minutes." He crammed an entire cracker into his mouth and started hooking up his laptop to the large monitor on the wall. Since they weren't working with classified evidence, they were allowed to use their own electronics in the building.

With all that had happened, she'd almost forgotten about the call. Chase liked to check in with the team every other day, but yesterday afternoon he'd texted about a mandatory all-hands meeting. Maybe there had been a break in their murder investigation.

She hoped so. While she loved her teammates, she was tired of running the roads between here and Elk Valley.

Ian stood and drained his can of soda. "I'm going to step out and see if the chief is here. Maybe he'll have a bag of those biscuits." He left the room, shutting the door behind him.

Smart man. He knew the call would include classified intel, and he hadn't waited to be kicked out.

They logged on and, as soon as they appeared on the screen, team leader Chase Rawlston acknowledged their presence. "We're waiting on Isla. She had a tech issue."

There were a few tired chuckles. Ironic, since Isla Jiminez was their technical expert.

The team looked as exhausted as Meadow felt. The serial homicides were taking a toll, especially on members like Rocco, Chase and rookie Ashley Hanson, who were from Elk Valley and had a vested interest in the case. When the serial killer had popped up again ten years after the first three murders, the FBI had called Chase in to lead the Mountain Country K-9 Unit. As the Wyoming Bureau supervisory special agent, he was familiar with the area and with the investigation.

Isla appeared on the screen, her brown hair pulled back in a ponytail. "Sorry, guys. I let my laptop battery die."

Detective Bennett Ford laughed. "Now I've heard it all."

"Yeah," Deputy Selena Smith chimed in. "You can't harass us when we make technical errors from now on."

"As amusing as this is," Chase cut off the banter, "we've got some details to discuss. With Meadow and Rocco caught up in the middle of an assassination attempt on a witness fresh out of WITSEC who's now under attack again, we've all got better things to do than to chat our time away on here."

Nobody said a word. They'd already received

texts about the goings-on with Meadow and Rocco, and several had reached out. Because they were all tied up in their own investigations, they couldn't offer much more than moral support.

Isla took over the conversation. "I'm the one who asked for this meeting. I've got an update on Cowgirl and a possible lead on our killer."

Cowgirl, a therapy dog meant to help comfort victims and witnesses, had been gifted to the unit by Ashley's father. Within days, the K-9 had been dognapped from their HQ in Elk Valley—and the team had come to believe that the thief was the Rocky Mountain Killer. One of the photos that the RMK had taunted them with featured the labradoodle wearing a pink dog collar with the word *Killer* spelled out in rhinestones.

It was sick.

"Is she okay?" Ashley leaned closer to her camera. "I hate to think of her out there in this guy's hands. I mean, I know he seems to be taking care of her, but with her puppies due any day, what will he do to her? What's his endgame?"

They were all questions the team had wrestled with since Cowgirl had vanished.

For weeks, Isla had been trying to track down where the collar had come from. She'd learned little beyond the fact that it was a common item sold in gift shops along the Rockies, including in Sagebrush, Idaho, where a tip had been called in that Cowgirl had been spotted. Her pregnancy and the unique brown spot on her ear made her easy to identify, and they'd blanketed social media with descriptions, hoping for a hit.

"Late yesterday, I may have landed on something during a phone call with a boutique owner in Sagebrush. When I sent her photos of Cowgirl, she remembered her because of the markings on her ear and because it's rare to see a labradoodle as obviously pregnant as she is out and about. The owner said a tall, good-looking blond man bought the collar. He had on a hat and sunglasses, and she was more focused on the dog than on the man."

"Can we trace a credit card?" FBI Agent Kyle West hopped into the conversation.

"He paid cash. That also stood out to her since most of her customers are tourists who tend to pay with cards."

There was a collective sigh of disappointment.

"Oh, but wait," Isla singsonged. "I'm not

done. He stood out also because he had an unusual tattoo on his forearm. A knife."

It wasn't a lot, but it was something. At this point, every little bit helped.

"I've made sure that was added to our BOLO." Chase took control of the meeting. "We've updated the website and social media, also. Now, before we log off, I want to see what we can do for Meadow and Rocco while—"

"Chase?" Bennett Ford raised his hand as though he was in school. He looked grim, as though someone had delivered bad news. "I think we might have a problem."

Chapter Seven

Meadow leaned forward, and her toe tapped Grace's belly under the table. The K-9 stirred and rose, moving to stand beside Meadow with her head resting on her partner's thigh, watching intently for a command.

Absently, Meadow scratched Grace's ears, her eyes on the screen. Bennett had recently married Naomi Carr-Cavanaugh, their initial suspect in the murders. A month prior to the first killings ten years earlier, Naomi had been taunted by several bullies at a dance hosted by the Young Ranchers Club. Naomi had been a bit of a wallflower, but she'd accepted an invite to the dance from Trevor Gage, one of the more popular young men in the group. When she'd arrived, Trevor's friends had pounced, telling Naomi that Trevor considered her a joke and had only invited her to get her hopes up. She'd fled, devastated by their cruelty, and Trevor had left the dance not long after.

A month later, on Valentine's Day, the first three victims had been murdered. Seth Jenkins, Brad Kingsley and Aaron Anderson were lured to a barn via text messages sent from a burner phone: Meet me at YRC barn at midnight followed by a kiss emoji. The guys were known to be serial daters and dumpers, so there were a lot of suspects who might want revenge.

Including Naomi, who had every reason to use a romantic holiday to wreak vengeance on the young men who had humiliated her.

But when the unit investigated Naomi, then recently widowed and heavily pregnant, her alibis for all of the murders cleared her, including the three most recent ones. Additionally, the Colorado victim, Peter Windham, had been a friend of hers, leaving her with no motive for his killing.

Bennett's statement raised the level of concern for everyone on the team, though. He and Naomi had connected during the investigation when she was targeted by an unrelated killer. They'd married recently, and if he saw a problem, it was possible he'd learned new information about his wife.

Meadow prayed it wasn't so. They were so happy together. To think Bennett might suspect Naomi of—

"What are you saying, Bennett?" FBI Agent Kyle West spoke first, echoed by the mumbles of other members of the team. "Is Naomi okay?"

"She's fine. The baby's fine. The three of us are fine." The baby had been born shortly before their wedding. "It's more that I feel I should bring up, well, my brother-in-law."

"Evan?" It seemed unlikely Evan Carr was their killer. The original investigators had followed that road before, as had their unit, and they'd come up empty both times. "He had a solid alibi for the first set of murders." Evan had been with his girlfriend, Pauline Potter, that night, and she'd confirmed that.

"I don't know." Their rookie officer, Ashley Hanson, looked a bit uncomfortable in the spotlight. "I interviewed Evan a few months ago because his sister was a suspect. He was genuinely concerned about the murders and empathetic, aware of the pain the deaths had caused everyone. Elk Valley isn't that big. Everyone knows each other. And Evan wasn't even a part of the Young Ranchers Club. He ran with a different crowd. The YRC was Naomi's thing, and I don't know that they were close enough for him to seek vengeance on her behalf, not in such a violent manner, anyway."

Chase took the reins again. "Bennett, what makes you leery now?"

"I don't know." Bennett dragged his hand down his face as he leaned back in his chair, away from his laptop's camera. "I just want to stay above board and to be sure we've checked all of the boxes. In all fairness, he's a tall, good-looking blond guy, like the boutique owner said."

"So are you, Bennett." Rocco's comment was met with a few chuckles. "It's not exactly a unique description."

"No, but among our suspect pool who were around at the time and might have even the slightest motive, it's worth sending the boutique owner a photo just to rule him out conclusively. And honestly? Sometimes it feels like there's something I just can't put my finger on." Bennett sat forward. "I'm just trying to think the way I'd think if he wasn't my brother-in-law. When we finally arrest a suspect, I don't want a lawyer to point at us and say we might have played favorites. It might be time to interview Evan again, simply to take him completely off the list."

"I get it." Chase tapped something on his keyboard. "You have a photo? We'll have Isla reach out to the boutique owner with it. The guy was wearing sunglasses, but it's still worth a shot."

Picking up his phone, Bennett scrolled on the screen. "I've got a couple of photos." He held the phone up to the camera, revealing the image of a handsome young man with short blond hair.

"Send that one to Isla." Chase said. "There are a million other tall blond guys in the world, but you're right, he's close to the investigation and we need to make sure our ducks are in a row. You know where he is right now?"

"He travels a lot, so it's probable he's on-site with his recruiting company. I can check."

"He have a tattoo?"

"Not that I know of. And since he and Naomi have never been close and haven't spent any time together recently, I doubt she'd know, but I'll ask her. He's been so busy that he's been by only once to see the baby, and that was a brief visit."

"From what I've heard about Evan, he's not

the kind of guy to get inked," Rocco said. He'd know, having grown up in Elk Valley. Ashley nodded in agreement. While Evan had been several grades ahead of Rocco and Ashley, they all would have crossed paths in town. "He has a reputation for being business-focused and kind of straitlaced. A visible tat would be completely out of character. If I can, I'd like to get in on that interview, though."

"No." Chase shook his head. "I need you to stick with Meadow, and I think I want someone who doesn't know him to chat with him this time. I want a totally objective, clean-slate viewpoint so we can avoid future questions about bias."

Rocco nodded grimly. "Understood."

There was an uncomfortable silence. Chase rarely denied their requests.

Isla cleared her throat and looked into the camera. "In the meantime, I'll also put together a list of tall blond men who were members of the YRC or who were at the dance that night."

"Might want to expand that to the entire high school." Standing, Rocco looked at the camera. "Everyone knew what happened. And while Naomi sort of kept to herself, there were still some people who were pretty upset that anyone could be as mean as those guys were. Also, given their reputations for loving 'em and leaving 'em, we can't forget we could also be looking at a jealous boyfriend. This might not be about Naomi at all."

"That's right." Looking to the right, Chase appeared to listen to someone off camera. He nodded then turned back to the group. "Let's not get tunnel vision. I know it's difficult. We've got six dead and a threat to an unknown seventh. We can't afford to make a mistake. And, Meadow?"

"Yes?" A buzz ran through her as though she'd just been called to the principal's office. Getting called out by name in meetings wasn't something she was used to.

"You and Rocco stay on the line. I've got some resources for you."

A chorus of goodbyes bounced from the speakers, and one by one, the other members of the team disappeared until only Chase was left. "I've got a lead on a place for you to lie low, but you may want to recon it first. I'm going to text it to you. Keep in mind, my hands are tied in some respects, but I'll do what I can. I've talked to the local authorities and gotten you and Rocco clearance to help out with this, but you don't have full capability. The FBI isn't ready to jump in yet without more proof, so we aren't officially involved, but Isla is available to consult."

"Understood." Meadow glanced over her shoulder at the closed door then stepped closer to the screen on the wall and the microphone it contained. "Ian Carpenter believes his cousin is in trouble or in proximity to trouble based on a series of texts she's sent him. He's set up a meet with her this morning in Cattle Bend. I think we should be there."

"It puts you out in the open in a town where he's already been hunted."

"Hiding at my house didn't help him." She exhaled loudly. "I'd like to know how that happened."

"I'll see what we can do." Chase wrote something on a paper by his hand. "As far as taking Ian out in public, I'm unsure."

When she looked at Rocco, he nodded grimly as he stepped up beside her. "We have no hold on him. He'll go on his own if we don't back him up, and that's not wise. He's a former law enforcement officer, and he's worked with Meadow before. We can't let a brother go in without covering him."

"No, you can't. If something were to happen to him neither of you would ever be able to wash his blood off your hands." With a tight expression, Chase gave a quick nod. "Do what you need to, but be careful, and I'll chat with the higher-ups and try to get you tapped into more of our resources. Keep me updated."

"Thanks, Chase." Meadow killed the call and turned to Rocco. "You don't have to get involved. You can stay here in Glacierville and keep digging into Henry Mulder's murder, keep yourself out of the line of fire." There was no way he'd do that. Lying back when there was action happening wasn't like Rocco at all.

He grinned. "You know me better than that." As he unhooked the laptop from the big screen, he sobered. "You realize this whole thing is foolish, right? The best thing for Ian to do is to let us go in and see if we can find his cousin. Your bad guys might know who we are, but we're going to be a lot less recognizable to them than he is, at least at first sight."

"True." Maybe that was the thing to do. If they borrowed an unmarked car from Glacierville PD, maybe they could roll in and reach out to Ian's cousin on his behalf without exposing him to a potentially deadly encounter.

Meadow headed for the door with Grace close behind, prepared to call Ian back inside. Rocco's plan was solid.

The problem would be convincing Ian not to put himself in the line of fire.

The closer they got to Cattle Bend, the more Ian regretted agreeing to Rocco and Meadow's plan. In the back seat of an SUV with darkly tinted windows, he drummed his fingers on his knee and watched the world pass by. The vehicle they'd borrowed from the impound at Glacierville PD smelled of stale cigarette smoke and beer. When it came to the stains on the seats, he didn't care to hazard a guess.

None of that bothered him though. He'd been in a lot worse places, and he had bigger problems. He'd failed Meadow in a gunfight. Had folded under pressure.

Was he about to fail Brooke as well?

With his phone busted, he couldn't reach out to his cousin to tell her he was on the way. A few minutes earlier, in an effort to calm Ian's nerves, Meadow had called the diner to make sure Brooke was safely at work.

No one had answered any of the five times she'd dialed.

Ian's gut screamed something had gone wrong.

Meadow caught his eye in the rearview. She'd pulled her hair into a ponytail and was wearing a borrowed baseball cap and her sunglasses. "You okay back there?" She'd been quiet for most of the hour-long drive.

Rocco had been silent as well, but that was because he'd fallen asleep almost as soon as they hit the road. Law enforcement officers and soldiers could sleep anywhere, that was for sure.

Still, the silence in the car was weighted with everyone's physical and emotional exhaustion.

Exhaustion he'd foisted upon them when he'd dragged them into his chaos. The more he thought about it, the more he believed he could have saved himself in the forest. Instead, he'd panicked and called for backup. Now Meadow and her team were in the crosshairs, whether Ian liked it or not. Telling her to back off would never work. That was one thing he'd learned from experience.

"Ian?"

He might as well answer. Her persistence was legendary. "A lot is running through my mind."

"Well, one of those things had better not be regret for reaching out to me yesterday." She flicked a gaze into the rearview. "I'd be pretty upset if you were out there trying to fix this on your own."

"I don't doubt it." He tapped his knee, wishing she'd try to call the diner again. "Why wouldn't a business answer their phone?"

"Maybe it's the breakfast rush."

Maybe. It was nearing nine, and Cattle Bend was a rising tourist town, so it was possible. "It worries me since Brooke was so cagey about something being wrong. I don't like it." Especially not with a target on his back. Brooke had been convinced one of her close friends was talking to a predator online, and she'd reached out to Ian. Since she was the one person who seemed to care about him, Ian would move mountains to help her.

And, sure, maybe he'd been looking for an excuse to come back. Maybe he'd hoped to run into Meadow. Maybe—

"You don't think she's somehow landed on Silas's radar, do you?"

That thought had barreled through his brain sometime in the middle of last night, when he'd been too keyed up with adrenaline to fall asleep. "I'd like to think not. My family isn't close. Brooke is my mom's sister's kid, so she doesn't share my last name. I haven't been around her in a couple of years and only established contact again after Ronnie died. We text and email and talk on the phone. No letters to intercept. They'd have to be pretty astute to figure out there's a connection between us, but you never know. Silas is smarter than he looks."

"You're probably right." Meadow navigated the exit to Cattle Bend, coasting to a stop at the top of the off-ramp, where a red light shined. "If they had any clue Brooke was related to you, they'd have used that intel to draw you out last night."

True. "I don't think they were aware I was in town until they spotted me in Cattle Bend yesterday. I'd just parked in front of the diner and was about to head inside when they basically charged me with their vehicle. If they made their way back there and started asking questions…" Then the worst might have happened. If they started nosing around and connected Brooke to him, then she'd be in danger.

He should have told Brooke to lie low, but her number wasn't one he'd memorized. Her mother's house phone was disconnected, likely because they'd all moved to cell service. He had no clue how to reach out to his family without simply showing up on their doorstep. He hadn't spoken to most of them in fourteen years, not since Dean had died. When his cousin wrapped his car around a tree after a party, it had been the final cut that severed Ian from his family. Everyone had laid the blame at Ian's feet.

Everyone except Brooke. Even as a kid, she'd recognized her brother's partying ways and stubborn arrogance. Yes, Ian had been at the party with his cousin. No, he hadn't been drinking, although Dean had downed half the liquor cabinet along with who knew what else.

Ian had taken his cousin's keys, but he hadn't counted on Dean having the spare in his pocket.

Brooke had lost her brother that night, and she'd looked to Ian to fill the void.

Now, she might be in trouble, and he was failing her. "What if she's been trying to reach me? What if something—"

"We've got someone getting you a new phone so you won't have to go into a store and risk putting yourself in the open for too long. And you'll feel a lot better once Rocco and I get into that diner and lay eyes on your cousin. We can prove to you she's okay and set up a meet so the two of you can talk somewhere safe."

Assuming they weren't spotted by Silas or a lookout.

Dropping his head on the back of the seat, Ian closed his eyes. Since when was he such a pessimist?

His hand went to his abdomen. Since he took a bullet in a parking lot where he should have been safe. The world would have to forgive him if he didn't trust any promise that said things were going to turn out fine.

When the light turned green, Meadow didn't release the brake.

From the right, a siren wailed as a Cattle Bend police cruiser slowed at the intersection then rushed through.

Ian watched it speed up the road and around a curve. There was an adrenaline rush to law enforcement work that he didn't often feel anymore. It wasn't a high, but a feeling of heading into the fray, being the one to help. Although he was happy with his quiet life with the horses at the rodeo, the protector instinct still called to him.

Meadow eased off of the brake and made the turn toward downtown. "You don't talk about your family much. Do—"

"We there yet?" Rocco shifted and stretched, his voice thick with sleep.

Saved by the groggy bell. His family was the last thing he wanted to discuss with Meadow.

She pursed her lips, then her demeanor shifted. "You're worse than my five-year-old niece, Roc."

"So when I start whining about how I want a burger from the drive-through and the little toy that comes with it, you won't be surprised." He stretched, pressing his palms against the ceiling, then looked over his shoulder at Ian. "Is the coffee any good at this diner where your cousin works?"

"Never been there. It's fairly new. Guy who used to run the kitchen at one of the ski resorts opened it up a couple of years ago, and it got popular pretty quickly." At least according to Brooke. She'd told him a while back that tips were good. "It's on the north end of the main road, on the right. When we set up a time to meet, she said we'd have to park in the back because they've eliminated street parking. Cattle Bend is getting more tourists since they revitalized the downtown."

Having seen the money coming in from travelers who were looking for the old-fashioned Western town experience, Cattle Bend had built facades and worked to attract independent business owners and restaurateurs to the area. He'd hardly recognized the place when he'd arrived yesterday. They'd really changed so—

"Uh-oh." Rocco lowered his arms and leaned closer to the windshield.

Dread pooled in Ian's stomach as Meadow inhaled deeply and gripped the steering wheel with both hands.

Ian forced himself to look out the front window as the main street through downtown came into view.

Three police cars blocked the road on the north end. A fire truck and an ambulance were also on scene...

Parked directly in front of the diner.

Chapter Eight

Meadow pulled in behind one of the police cars, her intuition running on overdrive.

This was about to be very bad for Ian.

Rocco was out the SUV and holding his identification up to an approaching officer before Meadow could kill the ignition.

She unbuckled her seat belt and turned to Ian. "Stay in the vehicle."

"No way I'm—"

"Stay. In. The. Vehicle." Her voice was hard, the one she used on suspects who weren't cooperating. "Use your head. If this is about Brooke, then it's likely Silas, Des or someone working for them who is keeping an eye out for you. Stay low. Don't move unless Rocco or I come for you. No arguments." She pegged him with her sternest gaze. "Tell me you understand and you'll do it, because I'd hate to pull that whole

TV cop thing and handcuff you to the steering wheel."

The vague attempt at humor didn't land. Ian stared at her for so long she was certain he was going to buck. Finally, he huffed a loud breath. "Fine. I get it."

She laid a hand on his knee. There had to be a way to ease his pain, which tugged at her heart. "I know you want to go in with a full head of steam to make sure Brooke is okay. This may not be about her at all. Just hold still until we know. I don't need you getting hurt." The day he'd been shot had gutted her, and she still had nightmares about it. She certainly never wanted to relive it. Believing she was close to losing someone who'd come to mean so much—

No.

Meadow shoved the emotions aside. Whatever was happening in the diner needed her full attention. Any past or present feelings for Ian could wait in the back seat with him.

When she joined Rocco at the rear of the SUV, they leashed Cocoa and Grace then headed for the perimeter, where emergency personnel moved between vehicles and the building with a frightening sense of urgency.

Bringing the dogs would blow their attempt to lie low, but they rarely left their K-9 partners behind. She scanned the area, searching for anyone watching too closely. Red, white and blue lights from first responders' vehicles flashed off of buildings and faces. Among the crowd of about twenty who had gathered, no one seemed overly interested in them, and no one was watching their SUV.

They showed their credentials to the Cattle Bend police officer standing guard, then Meadow hung her badge around her neck as she slipped under the tape with Rocco close behind. They were in civilian clothes, having hoped to keep anyone who might be a threat from immediately recognizing them. That hope was gone.

Inside the diner, chaos had left its mark. Several tables were overturned, their chairs flung onto their sides. Behind the counter, the jagged edges of a large shattered mirror clung to the teal-colored wall, while shards of glass were scattered across the counter and floor.

Rocco shot her a worried look.

"Deputy Marshal Ames." At the familiar voice, Meadow turned and found Cattle Bend Police Chief Gloria Montgomery striding to-

ward them. The woman was tall with posture
that made Meadow envious. She walked with
the grace of a supermodel. Her blond hair was
in a low bun on her neck, and the polished look
only added severity to her grim expression.

Chief Montgomery nodded to Rocco but
addressed Meadow. "What brings you to our
crime scene?" It was a friendly question, a curiosity, not a challenge.

"Honestly, I wasn't aware I would be walking into a crime scene." Meadow didn't want to
leak too much of Ian's story, since they needed
to lie low, but she also didn't want to be eva-
sive. "I'm here on unofficial business, looking
for a friend who's a waitress. Brooke Hawlett."

Chief Montgomery's mouth opened, then
closed. Her expression tightened as she glanced
at Rocco before meeting Meadow's gaze again.
"You're sure this is unofficial?"

Rocco's posture tightened, but he said nothing. He'd heard the odd undertone to the question as well.

Likely, he sensed the same tension Meadow
did. "Chief, are we stepping into something we
should know about?"

"What's your business with Brooke Hawlett?"
Where there had been a friendly, open expres-

sion moments before, a shadow now crossed the chief's face.

It took everything in Meadow not to buck at the question. This was Cattle Bend's crime scene, and it was their territory. She enjoyed a friendly relationship with all of the law enforcement in the area, and she didn't want to jeopardize that by popping off over a simple question. But she felt stonewalled, as though the chief who was usually so forthcoming was withholding information or stalling with her answers.

Meadow wanted to get to Brooke then get moving so Ian was out of harm's way, but as she surveyed the room and measured her words, she saw no one who matched the photos he had shown her.

Where was Ian's cousin?

Taking a deep breath, Meadow forced her voice to remain even. "All I can say is I have a friend who's worried about her. This person believes Brooke may be in trouble and wants to be sure she's safe. This is more of a…courtesy wellness check." As much as she wanted to step closer and crowd the chief's personal space, Meadow held her spot. "Is she safe?"

"What made this person assume Brooke might be in trouble?"

Okay, enough was enough. Ian had been in

the car too long. They were standing in the middle of a crime scene.

And there was no way to know who was watching.

It was clear Brooke had been involved in whatever incident had destroyed the diner and brought the police onto the scene.

"With all due respect, Chief, I'm on a time crunch. I've got a dangerous situation that's evolving rapidly, and I need to talk to Brooke Hawlett as soon as possible. I'm asking for some leeway here."

"And I'm trying to solve a kidnapping."

Rocco muttered something under his breath as Meadow took an involuntary step back at the force of what wasn't spoken. "Someone took Brooke?"

"Pretty violently." The chief gave a curt nod and seemed to come to a decision. "Two masked assailants pulled up to the front door about fifteen minutes ago, shot up the place and grabbed Brooke. She fought every inch of the way, but…" The chief gestured toward the overturned tables. "It was over in under a minute. We've got a BOLO out for a dark four-door sedan headed south out of town. So far, no hits."

Meadow balled her fist around Grace's leash.

They were too late. There was almost zero doubt Silas or someone working for him had taken Brooke.

But had Silas targeted Brooke for trafficking? Or was this an attempt to draw Ian out of hiding? Given the very public nature of the snatch and grab, it was likely about Ian, which meant the danger increased the longer he was in public. "What else have you got?"

"We've just started talking to witnesses, and I've got one of my guys viewing security-camera footage, but it seems they headed directly for Brooke as though she was the target." Chief Montgomery stepped closer and lowered her voice. "Maybe you've heard or maybe not, but we've had several young people vanish in the past four months. All around Brooke's age, but the others weren't taken like this. A couple were lured by an online predator. One was homeless and frequented a travel plaza near the interstate. One disappeared from a party where there was a steady flow of alcohol and drugs. Up until today, I thought we might have a serial killer on our hands, and when I saw you walk in with your federal agent self, I pretty much decided my theory was right."

"You were wrong. We're not dealing with a

serial killer." Rocco spoke for the first time. His expression tight, he looked to Meadow for confirmation it was time to share what they knew. When she nodded, he turned to the chief. "Silas Thornton has been spotted in the area."

Chief Montgomery held up her index finger, her head tilted as though she was trying to process the information. She almost spoke, then she pointed to Rocco as though she was having to wade through shock. "Silas Thornton is long gone. The scourge of that family was burned off when he died in an explosion and his father died in prison. It took years and a joint operation to shut them down. Silas is not back in action."

"I don't blame you for wanting it to be a mistake." The Thorntons had robbed the outlying towns around the city of Missoula of any sense of safety and security. They'd trafficked countless young women and men through the area, holding them in warehouses and other spaces scattered around Missoula. Occasionally, they'd hunted in the region, picking off vulnerable teenagers. Though they typically sought runaways, they sometimes lured other victims as well. There had been a collective sigh of relief when the organization was torn apart. To think they were active again in the same location was unimaginable.

"What proof do you have?"

"A reliable witness has laid eyes on them. I've heard their voices and enough of their own words to believe it's them."

"Them?" Chief Montgomery's eyebrows knit together. "Who's with him?"

"Desiree Phelps."

"Wow." The chief puffed out the exclamation. "The team is alive and well and working again."

"And out for blood. They've attacked a witness, and last night, they made a run at the same person when he sought protection at my house."

"That was you last night? I heard about the call for Glacierville PD and Peak County, but I hadn't been briefed on any details."

There was no time to offer them now. They needed to get moving. The longer they stood around talking, the larger Silas's head start grew. "We're working with a unit investigating the Rocky Mountain Killer, but we have some leeway on other cases as well. I'm going to call my team leader and see if we can officially assist." Given the violence of the crime and their suspicions, it might be enough to get the feds involved.

Chief Montgomery nodded. "I have a feeling I'm going to want you guys here. Let's shut this down before it goes too far."

And before Brooke was killed.

What was taking so long?

Each sweep of the second hand on his watch took hours. Every one of the ten minutes since Meadow and Rocco had disappeared inside the diner had hit him like a body blow.

Was Brooke hurt? Why hadn't Meadow stepped out with an update?

Ian reached for the door then let his hand drop to the stained upholstery. As much as he wanted to rush in and save the day, he could land them all in hot water if he showed his face. For all he knew, Silas and Des had created a commotion simply to draw him out. There could be a sniper on a rooftop, an assailant with a knife in the crowd...

Without knowing who, if anyone, Silas had on his payroll, there were too many unknowns. Anyone could be a killer.

He hadn't felt this helpless since he'd awakened in the hospital attached to so many tubes and wires that his initial foggy thoughts had made him believe he was hooked up to the Matrix. Ever since that day, he'd controlled every situation.

The past sixteen hours had proven control was an illusion. There was nothing he could do to manage the increasing chaos surrounding him. The longer he sat, the more convinced he was Brooke was in danger, but if he left the vehicle...

He could relive the feeling of a bullet slamming into him, only this time, the lead might finish its job.

His jaw clenched. Was this what he'd been reduced to? He'd once taken an oath to protect and serve; now he was bowing to fear instead of helping the one person in his life who'd never turned her back on him.

Ian shoved the car door open, stepped out and charged up the street. He ducked under the police tape and headed for the diner's open door like he belonged there.

He almost made it.

Two officers flanked him before he could cross the threshold.

The one to the right stepped into the doorway, while the one to the left took up a position beside him. "Sir, I'm going to need to see some identification."

The guy wanted a badge, something Ian hadn't carried in two years. While he wanted to charge forward, he didn't want the handcuffs that would follow. Inhaling deeply, he held his hands away from his body to indicate he was no threat. "I have a driver's license in my wallet in my back pocket, but I don't have my badge." *Or any badge at the moment.* "I'm with the deputy marshal who's inside, Meadow Ames."

The cop blocking his way raised an eyebrow. His blue eyes held a heavy dose of skepticism and wariness, a look Ian himself had worn on more occasions than he cared to count. "I suggest you go back to your vehicle. This is an active crime scene."

An active crime scene where his younger cousin worked. Ian wanted to shove past the guy and call out for Brooke. Instead, he scanned the interior of the diner, finally spotting Rocco and Meadow near the counter at the rear. "Meadow!" Her name echoed off the walls.

She turned quickly, her ponytail swinging, and her expression morphed from curiosity to anger.

Yeah, he'd pay for not following orders,

but he'd deal with that later. "Tell them to let me in."

He'd read about people whose anger looked like a thundercloud on their faces before, but he'd never seen it until now. If a face really could storm, it was highly likely he'd have already been struck by lightning.

She stopped behind the officer at the door. "I ought to have them arrest you. You'd be safer from yourself behind bars." When the officer moved his hand to his hip, she shook her head. "No. He's with me and Officer Manelli. You can let him in."

With a curt nod, the two officers stood down.

Before Ian could move, Meadow grabbed him by the wrist and dragged him to a wide wall between the two front windows. "Have you lost your mind?" The words barely made it through her gritted teeth.

The last thing he was worried about was Meadow's ire. "Where's Brooke?"

He tried to step around Meadow, but her palm against his chest shoved him against the wall. "Ian, stay away from the windows. If you can handle that, I'll bring the manager over, and we can talk about what's going on." The pressure on his sternum increased. "Are we clear this time?"

"Crystal." The humiliation of being talked down to burned the back of his neck. She might have been his handler on that op, but she didn't get to boss him around now.

Except...she was right about staying away from the windows. His shoulders lost some of their defiance. "Where is she?"

The pressure on his chest decreased, but Meadow didn't move her hand. Instead, her fingers curled as though she could wrap his heart against her palm to protect it from whatever happened next.

Well, she didn't need to protect him. "This mess in here... Someone took Brooke. By force." He was going to be sick.

Meadow swallowed hard. "If it helps, she fought them all the way."

He looked away, staring at the remains of a shattered mirror behind the counter. Brooke had lived a hard life with con-artist parents who had been neglectful before Dean died and who had canonized her brother after, constantly ignoring her in their grief and anger. That she was a fighter didn't surprise him, but such a trait could either save her life or get her killed.

Meadow's fingers tightened against his chest, her palm warm and her touch somehow soothing.

When Ian turned his head, she was watching him as though she wanted to speak, but then she simply dropped her hand and motioned for Rocco to join them.

He crossed the diner, stepping around an overturned table, followed by a man who picked his way across the room to avoid stepping on the debris that littered the tile floor.

For the first time, the trail of destruction came into focus. The broken mirror, the scattered tables and chairs... Brooke truly had done all she could to save herself, but someone had clearly come in with a mission.

He had a horrible feeling he knew who it was.

The manager, a middle-aged man with dark hair that had begun to gray around the temples, gathered in the huddle with Meadow and Rocco. His face was pale from what had clearly been a traumatic experience.

Meadow took the lead. "Mr. Pullman, this is Ian Carpenter. He's—"

"Brooke's cousin." The manager's expression collapsed. "I'm so sorry—"

"How did you know that?" Ian's chest squeezed. Nobody should know his name, let alone his relationship to Brooke. "Who told you?"

"I..." Mr. Pullman's head jerked back as though Ian had slapped him. He looked to Rocco as though seeking permission to speak and received a terse nod. "She...she mentioned you a couple of days ago. Said she had a cousin who used to be a deputy and she was worried about one of her friends who was talking to a guy online. She thought it sounded suspicious, but her friend wasn't listening and neither was her mom, so she'd reached out to him."

Ian sagged against the wall as his stomach crashed to his feet. After Ronnie Thornton died in prison, Ian had planned to stay in his new life in Texas. When he'd reached out to Brooke to let her know he was safe and they could resume contact, he'd asked her not to talk to the family about him. He hadn't thought there was a need to caution her about mentioning his name in public. "Did anyone overhear her? Ask her about me?"

Pullman's eyes shifted sideways, as though he didn't want to say what he remembered.

Ian felt like shaking him. Did this man not

understand the urgency? Forcing himself to remain calm, he balled his fists instead.

"Anything will help." Meadow's voice was more gentle than Ian's would have been.

"I guess you'd told her you were coming into town, and early this morning, she was pretty excited. She was talking to me and to a couple of her regular customers about it."

"Who were those regulars? And were there any strangers around when she was talking?" Surely Silas and Des weren't hanging around town on the regular, but they could have dropped into the diner while they were scouting locations, or they could have been the online boyfriend Brooke was concerned about and had been in town to work one of their heinous plans.

"I can make you a list, but none of them would do what those thugs today did to Brooke. It was mostly the old-timers in here when she was talking. But… I mean, there are always tourists around, so yeah, there were a few strangers, too."

"One of the Cattle Bend officers is in the back, running through the security video." Rocco was already backing away. "I'll go have him dial back to yesterday, see if they see her talking to anyone else or if there's anyone we recognize on the feed."

"Anyone you recognize?" Pullman straightened, his expression hard. "Is there a reason a federal agent is here? What do we not know? What *should* we know?" His voice was rising as his shock and fear morphed into doubts and anger. "Are our kids in danger again? We just went through this with—"

"Mr. Pullman." Meadow laid a hand on the man's shoulder, and he instantly quieted at her voice, which was somehow both authoritative and soothing. Even Ian couldn't help responding to it. "All we have right now is speculation, and we can't make official comments based on speculation."

"Wait. Ian Carpenter. I just remembered why your name sounded familiar when Brooke mentioned her cousin." Pullman's head whipped toward Ian. "You're the deputy who got shot after the Thornton investigation. The one who was undercover with them. It was all over the news." He stepped closer. "Are they back? Did you mess something up and they walked?"

"Mr. Pullman, I suggest you step down." Meadow held her arm between the manager and Ian, creating a barrier. "Ronnie Thornton died in prison three months ago, and all reports say his son was killed in an explosion. The rest of his crew were arrested or scattered in the aftermath."

Pullman never pulled his gaze from Ian's, his chest rising and falling with ire. He looked like a man who thought Ian might be guilty of crimes he was afraid to speak out loud. Finally, he sniffed, "Maybe so, but there are girls missing in the area, just like last time. And if the Thorntons are somehow back?" He shoved his finger into Ian's face. "Then it's your hands that are covered in blood."

Chapter Nine

Meadow watched the side mirror as Rocco navigated a curve. They'd made it to the outskirts of town without picking up a tail and were heading through the mountains toward the highway. Their trip would end in even more dangerous territory, the county sheriff's office, the place Ian had been shot by one of Ronnie Thornton's hired guns.

It was also the easiest place to start searching for clues in the recent disappearances. If they could find a thread connecting them, they might be able to trace where Silas and Des had taken Brooke.

It was all they had.

In the SUV's cargo area, Cocoa and Grace rested, ready for action should they be needed.

Ian was silent. He was understandably concerned about his cousin, but it was tough to tell if he was harboring some anger that added to his silence.

If it did, Meadow couldn't blame him. The manager had blasted him for something that wasn't his fault. It had taken all of her restraint to hold her tongue.

Worse than the manager's behavior was her own. She'd essentially backed Ian into a corner and treated him like a subordinate at the crime scene. Although he'd been reckless, her actions had been disrespectful. As a colleague and a friend, she'd been wrong.

Volcanic rage had surged through her when he appeared in the doorway. What was he thinking, putting himself in harm's way? It wasn't until she'd shoved him away from the windows and felt his beating heart under her palm that the truth had struck…

She wasn't angry. She was terrified. The thought of a bullet flying through the air toward him, of losing him for real, had jerked her emotions out from under her.

The question was…why? She'd long ago buried any feelings that had surfaced while they were working together.

Yet every time he was nearby, something stirred.

Something he would never feel in return.

Rocco cleared his throat, pulling Meadow out of her spiraling. "You okay, Ian?"

Meadow turned to where Ian rode behind Rocco. His gaze met hers, steely yet pained. "I should have gotten to Brooke sooner."

"You'd be dead." Rocco was too matter-of-fact. "The point was to draw you out."

Security footage had shown the attack, and the builds of the assailants matched both Silas and Des.

"You know he's right." Meadow tried to gentle her tone. "The upside is they'll keep her alive as long as they need her as bait."

Ian frowned. "But what will they do to her?"

His concern was valid. The Thorntons hated Ian. His undercover operation had been the bomb that splintered their organization. They might take their wrath out on Brooke.

"She doesn't deserve this." Ian stared out the window. "I should surrender."

"No." The word exploded from Meadow. Even Rocco jerked at the force of it. "They'll kill you, then her." More than anything, she wanted to touch him, to offer some comfort, but after the way her heart had twisted at the diner, she was afraid to. "Your emotions are clouding your judgment."

Hello, Pot? Meet Kettle.

"I should be doing something, not sitting here as a passenger on this road to nowhere." Ian's eyes blazed. "She's counting on me to find her, and what am I doing? I'm—"

"Doing what it takes." Rocco's voice was cool rain to Ian's raging fire. "We're going to comb through case files, pinpoint a central location, then move."

"I've got people in Missoula checking out Silas's old stomping grounds. It's possible he's headed for what's familiar." Meadow had reached out to the Marshals and local law enforcement. They had cruised by the Thorntons' former stash houses, though most had either been destroyed or auctioned. If Silas wanted to resume operations in Missoula, he would be hard-pressed to find a place.

Which meant he'd have to start over somewhere new. There were several young people missing from the surrounding areas, so what if the Thorntons were connected to all of that? "Why is Silas spending so much time around Cattle Bend?"

Rocco navigated a turn onto a two-lane road that ascended the mountain. "You thinking out loud?"

"More like brainstorming." Meadow shifted so she could look at Rocco and Ian, who still wore a mask of anger. Maybe getting him involved would help him to feel as though he was doing something constructive. "Silas can't return to any of his known locales. He's having to start fresh, which means obtaining a whole lot of property at once in order to build a network of stash houses."

"And not in his name or any known aliases." Ian sat forward, engaging with Meadow's thought process. He wore a look that said he was chasing an idea. "He'll have a shell corp or a new false identity, and he'll snap up properties somewhere that won't raise red flags."

"Somewhere like Cattle Bend." Meadow nodded. He'd boarded her train of thought.

"Okay," Rocco jumped in. "Why Cattle Bend?"

Ian leaned forward until his seat belt stopped him. "A few years ago, Cattle Bend was a dying town as coal mining dried up. The crime rate was rising. The population was moving to greener pastures. It was headed for ghost-town status."

"Until a group got together and decided to develop a new source of revenue," Meadow said. The many special elections and county meetings had made the Missoula news.

Ian nodded. "Ultimately, the town's council reached out to developers, pitching the area as an outdoorsy and artsy tourist destination like Whitefish is. Coffee shops, fishing guides, galleries... Tax breaks for small businesses brought people flocking in."

"Got it." Rocco glanced in the rearview, then joined the brainstorm. "Lots of people buying up lots of property all at once. Someone like Silas would have no problem building a network of stash houses without anyone batting an eye at the new player snatching up real estate."

"Bingo." Meadow pulled her phone from her pocket. "I'll have Isla dig into property purchases and rentals over the past two years."

"How long will that take?" It was hard to tell if the air around Ian was tight with impatience or concern.

"Hopefully not long." When Isla answered, Meadow focused her attention on the call. "It's Meadow. How fast can you can run a records search?" She ran down the events of the morning and what they were looking for.

"A couple of hours? Sooner if a pattern emerges. It'll require me to pull all of the real estate transactions for the past couple of years and to trace the purchasers to find red flags. Tough to say how long that will take. And... are you alone?"

"No. Why?" Meadow tried to decipher Isla's tone. "All good on your end?" She didn't want to attract attention, but she also wanted to know how Isla was doing. Their tech expert had been through a lot recently, and she often confided in Meadow.

She pressed the phone to her ear, trying to keep the guys from overhearing.

"All good." The words were bright.

Too bright. "Not buying it." Hopefully, the comment was vague enough for Rocco and Ian to think it was professional and for Isla to understand it wasn't. Isla clearly needed an ear.

The silence was long and void of the typical tapping that came as Isla clicked at her keyboard while she talked.

"Isla?"

"It's just..." Her teammate's sigh was heavy. "I was looking into who might have lied to the adoption agency about me having a drinking problem. I've gotten nowhere, and it's weighing on me."

"Oh." Meadow's quiet exclamation caught

Rocco's attention. He pulled his gaze from the rearview to glance over with a silent question. Meadow mouthed the word *foster*.

Rocco gave a sympathetic nod, turned back to the front, then checked the rearview again. His brow furrowed, but he said nothing.

Five months earlier, Isla had been approved to foster a baby girl named Charisse. Days before the placement, an anonymous tipster told the adoption agency Isla was drinking heavily and using illegal drugs. Because of her job, the agency had been leery of the accusations but had to act, placing Charisse with another family who was now in the process of adopting her. The events had devastated Isla and started her on a search for who would be so cruel to her. Isla was so good-natured and sweet that the list was short, though it did include three ex-boyfriends and a cousin who'd cut ties with her over a family issue.

"You came up empty on your searches?"

"All three of my exes seem to be in happy relationships," Isla said. "My cousin's boyfriend, the one I didn't want at Thanksgiving after I found out he was wanted on a slew of minor charges, is back in jail after violating parole. It wasn't him, and she and I had a decent conversation that leads me to believe it wasn't her either. I'm nowhere."

"I'm sorry." If only they could do more, but their resources were focused on finding the Rocky Mountain Killer and on the other cases they were working, including Ian's. "I wish I could give you a hug."

Rocco shifted in his seat, drawing her attention, then jerked his thumb toward the back window.

Dread pooled in Meadow's stomach. "Isla, I have to go." She pocketed her phone and turned to look behind them.

Brow furrowed in confusion, Ian did the same.

A white sedan appeared around a curve, roaring toward them at breakneck speed.

Meadow whipped toward the front. "Rocco?"

"I saw him a couple of miles ago. He was hanging back as we came out of town, but he matched every turn I took. Now?" Rocco gestured toward the area around them. They were on a winding stretch of road that meandered up the mountain before it would drop down again near the highway. No houses. No businesses. Thin traffic.

Meadow turned and let her gaze sweep past

Ian to watch the car close the distance. It disappeared briefly as Rocco took a turn then accelerated, seeking to put distance between them.

The car appeared again, gaining on them rapidly.

They were secluded. Without backup. Meadow pulled the phone from her pocket and dialed 911. Hopefully someone would arrive quickly, because she hated the thought of a shoot-out. It was the thing she wanted to avoid the most.

But they were isolated and alone right now, and if anyone wanted to eliminate Ian, now would be the perfect time to strike a fatal blow.

Not again.

Was he really being chased through the mountains again? Silas and Des were far from creative, that was certain. Still, the threat fired adrenaline into his heart with a painful jolt. He was already wrestling with a return to the sheriff's department where he'd been shot. The last thing he needed was more stress. While he was in the capable hands of two fellow law enforcement officers and knew how to defend himself, the PTSD reared its horrible head and muddied his emotions and thoughts.

If this kept up, a heart attack would take him out before Silas ever could.

Meadow ended her call to emergency services and turned toward him. "Rocco's the best driver on our team." Her voice was tight. It was tough to tell if she spoke the truth or was simply trying to convince them all that this would end okay.

He prayed it would.

"And it's a good thing this was a drug runner's car. The engine is souped up and ready to fly." Rocco punched the gas to emphasize the statement, and they shot forward at speeds that were on the edge of sanity.

The white sedan lost ground. Ian strained to see the driver, who seemed to be alone in the vehicle. He needed to focus on the tactical, treat this like a job and not a threat to his life. No emotion. Just business.

With the way both vehicles were whipping around turns, focusing was difficult. "I can't tell if the driver is a man or a woman." He faced forward, trying to ward off motion sickness before it could kick in.

"Same." Meadow looked at Rocco. "Think they know where we're headed?"

"No." Rocco navigated another curve, his

jaw tight. "If they did, they'd have waited for us there and—" Glancing in the rearview at Ian, he bit off the rest of the sentence.

Not that he had to say it. *They'd have waited for us there and ambushed us.* Just like the day he'd been shot.

He was going to be sick, and it wasn't from the wild ride through the mountains. What was he doing? Maybe he should let Meadow tuck him away in a safe house somewhere until this was over.

But no. Brooke needed him. He pulled in a deep breath and exhaled through pursed lips. There wasn't time to pull over and let him lose his breakfast. "Can you shake them?" His clenched jaw made his voice sound unnaturally deep.

"Don't need to do that. Just need to keep them at a distance until backup shows up, and we let overwhelming numbers tell them this is a very bad idea."

As if Rocco's words had spoken them into existence, two sheriff's SUVs appeared around the next turn, lights blazing and sirens blaring.

Rocco eased up on the gas. "Given that we've got their prey in our vehicle, I think the best course of action is to let the sheriff handle the chase."

"Agreed." Meadow's voice was tight.

Whipping around, Ian stared out the back window. As the white sedan appeared around a curve, the driver slammed on the brakes at the sight of the approaching SUVs. The car spun around and, smoke spewing from the tires, roared in the opposite direction, the deputies in pursuit.

That had ended much too easily. He settled back into the seat, trying to center his emotions. "They'll try again."

"Hopefully the sheriff will catch up to them but, if not, we'll be ready for them." Meadow's gaze bored into his. "We're going to keep you safe. I promise."

It was humiliating. He should be the one offering protection, not be the one so weak that he had to receive it.

The remainder of the drive was silent. Meadow continued to face the rear, eyes focused out the back window as she watched for another tail. Rocco made it to the highway and headed west toward Summit Road, where the sheriff's department was just off the exit.

Ian stared out the side window, avoiding

Meadow's eyes. He had enough roiling around inside of him without adding Meadow to the mix. Too much was happening too fast, and he desperately wished he could run back into the bunker and take shelter until this was over.

Brooke needed him, though.

As Rocco pulled off the highway exit, the imposing brick building that housed the sheriff's department came into view. He forced himself to look at it, hating the tightness in his chest. The feeling his heart was going to beat itself to death. The clamp around his lungs that kept him from taking a satisfying breath.

Now that their pursuer had disappeared, the adrenaline had subsided and left space for the memories and fears to grow. His chest felt like it might explode from the pressure the past exerted on his heart and lungs.

He forced himself to sit back and take a deep breath. There was no way he was going to tell Rocco and Meadow he was about to come unglued. This was foolishness.

Except it wasn't.

He hadn't been to the literal scene of the crime since the day EMTs had loaded him into an ambulance and rushed him away from the parking lot where he'd been gunned down by one of Ronnie Thornton's henchmen. Ian had been hailed a hero for facing death in the race to dismantle the crime syndicate that had wreaked havoc on the area, but he'd never felt like a hero.

No, he felt more like a terrified little boy who'd been punched by a bully one too many times and had curled up in the corner to ward off the next blow.

In the past twenty-four hours, he'd been chased down a mountain and through the forest. Had been responsible for his cousin's violent kidnapping. Had been pursued once again. And he'd been shot at twice.

They'd passed his worst nightmare hours ago. A bullet flying in his direction, ripping through him before the sound of the shot reached his ears was the horror that often left his body coated in sweat.

This was the thing that might break him.

As they slowed in front of the low brick building, he tried to keep his eyes away from the scene of his near death, but his mind betrayed him and turned his gaze toward the side lot where the deputies parked their SUVs.

It was no longer visible. The chain-link fence topped with barbed wire was gone. In its place, a high brick wall shielded deputies from the street and from anyone who might want to harm them as they came and went from the building.

At least his experience had done something to protect others, but the thought was cold comfort when memories assailed him with each rotation of the SUV's tires.

As Rocco parked the car, a large iron gate came into view. Through it, Ian could see the small lot and the corner of space number seventeen, where he'd come close to taking his last breath. He had very few memories of that day, but the ones that arose shot through him like lightning, just like they did in his nightmares.

He'd just stowed his gear and shut the SUV's door when something punched him in the gut, hard. A gunshot echoed off of the building. His Sig was in his hands before he realized he'd moved, the action reflexive. Adrenaline pulsing through his veins, he'd scanned the chain-link fence as other deputies came running, shouting, their footfalls melding with the sound of his own pounding heartbeat.

There. A man stood at the fence, rifle raised, prepared to fire again. The look of cold, deadly determination in his eyes was seared into Ian's memory.

So was the need to save his fellow deputies before the shooter could pull the trigger again.

He fired.

His gunshot mingled with those from fellow deputies who'd arrived to protect one another.

Ian never saw the guy fall. Never knew whose shot ended the assault. His body had suddenly gone cold. Shivering cold. Damp warmth spread across his abdomen as his knees wobbled then dropped him to the blazing hot asphalt. He'd looked down, captivated by the dark red seeping through his shirt, across his stomach. So much red. So much... So much he couldn't connect to reality. This wasn't happening to him, was it? He was watching a movie. Reading a book. This wasn't—

"Ian?" A warm touch on his knee dragged him to the present.

Meadow eyed him with concern, her fingertips resting lightly on his kneecap.

Rocco was watching him in the rearview mirror. "You okay, man?"

Closing his eyes, Ian exhaled slowly, sliding his hand along his thigh until he found Meadow's fingers and wrapped his around hers. He'd done the same thing in the hospital, when he'd awakened to find her sitting at his bedside, her fear and concern etched in deep lines around her eyes and mouth.

Now, as then, her touch said everything was going to be okay, that he could do this.

When he opened his eyes, she was still facing him, but she was staring at their entwined fingers, her expression unreadable.

It took Ian a second to make his mouth work. His tongue was so dry. How long had he been staring into the past? Maybe he should feel embarrassment, but he couldn't muster the emotion. It was taking all he had to survive. "I'll be fine."

"You haven't been back here since that day, have you?" Meadow's fingers tightened around his.

He'd missed this. Had missed her. The way she seemed to know what he was thinking. The way her hard edges concealed and protected her soft heart, something he suspected very few people realized. He'd missed...her. The way she made him feel things no one else ever had.

He'd been thinking about her in the moment the bullet had pierced his spleen. Had been considering calling her when he got into his vehicle. A call that might have changed things between them forever. For the better if she'd accepted his invitation to an actual date. For the worse if she'd let him down easy and said their partnership had been strictly professional and she was ready to move on.

He jerked his hand from hers. How had he forgotten those thoughts? Forgotten Meadow had been on his mind in the seconds before his life changed forever? If he'd been focused on his surroundings instead of on her, he might not have missed the gun trained on him. He might not have been responsible for putting his colleagues in the line of fire.

He'd known back then she was a risk. Relationships weren't for guys like him, who had never been taught empathy or love.

So, yeah, he didn't need to touch her or be touched by her. "I'll be fine." He repeated the words, hoping she'd buy them, then turned toward the car door. In the process, he caught Rocco's eye in the mirror, still watching, but this time his gaze held suspicion and a question.

One Ian had no intention of answering.

Instead, he scanned the immediate area, searching for danger, then forced himself to do the impossible.

He opened the car door and stepped into the bright sunlight, his feet landing on the very same pavement where he'd nearly died over eighteen months earlier, his body tense in case the Thorntons had followed him and were looking to bring his story to a not-so-poetic end.

Chapter Ten

Another conference room, another batch of files.

Five folders lay open at evenly spaced intervals around the polished wood table at the Peak County Sheriff's Department. While digital records were growing in popularity, Meadow preferred to put her hands on actual, handwritten reports.

The five folders, three thin and two thick, pierced her heart with pain and anger.

Pain. Four females and one male, ages ranging from midteens to early twenties, all missing.

Anger. Three had vanished after arguments with their parents. Two had been chatting with strangers online and made plans for secret meetings before disappearing.

Someone had stolen them and their innocence.

That anger layered on top of rage over that

white car's pursuit of them. Had they not been in a souped-up former drug dealer's vehicle, there was no telling how that chase would have ended.

They might all be dead.

And it wasn't over. When the deputies had reported in, the news hadn't been good. The driver gained enough distance to ditch the car on the edge of town and to disappear among the crowds of tourists. Whoever had tried to hunt them down was still at large.

At the news, Rocco had walked outside with Cocoa, claiming he needed fresh air and clean headspace.

Ian sat at the end of the table, head bent over the file for eighteen-year-old Cassidy Michaels. He was buried in the work, probably using the research as a tactic to avoid emotions whipped wildly by a near-death experience in the past and too many close calls in the present.

Meadow shoved the file on seventeen-year-old Robert Moore toward the center of the table and stood, pacing to a window overlooking a courtyard. She needed to clear her mind, to stop the racing thoughts conjuring horror stories about where these kids might be and who they might be with.

To shove aside the guilt that had chased her for hours.

They'd failed the people in this area when they failed to realize Silas and Des were still alive.

How many families had been destroyed because of the Thorntons? How many more would live with terror and pain?

She dragged her hands down her face, avoiding her reflection in the glass as she stared outside.

Pressure against her knee dragged her attention to where Grace sat, leaning in as though she knew Meadow needed support.

Meadow squatted and took the K-9's face in her hands, resting her forehead against her partner's. "You just know, don't you?" She closed her eyes, letting Grace offer the comfort that only she could. It was moments like this when she realized how vital therapy dogs like their missing Cowgirl could be. Hopefully, they'd locate the labradoodle soon.

"It's rough, I know." Ian's voice came from above, low and calming.

Rocking back on her heels, she looked up at the man she'd once loved. The one who had vanished in pain and had returned to even more pain. "I'm sorry." This was her fault. She'd been one of the leaders of the team taking down the Thorntons. If she'd done her due diligence instead of—

"Knock it off." Ian plopped onto the gray carpet beside her and rested his wrists on his bent knees. "Can I get in on the emotional support?"

Meadow smiled when Grace tilted her head toward Ian as though she'd understood his words.

Ian scratched Grace behind the ears. He'd relaxed slightly once they'd entered the conference room. Before they'd stepped inside, he'd asked for his presence to be kept quiet. Meadow had relayed the request to the sheriff, who'd shielded their way to the conference room and shut the door after a brief conversation with Ian.

She understood. What he'd experienced had been traumatic. Moving to Texas in WITSEC had left a lot of open endings. Brooke's kidnapping and the need to return to the scene of his shooting had taken an emotional toll. She couldn't blame him for not wanting to pile reunions on top of it. Even the mightiest of warriors could only take so much upheaval in one day.

She'd seen the turmoil roiling through him as they pulled into the parking lot. She'd touched his knee then immediately wished she hadn't. Her intent had been to offer comfort, but when he'd looked up at her, there had been something besides pain and fear in his expression. Something that echoed the things she'd once felt for him, things she might be feeling again, if she was being honest.

Grace shifted her attention from Meadow to Ian, angling toward him so he could more easily scratch her ears.

He seemed to be focused on the K-9, which gave Meadow the encouragement to speak freely. "I'm sorry for bringing you here. I should have considered how hard it would be."

Ian ran his hand down Grace's neck and scratched her shoulder as though he wasn't really focused on the K-9 but was seeking a distraction while he sorted thoughts. When he spoke, it was toward Grace, though the words were meant for Meadow. "I'm a big boy. If I thought I couldn't handle a ride-along, I'd have told you."

"You'd have told me, or you'd have told Grace?" The moment needed some levity.

Ian grinned. "Clearly Grace is the one in charge."

"She'd like to think so." Meadow sat back on the floor to give her knees a break and to open up a few inches of distance between them. There were things she needed to say. "I know you want to charge out there and find Brooke. So do I. But—"

"But I also know that would be the worst thing we could do. It would get me killed. Or you." Dropping his hands from Grace's neck, Ian pivoted to face Meadow. They both sat cross-legged, truly, fully face-to-face for the first time in years.

Grace lay down with her back against Meadow's hip, exhaling a contented sigh.

It was a sentiment Meadow could appreciate. Something about being in Ian's presence, alone in the quiet conference room, left her wanting to settle in and rest as well. Even with danger swirling outside the door, this space felt safe, separated from everything that was happening out in the world.

It was a foolish thought, and the kind of distraction that got people killed in the heat of battle.

But this wasn't the heat of battle. This was the four safe walls of the county sheriff's department, where they were temporarily shielded from outside threats.

Meadow didn't realize she was staring at him until his head tilted slightly, his gaze never breaking from hers. "What's going on in your head?" The question was low and gravelly, coming from somewhere deep inside of him.

It demanded the truth. Did she dare say it? "Coming here wasn't easy for me, either." She'd wanted to speak normally, but the words exhaled on a whisper. "I lost you that day."

Ian's lips flattened, his gaze turning toward the ceiling. Several emotions flashed across his face before he dipped his chin and leaned closer, his eyes capturing hers. "You really didn't."

She shouldn't be saying or feeling any of this. Meadow looked down at her fingers where they rested on her ankles. Their relationship had remained largely professional on the outside, though everyone knew they'd developed a deep friendship while they worked together. It was her heart alone that had tripped into something more, and that should be her secret to bear forever. She couldn't foist her emotions onto him. It was unprofessional. Some might say it was weak. Others would—

"Hey. Look at me." When she didn't move, Ian hesitated before he continued to speak. "I never had anybody I could count on. You know that. When I was undercover, I counted on you.

I just didn't realize how much until I woke up in the hospital and..." He reached over and wrapped warm fingers around her wrist. "And you were there. The first person I saw."

Closing her eyes, Meadow dug her teeth into her top lip. She should back away, stand, get back to digging through files for answers. This was silly. They were in the middle of searching for his cousin. She was a professional, right?

Wasn't she?

So why did she come unglued whenever Ian Carpenter was around?

"You were there, Meadow, when I needed you. I'm not used to someone caring about me. I didn't know what to do with that then." He withdrew his hand, letting the air in the room cool her wrist, but almost immediately, his fingers touched her chin, lifting her face to his.

When she opened her eyes, he was closer than he had been before, his gaze roaming her face. "I don't know what to do with that now either." He leaned in and brushed a kiss on her forehead, then rested his cheek against hers. His hand slid to the back of her neck beneath her ponytail, drawing her all the way in. He simply rested with her and breathed.

Tears stung the backs of her eyes, but she

couldn't sort her emotions to figure out why. There was just Ian, this moment and something so much more intimate than the kiss she'd half thought he was about to offer. Sliding her hand along her knee, she found his free hand and held on as his fingers tightened on the back of her neck.

She let him have the moment, and she allowed herself to sink into it, wondering if he could read her mind and understand the things she wasn't saying.

Wondering if he was thinking the same thoughts. If he was, then—

A door slammed up the hallway.

They jerked back simultaneously, her head whacking the wall behind her as Ian jumped to his feet like he'd been pulled up by his collar.

Grace leaped up as well, ready for action.

Taking a deep breath, Meadow re-centered her thinking and laid a hand on Grace's head, commanding her to sit.

Rocco's voice drifted up the hallway, coming closer. "I can't believe it. I mean, if you go to the funeral home, let his family know I'm thinking of them." He appeared in the doorway pocketing his phone, his forehead creased.

"Roc?" Meadow's focus shifted to her teammate. "What's wrong?"

"Just…" He shook his head with a shudder. "There was a fire last night in Elk Valley. The former high-school baseball coach died."

"Oh, man. I'm sorry." She winced. The people of Elk Valley had already endured so much. Now this? "Did you know him well?"

"Everybody knew him. I didn't play baseball, but he taught my driver's ed class. It's just a shock on top of everything else, you know?" Reaching for the bottle of water he'd left on the table, he took a long sip. "I just need a minute."

"Sure, anything you—" A loud buzzing shattered the sentiment.

Meadow pulled her phone from her leg pocket, glancing at her screen.

Isla.

Unable to look at Ian, she focused on Rocco. "You may not get that minute. It's Isla."

Rocco nodded as Meadow answered the call. "If you have good intel, I'm sending you chocolate." Her voice was strained, but she ignored it. Hopefully, Isla would, too.

"Ooh. You know I'm always down for chocolate. But first, I know how they tracked you to your house."

"How?" They hadn't been followed. And there was no way Des or Sils had put a tracker on them.

"When we went to retrieve your SUV from the parking lot, someone had busted the window. If you had anything in there with your name on it, you'd have been a snap to track. It doesn't take much to locate someone's address online."

Meadow dropped her head back and stared at the ceiling. Really? Her vehicle? Why did the bad actors always want to mess with her vehicles? "Let's keep that quiet." Rocco would never let her hear the end of it. "So, what else have you got?"

"I've got exactly what you need." Isla's voice was grave. "Answers."

"Skyline-Horizon Properties." Rocco hooked his laptop to the big screen, and instantly, a web page appeared.

Ian admired Rocco's ability to switch gears after the news he'd received, but it was something they were all trained to do, even when it was tough to box up the feelings.

Rather than offer condolences, Ian studied the screen, attempting to clear the clutter from his mind so he could absorb what he was seeing.

They'd returned to the Cattle Bend Police Department immediately after Isla's call, needing the technology Rocco and Meadow had stored there to continue the investigation. The sheriff had promised to send copies of the files on the missing men and women to them, though they'd yielded little clear intel so far.

Skyline-Horizon might be the link they needed, though. Isla had uncovered a newcomer to the scene, one who hadn't been buying open land around Cattle Bend or other nearby towns, but who had been snatching up vacant buildings and outlying properties that held existing structures.

As Ian sat forward in his chair and braced his elbows on the table, Rocco projected a map onto the large screen. "Isla put this together, and I'm pretty sure it tells us everything we need to know."

"A picture's worth a thousand words." Meadow walked closer to the screen, and the lines around her mouth deepened as she ran her finger down a series of pins dropped on the map. "There are eleven properties. The line originates with a cluster of properties in Cattle Bend and runs almost due south with a string of individual holdings through Colorado and New Mexico to the Mexican border."

"It's a pipeline." Ian laced his fingers and held his hands together tightly. "The source is in Cattle Bend." His stomach roiled. If the Thornton syndicate was truly behind these recent land purchases, they were definitely firing up their horrifying "business" again. Given the extent of the network they were building, Brooke could be anywhere by now.

But where were they getting the money? Their assets had been frozen or seized following the initial investigation and their deaths. Either they'd hidden some accounts very well, or they had someone bankrolling them.

That question could wait. Right now, finding Brooke was the priority.

Twisting her lips to the side, Meadow studied the map. "Okay, so, let's take emotion out of the equation."

"Looks like my cue to step up. The two of you are too close to this." Rocco stepped to the other side of the screen and looked at the map, not at Meadow.

The way her head jerked toward her teammate, she'd heard the unspoken accusation as well. Rocco believed Meadow was emotionally caught up in this situation, just as Ian was. Which meant, even though he'd been distracted, Rocco had sensed the undercurrent between Meadow and Ian.

The current had almost driven him to kiss her earlier. Surely Rocco hadn't seen that. They'd been sitting on the floor out of view of the door, and Rocco hadn't returned to the room until Meadow was standing. He hadn't seen any of that moment.

But he'd likely tuned in to the emotion that had led to it. There was a thread drawing Ian to Meadow, and, the way she'd reacted, it was tugging her toward him as well. Sitting so close to her, he'd needed to make a connection, to feel something bigger than what they'd shared in the past, something that had been simmering inside of him for so long that he couldn't pinpoint when it had begun.

But it was definitely there. Her memory had chased him all the way to Texas, even when he'd done his best to forget her. It wasn't until he'd looked her straight in the eye, close enough to hear her breathe, that he realized how deeply she'd been ingrained into his thoughts. For a moment, he'd thought she might kiss him…or he might kiss her.

But he'd craved something more. Something that made a kiss feel like it would be *less than*. He'd craved simply to soak in her presence, to be close without asking anything of her. To feel...connected.

To kiss her would have been different than to simply breathe with her.

He'd never felt anything like that before. His family had left him with bruises that had never healed, scars that covered festering wounds. He'd had his share of kisses and more in a frenzied attempt to fill the void in his heart. Those encounters had never worked. They'd left him colder than ever.

But then he'd met Meadow.

No one had ever stood up for him. No one had ever cared if he lived or died. No one had ever sought to connect with him on a level that said he mattered, he had value, he was loved.

Meadow had. She saw him. Really saw him. She heard him when he spoke. Cared enough to ask how he was feeling. Put her whole life on hold to stand beside him, both in the hospital and now, when he needed her the most.

When Brooke needed both of them. No, she needed *him*. His cousin was the one other person who had, in the selflessness of her child-like love, been able to reach his heart. Now, here he was worried about his own safety and whether or not Meadow would check *yes* or *no* if he passed her a folded note.

He pulled his hands apart and shook them out, trying to loosen the tension in his fingers and to focus on the intel that might lead them to Brooke.

Meadow and Rocco stared at the screen, talking about the map in low tones.

Ian studied the blue pins dropped along a route that would drag stolen young men and women away from their loved ones and into lives of horror.

They'd stopped the Thorntons once, and it had nearly cost him his life. Could they do it again?

They had to. Those blue dots represented fear and pain and suffering. Terrors beyond comprehension.

At one of them, Brooke was likely locked away. Scared. Lost. Maybe even hurt.

Ian shot to his feet. The time for sitting still was done. They had to move. "Where is she?" The words shot out as quickly as he'd stood.

Meadow and Rocco both turned, and

Meadow almost looked pained. She'd fix this if she could, he had no doubt.

He stalked to the screen and stood between them, staring at the cluster of dots in and around Cattle Bend. He jabbed his finger against the screen. "They're holding them near here. I don't think they're actively moving anyone yet."

"What makes you say that?" Rocco looked skeptical, but he was listening.

A gut instinct, mostly, but the longer Ian stared at the map and the more he considered the situation, the more he understood what his subconscious was seeing. "Hear me out…"

Meadow leaned against the wall and crossed her arms, studying him as though she could read his thoughts before he spoke them.

Ian charged ahead. "These kids all went missing within the past few months. When were these properties snapped up?"

Glancing at her phone, Meadow scrolled through the notes Isla had included with her email. "Rocco, put up the image labeled *timeline*."

The screen changed only slightly. The same map appeared, but this time, dates were posted beside each of the pins.

Ian scanned the image, certainty growing in his gut as the dots began to form a picture. There was a chance of saving Brooke and the others, but only if they moved quickly. He pointed to the cluster of holdings in Cattle Bend. "All of these were purchased six months ago, within a few weeks of each other. Because it happened during what amounts to a modern-day land grab, no one batted an eye." He dragged his finger down the map toward Mexico. "Each of these were randomly purchased during the same time period, with the last purchase only being finalized in the past week."

"I see what you're looking at." Meadow pushed away from the wall and stood beside him. Her shoulder brushed his, and he did his best to remain focused on the task at hand. "Their network may not yet be fully complete, but they're already gathering up their *inventory*." Revulsion coated the last word. Men and women like Silas and Des regarded people as objects, not as living, breathing humans. This was why they needed to be stopped, no matter the cost.

Disgust flooded Ian's veins. "There's a big gap

near the New Mexico–Colorado border, which indicates they haven't completely finished their pipeline. They're missing a few key pieces."

"Which also means they're likely holding their victims in Cattle Bend, where they have more space to house them until they're able to move them." Rocco's declaration was angry, heated with loathing. "More places to move them if someone close by gets suspicious."

"Des and Silas both had time to hunt me down in the woods and to personally go after Brooke, so I doubt they're overseeing an operation with a lot of moving parts yet. They might have a henchman or two on their payroll, but it's probable they don't have a fully working organization in place." He hoped. "The trick will be figuring out which of those places they're using without Silas or Des getting wind of our presence. If they have any help at all, they'll find out quick if we roll up and do a full-on search at any location."

"It's too many places to put enough teams together to hit them all simultaneously." It was clear Meadow was thinking, but it wasn't clear the direction her thoughts were going.

"So what's the plan?" Rocco was as ready to

roll as Ian was. "Obviously, we'll reach out to local law enforcement and to the feds, but I'm not certain they'll get involved yet, since we're operating on conjecture. We might be on our own a bit longer with our team tossing us a few favors."

Meadow pressed her lips into a tight line as she stared at the screen, although Ian doubted she was really seeing it. With a deep breath, she looked at Grace, who had settled onto a blanket in the corner, then turned toward Ian.

He turned as well, putting them face-to-face, trying to read her mind.

"Grace is trained to track." She said the words slowly.

Ian arched an eyebrow. Why was she telling him something he already knew?

Unless she was thinking of using Grace to sniff out each location on a quick search for the scent of one of the victims.

In a quick search for Brooke.

Which would require them to have something of Brooke's for Grace to sniff in order to track her.

Ian looked away from Meadow. If she saw

the hesitation in his expression, he wasn't sure how she would handle it.

Because what she was asking of him might be close to impossible.

Chapter Eleven

With all of his heart, Ian wished he'd gone with Rocco in their ratty loaner SUV instead of hopping into the unmarked SUV on loan from the sheriff's department with Meadow. She'd relayed their findings to the Cattle Bend police and to the Peak County sheriff, but she'd asked them to merely pull surveillance until they could determine for certain where the Thorntons were holding their victims.

As she pulled into the driveway of his aunt's house and shifted the vehicle into Park, Ian's stomach churned. He might just be sick.

He should have sent Meadow to the house without him. The Hawletts preferred to keep their lives and their lies as far from law enforcement as possible, and they'd proven time and again that Ian and his badge represented their idea of the lowest kind of scum. Not only had he chosen a life in law enforcement, but he'd also had the audacity to be true to himself by standing up against their petty crimes.

A traitor. A turncoat. The same words Silas had used for him.

They'd called him arrogant and prideful and a moral fanatic. Every family gathering had led to him being ostracized and verbally abused, even as a child who knew they were doing wrong when they bragged about the people they'd conned.

Brooke had been cut from the same cloth as him, appalled by the family's behavior, and Ian had done his best to shield her from the cruelty they used to cover their guilt. Likely, that was the reason she'd bonded with him.

When Dean died, it had been easy for the family to heap blame on Ian for the accident he'd tried his best to prevent.

Meadow had dubbed him *Outsider* when he was undercover. She'd had no idea how right she was.

Shutting off the engine, Meadow turned to him. She'd put her badge in her pocket and had removed the identification from Grace's harness. Their plan was to approach with the least threat to his family as possible, which meant not identifying her as a marshal until it became necessary.

But Ian? They'd recognize him the minute he left the vehicle. There was no telling what kind of altercation would result.

The family was already watching. The curtains near the front door of the nondescript two-story brick house shifted and fell into place. If they hadn't already figured out who he was, they'd know soon enough. It was surprising no one had stepped onto the small front stoop with the iron railing to scream at him.

"You okay?" Meadow didn't touch him. Instead she rested her hands in her lap, studying him carefully.

Ian stared at the front of the house. "Nope." Might as well be honest. "I should be at the safe house with Rocco, not here." This was the most dangerous place he'd likely ever be, about to enter the lion's den of his family's loathing. Even bullets didn't cause as much pain as their ostracism.

"You're not who they say you are."

His head snapped toward her. What did she know of his past? Of how he'd been cut off from everyone? How he'd been verbally beaten? What he'd endured at—

A sudden memory charged forward with almost digital clarity. He'd always remembered her beside him when he'd awakened in the hospital. Now, as though someone had opened a dam in his brain, he could hear himself under the influence of pain and medication, telling her the entire horrible story of his life. His stomach clenched. "I told you."

She merely nodded.

"All of it?"

"I don't know what *all of it* would be, but you said a lot." She looked down at her hands. "When you woke up in the hospital, you pretty much laid it all out there. I know what this is costing you today. I know Brooke means a lot to you, or you wouldn't risk walking to that front door."

Part of him was relieved someone else knew. He'd been hated and blamed, first because he looked too much like the father who'd abandoned the family, and later because he'd spoken up against the petty cons his mother and her sister were running.

And because he'd failed to stop his cousin from drinking, driving and slamming his car into a tree. That night had been the breaking point, when his aunt had screamed at him in front of an entire hospital waiting room. *Where was your goody-two-shoes behavior tonight? If you were as righteous as you pretend to be, you could have stopped this.*

His own mother hadn't even bothered to speak to him. She'd simply offered him an obscene hand gesture, then turned and walked away, not caring that he was grieving as well. That he was burdened by his own misplaced guilt.

They'd barred him from entering the funeral.

He hadn't seen them since. Only Brooke, wise beyond her young years, had reached out to him after she saw his name on a social media post. He needed his cousin in his life, and he needed to keep her safe. While he had no doubt Meadow could get what she needed from his family, the drive to rescue Brooke pushed him to be involved.

The longer he sat terrified of the past, the less time they had to secure his cousin's future.

"Let's go." Ian shoved open the door and strode toward the house, leaving Meadow to follow. He couldn't lean on her as a crutch. Some things, he had to do for himself.

She caught up quickly, having left Grace in the air-conditioned SUV. When she fell into step beside him on the sidewalk, she rested her hand between his shoulder blades. Not a word was spoken, but the silent *you're not alone* made him want to stop and pull her close, to soak in her presence until he could handle whatever came next.

They were halfway up the walk when the door flew open and a woman stepped onto the porch.

Ian stopped, shock at the sight of his aunt drawing his muscles to an immediate halt.

Tall and thin, Sylvia Hawlett was the spitting image of her older sister, Ian's mother. The only difference between them was Sylvia's dark hair, which stood in stark contrast to Rena's platinum blond. It was clear Sylvia dyed it to hide her age, as it seemed unnaturally dark. She was still trim and well put together, a trait her sister had never shared.

Her perfectly made-up face was contorted in rage when she stalked down the steps toward Ian. "You have more of a spine than I thought, showing up here today." She spat the words with enough venom to burn a man on contact.

Ian stopped walking as each syllable blistered his skin. He said nothing. As often as he'd endured the wrath of the Hawletts, it shouldn't still sting.

But it did.

Beside him, Meadow stood still, her posture relaxed. It was a tactic to keep the enemy off guard. Beneath her poise, she was coiled and ready to strike if the situation warranted action.

A small group of people stood inside the doorway, watching the scene unfold, but none of them triggered immediate recognition. They could have been strangers, though he had no doubt it was his own flesh and blood waiting for him to be gutted in the arena of battle.

Sylvia stopped six feet away, her fists clenched at her sides. "Where is my daughter?" The hissed question dripped with the poison of her hatred.

Meadow responded before Ian could. "That's what we're here to find out, Ms. Hawlett."

The wrath turned to Meadow. "And who are you? If you're defending him because you're dating him, then you should know the kind of man he—"

"Enough." Attacking Meadow was more than Ian would allow. "*Deputy Marshal* Ames is investigating Brooke's disappearance." It didn't matter any longer if they knew Meadow was in law enforcement. His family had run rough-shod over him, but he would not allow them to disrespect her, not while he could do something about it.

His aunt's gaze swung back to him, and her voice dropped impossibly lower. "You brought a US Marshal into this?"

He bit down on the words *she's a friend*. That would only serve to drag them back to his aunt's initial suspicions.

"I don't know why you bothered." Sylvia's chin tipped up, and her haughty expression reset itself. Even in the face of her daughter's disappearance, she wallowed in disdain for her only nephew. "I have every idea you know where my daughter is. I was about to call the sheriff about you, but you've saved me the trouble." She turned to Meadow. "Deputy, there's no need to investigate further. This man took my daughter. He's the one you need to arrest."

The hardest fight of Meadow's life was the one she currently waged within herself. It was taking all she had to hold her expression at neutral. She swallowed the words she wanted to fire at Ian's *aunt* and opted to stare the woman down instead.

The first to look away would lose.

Sylvia blinked, turning to Ian. "I know you have Brooke. Coming here is a way to cover your—"

"Ms. Hawlett." Meadow hit the name hard. "That's enough. There isn't a shred of evidence to point to Ian being involved with Brooke's disappearance." After her earlier comments about them dating, there was no way she was going to tell this woman Ian had been with her at the time of the abduction.

"He's been in contact with my daughter against my wishes. We've found emails on her laptop and are looking at our cell phone bill now to see if the number she's been texting belongs to him. Reaching out to young women in secret. Isn't that how all *predators* behave?"

Ian flinched. The blow had landed.

Meadow spoke before he could say something that would express either his hurt or his anger and turn this situation even more volatile. "Mr. Carpenter has a solid alibi, and we know about the communication between him and your daughter, which is completely aboveboard." They'd combed through the emails and texts the night before, searching for clues. "We're here because I'm a K-9 officer, and we'd like to see if we can locate your daughter by tracking her. The county doesn't have that capability, and I'm offering my services. We believe, given something of your daughter's that would allow my partner to follow a scent, we can locate Brooke."

Sylvia Hawlett stared at Meadow, her expression as sharp and rigid as a knife. It was possible she was about to kick them off of the property.

Meadow didn't break eye contact.

Without warning, Sylvia's chilled demeanor melted. Her jaw slacked, and tears stood in her eyes. She began to shake. "My daughter... You could find my daughter?"

Compassion softened Meadow's anger. No matter what the Hawlett family had done, this was a woman whose daughter had been violently kidnapped. She was worried and afraid, and that deserved a measure of mercy and concern. Meadow glanced at Ian.

His head had tilted to the right slightly, and he eyed his aunt's breakdown with a practiced expression, almost as though he was judging the authenticity of the emotions. The opposite of his aunt's demeanor, his jaw was tight and his shoulders rigid, as though he was holding himself back.

When he caught Meadow's eye, she gave him a brief nod. This moment was his to navigate. She prayed God would use it to begin to heal him and his family, knowing that was the kind of work only God could do. If nothing else, she prayed this moment would be one of compassion.

With a soft exhale, Ian tentatively laid a hand on his aunt's shoulder.

She immediately stepped toward him, accepting his embrace as she cried on his chest. "I just... I just want her to...to be safe."

Ian's eyes slipped shut, and while his posture remained stiff, he accepted his estranged aunt's grief.

Unwilling to intrude upon a moment when God was clearly at work, Meadow scanned the area. No one came out of the house, although they could be seen at the storm door and the front windows. It seemed the Hawletts weren't willing to extend a proverbial olive branch to Ian, even given the pressing nature of the situation.

The house was well-kept and spoke of money. Not millionaire kind of money, but a comfortable living. From Ian's stories, she knew their income had come largely from conning tourists in nearby Whitefish, bilking charitable people online and embezzling from various organizations. There had never been enough proof for the Hawletts to be brought to justice. Even Ian's testimony couldn't be counted on to bring them punishment for their crimes.

Now wasn't the time. Time was of the essence if they wanted to find Brooke before the Thorntons pushed her down their pipeline and into oblivion.

Meadow cleared her throat as Sylvia's storm of tears subsided.

The older woman sniffed and backed away from Ian, smoothing her floral shirt as though she was dusting away contaminants. She didn't look at her nephew. Instead, she faced Meadow and swiped the tears from her cheeks. "What do you need, Deputy Marshal?"

So that's how it's going to be. The woman had stormed her tears onto her nephew yet offered him no grace in return? In a different situation, Meadow would have so many words for—

Baby steps. The words sank into her mind, coming from who knew where, although she suspected God was admonishing her. Let Him work it out. It wasn't her job to pull an apology from the Hawletts or to broker a reconciliation

Ian might not want. Her sole task was to bring Brooke home safely.

She swallowed her emotions and cleared her throat. Normally she had a whole spiel she went through, but today she didn't have the energy. "I need something Brooke has worn recently and often. Or, if you haven't changed the sheets on her bed, her pillowcase would work well. The more contact she's had with the object, the more it will hold a scent." She pulled out an evidence bag she'd stowed in her back pocket. "If you can take me to the object, I can—"

"No." The edge returned to Sylvia's expression, though it was not as sharp as before. "I don't give law enforcement permission to enter my home." She held out her hand, palm up. "If you give me the bag, I'll bring something out to you."

That was perfectly within her rights. Since the bag was meant merely to preserve the scent and not to protect evidence, the request wasn't problematic, though it was annoying.

Meadow passed the bag to her with quick instructions on the best way to collect the item without muddying the scent, then walked toward the SUV when Sylvia disappeared through the front door.

Ian leaned against the passenger door with his arms crossed, staring at the house next door.

Giving him a minute, Meadow continued to watch the front of the Hawlett house. What was going on in there that required such vigilance from those inside? What were they afraid she'd see if she walked in?

"Whatever they're hiding, it's of the white-collar crime variety." Ian's voice was low, grating across the words. "Likely the only reason she wouldn't let you in is fear something incidental might incriminate them, not because they're actively in the process of committing a crime." His forehead creased. "And, you know, they don't want to risk getting the stench of me into their inner sanctum."

"Ian…" She moved to touch him, but with prying eyes on them, that wasn't the best idea if she wanted to maintain the sense of professionalism they'd cultivated. Still, his pain crossed the distance between them to rest like a heavy mantle on her shoulders. "I know this isn't easy."

"I shouldn't have come. It made everything harder. You'd have had an easier time if I hadn't been a distraction."

"I doubt it. I think you jolted your aunt out of the emotional box she's built. Seeing you threw her off-balance. She never would have broken down in front of me and might have denied me completely. At least—"

"Don't say it." He pushed away from the truck and paced a few steps to the edge of the driveway, still staring at the next-door neighbor's house. "She only accepted comfort from me because I was convenient. Believe me, if she'd been anywhere near her right mind, she'd have put a fist in my face instead. It wouldn't be the first time."

The front door opened, and Sylvia appeared.

Ian walked to the rear of the vehicle and out of sight before Meadow could react to his stark declaration. The last thing he needed was another interaction with his aunt, even one of indifference.

Meadow met Sylvia on the sidewalk and took the bag, which now held a light blue sweater. "I can't promise this will be returned to you."

"Just find my daughter." Sylvia had reverted to the clipped anger she'd displayed initially, but her gaze drifted to the vehicle, lingering where Ian stood out of sight. Something seemed to soften, and she looked back to Meadow. "Thank you." Without waiting for a response, she turned and walked into the house, shutting the door firmly behind her.

Chapter Twelve

The sound of his aunt's sobs lingered in Ian's ears as they pulled into Cattle Bend on the main road. Her willingness to let him comfort her had shocked him. Her quick reversal into icy disdain had been expected.

Still, the chill had burned in a special way, coming after a moment when someone in his family had touched him for the first time in years. What was he supposed to do with that? Go back to the status quo? How? Brooke was missing. It would be so much easier if the family could pull together during the search, but it was clear that wasn't going to happen.

The SUV had been silent for the twenty-minute ride to town. Ian was mortified at the things he'd confessed to Meadow, including the physical abuse he'd endured at the hands of his mother and aunt. That was the one thing he kept buried, the one thing he never dwelled on even in his lowest, darkest times. The memories had clearly been there, festering, because they had bubbled up in a horrible moment of confession.

Meadow slowed as they neared the diner, where crime-scene tape fluttered in the breeze that funneled up the narrow street. Several official vehicles remained on the sidewalk as the crime-scene team gathered evidence.

"Which site are we going to go to first?" He needed to say something. If he didn't, he'd demand Meadow pull over so he could charge into the diner. A weird glitch in his brain wondered if he could turn back time and rescue Brooke before the abduction occurred. There was another irrational part of him that believed he could walk into the restaurant and find Brooke waiting for him as they'd planned.

"The bank building at the corner of Reyes and Third. Since it has a vault…"

A vault. What was happening to Brooke as they drove around searching for her? What horrors was she enduring?

He should have seen her immediately and not let Silas and Des chase him into the hills. If he had, he could have stopped whatever nightmare she was currently fighting to survive.

Meadow didn't seem to notice he was battling waves of nausea over his responsibility for Brooke's plight. She didn't even look at the diner as she cruised to the end of the street and took a left into an older section of town where revitalization had been slower. Several small restaurants and shops were already bringing life to pockets between vacant storefronts, so it wouldn't be long before this area was hopping as well. For now, it was a hodgepodge of old and new, of vibrant life and eerie desolation.

At Reyes and Third, Meadow rolled to a stop at the sign and surveyed the front of the old Cattle Bend Savings and Loan. The three-story brick building stood silent sentry, its windows covered with brown paper on the inside and the doors chained shut on the outside. "Local law enforcement has cruised by this site looking for signs of activity, but they haven't attempted to engage. The last thing we want is to send in the cavalry to the wrong place and put the Thorntons on alert."

There was no telling what they'd do to Brooke and the others if they realized their safe houses had been compromised. They'd either move immediately or...

Or do something so much worse.

Turning left, Meadow drove past the alley behind the bank. Trash littered the area, and construction debris from the storefront next door crowded the space. A couple of men in paint-spattered clothes stood near a doorway farther down the alley, clearly taking an early afternoon break.

Was this the place? His intuition said no. "It's not likely they'd use a stash house near a busy worksite. There's too much risk of being seen or heard by the crew doing renovations."

"You're probably right, but I'm still wondering about that vault."

A bank vault would likely be dark, airless and soundproof. He didn't want to think about Brooke locked away behind a heavy steel door, panicked and fighting for breath. "There's a camera mounted above the door of the shop next to the bank. I seriously doubt Silas would bring his victims into a space with built-in surveillance."

"Unless it's his surveillance." Meadow was deep in thought as she parallel parked in front of a coffee shop up the street from the bank. She tapped the steering wheel as she stared out the windshield. "I want to get Grace out with her super sniffer and walk back to the bank, see if she picks up on anything. I'll talk to those workers and see if they've noticed suspicious activity or heard anything that concerns them."

There was no way he was sitting on the sidelines. Ian reached for the door. "I'm going with—"

"No, you're not." Laying a hand on his bicep, Meadow tugged gently, pulling him back into his seat. "You're highly recognizable to Silas and Des and to anyone they've managed to hire onto their crew. One look at you snooping around a building they own and they're going to know we're onto them." She pointed out the windshield. "The diner is at the end of the street in your direct line of sight. If you're spotted, they'll think you're here because the diner is here, not because we're checking out the bank." Her grip tightened. "I know this is hard. I know you want to take action. You love your cousin and want her to be safe. This is the only way."

Anger surged through Ian. He hated being chained up. Hated being the catalyst for Brooke's suffering. Hated that Meadow was right. As much as he wanted to be in the open kicking down doors, he was a hindrance, not an asset. "Take me to the safe house, then you can investigate without me getting in the way."

Was he whining? Because even to his own ears, it sounded like he was whining.

Meadow arched an eyebrow. "I know you. If you were locked up in a safe house, you'd go stir-crazy and wind up taking matters into your own hands. You'd last about thirty minutes, tops. Besides..." She released his arm and reached for her door, effectively turning her back to him. "I need you with me."

She was out of the SUV with the door closed behind her before Ian could process what she'd said.

She needed him.

He stared out the window but saw nothing, drowning in her brief confession as she opened the rear lift gate, leashed Grace and allowed her to sniff the sweater, then headed down the street.

Meadow needed him.

Other than on the job, he was pretty sure no one had ever needed him before. And, really, had the job needed him? He'd disappeared into WITSEC, and the sheriff's department hadn't fallen apart. His family had certainly never needed him as anything other than their whipping boy. Brooke hadn't needed him, even though she'd reached out and kept in touch with him and had loved him as her family.

But *need*?

Meadow was a woman who had it all together. Who charged into life and took care of business while having compassion for victims and their families. She possessed a strong faith, a strong family and a strong friend group. She was not someone who needed to lean on another person.

But him? He'd drawn strength from her in the hospital and in this current trial. He had unknowingly been bolstered by her memory when he'd started over in Texas. He'd called her when he was in danger, and she'd come running.

He needed her, but he'd never considered the sentiment might run both ways.

What could Meadow possibly need him for? He couldn't offer her anything. He had no real home. No sense of family and, honestly, no sense of identity outside of his work. When it came to having something of value, he was definitely the least of everyone on the planet. No worth. No purpose.

Worth. *Purpose*. When he'd started going to chapel with the rodeo, those words had been tossed around quite a bit by the guys who led the services. Ian had scoffed at them. God existed, but what did He need a guy like Ian for? Why would He care what happened to a guy whose family didn't even love him? God had created him, sure, but then He'd taken His hands off and let Ian run the race alone.

Except...

Brooke loved him. Meadow seemed to care. If they could find some nugget of value in him, then maybe there was something to that verse Hayden, one of the younger guys, had stitched onto his chaps. Something about God knowing all of his days before he was born and writing them down in a book.

If that was true, then God was well aware of everything that would happen to Ian in his life. The shooting. The family trauma. Everything.

Maybe God wasn't so hands-off after—

A shadow fell across the interior of the car.

Something hard tapped on the passenger window.

Ian whipped toward the sound and stared straight down the barrel of a pistol.

Lord, if we could find Brooke at this first location... It was a desperate prayer, but one Meadow sincerely hoped God would answer. The minute hand was spinning faster, and the longer they took to find the stash house, the more hope of finding Brooke and any other victims diminished.

Grace didn't alert along the sidewalk, though she kept her nose to the ground and sniffed away, diligent in her job and wanting the treat that came from successfully completing an assignment.

Meadow watched her and also scanned the surrounding buildings as she plotted a strategy for approaching the men in the alley. When it came to disarming potential suspects or witnesses, sometimes the best thing to do was to play to the stereotype. *Girl who needed help with her runaway dog* gave her a defenseless air, one that tended to win over both men and women if it was played right.

At the corner near the alley, Meadow slowed and allowed Grace to see the men. She crouched beside her partner and unhooked the leash from the K-9's unmarked harness. "Grace. Greet."

With a joyful leap, Grace bounded up the alley toward the workers, tongue lolling like a happy pup on a romp.

Meadow waited a beat before pursuing, purposely calling her by the wrong name and using the wrong commands. "Tally! Stop! Leave those men alone!" She waved her arms. "She's safe, I promise. Just friendly. Can you grab her?"

The men stepped into the center of the alley to block Grace's path, and the dog leaped onto the younger one's chest, then dropped down to roll onto her back as though all she wanted was belly rubs from her new friends.

The older of the two workers chuckled. Shoving his hat back on his head, he squatted and obliged Grace with a belly rub with one hand as he grabbed the handle on her harness with the other. "Looks like she got away from you."

Meadow approached, pretending to be breathless from the chase. She passed the leash to the man holding Grace's harness, then leaned forward with her hands on her knees as though she needed to catch her breath. "She jumped out of the SUV before I could leash her. She's a little escape artist."

The man clipped her leash, then handed the end to Meadow as he stood. "I wouldn't call her *little*. What is she? Looks like a Weimaraner but her color's wrong."

"Yeah, I guess she's not so small anymore."

Meadow smiled as she looped the leash around her arm. "She's always going to be my baby. And she's a vizsla. You know your dogs if you thought she looked like a Weimaraner. They're cousin breeds and often confused."

"My brother has a Weimaraner. Pretty dogs."

The alley was darker than the sun-soaked street, though the temperature was hotter here where no breeze stirred. It smelled of paint, sawdust and stale air. Meadow looked around as though she was seeing the alley for the first time. "Sorry to bother you guys. I was going to walk her up the main street, but it looks like the police are doing some kind of investigation. You guys working on one of the stores or something?" The easiest way to get information was to play ignorant.

"Yeah. Lots of sirens earlier. Not sure what it was about, though." The younger guy stepped up. He was younger than she'd initially thought, probably only sixteen or seventeen, and he had all of the youthful swagger that would make him think he could impress the ladies. "I thought about walking over there and seeing what was up, but my grandpa needed my help, so I hung around here."

Meadow almost smiled but bit back the grin

and snapped her fingers to call Grace to heel. There was no need to encourage the kid.

Not that he needed it. He kept right on talking. "We're about to open an organic butcher shop. We have a small farm outside of town. Beef and pork and some truck."

"Truck?"

"Vegetables." The older man practically rolled his eyes at his grandson and gave Meadow a slight, apologetic smile. He knew what was up. "We've always sold at the farm, but with the town growing and us being a good half an hour away, we figured we'd give it a shot."

"That sounds cool. I'll have to check it out." There were several small farms around the area that sold to the public, but since she didn't actually cook, she'd never paid them much attention.

Rocco would love a place like this. It had all of the farm-to-table things he enjoyed so much. She could really afford to learn a few cooking tricks from him, but that wasn't why she was here. There was so much more than her cholesterol at stake.

She scanned the alley and let her gaze linger on the bank. "Anything going on in this building? Looks like it's ready for something to go into it as well."

The younger man shrugged. "Dunno. We heard some corporation bought it, but nobody's been around since we've been here working. It's been quiet. We're all waiting to find out. Lots of people convert old banks into restaurants or wedding spaces, so who knows?"

"I hope it's a restaurant." The grandpa arched an eyebrow. "If it is, maybe we can cut a deal with them as exclusive suppliers or something. Restaurants and grocery stores are where the real money is."

It was clear she wasn't going to get much information out of the two of them. She'd gotten what she needed anyway. The bank could be crossed off their list. "Well, I wish you the best." Meadow clucked to Grace, who stood, ready for action. "I'm going to get this energetic little girl moving so maybe she'll calm down this afternoon. It was nice meeting you."

"Same to you." The older man shoved his grandson toward the rear of their store before the young man could speak. It was clear grandpa understood the awkward flirting and was putting a stop to it in a quiet way.

Yeah, Grandpa was going to have his hands full with that kid.

Meadow bit back a grin.

As soon as they disappeared into the building, Meadow knelt in front of Grace and pulled the bag containing the sweater from her backpack. She let her partner have a good sniff, then gave her the command to search.

Grace inspected the area as they walked toward the street, nosing around in trash piles and construction debris, but she never alerted, not even at the door to the bank. Clearly, this wasn't the site they were looking for.

At the alley's entrance, she knelt, passed Grace a treat and praised her work, then turned toward the borrowed SUV. It would be good to have her K-9 SUV back with all of the comforts and alarms for Grace. Traveling incognito had its downsides, but they'd have to deal with those as they headed to the next location, an old hardware store on the outskirts of town.

As she stood, the shadow of a person moved on the sidewalk at the passenger side of the vehicle. Had Ian once again disobeyed what amounted to an order and stepped into the open? It would be so like him to—

Someone moved in the passenger seat. No, Ian was still right where she'd left him.

Meadow commanded Grace to heel then reached for her sidearm at her hip. It could be innocent, someone asking for directions or curious about the commotion at the diner.

Or they could have stepped straight into the lion's den…and she'd left Ian without backup.

She fought to keep her pace steady, not wanting to draw attention to herself. If Silas and his crew were watching, they'd know she was nearby. She might be less recognizable to them than Ian was, but they'd still figure out she was with him if she made a wrong move. She kept Grace on the opposite sidewalk as though they were simply strolling around town. She prayed for Ian's safety and that they could get out of this alive.

Sliding the leash to her wrist, she pulled out her phone and thumbed a quick text to Rocco, asking him to contact the Cattle Bend PD. They were close, just a few hundred feet away at the diner, so backup could reach them quickly. As soon as Rocco confirmed, Meadow pocketed her phone and walked past the SUV, not looking toward it although she watched it from the corner of her eye.

There was definitely someone standing near the passenger door.

At the corner, she crossed the street, allowing her to get a good look at Ian's position.

Her stomach sank as adrenaline surged.

A man she didn't recognize stood close to the door. It was clear he was armed, though the way he stood shielded the weapon from view.

He could pull the trigger any second.

It was time to drop all pretense.

Commanding Grace to stay, Meadow dropped the leash and ran toward Ian. "Ian! Duck!" She raised her weapon. "Federal agent! Drop your weapon!"

The man startled and whirled toward her, his pistol aimed straight at her center mass.

A gunshot cracked before she could fire.

Chapter Thirteen

Ian shoved the door open as hard as he could, knocking his attacker sideways as the man pulled the trigger. The shot he'd fired at Meadow exploded against the building beside them, raining brick debris to the sidewalk.

The man stumbled and almost went down. It wasn't much, but it was enough.

Ian was out of the vehicle and around the door before the man could regain his footing. He drove an uppercut into the assailant's jaw, whipping his head backward.

The gun clattered to the ground. The man's dark eyes glazed as he wavered, dropped to his knees, then pitched forward onto his face.

Kicking the gun toward Meadow, Ian looked down at the man he'd bested. The man who'd pointed a gun at his face. The man who could have killed him...and Meadow.

He'd been only inches from the gun this

time. Inches from the bullet that could have ended everything.

Nausea tried to double him over. As quickly as his energy had surged, it flagged, dragging the strength from his joints in a tidal wave of fear.

A pistol. He'd faced down the barrel of a pistol. Again.

Ian gulped air. Training had kicked in and allowed him to take down the bad guy, but in the aftermath, he stared into his worst nightmare. His pulse rate shot up. His breaths quickened. His superheated skin sheened with sweat.

As Meadow pressed a knee into the man's back and dragged his arms behind him to cuff his wrists, she looked up at Ian. "Sit. Now. Breathe. Head between your knees. Breathe, Ian!"

The words cut through the darkness swirling at the edges of his vision and beat their way through the roar in his ears. He dropped to the seat of the SUV and leaned forward.

From his left, shouts and pounding footsteps approached, but he couldn't see around the door. Sound and sight blended into one sense, a cacophony of noise and light that his brain refused to process. He simply stared at the curb beneath his feet and focused on breathing. *In. Out.*

Voices and motion swirled, then the SUV rocked as the lift gate opened and shut.

Then... Meadow. She sat on the curb in front of him, looking up into his face. "How's it going?" Her voice was soft and comforting. She reached up and laid her hands against his cheeks. They were cool against his warm skin, easing some of his fear and drawing him back into reality.

Horrifying, humiliating reality.

He'd panicked in front of her.

As the fog cleared and his senses settled, inadequacy screamed in his head. The very worst of his weaknesses, the largest failure inside of him, had torn loose and roared out to be witnessed by the person he wanted to impress the most.

Her thumb stroked his cheek, and her gaze held his. "Thanks for saving my life. I might have hesitated to fire in the middle of town like this."

She was lying. Meadow was a crack shot who wouldn't have missed her target.

Behind her, several Cattle Bend police officers hauled the man to his feet, though he wobbled from the blow Ian had dealt. One officer stepped closer. "We're going to have him checked out by the paramedics then take him to the station. You need medical transport?"

"No." Meadow dropped her hands to Ian's knees as she looked up over her shoulder at the officer. "We'll be there shortly. I want to see him questioned as soon as he's processed. He might know where Brooke Hawlett is being held." She started to turn back to Ian, then stopped. "Hey, do you have enough manpower to post someone about twenty feet away from us until we roll out?"

"Sure do." The officer motioned to one of the men, then they all disappeared from Ian's line of sight.

Ian let his head fall forward. "I let the guy sneak up on me."

"I left you alone." Meadow tightened her grip on his knees. "This isn't your fault. We're doing the best we can, but our best isn't good enough when we don't know what we're up against. Your timing was perfect just now. You saved me and maybe even someone out on the main street if that bullet had made it past me." She angled her head until he had no choice but to focus on the sincerity in her expression. "Ian, you're still trained in law enforcement.

You're still *you*. Your instincts kicked in, and you came through for everyone. Fear is natural. It's nothing to be ashamed of. Nobody faults you for not wanting to take a beating from a lead fist again."

Thoughts spun in his head, and emotions raced through his heart. Ian closed his eyes, trying to shut out the external stimuli, focusing on Meadow's touch instead. She was the one person he wanted to impress...

But she was clearly the one person he didn't *have* to impress.

She already believed in him. Already saw a hero in him, just as he saw one in her.

She didn't fault him for his weakness. She didn't even view his fear as weakness. She embraced him for who he was, scars and all.

He hadn't cowered when he'd come face-to-face with a pistol's barrel. He hadn't flinched when Meadow was in danger. He'd reacted. He'd protected. Only in the aftermath had he come unglued.

Maybe he was healing after all.

Inhaling deeply, he opened his eyes and found Meadow still looking up at him.

Life. Survival. They surged through him. He

was truly healing, had truly survived another close encounter with death.

Maybe the cowboys at the rodeo were right. Maybe God had something for him and was keeping him on this earth, putting one foot in front of the other, for a reason.

Maybe…

He was caught up in Meadow's blue eyes, so close. So sincere. So…alive.

He had the irrational urge to kiss her. To drive home the truth he was alive and so was she, and maybe there was something on the other side of this for him. For *them*.

Meadow's head tilted slightly, and her expression softened.

But then, so fast he wondered if he'd imagined the moment, her mood shifted to a no-nonsense, all-business investigator facade. Patting his knees, she stood. "If you're good, we need to get to the courthouse, where the police department is. We made a spectacle of ourselves out here, and now we've apparently got one of Silas's men in custody. Word's going to get back to him fast. While he'll likely think we were here because of the crime scene at the diner, we don't need him getting suspicious about our presence before we can recon the rest of the sites." Tapping the door with her fist, she walked away and spoke to the officer standing guard.

Ian watched as he turned in his seat and shut the car door, forcing himself away from his heart and into his mind. They had a job to do. He had a cousin to rescue.

Meadow had been right earlier. The man who'd tried to kill them might know where Brooke was. That needed to be his primary focus.

That and the truth… He was still a man without a family. One who didn't know how to love.

One who would never be worthy of a woman like Meadow Ames.

On the other side of the one-way glass, Van Moore stared at the detective across the table from him with steely eyes. Other than asking for a lawyer, the thug who'd taken a shot at Meadow hadn't said a word since they'd led him into interrogation.

It was taking all of Meadow's restraint not to charge into the room television-detective style and back Van's smug self against the wall with her forearm against his throat.

Ian stood stiffly beside her, likely battling similar thoughts. "He knows something." He ground the words through clenched teeth. "And I'm willing to guess he's the one who was chasing us through the mountains after we left the diner."

"Both of those things are likely, but we have no leverage to get him to talk. As far as we know, there's nothing that makes him more afraid of us than he is of Silas or Des." The two were known to be ruthless. The Thorntons had proven they could reach anyone, even behind prison bars. Before his death, Ronnie had ordered hits on several of his former henchmen who had been arrested after the initial raid. Officials were still trying to figure out who had fed him information and how he'd been able to have them killed in jail.

Now that they knew Silas and Des were alive, the *who* was obvious. The *how* might forever remain a mystery.

"How long before you hear back from your people?" Ian stared intently through the glass as though he could will Van to speak. "Maybe we need to let him sit here and stew while we go out and keep searching."

But where would they search? There were

no signs of life at any of the other locations law enforcement had surveilled. "Look, Isla's good at what she does. She'll get back to us fast." Meadow had passed on everything the police had given her about Van. Isla could dig up intel faster and search deeper than a local PD. "Also, I'm not so sure about taking you out with me again. It might be time for both of us to move to the safe house and to let others do the foot-work."

"No." Ian looked at her for the first time since they'd entered the small room. "I want to be involved, not tucked away somewhere consuming oxygen while other people take on the risk for me."

Meadow dug her teeth into her tongue and counted to ten while she formulated her next words. "You could have died today."

"So could you."

She likely would have if he hadn't reacted so quickly, but that wasn't a thought she could allow to settle if she wanted to stay focused. "Rocco can take point on the search while you and I take a breather at the safe house. Three other members of my team are on the way here to help out. They'll be here late tonight."

"Those are wasted hours Brooke probably doesn't have."

He didn't need to keep telling her. The time bomb ticked in her brain so loudly it was shocking the clicks didn't echo off the walls in the small room.

On the other side of the glass, neither the detective nor Van had moved in what felt like hours. They both sat back in their chairs with their arms crossed over their chests, staring at one another as though waiting for the other to blink first.

"Aren't you going to do something?" Ian turned fully toward her, his hands clenched at his sides. "I can't stand here. There's got to be—"

Meadow's phone buzzed, the soft sound loud in the cramped room. With a hard look to stem any more of Ian's words, she pulled it from her pocket and held it up to show him Isla's video call request. "She's got something."

"Finally."

Tightening her jaw to keep from defending her friend by reminding him it had been less than an hour, Meadow tapped the screen so Isla's face appeared. "You're on the line with me and Ian."

"Anybody else?" Isla leaned closer to the phone she kept in an elevated stand on her desk by her computer screen, her brunette ponytail swinging. She likely had intel she didn't want overheard.

"Nope. We're in interrogation watching the silence on the other side of the glass."

Isla sat back in her chair, allowing a broader view of her office behind her. "I'm not surprised he's being stoic and silent. Van Moore is hard-core. I'm surprised Silas was able to get him on the payroll, to be honest. His services don't come cheap."

"Great." Venom laced Ian's soft exclamation.

Venom that Meadow could almost taste in her own words. "So Silas and Des might be further along in building up their network than we initially thought?"

"Tough to say?" Isla rarely expressed such uncertainty. "They could have thrown all of their eggs into the Van Moore basket, making him their only muscle. It's interesting, though…" She leaned closer with a glint in her eye that said she had tantalizing tea to spill. "Van Moore and Desiree Phelps do *not* get along. It seems they were a bit of a couple at one time…until she double-crossed him after a job they pulled together before she worked for Ronnie Thornton. She wanted all of the take for herself. She hung him out to dry, and Van spent a couple of years in prison before he was released on a technicality."

"That's definitely cause for bad blood." Ian winced, his anger fading as they made progress with new information.

"Yet it appears Silas has him on the payroll?" That made no sense. Des was Silas's right hand. She'd been with the Thornton organization from the beginning. Why would Silas hire someone who would cause friction within the group when they were navigating a rebuild? "We're sure Van is working for the Thorntons?" Was it possible there was another player in the game?

"I was able to access Van's phone records, and I already had Silas's from our earlier search. Des's, too. Silas has been in contact with Van repeatedly over the past month or so. Des? Not once."

"None of this adds up." What was Silas doing? The only way this made sense was if Des had somehow crossed Silas, and he was looking to cut her out by hiring different muscle, or…

"Hey. When did Van Moore get out of prison? Before or after Des faked her death?"

"Hang on." Isla's focus shifted to the left, toward her computer screen. She typed then scrolled. "Looks like he got out about three months after." Her gaze shifted back to the phone, a sly smile lifting one corner of her mouth. "He probably believed Des was dead, so he never exacted his revenge."

"Now he knows she's alive, so he's ready to move. I'm thinking Silas is up to something." It was possible Silas was playing his most trusted associate and her most hated enemy against one another to gain an unknown advantage. But what? "Who are Van Moore's other known associates? Let's look at his more recent activities, just before he hitched his wagon to Silas."

Going back to her computer, Isla's eyes shifted as she read. "Most of the intel I dug up has him around Chicago until he fell off the grid around the same time he started talking to Silas. I've got surveillance images of him with the Biancos, some of it going back several years." Grabbing her phone, she held it so they could see the stills from security-camera footage on her screen.

Ian leaned in to get a better look, his shoulder brushing Meadow's. "What are the Biancos known for?" Dread seemed to drag his words down, as though he already knew.

Meadow had a sick feeling her thoughts matched his. "It's human trafficking, isn't it?"

Her expression grim, Isla nodded. "They started out in drugs decades ago, setting up pipelines through the Canadian border. Drugs are a one-time commodity, though. You sell your inventory, it's gone, and you have to obtain more."

"People are different." Ian spat the words and walked to the glass, though Meadow doubted he saw anything on the other side. "You can sell them for a one-time payment, or you can rent them out over and over again for a steady stream of income."

It never failed to sicken her, the absolute disregard for human life and spirit. How criminals treated living, breathing humans as products. It was heartless and cold and downright evil. *Oh, Jesus...* There was no other prayer.

Her stomach turned in on itself. Even if they rescued Brooke, there were thousands upon thousands of others around the world suffering the horrors of modern-day slavery. There was no way to rescue them all.

She needed to focus on the ones she could help before she drowned in futility. Meadow glanced at Ian, whose posture was rigid not in anger, but in pain. They had to rescue Brooke or he'd never survive the guilt he had imposed upon himself.

She forced her mind onto the job, onto the trail of what Silas might be up to. "It's likely Silas has partnered with Van, who has access to resources with the Biancos that can help him spin up his operation faster."

"Right."

Ian stepped back into the conversation. "So either Silas is double-crossing Des and has promised to hand her over to Van once he gets what he wants…"

"Or Silas and Des are making Van believe he's being offered revenge on a silver platter and plan to off him in the end." Meadow shook her head slowly. "That's a risky proposition. If Silas and Des turn on Van, it's possible the Bianco family will hunt them for blood."

"This is twisted." Ian exhaled loudly.

It was. "Either way, Van Moore and possibly the Biancos are involved." Which meant they still had hope of locating Brooke. "Isla, find me—"

"I'm two steps ahead of you." When Meadow's phone pinged with an incoming email, Isla grinned. "I've sent a list of properties owned by the Biancos' known shell corps. Two of the addresses are properties they've bought in the past month near Cattle Bend, a mining company and a warehouse."

A charge of *knowing* zipped through Meadow. The other sites they had been surveilling had come up empty. Given this new information about the Bianco family's involvement, it was obvious, to everyone involved. Most likely, Brooke was going to be in one of those two places.

Ian knew it, too. He looked at her above the phone, his expression resolute. There was no way he was going to go quietly to the safe house now.

"You're the best, Isla." Meadow blew a kiss at the phone. "When I get back, you're getting coffee and a long conversation."

A shadow crossed Isla's face. "I'm going to need that conversation."

They might be sitting on a ticking time bomb, but something was going on with Isla, and it was more than the anonymous tip that had ruined her chance to foster a baby. Meadow looked at Ian, who'd paused halfway to the door. "Has something else happened to you, Isla?"

"It's nothing."

"Isla…"

"Fine." Isla glanced away from the camera and then back again. "There's nothing to be done about it now, but someone called my bank and impersonated me. Told them I'd lost my wallet and needed all of my cards canceled and my accounts put on hold."

"Isla, no." This was the last thing she needed. "Who would do this to you?"

"I don't know. And look, it's a nuisance and nothing near as big as what you've got happening right now. Don't worry about me. It'll be fine." She offered a thin smile. "I've got a few other angles I can work, maybe see if they're communicating on any dark-web sites. Let me know if you need anything else. I'm all in on helping you shut this ring down."

Before Meadow could respond, the call ended.

The foster process weighed heavily on her friend, and now all of these strange attacks kept hitting her. Meadow would have to make sure to keep that promise of quality time with Isla when she made it back to headquarters. Although the team was close-knit, it wouldn't hurt for Isla to have all of them as listening ears.

But for now, there was a more dangerous situation at play. Meadow turned to Ian, but he was already heading out the door.

He motioned for her to follow. "Let's move."

"Slow your roll, McQueen." Rushing into the unknown would get them nowhere but dead. "We'll be wheels up as soon as I lay some groundwork. We'll have some unmarked local law enforcement cruise by to scout one location, and we'll take the other so we can hit them both at once. I want Rocco with us, and I want backup. There's no telling what we're getting into. Besides…" She walked to the window and looked through. "I think we can get some added intel by working the Des angle against Van. And I think our weak link on the inside is Des. We might be able to leverage that."

If they could, it might get them through this night without one of them getting killed.

Chapter Fourteen

Van Moore hadn't cracked.

As darkness fell, Meadow navigated toward an abandoned coal-mining operation about half an hour outside of town, watching the sky fade to black. It had taken several eternally long hours to put all of the pieces into play. Surveillance had revealed activity in the old mine shaft, and while one team of law enforcement officers from various agencies headed there with Meadow, Rocco and Ian, another team moved on a warehouse between Cattle Bend and Missoula. While it appeared to be empty, they didn't want to take any chances.

Ian rode silently in the passenger seat while Rocco manned a laptop in the back, keeping track of the moving pieces and waiting to see if either Des or Silas powered up their cell phones, giving away their location. They'd been dark since Brooke's kidnapping.

No one had spoken outside of a few updates from Rocco about team positions and ETAs. They were on their own, headed to meet the special response team from the state highway patrol and federal agents from Missoula. In half an hour, this should all be over.

Hopefully without having to involve the coroner.

Meadow shook off the thought and laid a hand on Ian's wrist. "You doing okay over there?"

In the rearview, Rocco looked up with mild interest, his face lit by the laptop screen.

Okay, he'd seen her touch Ian. So what? She shouldn't, but she couldn't help it. He was hurting. She wanted to fix it.

She'd always wanted to fix his hurts.

There had been a wounded air about him from the moment she'd met him. The more they'd worked together, the more she'd fallen for him. He claimed he wasn't one who got close to people, but he'd reached out to her on more than one occasion. Had shared his thoughts and cracked jokes that made her laugh until she cried. He'd had a reckless attitude about him when he first went undercover, a half-wild manner that had made her wonder if he cared whether he lived or died.

Until that bullet had almost ripped him from this world. In the hospital, she'd recognized the fight in him. He had a will to live. She didn't know where he'd found it, but he'd found it.

He'd seemed relieved to see her at his bedside when he awoke after the shooting. And he'd spoken more about God lately, though it seemed like a distant relationship.

At least it was something more than he'd had before. She prayed he'd eventually realize how much God loved him.

Maybe then, he'd realize other people loved him, too.

Ian shrugged away and turned to look at Rocco. "What's our ETA? And is the rest of the team in place?"

Nothing had changed in the three minutes since Rocco had last given an update, but Meadow heard the purpose behind the question loud and clear… Ian wanted to focus on the job ahead, not get tangled up in thinking about her.

Message received, and rightly so.

Meadow moved her hand to the steering wheel while Rocco answered as though he hadn't just handed out that info. "The team is in place and waiting for us to arrive. Meadow will act as team leader. We're about eight minutes out."

Ian was going to feel every one of those eight minutes keenly.

He nodded. "Any sure sign of Brooke or the others?"

"Negative. But they are reporting movement in the mine shaft. The other team says their location is silent. No one seems to be— Hang on." Rocco pressed his earbud deeper into his ear, listening. "Pull over. I'm transferring this call to the car's speakers."

Ian and Meadow locked eyes as she pulled to the side of the narrow back road, moving the tires from the edge of the pavement as far as she dared.

By the time she shifted into Park, Isla's voice was coming through the speakers. "You're headed into an ambush. I've notified the team already. They're pulling back. Silas has a bunch of local muscle waiting to slaughter anyone who gets near that mine shaft."

Ian pounded his knees and stared out the side window, the air around him practically humming with tension.

"But…" Isla rushed ahead before Meadow could react. "I think I know where they are."

"Where?" Ian whirled toward the speaker as though Isla could see him. "Give us something. Anything."

"O-okay," Isla stuttered, likely shocked at the sound of an unknown person spouting orders. She took it in stride, responding as though Ian had a right to demand answers from her. "You guys need to turn around and head to the address I'm texting to Rocco. I've got backup headed your way, but given how thin you guys are spread and the direction you're heading, you'll probably beat them there."

"Got it. Putting it into GPS. It's twelve miles in the direction we just came from, at an old truck stop by the highway." Rocco was fully focused. "Isla, how confident are you about this?"

"I'll give you a 95 percent chance of finding Brooke and a couple of others there, but you have to hurry."

Hanging a U-turn, Meadow roared toward town, pushing the limits on the SUV. If Isla said they would find Brooke there, she trusted her. Still, what were they getting into? "Where did you get your intel?"

"Short version? Des and Van have been communicating on the dark web. I managed to crack a direct message thread between the two of them. Turns out, Van knew Des was alive the entire time. They've been communicating for years, and she was even bold enough to visit him in prison several times. Their plan is to get the pipeline set up then take down Silas, all the while making Silas think *he's* the one working with Van behind Des's back. Des and Van will run the Bianco family's new Western operations, while the rest of the family maintains the Eastern arm. Guys, this text stream is a gold mine. I've got enough to take everyone down, including the Biancos. Finally."

While that was certainly good news, this was worse than Meadow had ever imagined. It was sick on a thousand levels. "So Des doublecrossed Van, he went to prison, but they're still working together?"

"Girl, based on some of these messages, they're more than working together. They give me the ick."

"So how do you know where we're headed is the right place?" Ian gripped the handle above the door, hanging on as Meadow took the curves faster than safety dictated. Hopefully, the K-9s were hanging tough in the cargo area.

"They talked openly in these messages about buying this one property under a different identity. It's separate from both the Bianco shell corp and the Thornton shell corp in order to prevent Silas from finding out about it. Des is there with three victims, one of which is Brooke."

"They really did get candid in those texts."

"They didn't see me coming, that's for sure. They thought they were safe to say whatever they wanted. Des talked Silas into setting you up for an ambush at the mine shaft. He thinks Des has the girls at one of the Thornton stash houses. He's at the mine, ready to exact the revenge he believes Des set up for him. The real plan is to take Ian down and to kill Silas in the cross fire. But, guys? You need to hurry. They plan to move these victims within the hour whether Van is there or not. They've built in all sorts of contingencies."

"So why did Van come at me today? It got him caught."

"Not sure. Looks like he simply saw a chance and took it, maybe planning to take you to Silas then kill both of you without all of this drama. I do know they overheard Brooke talking at the diner, and taking her was a way to get you involved. Silas is consumed with revenge, and Des is exploiting that to keep him from figuring out what's really going on."

This was a twisted path none of them had seen coming. "Isla, you're a rock star. Never leave us." She'd just saved their lives and the lives of the captives at the truck stop.

"Just doing my job." There was an under-current in the words that likely had everything to do with the personal stress she was under. When she glanced in the rearview, it was clear Rocco had heard it, too. "I'll inform the other team you're on the way. You'll have to park in a wooded area about a quarter of a mile before the truck stop to avoid detection. I've highlighted the area on a map I sent to Rocco. Check in soon. Be safe."

"Unless forced, we won't go in without backup. Thanks again, Isla."

None of them spoke as Meadow wound through the back roads, following Rocco's directions as she headed for the wooded area near the truck stop.

Once there, Meadow located a narrow trail that led into the woods, killed the lights and pulled the SUV in. Quickly, they geared up in their bulletproof vests, including one borrowed for Ian from the Cattle Bend PD. They checked their weapons and leashed the K-9s. Meadow grabbed the small bag that held Brooke's sweater then they made their way along the edge of the wood line, navigating by moonlight.

The moon was a blessing and a curse, lighting their way but making their shapes and shadows obvious to anyone watching for them.

Hopefully, no one was on the lookout. If Silas and Des believed their ambush plan was working, they'd be focused on the mine. Des wouldn't be concerned about a location she believed was entirely secret.

Please, God, let it be so.

The roar of cars zipping along the highway grew louder as they neared the clearing where the abandoned truck stop stood. The woods ran right up to the concrete parking pad. Weeds grew between cracks in the broken and uneven surface. That would make it difficult to move quickly. One bad step could break an ankle or take a person to the ground.

The building itself was silent, the windows boarded up long ago, which kept them from seeing inside.

It also kept whoever was inside from seeing out.

Ian tapped Meadow's shoulder, then pointed.

At the edge of the front window, a thin sliver

of light shone. Someone was definitely in the broken-down square red building.

Keeping to the edge of the trees, they moved toward the rear of the building. A sedan that matched the description of the one involved in Brooke's kidnapping was tucked behind an old car wash. Inside, a box truck sat with its engine running. It would be invisible from the road, blocked from view by the main building.

Meadow exhaled through pursed lips, releasing the dread and relief that tried to clamp down on her heart. They were nearly too late… but they'd made it. Now wasn't the time to let emotion take control. Now was the time to be tactical and methodical.

She backed into the cover of the trees and addressed her small team. "I'm going to take Grace around and see if she picks up Brooke's scent at the car, just to be sure. Beyond that, we'll wait for the team to arrive."

Ian straightened, moon shadows doing nothing to soften his tense features. "But—"

"Racing in alone and blind could get everyone killed."

Rocco looked toward the building. "Cocoa and I will see if we can gather any useful intel. How many players are inside, where Brooke and the others are. Once the team gets here, we can move in."

The plan was dangerous but necessary. "Just be sure to—"

A crash and a scream shattered the stillness. A female ran from the rear of the building, racing toward the highway.

A gunshot cracked and the figure dropped to the ground. Motionless.

Gunfire.

Bullets.

A body lying motionless in a parking lot.

Ian jerked as though an invisible force grabbed him by the neck and snatched him backward in time. As the gunfire echoed, memories rushed forward, layering over the present until he wasn't sure if he was the victim or the witness.

But as the sound died away, the memory died with it.

Clarity returned in a rush as shocking as the gunshot.

That could be Brooke.

This wasn't about him. This was about her. About his makeshift team.

There were only three of them against an

unknown foe, and he couldn't let them down. If he did, one of them could die.

Meadow could die.

The thought shifted his heart into overdrive and fired fear into the deepest reaches of his mind. He went emotionally numb, something he'd only experienced on a handful of occasions in the heat of overseas combat.

Meadow was already on the move. "We can't wait. We have to go in." She looked back. "Rocco, take the front as planned. I'll go for the girl. Ian, cover me from the rear of the prop—"

"I'll go for the girl." He was already in motion, weapon drawn. "It might be Brooke." Meadow had to understand what drove him. His cousin might need him, and come death or life, he was going to be there for her. She was the only one who'd ever loved him for who he was.

Except, possibly, Meadow.

She hesitated, watching him. Time seemed to slow, and she moved to say something, her hand hovering in the space between them.

But the moment passed. She drew her sidearm and headed toward the rear of the property. "I'm going to disable the truck, then I'll have your back. Don't move until you hear the engine stop." She looked at him, her face in shadow. "Be careful. You'll be in—" Her expression turned to worry before she reset it to a hard-core law enforcement mask.

Still, her unspoken words rattled in his skull. *You'll be in the cross fire.*

No doubt. Once that engine stopped running, whoever was inside might be alerted to their presence. If the bullets started flying, he'd be between Meadow and Des.

But that couldn't stop him. He'd been living for himself for years, driven first by the belief his life didn't matter, then by the fire of fear.

Fear for himself had driven him away.

Fear for his cousin had brought him back.

It was time to step up and reclaim who he was born to be. One of the cowboys at the rodeo had said everyone was formed with a purpose. They were all here for a reason.

Maybe it was time to believe it.

Lord, keep us safe. Get us out of this alive. And whoever that girl is, let her be okay. He couldn't bring himself to accept it might be Brooke bleeding on pavement still hot from the earlier July sun.

To the right, metal squeaked. Half a minute passed, maybe more, then the hum of the truck's engine died.

Now or never.

No shadows covered his approach across the open pavement, so he stayed as close to the center of the building's side as he could. That should keep him largely out of sight of the doors at the front and rear until he was in position.

At the corner of the building, he pressed his back against faded red cinder blocks and caught his breath. He needed to be steady to get that girl out of this alive.

Holding his Sig at the ready, he peeked around the rear of the building, first at where the door should be, then at the person on the ground.

She was moving, dragging herself slowly toward the woods, heading in his direction. She was forty feet away, and if the person who shot her returned, they'd have Ian squarely in their crosshairs.

If he wanted to save her, then he had no choice but to give away his position.

Looking toward the van, he tried to get a high sign from Meadow, but he couldn't see her.

He was on his own. Where was their backup?

Fear tried to worm its way up his throat. It

squirmed in his chest and threatened to choke him. Breathing deeply, focusing on the struggling woman, he said another quick prayer. Only God could get them out of this.

Ian couldn't let her die, and that was exactly what would happen if he didn't find the strength to move.

Before fear could get a tighter toehold, he rounded the corner, sticking close to the wall, trying to keep his breaths from racing out of control.

The rear door of the building was closed. The windows were boarded up. If he moved quickly, he might be able to save them both.

With one final prayer, he raced forward and dropped beside the girl.

She'd stopped moving, lying cheek-down on the pavement. Light brown hair spilled around her, matted with blood.

It wasn't Brooke, but that brought little relief. This young woman was injured. Somewhere behind those thick concrete walls, his cousin was still a prisoner.

But before he could rescue Brooke, he had to get this victim to safety.

Ian glanced at the door, then back to her. He laid his fingers at her throat and found a thready pulse, then shook her gently. "Hey." He leaned close to her ear and whispered, "Can you walk? I'm here to help."

Nothing.

He'd have to carry her.

Closing his eyes, he tucked his gun into its holster, fighting a wave of panic. If someone came out the door while he was carrying an unconscious woman, he'd be unable to reach for his weapon—

No.

He had to trust Meadow and Rocco were out there and had his back. He had to trust the things he'd heard about God over the past two years. That verse Hayden had on his chaps, the one about God knowing his days.

He was important. Known. Loved.

He had a purpose.

Maybe it was to save this girl at the expense of his own life.

Maybe it wasn't.

But in this moment, there was no denying the call that was directly in front of him.

Quickly, he rolled the girl over and scanned her for wounds in the moonlight. Blood seeped from her shoulder. She was likely in shock.

A firefighter's carry was out. He could hurt

her worse. Instead, he cradled her against his chest and jogged toward the shelter of the trees.

He made it to the corner of the building before the girl stirred and jerked.

Then screamed.

"Shh... Shh..." Ian fought to hold her as she struggled. There was no way to quiet her, nothing he could do to silence her panicked shrieks. "I'm here to help."

Still, she fought and wailed.

He rounded the corner of the building as the back door squeaked open. Footsteps crunched on gravel slowly at first then faster, following the cries of the young woman in his arms.

In seconds, they'd be dead.

She screamed again, but the sound died abruptly as though the volume had been cut. She went limp in his arms. Still breathing, still moving, but she'd apparently exhausted her oxygen.

He leaned forward, preparing to settle her to the ground. Maybe he could draw his weapon and—

Footsteps beside him. He whipped around as quickly as he could with the weight of the girl in his arms.

Rocco approached with Cocoa at his side. "Thought you could use a bodyguard."

"Dude, am I glad to see you." Other than Meadow at his hospital bedside and in the woods just a couple of days ago, he'd never been more relieved to see another human being. "She's alive. Looks like a shoulder wound. Probably going into shock. What's our situation?"

Two gunshots echoed. Tough to tell if they came from the building or the trees.

Ian jumped and almost dropped the woman.

Someone cursed, and the back door slammed. The shots must have been cover fire from Meadow.

Ian nearly collapsed in relief.

Rocco reached for the young woman. "We're directly under a cell tower, so no service. No idea where backup is. We're out of time. I'll take her. You get inside. I saw two young women through the crack between the board and the window, and one of them looks like the girl in the photo of Brooke. Both are alive. Didn't see any extra guards, but that's not much help. We've made our presence known. Also, watch yourself. Cocoa alerted to an accelerant, though it could be old from the time when this place was an active truck stop."

So they were battling guns and the threat of fire, and they'd lost the element of surprise. Those women were in more danger now than ever before.

Ian passed the young woman to Rocco, who headed for the relative safety of the woods with Cocoa close behind.

Ian moved toward the front, urgency pushing him forward. If they didn't move quickly, Brooke and the other girl would be dead as soon as Des could pull the trigger.

Ian crept along the wall and peeked around the front of the building.

Nothing moved in the moonlight. With the wide parking lot to the front and the highway to the other side, there were few places for a sniper to hide.

That didn't mean there wasn't one, but if there was, he'd have taken out Rocco. Entering from the front was likely their safest bet.

Ian ducked below the window level and passed the glass double front door. Though the glass on one side was cracked, the doors were chained and locked, then boarded up from the inside. No good entry point there.

At the far window, he crouched by the thin gap between the wood and cinder block and peered inside, searching the sliver of room he was able to see.

The part of the old convenience store that was visible was filthy, littered with trash and layered with years of moisture and grime. The light was dim and flickery, emanating from an old oil camping lantern on a shelf that probably once held snack food.

No sign of Brooke.

Shifting to the left, he tried another angle.

There.

Bile rose in the back of his throat.

In the old refrigerated units along the back wall, Brooke and another girl were imprisoned behind grimy glass doors, huddled in the space where sodas and beer used to be displayed. It was like a sick museum piece, a prison on display. One door hung open, likely where the third woman had been imprisoned. Des had probably been moving her to the truck when she broke away.

Des was nowhere to be seen, but that didn't mean she wasn't on her way in to murder her prisoners. He had to move, even without backup.

If only he could signal to Brooke he was nearby, but she was curled into a ball, her arms wrapped around her legs and her chin resting on her knees as she stared blankly at the refrigerator door.

Reluctantly, Ian moved to the front doors, inspecting them. There was no way to break the heavy chains, but the boards behind the glass appeared to be plywood, and the doors themselves had not weathered well. If he could shatter the glass that was already damaged, he might be able to kick the plywood away from the wall.

It would take several blows and possibly a gunshot. Would he be able to breach before the noise brought Des running?

Did he have any other choice?

Backing away to avoid ricochet, he lifted his pistol, aimed at the corner of the cracked door...

And fired.

Chapter Fifteen

Crack!

Meadow jumped as a gunshot rang out from the front of the building. Grace had just alerted to Brooke's scent, and now she watched Meadow, anticipating a treat that wasn't coming.

Crack! Crack! Crack!

Three more pops in rapid succession. A series of hollow thuds followed.

Meadow motioned for Grace to heel then peered around the back of the box truck. She couldn't see what was happening. Rocco and Cocoa were entering the woods with the girl, which meant Ian had moved to the front of the building.

Beyond that, she was in the dark. Literally.

She needed to do something.

Either those gunshots meant Des had done the unthinkable, or Ian was creating a distraction so Meadow could approach.

Whichever it was, she had to move now.

With one last scan of the area, Meadow rushed around the vehicle toward the open space between the car wash and the main building with Grace beside her. There was nowhere to hide and no time to take it slow. This was what she trained for, what she had prepared to do for her entire career...

Put herself and her partner in the line of fire to save another person.

Tensed against a potential bullet, she charged into the fray.

The bullet never came. She ran until she hit the back of the building, taking only a moment to catch her breath and to check on Grace before she eased along the warm cinder-block wall to the door.

In her rush to defend the front, Des had left it unlocked.

Either that, or this was a trap. They'd assumed Des was alone. They could be dead wrong.

Motioning for Grace to sit, Meadow allowed her partner to sniff the sweater once again, then commanded her to investigate the door.

Immediately, Grace sat and looked up at

Meadow, waiting to receive a treat for a successful search.

Brooke was inside.

With a quick pat to Grace's head, she passed on a small treat.

Standing to the hinge side of the door, Meadow readied her pistol then extended her arm, pulling the door open with the other.

Two gunshots sounded.

She flinched, but the shots hadn't been aimed at her and Grace. They came from the front of the building.

Another thud reverberated in the building. Another gunshot rang out.

Pulling in a deep breath and releasing it slowly, Meadow steadied herself and stepped into the room, gaze sweeping from left to right as Grace trotted beside her.

The storage room was lit by flickering overhead fluorescent light. It was empty save for several broken shelves that held old tools, ancient auto fluids and discarded parts. A tiny bathroom on the right stood empty.

She hurried to the door in the center of the wall, nestled between shelves. She was in a fatal funnel with nowhere for her and Grace to take cover as they advanced.

Stepping into a short hallway with a closed door on each side, she paused, looking straight through to the front door. Another thud, and the wood at one side of the door cracked, the plywood sheet falling crookedly.

Two more gunshots, this time from the inside. Two bullets splintered the wood.

Ian was coming in, and Des was determined to stop him.

Ian would never survive, and he had to know that, yet he was doing what it took to rescue his cousin. He would be exposed if he came through that door, wide-open to the line of fire.

The advantage belonged to Des...

But Des didn't know about Meadow.

Creeping to the door, Meadow peeked into the storefront.

Des had concealed herself behind the counter, gun at the ready, less than six feet away.

Meadow had to move before Ian came through the door and sacrificed his life. One quick prayer. One deep breath. "Federal agent!" She stepped into the room, Glock leveled at Des. "Put down the weapon!"

Rolling to a seated position, Des fired as Meadow's finger squeezed the trigger.

Indescribable force slammed into Meadow's chest, blowing the air from her lungs and staggering her backward. She hit the doorjamb and dropped to her knees, clawing at her chest, trying to make her lungs expand. Gasping. Suffocating.

A guttural cry tore the air. Hers? Someone else's?

Other screams blended with the ringing in her ears in a horrifying symphony.

More gunshots. An explosion. Shrieks. Shouts.

Grace shoved her nose against Meadow's face, whimpering.

Meadow tried to jerk her head away as she dug at the pressure in her chest, desperate for air.

"Meadow!"

The sound of Ian's voice jolted through her and she gasped, allowing her lungs to fill. On hands and knees, she heaved in air, fighting through pain to get the oxygen she needed.

Was that…smoke? Was it real or was she hallucinating?

She inhaled again, her throat burning.

The smoke was real.

Clarity rushed in. *Des*.

Des's shot hit her in the vest. She had to defend herself. To defend Ian. Where was her gun?

There. She reached for it, but feet appeared between her and the weapon. She tried to come up swinging, but the pain in her chest was too great.

And then… Ian. He lifted her chin. "Look at me, Meadow. Can you get up? I need you with me."

She nodded, the sight of him clicking reality into place. Her breath was constricted, but at least she could focus. "Des. She…"

"She's no longer a threat, but her second shot went wild. Hit the lantern. We have to move. To get the girls out. Now."

Calling on every reserve she had, Meadow grabbed Ian's hand and let him pull her up. Her eyes stung as smoke thickened the air.

Grace took her place by Meadow's leg, watching and waiting for the next command. Her partner was brave and undeterred by the danger.

Fire licked the walls at the front of the building, feeding on trash, dry wood and discarded containers of auto fluids.

The sight and smell propelled Meadow forward despite her pain and breathlessness. "Where are—" Her head spun. Two young women, locked behind glass. They banged the doors of the old refrigeration unit, screaming, crying. *The girls.*

Thick chains woven between the handles secured them inside.

Meadow turned quickly, her vision whirling from pain and fumes. This was more than simply smoke. Something chemical was on fire. There was no telling what they were inhaling. Her eyes watered and her lungs burned with the stench and the smoke. The room wobbled, and her already labored breaths grew shallow.

Ian grabbed her arm. "Stay with me, Meadow."

She was trying. Oh, she was trying. But the darkness was closing in.

Sensing Meadow's distress, Grace leaned against her leg, pressing in tightly as though she could support her.

Meadow hardly felt it. She stared at the frantic young women, trying to form a plan. They couldn't shoot the glass, not without a risk of ricochet hitting the captives or themselves. Double-pane glass was a beast to break without something to concentrate the blow.

"We need something sharp." Ian looked frantically around the room, but the smoke was thickening.

Something sharp.

The tools in the back room.

Meadow stumbled, righted herself and wrestled pain and lack of oxygen to make her way, half doubled over, to the storage room. Grace kept nudging the back of her leg as though she was herding Meadow toward safety.

The air was clearer, but that didn't make it any easier to breathe through the agony that seemed to splinter her side with every inhale.

She grabbed a hammer and a screwdriver and made her way into the smoke, hunched over, moving through a thick sludge of half consciousness. Holding out her offering to Ian, she sagged against the wall.

He braced the screwdriver against the bottom corner of the glass door and looked up at his cousin. "Brooke, back up as far as you can."

His shout was lost to the roar of flames and the thunder in Meadow's skull.

Ian pulled back the hammer and drove it into the screwdriver.

Glass shattered and rained onto the concrete floor.

Meadow collapsed with it as the world turned black.

Brooke flew into Ian's arms as Meadow sagged to the floor and Grace took up a protective stance by her stricken partner. The K-9 looked to Ian as though he would know what to do.

He didn't.

Like a drowning victim, Brooke clung to him, wrapping her arms tightly around him. She shook with gasping sobs driven by panic and smoke.

It ripped his heart out to pry her arms from around his neck. He placed his hands on her cheeks, forcing her to look him in the eye. "Brooke. Listen. Listen!"

His shout seemed to shatter her panic. She stood in front of him, shoulders heaving with rapid breaths, eyes wide, cheeks wet with tears.

"Good." Ian rested his palms on his cousin's cheeks and pressed a kiss to her forehead, relief coursing through him. She was safe.

But Meadow, Grace and the young woman who screamed from the other refrigerated unit were still in danger. The room grew hotter, and smoke depleted the oxygen. "Go to the back door. Help is on the way."

Her head swung back and forth as her eyes widened with worsening panic. She moved her lips as though she wanted to protest.

"You can do this. You're strong. I know you can. I have to get the others out."

With a gasping breath, Brooke finally nodded, her damp cheeks slipping beneath his palms.

Sirens screamed through the roar of the flames. Squealing tires and racing engines were barely audible. "Help's here. Go to them. You're safe. I'll be out before you know it."

And if he wasn't, she'd always know he'd loved her enough to return for her.

One more hesitation, then Brooke pulled away, disappearing into the back room, hopefully headed for freedom.

Bending to retrieve the screwdriver and the hammer, Ian gulped cooler air near the floor, refusing to look at Meadow where she'd heaped to the concrete.

Grace stood guard, barking as though Ian didn't understand the urgency.

He more than understood. If he looked at her, though, he'd lose focus. Whatever was wrong with her, he couldn't help until he freed the other young woman. His heart and mind balked at the idea of turning his back on Meadow, even for a moment, but he inhaled one more burst of relatively smoke-free air and moved to the next refrigerated unit.

The woman inside had already slid into the

far corner, huddled on the slimy floor with her head bent over her knees. Either she'd heard Ian's earlier instructions to Brooke, or she'd given up hope and was waiting to die.

Wedging the screwdriver against the corner of the glass, Ian pulled the hammer back and drove it toward the handle.

The flickering light from the fire and the eye-watering smoke and fumes threw his aim off. He smacked the door. The hammer bounced off the glass, cracking him on the hand that held the screwdriver.

Wincing, he bit back a cry. He had to free this prisoner. Had to move fast. Had to get to Meadow.

With a roar from deep inside his chest, he smashed the hammer against the screwdriver handle.

The window cracked but didn't shatter.

Abandoning the screwdriver, Ian dropped to his hands and knees seeking cleaner air and better sight. He pounded the cracked window with the hammer until the glass shattered, falling around him like crystal rain.

The young woman scrambled to her feet

and shoved Ian to the side, bolting toward the flames, frantic to be free.

"No!" Ian leaped to his feet and grabbed the panicked woman around the waist. He hauled her against him. "No! You have to get out. You can't go that way. You're free now. I'm going to get you to somewhere safe!"

She fought, kicking and screaming and crying, hysterical and likely unable to even hear him.

He couldn't release her to attend to Meadow. She might run headlong into the flames.

No, he'd have to carry her to safety, leaving Meadow behind.

Could he?

His heart shattered like that glass.

The girl wrestled and struggled, landing an elbow to Ian's ribs so sharply he almost dropped her.

The pain galvanized him into action. Lifting her feet from the floor, he carried the panicked woman into the dark storage room and sat her feet onto the floor, shoving her toward the exterior door and freedom. "Run! Get out of here!"

She stumbled, looked back at him with a

stricken expression, then raced through the rear storage room and out into the night, where red, white and blue flashes of light indicated help had arrived.

He didn't take time to feel relief. Instead, he turned back to rescue Meadow.

The smoke was thicker than ever, the acrid chemical odor overwhelming. Dropping to his hands and knees, he crawled toward the refrigerators, feeling his way along the floor as the smoke filled the room.

Grace appeared in the flickering darkness, licking his face and tugging at his sleeve, urging him forward.

A hand appeared on the concrete before him. Meadow's hand.

As his breaths labored, he wrapped his fingers around her wrist and backed away, then tugged her limp body toward him. He didn't dare stand and pick her up. They'd both suffocate.

Dirt and grit dug into his jeans as he scooted back a few more feet and dragged her with him.

Grace kept a slow pace and barked an alert that sounded more like a command to keep moving.

Lord, let her be alive. Let her make it through this. You got Brooke out of here, get us out of here. Please.

The prayer looped in his head, sincere in its repetition. Over and over he tugged, the faint feel of her pulse tapping unevenly against his palm.

The room was unbearably hot. The inches were hard-won, and her lifeless weight grew heavier as lack of oxygen drained his strength.

Please, God. He tugged again, her wrist slipping in his sweat-soaked palms. *Please. Don't let me realize I love her just to lose her.*

He did love her, and he should have told her sooner. When that had happened, he had no idea, but the emotion drove him to keep going, inch by inch, to keep pulling them both toward freedom.

He'd loved her when he saw her in the woods days ago. When he'd left for Texas and even before. The emotion had crept up on him, sneaking into his heart so stealthily, so unfamiliar, he'd failed to recognize the warmth and longing he felt toward her for what they were.

Love.

With a guttural cry, he tugged her into the storage room, but the smoke had begun to fill that space as well.

The fluorescent light flickered and died.

Grace continued to bark.

His strength was sapped. It felt as though he'd been dragging Meadow in darkness through a thick swamp of mud for years. Time was irrelevant. Space made no sense. His ears rang and his brain fogged. He had no idea if he was moving backward or forward or—

Strong hands gripped him under the arms and tugged him upward.

Meadow's wrist slipped from his grip. *No!* He tried to cry out, tried to fight, but his muscles were water. His words were gone. He was somewhere between life and death, awake and asleep.

He'd been here once before, staring up at a clear blue sky from pavement as the blood seeped from his body and his life drifted away. He'd thought of Meadow then.

Why now, when his life was leaving him again, did he suddenly remember?

Muffled sounds. His body moving on its own, bumping across the floor as a force dragged him backward.

Fresh, clean air hit his lungs. The hands moved away. He was flat on his back on the warm pavement. Staring up at the stars as they faded into darkness.

He'd been here before.

Meadow...

Chapter Sixteen

Everything hurt.

Literally *everything*.

Meadow's lungs burned. Her head pounded. Her arms and legs were lead. Even her eyelids fought every attempt to open them.

"Here she is." A gentle female voice spoke above her, and the light seemed to dim as someone leaned over her. "She's coming around now."

Who was this person in her...in her—where was she anyway?

When had she fallen asleep?

She managed one blink and caught a flash of bright light.

Light. Fire.

Fire. Ian.

Brooke. The other girl.

They had to get out! "Ian." His name croaked from her dry throat. Was he okay? Had she lost him again, this time forever? Tears leaked from her eyes and ran into her ears. She'd never told him—

More soft words and then another presence beside her. A hand rested on her arm. "It's me. I'm fine. We're all fine."

Ian.

Meadow turned her head toward the warmth of his hand. "You're here." Her voice croaked. Maybe the words hadn't even come out.

"Not planning on going anywhere."

"Good." While her eyes refused to open, the corners of her mouth tipped up. "'Cause I love you."

Sleep overtook her, and the next time she awoke, it was to filtered light. Her throat was dry and her head pounded, but her brain seemed to be on line. "Where am I?"

"Hey. You're back." Ian's soft voice came from her left, and then he appeared, leaning into her field of vision. "You're at St. Patrick Hospital in Missoula. You broke some ribs and punctured a lung when Des shot your vest at close range, and you inhaled a hefty dose of all sorts of chemicals." His voice sounded as raw as hers felt. "You had a quick surgery to do some

repairs, and you'll feel like a horse kicked you
for a while, but you'll be fine."

Everything rushed in. The fire. The gun battle. The young women behind glass. "Help me
sit up."

Ian pushed the button on her bed and raised
her head until she was partially upright. The
pain as her ribs shifted was dull, but that was
likely due to whatever was dripping from the
IV bag by her head.

Ian helped her sip from a cup of the sweetest,
coolest water she'd ever tasted. It slipped down
her raw throat like balm, giving strength to her
voice. "Brooke and the others? And what about
her friend, the one she was worried about?"

He set the cup aside. "Brooke's fine. She's
up the hall with…with her mother and will be
released tomorrow. The other woman, Trinity
James, is in a room with her parents. Cassidy
Michaels was the shooting victim. She took a
hit to the shoulder but came out of surgery and
will recover after physical therapy. Once Van
figured out there was no hope for him unless
he cut a deal, he gave up the location of the
remaining missing persons, and they're being
reunited with their families as we speak. Her
friend is safe as well. Silas, Des and Van got so

wrapped up in taking out their revenge on me that they never pursued a meeting with her."

She couldn't have asked for a happier ending. "And Grace?"

"Chilling with Rocco at your place."

Tension leaked from her shoulders. Until it released, she hadn't even realized she'd been carrying it. The girls were safe. Her partner was safe. "Des? Silas? Their crew?"

"Des won't threaten anyone anymore." He glanced away then back to her. "Silas and the three hired guns he had with him were picked up at the mining shaft. Based on the intel your friend Isla uncovered, an operation has been set into motion against the Bianco organization. We did a lot of good in the past couple of days."

"And nearly died doing it." Ian had to have faced his worst nightmare, with guns blasting and fire raging. It felt good just to be in his presence, to see he was alive and okay. "How about you? How are you?"

"I'm good. Scratchy throat. Sore chest. I fared better than you did."

"I meant how are you in here?" She lifted her hand, partially tethered by the IV, and touched his temple, then let her palm slide to his cheek. "You've had a rough few days."

He grasped her hand and lowered it to the bed, carefully twining his fingers with hers. He smiled as he stared at their hands, his thumb running up and down the side of hers to create all kinds of warm fuzzies that defied the pain-killers coursing through her body.

She could certainly feel the things he wasn't saying. "I'm doing pretty okay. I mean, I'm a long way from being totally fine, but I think I see a path in that direction. I finally realized it's not about me. I was willing to…to face Des's bullets to rescue someone else, someone I care about." He shifted his gaze to hers. "Two people I care about."

"You laid down your life for your friends." It was like the Bible verse said. That was the greatest love, and Ian had found it. Hopefully, he realized the verse applied to him, too. That Jesus had laid down His life for Ian.

"For my cousin." He held her gaze. "For you. You're more than my friend, Meadow. And…" His soft smile morphed into a mischievous grin. "From what you said when you were still a little loopy, I think you'd agree."

"What?" Grogginess blew away. Meadow tried to sit taller, but she couldn't. What did he know? What had she said under the effects of painkillers and anesthesia? Pulling her hand from his, she raised the bed until she was almost eye to eye with him. "What? Ian..." She put all of the threat she could muster into her voice. "What did I say?"

He leaned closer, resting his lips against her ear. "That you love me."

Her eyes slipped closed. Maybe if she tried really hard, she could find what little bit of anesthesia was coursing through her and slip back into unconsciousness. Maybe when she woke up, she'd be back in time somewhere before she'd let that slip.

Ian wasn't a guy who wanted love. He wasn't a guy who believed he was worthy of it. If he thought she was in love with him, he'd bolt.

Except...he hadn't.

When she opened her eyes, he drew back slightly so she could see his eyes. For the longest time, he simply scanned her face as though he could lock this moment in his heart forever.

Either that or he was looking for a gentle way to let her down. She'd backtrack, save him the trouble. "Look, I—"

"I love you, too, Meadow Ames." Leaning forward, he pressed a gentle kiss to her forehead, his voice a low whisper. "That's all you get from me until we're out of here and can talk somewhere more private, like a spider-infested bunker."

All of her emotions choked on a chuckle. This was Ian. The man she loved. The one who apparently loved her back. He was not going to dive headlong into the mushy and the gushy.

At least, not yet. She had a feeling it lived inside of him somewhere, though. It was going to be fun bringing that out. "About those spiders, Carpenter. I'm not sure I love you that much."

"Keep insulting me, and I'll go live in that bunker."

When he started to back away, she laid a hand on the back of his neck and pulled him close, pressing a kiss to his forehead. "Only if you take me with you."

"I think I can do better than a—"

"Yuck and gag and ick and all of that stuff." Rocco's voice from the door cut short any further *mushy and gushy*. "It took you guys long enough, but seriously, it can wait."

"You're an uninvited guest, Roc. You can leave just as easily as you arrived." Meadow tapped her forehead against Ian's then dropped her hand as he sat back in the chair.

Rocco stepped into the room, his smile betraying his words. Walking over to stand beside Ian, he looked down at Meadow. "I hear you're going to survive."

"Yeah. You can't lay claim to my gourmet kitchen just yet."

"Such a waste on you." He bumped a knuckle against her shoulder, sobering. "Glad you're okay, M." Clearing his throat, he backed away and studied her IV. "How would you feel about putting a nice *pomodoro* sauce in this thing? See if we can give you Italian blood?"

Ian pretended to gag, and Meadow winced. "That's disgusting. Where's Grace?"

"In my SUV with Cocoa."

They'd be fine there, with the dedicated AC unit, built-in water bowls and alarms that alerted their phones in case of emergency.

Meadow ached to see her partner, but she wouldn't push it by asking for her in the hospital. "Hey, Roc, speaking of food, I won't deny you if you want to cook me a big ol' Italian meal when I get out of here."

Rocco settled on the bed by her feet and thumped her shin. "I would love to. Your kitchen is..." He offered an exaggerated chef's kiss then grew serious. "I'll have something ready tomorrow when you get home, but then I'm out the door."

"Why?" Meadow managed to sit up slightly, although the move cost her. "Did we find the Rocky Mountain Killer?" Her gut sank, horrid thoughts blending with the slight nausea she was already feeling. "Did he strike again?"

"No." Rocco's demeanor crumbled. Something was wrong. "Chase wants me in Elk Valley. I know the place and the people well, so he's asked me to come back."

"Why? What's wrong?" With a quick glance at Ian, Meadow held her hand out to Rocco. Something was bothering him. Could it be...? "Is there news about Cowgirl?" If their calculations were correct, the missing therapy dog had likely given birth already. What would a murderer like the RMK do to Cowgirl and her pups?

Rocco shook his head. "No word."

Her stomach sank. "Your family? Are they okay? Is it about your dad?" Rocco still grieved his father and believed the stress of the unsolved RMK case had driven him to an early grave.

"Everybody's fine." Pulling his hand away, he stared at his feet. "We have another potential suspect. Ryan York. His sister Shelley died by suicide after Seth Jenkins, our first victim, broke up with her."

Another suspect was good news, but Rocco wasn't acting like himself. Something was wrong. "So Ryan might be seeking revenge?"

"Possibly. He left Elk Valley shortly after the initial murders, so Isla is tracking him down. Preliminary info says he's got a Glock 17 registered to his name and get this…he's tall and blond."

Her heart kicked up a notch. Did they finally have a decent lead? "Tattoos?"

"Not at the time he left town, but now? Who knows?" Rocco dragged his hand through his hair. "It's a thin lead, though. He's got motive for Seth's death, but he wasn't affiliated with the YRC, so why kill the others? And why now?" Something more haunted his expression.

His pain was so palpable, Meadow wanted to hug him. When one of her teammates hurt, so did she.

He was likely thinking of his father, who'd investigated the case originally and had died with the killer still at large. Rocco had always attributed his father's heart attack to the stress of the unsolved murders, and he sought to bring closure to the work his dad had started. "Roc, you okay? I can be out the door as soon as they release me." She needed to be of use, to help her team wrap this thing up.

"Chase would never let me hear the end of it. You've been ordered to take leave, rest up." He offered a weak smile. "And I'm fine. It's just that the town's on edge, struggling with the murders. It's opened a lot of wounds and brought in a lot of fear. And now...they think the fire that killed the baseball coach was arson."

The adrenaline surge she'd felt at the news of a new suspect crashed. "Roc, no. Why?"

"Because there was another fire that killed the owner of a feed store. Both were deliberately set. Both are being investigated as homicides."

This couldn't be happening. It was heartbreaking. The last thing Elk Valley needed was more fear, more death. "I'm sorry."

"Yeah, so on top of the first serial killer, the town is dealing with a serial arsonist-slash-murderer." His gaze wandered the room. "People are scared. And you know that multiyear high-school reunion the EVHS alumni committee was planning? They've decided not to postpone it. The committee believes the town 'needs something positive to focus on.'" Rocco practically sneered.

"What?" Meadow sank against the pillow. That was utterly foolish. "Do they not understand the danger of that many people coming together all at once, many of them linked to the Young Ranchers Club and the murders?" *What are they thinking?*

"It could be our killer's dream come true."

Could a town handle so many tragedies at once? It would be a test of Elk Valley's resilience, most definitely.

"But hey!" Rocco brightened and turned his attention to Ian. "Chase said something else. Our team leader is interested in your résumé. If you're tired of the horses in Texas, he'd like to chat with you about your skills. The team could use a guy like you, and I need a good prep cook, so if you can dice onions, you're in."

Meadow scraped her teeth lightly along her dry tongue. Given Ian's trauma, Chase would likely recommend some counseling before he would be fully involved with the team, but he'd be a great fit. Ian's answer to that proposal would tell her a lot about their potential future.

He didn't look at her, focusing instead on Rocco. "Ya know..." He reached over and squeezed Meadow's fingers. "I always wanted to learn how to cook."

Ian walked up the hospital hallway, feeling more like himself than he had in years.

If he was being honest, he felt more like himself than he ever had. A clean shower and a good night's sleep in the guest bed at Meadow's home had done wonders for his mental clarity.

Knowing Brooke was safe had done wonders for his emotions.

Realizing with certainty God loved him and was holding his life in His hands had done wonders for his soul.

And a long talk with a still groggy Meadow before he'd left for the night had done wonders for his heart.

He loved her. How he'd managed to deny that truth for so many years was beyond his comprehension, but he did. She was a gift handed to him by the God who loved him more than he deserved. To know she'd loved him years ago...

Part of him regretted the time he'd spent cut off from her in WITSEC, but it had been for the best. He'd grown as a person, had drawn closer to God, had begun, even without realizing it, to love himself and to accept the love of others as he'd worked with horses as broken and wounded as he himself had been. God had been preparing him to love and be loved by a woman like Meadow.

Now that she was about to be discharged from the hospital, he was more than ready to make up for their "lost" time. Nobody knew him like she did. Nobody loved him like she did.

But someone else did love him.

Brooke.

His cousin was recovering a few doors down from Meadow, yet he hadn't seen her since he'd pulled her out of that horrible refrigeration unit. Rocco had said she was asking for him, but he hadn't been ready to run the gauntlet of his family the day before. All he'd wanted was to be with Meadow and to bask in the glow of their declared love and of the obvious love God had for both of them.

But now?

His footsteps slowed near the door to room 219. Soft voices drifted into the hall from inside.

Someone was with her. Maybe he should wait until they left.

If he did, his fragile bravery would shatter

like the glass of that refrigerator door, and he'd never be able to put the pieces together again.

No, he had to go in now. To prove to his cousin she meant more to him than his fears and family pain. She needed to know he cared and she was special.

God, help me. Pulling in a deep breath and straightening his spine, he stepped into the room.

Brooke's face lit like the sunrises he'd often enjoyed over the plains in Texas. "Ian!" She stood from her perch on the edge of the bed, dressed in leggings and an oversize T-shirt, clearly about to head out the door for home.

She practically jumped on him, wrapping her arms around his neck like the exuberant toddler she used to be. "I knew you'd come! I knew you would. I asked you for help, and you came." Her voice was filled with joy, though damp tears soaked through his shirt to his shoulder.

Ian forgot everything else. This little girl…

Not a little girl anymore. In the years since he'd last seen her, she'd grown into a young lady. One who had his heart wrapped around her little finger the way a little sister would have. Holding her as she cried, knowing she was safe… Her tears of joy and relief went a long way toward healing his wounded heart.

It no longer mattered what his family believed about him. Brooke believed the best.

He sniffed back his emotion, totally unwilling to give in to tears as long as he had an audience. "Hey, I did my best."

"I knew you'd find me." Brooke backed away, swiping at her face. She looked haggard and tired, the ordeal having taken a toll, but her expression was joyful. "I never doubted it. I was telling Deputy Marshal Ames that when you came in."

Ian's gaze swung to the chair beside the bed, and the sight there sent his heart into a double thump.

Sure enough, Meadow sat straight-backed with her forehead creased in pain, though a smile lit her face. She rose slowly, standing before Ian could offer help. Waving him away, she walked to the door. "I was just chatting while Brooke's mother is getting the car. I need to go back to my room. They'll be in with my discharge papers soon, then I'll be ready to go home." She stopped long enough to kiss Ian's cheek. Far from the fire funk she'd smelled like yesterday, she now wore the scent of soap and

mint and maybe even freedom, since her fond-
est desire was to get out of the hospital and back
to Grace, who was waiting at her house with
Rocco.

It was tough to pull his attention back to
Brooke once Meadow exited the room.

When he did, his cousin tilted her head with
a knowing grin. "You *l-o-v-e* the deputy marshal."

"Stop it." He motioned for Brooke to sit on
the edge of the bed then took the chair Meadow
had vacated. "How are you doing?"

Her expression clouded. "I don't want to
talk about it yet." She charged ahead before
Ian could speak. "A social worker came in and
let me know how to get counseling, and I'm
going to do that. Right now, I just want to get
out of here and…" She pulled in a long breath.
"That's kind of what Meadow and I were talking about."

Meadow, not *Deputy Marshal*. Interesting.

"I'm nineteen now. I know what happens in
our family. I know the things they do and…"
She looked away, staring at the blank television
screen. "Mom wants to talk to you, to thank
you and maybe more, but she's afraid of losing
her *livelihood*." The word dripped sarcasm. "She

and Aunt Rena are too in love with money to stop conning people. I've put up with it for too long. Maybe someday she'll come fully around, but she's grateful to you for finding me."

Ian stared at the young woman in front of him, pained by her family's actions yet still behaving as a loving daughter. "I'm sorry you've been caught in the middle all these years."

"I chose to be, even though I was a kid. My mom is my mom, but you were always important to me." Brooke turned to him, her brown ponytail swinging over her shoulder. "I hated when you left, but now that I'm older, I see how they treated you and the position you were put into. You went out of your way to love me and to let me grieve Dean. You weren't selfish. You cared about me as a person. So many times, I wished I could have lived with you instead of them, and then you were gone. That was hard. Hearing from you again a few months ago was…good. Really good." She smiled. "And I've made a decision."

"About what?"

"I'm moving out of Mom's house. Mr. Pullman has an apartment above the diner. He'll let me live there in exchange for me opening or closing every day. It'll free up some of his time. It's time I confronted what our family is doing, even though I still love them."

"It won't be easy." Ian's heart swelled with pride. She was taking a stand against wrong, but she was doing it in a way that respected her family as well. He could learn a few things from his younger cousin. "I'll be around now. I'm here if you need me."

"Just like always." She leaned closer, her grin full of mischief. "Maybe you'll be living near Cattle Bend?"

Ian tried not to let his face give anything away. He owed it to Meadow to talk to her first.

He stood. He should leave before his aunt returned. While he planned to reach out to his family soon to see if they could build on the small hope Brooke had handed him today, right now was not the time to surprise her with his appearance. Emotions were running too high from the fright of Brooke's kidnapping.

Leaning forward, he pressed a kiss to his cousin's forehead. "Where I live is a conversation for the grown-ups, but I'll keep you posted."

She grabbed him in a brief hug before she released him. He was halfway out the door when she spoke. "I love you, coz."

Ian didn't turn. She might see the tears standing in his eyes. Tears of relief. Acceptance. Hope. "Love you, too, kid."

Outside Meadow's room, he paused to let his emotions settle. So much was happening so fast. He was feeling for the first time.

Love for his family. Love from God.

Love for the woman on the other side of that door.

The kind of love he'd never imagined would flow to him or through him.

He patted his jeans pocket, tapped lightly on the half-open door, then stepped inside.

Meadow was standing by the window, looking out at the world. "I'm so ready to get home. I haven't been away from Grace this long... ever." She turned, eyebrow arched in question. "How did it go with Brooke? She's a great kid."

Suddenly, he didn't want to talk about anything but them. Their future. With three long strides, he walked around the end of her hospital bed, wrapped his arms around her and kissed her the way he'd promised to the day before. The way he'd wanted to before he'd even *realized* he wanted to.

And she met him with all of the emotion he was feeling, leaning into him in a way that let him support her yet also held him up. The way it had always been between them.

The way it should be.

He had no doubt when he pulled the ring from his pocket she'd say yes. No doubt they would share a life together that was somehow both exciting and settled.

He was ready to come out of the darkness and the woods. Ready to love and be loved.

Now and forever.

★ ★ ★ ★ ★

Don't miss the stories in this mini series!

MOUNTAIN COUNTRY K-9 UNIT

MILLS & BOON

Showdown In the Rockies
Kathleen Tailer

MILLS & BOON

Kathleen Tailer is a senior attorney who works for the Supreme Court of Florida in the office of the state courts administrator. She graduated from Florida State University College of Law after earning her BA from the University of New Mexico. She and her husband have eight children, five of whom they adopted from the state of Florida. She enjoys photography and playing drums on the worship team at Calvary Chapel in Thomasville, Georgia.

Visit the Author Profile page
at millsandboon.com.au for more titles.

My brethren, count it all joy when ye fall into
divers temptations; Knowing this,
that the trying of your faith worketh patience.
But let patience have her perfect work,
that ye may be perfect and entire, wanting nothing.
—*James* 1:2–4

DEDICATION

For our wonderful family at Engage Church
in Tallahassee, our missionary friends in Africa
and Israel, and our incredible neighbors in
Shell Point, Florida. Thank you all for your kindness,
forbearance and unwavering love.

A special thank-you to Mike McElroy for his technical
expertise. Any mistakes are truly my own.

I continue to be blessed and thankful for
my wonderful family: Jim, James, Bethany,
Daniel, Keandra, Jeremy, Jessica, Nathan, Anna,
Megan, Joshua O., Bradley, Brayden and B.J.
Also, in loving memory of our son, Joshua Evan Tailer,
who will forever be in our hearts.

Chapter One

The man was dead.

His bare hand reached out and pointed awkwardly toward the tree line, the fingers curled as if grasping for something just beyond his reach. Blood was splattered on the snow around his body...*so much blood*.

An icy chill swept down Flynn Denning's spine as she refocused her camera. She had seen dead bodies before—unfortunately—at her new job as a detective in Tallahassee, Florida, but the horrific scene below still made her stomach twist into knots as the helicopter she was in flew over the unexpected and grisly sight. She wondered fleetingly if she would ever get used to seeing death displayed in such a macabre tableau. The bright snow contrasted with the dark red stains that covered a substantial part of the clearing. She hadn't known what to expect when she'd found the map of the Colorado Rockies and notes in her sister's house. The handwritten remarks were vague and mentioned a company named Bear Creek Vacation Rentals and a possible meth lab, but not much else. Flynn hoped that the notes and map had something to do with why her only sister, Erin, was now fighting for her life in the nearby hospital. Erin had been shot in the abdomen three days ago by an unknown perpetrator and still hadn't regained consciousness due to massive blood loss.

Flynn knew from the notes that her sister had been investigating a local drug cartel, but she had few details. Erin was also a detective, but she was employed by the local police department in the small town of Frisco, Colorado, and when Flynn had asked about the cases Erin was working on, the local force had been unable to link any of them to her sister's shooting. In fact, according to Erin's captain, they didn't have a single lead. They were digging into some of her past arrests, but so far, nothing had panned out.

The local team also knew nothing about Erin's drug cartel investigation, so Flynn had decided to take the bull by the horns and investigate the case herself—even if she did have only Erin's chaotic notes and a map to go by. She had to do something while her sister was lying in the ICU fighting for her life. Flynn had never been good at waiting for things to happen. She was a woman of action, and sitting around, hoping the local police force would catch Erin's shooter while she twiddled her thumbs, just wasn't going to work for her. Still, Erin had clearly been in the beginning phases of her investigation——her notes gave coordinates and vague hints, but nothing concrete. Apparently Erin had participated in a drug bust in Frisco, and one of the men she'd arrested had tried to secretly bargain his way out of a prison sentence by revealing more about the drug operation. When the attempt failed, the suspect later denied he had tried to make a deal, but Erin was good at her job, and had evidently started investigating his claims on her own. Flynn hadn't expected to find much on this helicopter trip, but now, after seeing the grisly scene below, she was sure that Erin had been on the right track.

Flynn glanced back out the helicopter window and snapped a few more photos. Why was a dead body way out here in the middle of nowhere, slowly being buried by the snow in the remote Rocky Mountains? How did the scene below tie into the drug cartel? Questions spun in her head. Flynn shifted slightly in the helicopter seat so she could determine the exact cause of death, but no matter what angle she chose, it didn't help.

She focused her camera on the snow and followed the dark streaks of red that marred the wintry scene. Maybe, just maybe, her photos could help local law enforcement figure out what had happened. She was well out of her jurisdiction, but she was still a skilled investigator, and she wanted to help however she could. If she came to them with real evidence, maybe it would lead to the arrest of whoever shot her sister.

She leaned forward, adjusting as the helicopter turned. They had come to another nearby clearing, about the size of a baseball field, circled with aspens and pines. They helicopter hovered about eighty feet over the snow, and Flynn grimaced at the sight.

There was more than one body.

"Do you see that, Derek?" She turned toward the pilot who was flying them over the area and pointed.

"Unfortunately, I do," he said tightly. Even through the metallic speakers on the headset, she could hear a protective edge in his voice.

"We're right over the coordinates you provided from that map you showed me. Is this what you expected to find?"

Flynn met his eyes for a moment, then shook her head. "My sister's notes were pretty vague. I wasn't sure what to expect, but it definitely wasn't this."

"What's going on?" Flynn's eleven-year-old nephew, Kevin, pushed forward from the back of the helicopter, trying to get a better view out the window. "What do you see? Is there something weird out there?" Instead of the ominous tones she'd heard from their pilot, Kevin's voice sounded more interested than he'd been in anything else they'd talked about today...or all week. According to Erin, Kevin had been struggling ever since his father had abandoned him and Erin over a year before. The boy had been sullen and moody. Flynn and Erin had discussed Kevin quite a bit over the phone, but now that Flynn was actually in Colorado and had been taking care of the youth while Erin was in the hospital, she was seeing his behavior in person for the first time since his father's unexpected departure. Counselors hadn't been able to help him so far. And now that his mother's life was in jeopardy, Flynn was worried that his emotional state was only going to worsen. On top everything he had already been struggling with, he had to be terrified that he might become an orphan, even if he was desperately trying not to show his fear.

A wave of regret swept over her. She wouldn't have brought Kevin with them if she'd known they'd find a murder scene up here. Surely he didn't need to be exposed to something so hideous. The boy had been so obstinate and difficult in the hospital, though, that she'd thought the helicopter ride would be a good distraction for him. Flynn had also hoped that during the trip, she would learn a clue or two about who had tried to murder her sister. Still, the scene below was nothing like she'd expected, and she wished she'd left Kevin with a friend back in Frisco.

She turned to the boy and chose her words carefully, not wanting to add to the boy's trauma. "Some people have been killed," Flynn said gently. "You don't want to see it. There's a crime scene down there."

"A crime scene? Here?" Kevin's voice showed his surprise, and when Flynn looked over at him, he looked a bit paler than before. "What happened? Can you tell?"

Derek turned but didn't answer the boy. He looked back at Flynn. "I count three. Is that what you see?"

"Yes," she replied. "Kevin, try not to look. I'm going to take a few more pictures for the police, and then we need to go back to Frisco and take my SD card to the authorities. They'll have to send a team up here to investigate." She snapped several more photos as Derek banked the helicopter and turned so she could photograph a different angle.

"Good grief. It looks like a war zone down there," Derek muttered, pulling her back out of her thoughts and into the here and now. "The victims were shot, that much is clear."

Now that they were closer, the manner of death was much more apparent. "You're right," Flynn agreed. "At first, I was afraid maybe a wild animal had gotten them." She paused. "I only made detective a few months ago, so I'm still learning. Did you come across scenes like this very often in the military?"

"Unfortunately," Derek said under his breath. Even though he had murmured the comment, the word still went through the headset loud enough for Flynn to hear the desolation in his voice.

She looked back at the scene below them. A copious amount of snow was pink or red near the bodies, and now that they were closer, it appeared that the victims had been trying to escape and had been shot in the back. Footprints from the attackers came from behind and then circled each of the victims. Two were wearing winter clothing, so it was hard to determine their race or even their sex, though by their size they all seemed to be adults. The first body she had noticed was dressed in jeans and a red-and-black flannel shirt. He appeared to be an adult male, with short-cropped black hair, but it was difficult to be sure.

Flynn turned her camera to a couple of buildings on the side of the clearing and nestled into the edge of the surrounding woods. There was a large log cabin–style house that had obviously seen better days. The structure looked abandoned and leaned slightly to the left. Several shingles were missing, and paint peeled from various spots on the dark wooden walls. The building was situated closer to the other side of the tree line and stood about a hundred yards away from where the bodies lay in the snow. There was also a pole barn with an attached structure farther down the valley, and something that could have served as a helicopter pad near the house in the middle of the field. The pole barn housed some sort of equipment, a large tractor and a host of other items including a broken-down truck that had obviously been there for quite some time. A couple of snowmobiles were parked near the house's front door, but they had a few inches of snow on them, as if they hadn't been driven in the last couple of days.

"What is this place?" Flynn breathed almost to herself.

"An abandoned home turned meth lab, if I had to guess," Derek responded. "Do you smell that?"

"Smells like cat pee," Kevin volunteered.

Flynn wrinkled her nose and shook her head. She had never spent much time around young boys, but one thing she knew without a doubt—Kevin seemed to have a fascination with nasty smells.

"That's ammonia," Derek confirmed. "The smell gives it away. Ammonia is one of the key ingredients for making methamphetamine. We came across a few meth labs in Iraq, and I recognize the smell. We need to get out of here. Labs can be really dangerous. If the cooks don't do everything perfectly, the whole building can explode. Not to mention the fact that three people were murdered down there and the shooters are probably still hanging around." He pointed at the cabin. "I see some smoke coming out of that chimney. We are not alone."

"I agree. Let's get out of here," Flynn said as she sat back in the seat. Had her sister known about this meth lab? Had the drug dealers shot Erin before she could investigate further and shut the lab down? Questions plagued her mind.

"How long were you in the army?" Kevin suddenly asked, leaning closer to the pilot.

Derek turned his head as he steered the helicopter and took a moment to respond. "Eight years."

"That's so cool," Kevin opined. "Where were you stationed?"

"I did three tours," Derek confirmed.

"What did you do over there?" Kevin asked, apparently unable to keep the enthusiasm out of his voice.

"I flew Boeing AH-64 Apache helicopters in the sandbox—mostly in Iraq," Derek answered tightly.

"Man, that is so awesome! Why did you get out? Flying for the army sure sounds like more fun than flying around these mountains all day for the tourists. This is probably the most excitement you've ever had in Colorado."

Derek pursed his lips and didn't answer. Flynn glanced at him expectantly, but it was clear from the look on his face that they had broached an area that he had absolutely no desire to discuss. Flynn hadn't seen Derek King since their college days, and she'd truly been surprised when they had arrived at the airport and seen him running the flight check on the helicopter. She had spoken with a female receptionist to make the reservation and had no idea King Helicopter Tours was owned and operated by her old boyfriend. Back in college, she and Derek had dated for almost three years before they graduated. They had even talked about marriage, but then Derek had suddenly broken up with her and joined the army, with very little explanation. The breakup had been brutal, and Flynn hadn't heard from him since. In her mind, the wedge between them had all boiled down to one central truth—he had chosen a military career over marrying her, and once he'd made the decision, he hadn't been able to get away from her fast enough.

She had eventually forgiven him and tried to

move on, but seeing him again brought feelings back that she thought she had resolved long ago, and the knot that formed in her stomach every time he glanced at her told her she hadn't quite gotten him out of her system yet after all.

She eyed him carefully. He was bigger now, had filled out quite a bit during his time in the military. His shoulders were broad and muscular, and his arms and legs were equally well-built and strong. He still wore his dark brown hair in a short style, and his handsome face had a few new lines of maturity and stress that only made him more attractive. He was also wearing a well-trimmed beard and mustache and looked the part of a mountain man instead of the former military aviator she knew him to be. His carefree swagger was gone, though, and he now moved with that military bearing that people outside the service could never quite duplicate. The posture was like a confidence that never wavered, no matter the circumstance.

She had to admit, even though eight years had passed, he was still one very good-looking man. His bold, rugged features and firm cheekbones lent him an air of authority. She also liked the way his dark blue eyes captured everything around him. She paused, thinking back to the last time she'd seen him. Despite their horrible breakup and the way he had so callously thrown their relationship away, she had still always remembered him as a fun and gregarious person. The man she had encountered today, however, was serious and subdued. She wondered at the change in him. Anyone who'd served in the military and seen action probably had horror stories replay in their mind from time to time. Maybe Derek had experienced a horrible event while on active duty that had turned him into this sullen and tight-lipped man. Or had there been something else in his personal life that had changed him? There was no ring on his finger, but from his current expression, it was clear she wasn't about to find out any of the missing details from his life. He seemed professional but also distant, as if he were somehow living in a shell, bricked off from the rest of the world.

She turned away and made an effort to study the landscape. Attractive or not, she knew instinctively she would never pursue any sort of relationship with Derek King ever again. She was done with relationships and men, and once her sister had recovered, she would be returning to Florida on the first available flight. Until then, taking care of her nephew and finding out who shot her sister were her only priorities. That was more than enough to keep her busy. She didn't need or want to give Derek King a second chance to break her heart.

Derek subtly shook his head as he piloted the helicopter. He was glad the kid was interested in the military. Despite the negatives, like losing friends and family during wartime, he truly appreciated people who wanted to serve their country. Still, he didn't talk about the army—not with anyone. They had trained him to fly during his initial entry rotary wing training at the US Army Aviation Center of Excellence at Fort Novosel, Alabama. After his third tour had ended in a devastating crash, he had gotten out early with an honorable discharge from his thirteen-year commitment and taken his piloting skills to the civilian world. That expertise was all he wanted to remember from his time in the service. The other memories were too painful to dwell on.

Flynn apparently picked up on his reticence and changed the subject before he had to come up with an answer to Kevin's question. "Did you note the coordinates of that meth house? We can call in the crime scene to the tower, right? Or should we just contact the police once we get back?" Flynn asked.

"Yes, I've got the latitude and longitude," Derek confirmed, grateful that the discussion had veered away from the army and into new territory. "I'll call these in to the tower right now. I'm sure they'll want to come check out this mess ASAP."

Suddenly, before he even had a chance to reach for his radio, he saw movement out of the corner of his eye. Two men, both dressed in dark, heavy winter coats, had come out of the house and were standing in the snow. They were also both holding high-powered rifles, and before he could react, they started shouting and pointing their weapons at the helicopter.

The first bullet ripped into the window by Flynn's head, causing a crack in the glass that looked like a lightning strike. More bullets followed closely behind the first.

"Look out!" Kevin yelled, panic tingeing his voice.

"Get down," Flynn shouted as she motioned for Kevin to move lower on his seat. Apparently, she still couldn't see the shooters from her angle, and she huddled against the door while also trying to get a better look at what was happening. Another loud bang cracked through the air, and the aircraft dipped precariously.

A buzzer sounded, and a couple of lights flashed from the dashboard. Derek responded immediately by turning the aircraft away from the shooters and revving the engine to escape the onslaught, but he wasn't quite fast enough.

Another bullet ripped into the back of the helicopter, and a plume of smoke began pouring from the engine, floating ominously toward the sun. Derek immediately corrected the flight trajectory, but there was only so much he could do as the aircraft limped away from the scene. At this point, he instinctively knew there was no way they were going to make it back to the flight line. All he wanted to do was get the helicopter as far away from the shooters as possible and find a safe place to land.

The gunmen fired several other shots, but Derek flew in an erratic pattern that he'd learned from the firefights he'd flown in the sandbox. No other bullets hit the helicopter, but he was losing altitude fast and trying to compensate as best he could as he studied the terrain. Smoke continued to billow from behind the helicopter and filled the air. If nothing else, he hoped it helped camouflage their exact location—at least a little—from the shooters.

"We've been hit," he said over and over again into his microphone as he tried to transmit their location and the call numbers from his helicopter to the tower. Static was his only response, and he wasn't even sure the tower was receiving his messages. Apparently, the radio had been damaged, or there was some other problem. A gust of wind lifted his helicopter and pushed him farther south than he wanted to go, and he quickly adjusted. He hadn't had to fly like this since his last flight in Syria, and he had to push away from his mind's eye images of the crash that had taken his friend's life. Jax Thomas had been his copilot and had been flying with him on that awful day when they'd taken fire. A bullet had caught their rear rotor and crashed the helicopter. Despite all his efforts, Derek hadn't been able to save his friend, and the crash still haunted him today. Guilt followed him around like a constant companion, robbing him of any joy that tried to trickle into his life. He didn't deserve happiness. His friend would never again be able to enjoy the good things in life, so why should he? The memory of Jax's death was like carrying a heavy stone around day in and day out. The painful recollections weighed him down, so much so that many times, he felt like he was just going through the motions as he tried to get through another day. Was this crash also going to kill someone he had cared about?

Another gust of wind took them higher, and he could tell that he was fast losing control of the aircraft. His speed increased, and smoke, burning smells and heat permeated the cabin. There had to be a fire in his engine compartment, and he studied his instruments carefully, trying to verify and isolate the problem.

He flattened his lips, and his jaw tensed. According to the readings, his entire engine was on fire. The heat in the cabin was almost unbearable.

Derek kept shouting into his headset, but there was no response from the tower. He tried one last time. "Mayday, mayday. We're going down!"

Chapter Two

Derek glanced over at Flynn. Her left hand grasped the seat beneath her, and her right grabbed the door frame for dear life. She was gripping the plastic handle so tightly her knuckles were turning white. Her curly light brown hair was pulled back from her face with a light blue headband, and her blue eyes had rounded so he could see the fear overwhelming her. She had a smattering of freckles across her cheeks, and each one stood out in contrast against the paleness of her skin—even more so now. His heart constricted as he felt beads of sweat popping out across his brow, and his jaw ached from gritting his teeth.

Derek turned and quickly moved his focus back to flying the helicopter and getting them on the ground. He couldn't lose Flynn and Kevin like he had lost Jax in the Middle East. He had to land safely. He quickly turned off his fuel, the heater, the defroster and anything else he could reach as he tried to keep the helicopter under control. They were dropping even faster, and he rapidly searched for a landing site that would be both safe and far enough away from the shooters that they would have a fighting chance to survive.

They came across a small clearing that just might work, and Derek pulled hard on the throttle, trying to decrease speed as he lowered the collective and aimed for the spot. He was losing his hydraulics and had to exert quite a bit of force to get the controls to work, but they slowly did as he required. As his hands worked the collective and the cyclic, he used his feet to operate the antitorque pedals to control the direction the helicopter was pointing in. Gently, he increased the pressure on the left pedal to swing the nose in that direction, trying to avoid all contact with the trees and a nearby outcrop of rocks. He hoped he was at least two hundred feet away from any obstacles that might cause him to crash and kill them all, or cause even further damage to his helicopter, but with the heavily billowing smoke, it was hard to get a read on their actual distance or location. He glanced again at his landing site that was on the right side of helicopter and grimaced as he adjusted the trim once again.

The airspeed dipped to about forty knots as he began his descent. Even so, the vertical speed was still a bit too fast, and he pushed hard on the collective control, but it was nearly impossible to lower the velocity much as gravity pulled against them. Derek frowned and pushed up on the nose, then breathed a sigh of relief as the airspeed dropped to thirty knots, then twenty. That movement obscured his vision of the landing area even further, but it was necessary to keep them from slamming into the snowy ground below.

The helicopter moved forward a few more feet, and Derek reduced the collective even more. He armed the parking brake, then eased the cyclic control back to reduce momentum. Then he slowly moved the stick forward to level the altitude. He kept the rate of descent as slow as possible, adjusting the collective as he did so, and felt the helicopter touch the ground. Derek wasn't sure how deep the snow was beneath him, but after another few seconds, he made contact with the earth itself and heaved an inward sigh of relief.

He verified that his parking brake was armed

and then reduced and cut all power to the helicopter. Thick gray plumes of smoke billowed around them as the rotors began to slow. He quickly unbuckled his seat belt and turned to Kevin.

"Hand me that fire extinguisher," he ordered brusquely.

Kevin was shaken, but Derek's firm voice shocked the boy into compliance.

Derek took the small canister, then met Flynn's eyes. "Both of you, please get out and get as far away from the helicopter as you can, but keep your eyes open for the shooters, and try to hold your breath as much as you can so these fumes don't make you sick." They both nodded, and he could tell by their expressions that they understood the seriousness of the situation and would follow his directions. He pushed open his door and jumped out of the helicopter, then released the catch on the engine compartment and started spraying the metal down with the white foam that came spewing out of the extinguisher. As he suspected, the smoke was suffocating, and he paused a time or two to draw his shoulder up to his mouth and inhale through the fabric of his navy flannel shirt, hoping to get even the smallest amount of clean air. His chest tightened as he struggled to breathe and handle the relief that was also coursing through him. They had made it safely to the ground, but the shooters might be only a few steps behind them. Tightness pulled against his chest.

He glanced over at Flynn, who had taken the boy over to the tree line. She still looked pale and terrified. Of all the women who had to lease his helicopter today, why did it have to be her?

Derek had loved her once, back in college, although he had given her up when he joined the army. Unfortunately, he'd realized he'd made a huge mistake the minute he got on that plane to go to basic training, but at that point, he'd already destroyed the relationship, and he'd convinced himself there was no turning back. He had been terrified of settling down and having a family, so he had escaped, and run as fast and as far away as he could. His life growing up had been no picnic—his father had been an angry and physically abusive man who had made Derek's life miserable until the older man had finally succumbed to a heart attack a couple of years ago. How could he guarantee he wouldn't be the same kind of parent? He'd never been good around children, and Flynn had wanted a family—complete with a dog and white picket fence.

He glanced at her again, and his grip tightened. He'd dated since then, telling himself that he'd finally gotten over her, but every woman he'd gone out with had always been a pale imitation of Flynn who had captured his heart all those years ago. She was the most beautiful woman he'd ever seen, with curly brown hair that begged to be toyed with and blue eyes the color of the sea after a storm.

He turned his head slightly, forcing himself to look away from Flynn and focus on their current situation. He had no business even thinking about Flynn right now beyond trying to keep her and her nephew safe. She deserved better than a has-been military pilot who had let his best friend get killed in the Middle East. The love he'd felt for her had never truly disappeared, but he couldn't pursue Flynn now...or ever. He'd already broken her heart once, and he knew she'd never trust him again.

Though they had landed and were all in one piece, Flynn felt paralyzed with fear. She had been alive for nearly thirty years and had been in mortal danger on more than one occasion on the job. However, having someone trying to shoot her out of the sky was a new experience that scared her on an entirely new level.

Unfortunately, their troubles were just beginning. They were near the top of a mountain peak in the Colorado Rockies with a damaged helicopter that she doubted would fly again before the engine received major repairs. They had no supplies that she knew of, killers were undoubtedly going to show up at any minute, and despite her coat and lightweight gloves, the snowy cold weather chilled her to the bone.

Not to mention the fact that her eleven-year-old nephew was standing beside her, and she was responsible for his welfare. Would they survive this?

She had to do this. Regardless of her own fear, she had to be strong for Kevin. She turned slightly so she could see the boy. His face was ashen and stood out in stark relief against his dusty blond hair and dark brown eyes. "Are you okay?"

"Yeah, but I don't think I ever want to ride on a helicopter again." Kevin shivered.

"Agreed." She had grabbed her camera bag before the two of them had run over to the tree line, and as she adjusted the strap on her shoul-

der, she noticed for the first time that Kevin
was also carrying a small bag.

"What have you got in there?" she asked.

"Just some snacks," he mumbled. "I figured
we might get hungry."

She gave him a reassuring nod as she quickly
took her camera strap from around her neck and
removed the SD card that contained the crime-
scene photos. She found a blank SD card in a
side pocket of her backpack and inserted that
into the body. Next, she slid the small card with
the crime-scene photos into a protective plastic cover and thrust it deeply into one of her
gloves. She stowed her camera back in her bag
and placed it by the trunk of a large aspen tree.
The backpack contained some pretty expensive
equipment, but she opted to leave everything
behind anyway. If she had to guess, they'd be
walking until they found help, and she didn't
want the heavy bag to hamper their escape.
It was hard to be so practical, but she figured
that since her life—and Kevin's—depended on
safely navigating down the mountain, she didn't
want to be hindered by the backpack or worry
about the contents as they traveled. She did
have a small waterproof pocket camera, which
she stowed in her jacket. She couldn't imag-

ine needing it but figured there was no harm in keeping it with her due to its slight size and weight. Hopefully, they would be able to return to the helicopter's crash site with help from local law enforcement and she could retrieve her bag again. But even if the camera didn't survive the cold or the elements, keeping the equipment safe wasn't worth her life.

They watched Derek from the tree line, which was about sixty feet away from the downed helicopter. He had finished with the fire extinguisher, and although the billowing gray smoke had lessened a bit and turned whiter in color, there was still quite a bit floating through the air. He shook his head, and Flynn could see his frustration in his expression and body language. She hoped he had insurance, but either way, this horrible event was going to put him out of business for days, if not weeks. She had no idea about his financial solvency but imagined a helicopter operation was not a cheap endeavor and retrieving the helicopter from this remote, snowy mountainside was not going to be easy. She hoped the bird was fixable, but another wave of guilt swept over her. Why hadn't she just stayed at the hospital with her sister?

As they kept an eye out, Derek grabbed a few things from the helicopter and put them in a navy backpack, then quickly headed toward them. "I'm really sorry about all this," he said quietly once he had joined them. "But don't worry. I don't have much that will help us, but I do have an emergency kit with a few vital items, and I know quite a bit about surviving in difficult situations. I promise I'm going to do everything I can to get us safely back to town."

"This is my fault, not yours," Flynn murmured. "Any chance you can fix that helicopter?"

"Not without help and some new parts. The bullets caused too much damage."

He ran his fingers through his short dark hair in a show of exasperation. "The first thing we need to do is put as much distance as we can between us and this helicopter. All this smoke is basically acting like a beacon for the shooters right now. Those guys could show up at any second. Are you ready to move?"

Flynn glanced at what Kevin was wearing and winced. He had not planned to be out trekking through the snow, and his clothes were better suited for hanging out with friends or watching a movie instead of spending any time outdoors. His jacket was thin, and although he had on a knit hat, he was wearing canvas tennis shoes and didn't have any gloves. "Yes, unless you have any warmer clothes in that helicopter for Kevin. He's not wearing much to keep him warm."

Derek shook his head. "Unfortunately, I don't, but he can take my gloves." He quickly stripped them off and handed them to the boy, who immediately put them on. "Okay, let's go." Derek motioned into the forest with his head, then started moving toward the trees, his motions quick and efficient.

Flynn and Kevin followed closely behind him despite his long stride. Her mind whirled as she watched him make his way through the snow. She glanced at Derek's sidearm that was secured at his waist, along with an extra magazine. The fact that he was armed made her feel somewhat safer, regardless of what he'd stowed in the backpack. She was a good shot herself, but she also knew Derek must have received extensive training in the military. She'd been angry when he'd chosen the service over their relationship back in college, but now she found herself thankful that he was so prepared. The trek back to civilization wouldn't be easy, but with Derek along, she acknowledged that they at least had a fighting chance. She was a Florida girl, born and raised, and only had a vague idea of what it would take to survive in the snow.

Suddenly, they heard voices closing in. Derek turned and motioned for them to follow him, and they quickly ran several yards and ducked behind a fallen log. Right before joining them, Derek grabbed a nearby fallen branch and used the dried leaves to brush the snow and hide their footprints. He dived into their hiding place just as two men emerged from the nearby trees.

"I see the helicopter," the first man said as he pointed toward the clearing. He was wearing a green puffy coat and jeans, a black knit hat, and thick leather gloves. "I told you I was going to knock it out of the sky." He laughed callously. "That metal bird is still smoking."

Flynn laid a careful hand on Kevin's back, hoping to reassure him. He was close in front her, and Derek was directly behind her, his body curled protectively around hers like a shield. She turned her head so that she could see into his eyes, and the confidence she saw there helped calm her racing heart, even as she stiffened at his touch. Despite her law enforcement training, she was scared—more for Kevin's sake than her own. She had to protect her nephew, no matter the cost. Derek said nothing, but reached for her hand and gave it a squeeze as he nodded slightly, apparently understanding her angst. He was so close, she could smell the mint on his breath and see the dark flecks in his stormy blue eyes. There was some awkwardness in his response, yet he still did his best to try to comfort her. Derek's touch made her feel safe, which surprised her, even though she'd flinched at the contact. She had been avoiding most touch for quite a while—especially by men—even if it was innocent or just a friendly gesture. Her attention went back to their pursuers, and she could hear their feet crunching in the snow as they approached.

"Yeah, yeah," the second man responded. He was wearing similar clothing but had on a blue jacket instead of green. "The helicopter is huge—at least as big as my truck. How could you miss? You're no sharpshooter. Anyone could have shot that thing out of the sky."

"I didn't just hit it," Green Jacket boasted. "I got the engine. That thing won't be flying for a while, I can tell you that."

The other man's voice sounded bored. "I couldn't care less. Let's just find the pilot and the passengers, finish them off, and get back to the house. It's freezing out here."

"Like they're gonna survive in this snow anyway," Green Jacket said with a grin.

The other man stopped only a few feet from where the trio was hiding. Flynn could just make out their shapes from her position on the ground. They weren't big men, but with the guns in their hands, they seemed larger and more threatening. She prayed silently and squeezed Kevin's shoulder in reassurance.

"Look, you idiot. They saw the meth lab. They saw the bodies in the field. They're witnesses, and we can't go back and get out of this snow until they're all dead. No loose ends, got it?"

"Yeah, okay. But it sure is cold out here. I'm telling you, they won't survive, even if we never find them."

"Just shut up and do your job." Blue Jacket shrugged and glanced around the area. "The others will be here soon. Let's get this over with."

Flynn tensed at the man's words, but Derek gave her shoulders a squeeze of reassurance. She knew, despite their past and difficult breakup, that he would do everything he could to keep her safe. The protectiveness was clearly visible in his eyes.

After a few minutes, the two men continued away from the small group, unaware that the people they were hunting for were huddling in the snow and hidden by the brush only a few feet away. Flynn glanced over at Derek, but he silently shook his head, letting her know it wasn't time to move just yet. She turned her head so she could see their adversaries. The man in the green jacket was a wild card and an easy target, but the blue-jacketed man was a more serious opponent, and both of them carried .30-06 Springfield rifles with scopes—very deadly weapons with quite a range.

A few minutes later, the men moved farther away, and Derek finally raised up slightly and sneaked a peek over the log. "Back up and crawl after me. Stay low and close," he whispered. He released Flynn's hand and began to crawl away from the scene, and Flynn and Kevin followed, trying to keep as low as possible. They hid behind brush and trees until they were a good forty feet from where they'd been hiding by the logs. Finally, a few minutes later, Derek stood and reached out his hand, helping both of them to their feet one at a time.

"Stay close, and stay quiet," Derek ordered in a whisper.

Flynn and Kevin nodded and followed Derek wordlessly into the forest, not even stopping to brush the snow from their clothes. Derek set a brutal pace, but the two stayed close, struggling some with the depth of the snow at times, but both doing their best to keep up.

They continued on for at least forty-five minutes, none of them saying a word as they trudged through the trees and the snow. The boy's teeth had started chattering, and Flynn knew her own face was pink from exertion and the cold. Thankfully, she had donned leather hiking boots for the trip on a lark, but Kevin's canvas sneakers were more suitable for a grassy field in summer than this heavy snow. They were soaking wet and his feet had to be freezing. Still, to his credit, he said nothing, although he did cup his gloved hands together and blow on them from time to time, then worked his fingers to keep the blood flowing.

They came upon another clearing, and Derek motioned for them to stop. "Stay at the tree line and out of sight. I see something up ahead," he said quietly.

Flynn nodded, then watched him head to

the eastern side of the field where a bit of blue was sticking up. A sickening feeling swept over her as she watched Derek approach the mound that was partially covered by snow. Kevin had sunk down to sit on a fallen tree trunk, and she moved to block his field of vision as she watched Derek move cautiously, then circle the darkened snow.

Across the distance, their eyes met, and Derek shook his head and rubbed his eyes. A sickening feeling twisted in her stomach.

Derek had found yet another dead body.

Chapter Three

Derek stepped carefully around the red that had splattered in the snow surrounding another gunshot victim. This body was a short young man, probably in his early twenties, with scruffy brown hair tucked loosely under a green knit cap. He was lying on his stomach and had been shot in the back as he'd run away from whoever had been pursuing him. Slowly Derek rolled him over, searching for any signs of life. His lips were blue, and his skin was pallid and mottled with sores, and he had damaged teeth, as if he used methamphetamine. Derek felt sure the man was dead, but reached for his neck anyway, feeling for a pulse.

There was no heartbeat. He readjusted his fingers, just in case, then pulled back. The young man was definitely lifeless, but his dark brown eyes still held a look of terror. Apprehension twisted in Derek's gut. He'd hoped to never see death again—especially so up close. He tried to push his anxiety aside and began searching the victim's body. He found a Smith & Wesson M&P Shield 9mm pistol in the man's waistband and pulled the pistol out and checked the magazine. The mag was full—eight bullets with an additional bullet in the chamber. Nine shots. Derek still had his own pistol with an extra mag, but with armed men chasing them, it would be good to arm Flynn as well.

She'd always been a tough, independent lady, and it didn't surprise him in the least that she had already become a detective despite her young age. As far as he knew, it usually took someone several years longer to reach that level in law enforcement, but Flynn was smart and driven—two great qualities that undoubtedly helped pave the way for her to reach her career goals.

Derek pocketed the new pistol. Flynn's firearm training would definitely come in handy if they met up with their pursuers before they made it back to town, and at this point, they needed all the help they could get to survive this challenge.

He glanced over at Flynn and Kevin, verifying that they were still safe, then searched the man's pockets, just in case he had an extra mag secreted somewhere on his body. There wasn't one, but he did find the man's wallet that contained a few bucks and an I.D. The victim's Colorado driver's license matched the face of the corpse. It was definitely the same man, despite the fact that the body now had the definite telltale signs of a meth user—he was thinner and had aged considerably since the photo was taken. Derek pocketed the license and replaced the wallet, hoping he would have the chance to give the card to law enforcement once they arrived safely back home. He hoped the authorities wouldn't have trouble finding the body, but if his adversaries tried to cover up their crimes, they would probably dispose of the bodies as soon as possible, and the license and Derek's eyewitness testimony could be all that proved the man was indeed dead. Somewhere, the victim might have a family who needed to know that this young man was never coming home.

He studied the man's body once again and made a swift decision. He'd already messed up the crime scene to verify the man was truly dead, and Kevin was freezing and was just a little bit smaller than the victim. He quickly pulled off the man's jacket, boots and gloves and headed back over to where Flynn and Kevin were still waiting for him at the tree line. He glanced at their clothing and noted Flynn's jeans, burgundy flannel shirt and T-shirt underneath. She also wore a decent winter coat and hiking boots, but the boy's clothing was completely inadequate.

"See if these fit," Derek said as he held the clothing out to Kevin.

Kevin raised his eyebrows, a look of disdain and horror on his face. "You're kidding, right? There's blood on those."

"Yeah, but they will keep you from freezing."

"I'm not wearing those, and you can't make me," Kevin said with a slight tremble in his voice. He was probably trying to sound defiant, but that goal was hard to accomplish with his teeth chattering because of the cold, and the sound he emitted was more of a whine.

Derek was ex-military—an officer. He didn't have time for obstinate kids, especially those giving an attitude when all their lives were at stake. He glanced over at Flynn and was about to blister the boy's ears when Flynn subtly shook her head. Her concerned expression gave him pause and held him back.

"Kevin, you don't have a choice," she said

softly, her tone filled with understanding but still laced with firmness. "I know it's tough, but your feet and hands will freeze without boots and gloves, and Derek needs his gloves back to protect his own hands. We don't know how long we're going to be up here on this mountain in this snow. It could take us days to walk down, and the temperature is already dropping pretty fast."

"When you get frostbite, you'll lose your fingers and toes. Without that coat, you might also lose your life," Derek added, his voice leaving no room for argument, a scowl on his face.

Kevin curled his lip. "There's blood on the coat, and a hole where the bullet went through the back."

"Yes," Derek agreed. "But there's only a little blood, and like I said, they will keep you from freezing to death."

Kevin took a step back, still not taking the items from Derek's outstretched hands. "I can't wear this stuff, Aunt Flynn," he whined, his voice sounding strangled. "It's gross."

"It's not up for debate. Put the clothes on. Now." Mindful of Flynn's concern, and the fact that her nephew's mom was still fighting for her life back in the hospital, Derek kept his voice firm but nonthreatening. For a moment, Derek thought the boy was still going to refuse. There was even defiance in the youth's eyes that burned with resentment, but finally he took the boots first and tried them on. They were actually a decent fit and only slightly too big, as were the gloves. The boy handed Derek's gloves back, and Derek quickly put them on.

"So what do I do with my old shoes?" the boy asked.

"Carry them or leave them. That's up to you," Derek replied. "Now try the coat."

Kevin balked, and even put his fingers through the bullet holes in the back panel, but wisely kept his mouth shut and finally acquiesced. The jacket was a bit large on him but still offered him more warmth that his own thin jacket could provide, and Derek knew that despite the blood, unless they were rescued pretty soon, the coat and other items could very well save the boy's life.

"All right. Let's keep going..." His words were cut off by the sound of a bullet whizzing by his ear and ricocheting off a nearby tree branch. "Get down!" he whispered fiercely, grabbing Flynn's hand and pulling her into a crouch behind a larger tree trunk. Bits of wood spit into the air and littered the snow right in front of them as another round hit the sapling close to the first.

"We know you're back there!" a male voice shouted from a distance. "We won't hurt you if you come out with your hands up now!"

Derek held his finger to his lips and shook his head. If they came out, they were as good as dead. It was painfully obvious that the drug dealers would do whatever was necessary to get rid of any witnesses to their criminal enterprise. He had a downed helicopter to prove it. They needed to get out of there—and fast.

Flynn's heart was beating so hard, she was sure the sound was going to get them killed. The pounding in her chest and the roaring in her ears were so loud she just knew they had to be audible to those around her. She'd been in tight spots before, but never with her nephew in tow and under her care. Her vision swam and the trees started spinning right before her eyes. How had this afternoon turned into a disaster so quickly? She had wanted to give Kevin a break from the hospital walls and distract him from his mother's situation.

Putting his life in danger had not been part of her plan.

She glanced at Derek, who was crouching next to her and taking stock of the situation. She could almost see his brain working, considering options, figuring out a plan of escape. She might not recognize this professional yet detached soldier as her boyfriend from her college days, but she couldn't have picked a better person to be stranded in the woods with. Despite the years that had passed, and her general distrust of men in relationships, she knew instinctively that the two of them would make a good team as they fought this adversary together. He moved slightly and handed her a pistol, and she gave him a smile, flipped the safety off and checked the magazine. Nine shots.

Things were looking up.

She met Derek's eyes, and he motioned for her and Kevin to follow him, crouching down and moving silently and quickly through the forest, away from the men with the rifles. There was no use having a showdown if it wasn't necessary, and her primary goal was getting Kevin to safety. They moved from tree to tree, using them as shields and camouflage as they tried to

put as much distance as possible between them
and the criminals pursuing them.

Dear God, please help us. The prayer was short
but heartfelt. She had been moving away from
God during the last few years, but she knew in-
tuitively that her reticence was a mistake. She
needed to draw closer to God, not pull away.
She needed God in her life more than ever,
especially now with a pair of killers bearing
down on them.

They had gotten about thirty feet away from
their original location when one of the shooters
opened fire again. Bits of bark rained down on
them as they raced from tree to tree, trying to
stay safe and ahead of the shooters' onslaught.

Flynn staggered over a tree limb and hit the
ground hard, but when a bullet hit a tree in
front of her, she realized that the fall had actually saved her life. If she'd been vertical, the
bullet would have no doubt caught her in the
chest. She pulled herself to her feet, ignoring the
throbbing pain that had begun in her left knee
when she'd landed, and kept running. Derek
was leading the way, and Kevin was between
them, and that was just the way she wanted it.
Derek would undoubtedly know the best way
to go, and she needed to have Kevin in front

of her and in her line of sight so she knew he was safe and keeping up with them.

Snowdrifts slowed them down—in some areas the snow was over a foot thick, and she struggled to pull her feet up and take the next step. The conditions made it hard to outrun the reach of the high-powered rifles the shooters were using. The only consolation was that the difficult environment was also slowing down their pursuers. The shots continued, and each bullet sent another jolt of fear thorough her as she ran. She couldn't lose Kevin, especially not when her sister was fighting for her life in the hospital. She had to keep him safe. The thought of losing both of them terrified her as the adrenaline pumped through her veins.

Suddenly, she saw Derek pull himself up short and stop. As she approached, she could see that he'd reached a ledge and there was apparently a drop in front of him. He grabbed Kevin and quickly pulled him behind a stand of bushes, and she joined them a few seconds later and looked down past their feet into the gorge that loomed below.

They were stuck. The area below was at least forty feet down—maybe even more. She had never been good at estimating distances, but the sight scared her. Rock climbing had never been her thing, but at least she was in fairly good shape—she could probably make it down without too much trouble. But what about Kevin? She took another look. In certain places, the snow had piled up against the bank of the ledge at the bottom of the gorge, but it was impossible to know how deep the slush was or what was beneath it. The three crouched down, trying to make themselves as small as possible as they figured out their next move. They couldn't go back. But how could they get down the ledge safely?

"Now what?" Flynn asked breathlessly, her eyes meeting Derek's.

"We climb down the rocks. There is no other option. The shooters have us pinned down." Derek looked directly at Kevin. "Can you handle this?"

The boy shrugged, but Flynn could tell he was putting on an act as he tried to infuse toughness into his voice. "Do I have a choice?"

"I don't see one," Derek mumbled, apparently more to himself than in response. His expression was filled with frustration. It was obvious that he shared Flynn's concerns about getting Kevin to the bottom. "Kevin, come behind me, so if you have any trouble, I can try to help you. There are some deep snowdrifts down there, so if either of you start to slip, try to slide toward one that can help cushion your fall." He swung his legs over the edge. "Okay. Let's do this. Grab the branches or other handholds when you can, and follow me down."

More bullets sounded around them, and stealth was immediately forgotten as they scurried over the ledge and started their descent. Flynn didn't have time to think about the distance between her or the ground—or the lack of handholds available on the snowy surface of the vertical rock wall. She just started climbing down, her mind focused on escape and making sure Kevin and Derek were nearby and safely descending.

Suddenly, her left hand slipped, and she searched frantically for a new handhold. Her glove grappled around the area, looking for anything that would help support her weight, but she found only dirt and bits of rock that dislodged and fell as she tried to grasp something new for support. Her right hand was holding a root that was protruding out a few inches, but even as she tried to find a new handhold for her left, she felt her right hand slipping down the root. The narrow stem was simply too small to support her, and she realized fleetingly that she was only seconds away from plummeting to the ground. Her body swayed, then started slowly sliding as the root slipped through her fingers and gravity pulled her down the face of the wall. She wanted to scream, but she swallowed the sound, unwilling to give her attackers any more clues about their whereabouts. Instead, she gritted her teeth as fear coursed through her veins, her jaw tight as she slid awkwardly down the rocky surface, unsure if she would survive the next few minutes.

Chapter Four

Flynn landed in a deep pile of snow and lay still for a moment, surprise mixed with relief making her breath shallow and fast. She was still alive. A quick but near-silent prayer of thanksgiving issued from her lips as she started to move, carefully at first, making sure there weren't any rocks or other solid hazards buried around her. She rolled to the right, the snow crunching beneath her weight as she struggled to her knees. A few seconds later, both Kevin and Derek were by her side, worry painted across both of their features.

"Are you okay?" Kevin asked, his eyes wide as Derek reached over and helped her to her feet. "I got so scared when I saw you fall! I thought you were dead!" He kept his voice low, even though it was filled with anxiety.

"I'm okay." She shook herself, trying to regain her bearings. "That was quite a ride." She whispered, knowing the gunmen were still close by and hunting them. She looked down at her jeans, where there was a small tear, and smiled to herself. God had truly been watching out for her. She could barely believe that after being chased through the woods and falling down the rocky ledge, she was relatively unscathed and had only a sore knee and a small rip in her pants to show for it. She said another silent prayer of thanks, then took a deep breath. "Let's get out of here before those killers follow us down."

Derek nodded. "Good plan."

She glanced at his expression and saw what she thought was genuine concern and something more filling his eyes. Before she could think that much about his countenance, he had already turned and started leading them away from the bottom of the rocky wall. Back in college, she could read him like a book. Now? She had no idea what he was thinking.

Suddenly, a bullet ricocheted off a nearby rock, and Flynn flinched involuntarily as she heard noises from above. Adrenaline coursed through her chest as she quickly motioned to her nephew to move toward the trees. He followed her directions, and she trailed closely behind him, searching the area above them for any sign of their attackers as she did so. She couldn't see them, but she could hear them shouting, and she figured they were just firing randomly, hoping to hit a target. She considered pulling her pistol and firing back but knew instinctively that she had little chance of hitting a target from this distance and angle, even if she did manage to get one of the criminals in her sights. Her pistol didn't have the range or accuracy of the rifles that the shooters were using. And with limited ammunition, there was no use wasting it when she might very well need it later on. Keeping her weapon secure, Flynn followed Kevin and moved to cover.

"They're headed west!" a man yelled, and his voice echoed off the canyon walls as another bullet followed closely behind the first.

Maybe they weren't shooting randomly after all. Flynn grabbed Kevin's hand and followed closely behind Derek, who had taken refuge behind an outcrop of rock as he waited for them to catch up. He motioned for them to follow him and headed deeper into the aspen forest at a fast clip. They used the tree trunks and brush as cover the best they could, and thankfully, the snow wasn't as deep here, so they were able to make good time and put quite a bit of distance in between themselves and the attackers. Eventually, the shooters stopped firing, and they could no longer hear their voices. Finally, they all paused and caught their breath, taking in their new surroundings while still being mindful of the threat behind them.

"Do you think they're still following us?" she asked cautiously.

"Yes, but I don't think they're willing to chance going down that cliff. They're going to have to find another way around to get down to this level. By the time they do, I'm hoping we'll be long gone." He avoided her eyes and turned. "Let's keep moving. The more distance we can put between us and them, the better."

They kept moving down the side of the mountain, hiking as quickly as they could manage for what seemed like hours. They said very little and stayed near the trees whenever possible. Thankfully, they didn't see their pursuers following them and heard nothing more. Even so, they knew the shooters had to be following them, closing in, dogging their heels.

For the most part, Flynn followed Derek's lead, but later that afternoon, when Kevin's stamina started to wane and his steps slowed, she waved to Derek and motioned out of Kevin's sight that they needed to talk. They had stopped a couple of times already to rest, but at this point, Flynn was convinced that Kevin was completely spent. The boy was only eleven, after all, and though he was of average height and build for a boy his age, he wasn't used to the strenuous activity of hiking through snow for hours at a time. He plopped himself down on a fallen log and his shoulders slumped. The stress from exertion showed in his haggard expression and exhausted body language. Flynn was tired herself, and her knee was throbbing. She couldn't imagine how Kevin was still managing to stay on his feet.

"We need to stop," Flynn murmured for Derek's ears alone, still very much aware of the necessity of keeping her voice low, just in case their enemies were in earshot. She motioned with her head, not wanting her nephew to hear her concerns, either. "Kevin can't go any farther." She swallowed and absently rubbed her leg above her injured knee. "I feel like we've been going in circles, but I'm sure you have a reason. Do you have plans for the night?"

"I do," he said softly as he raised an eyebrow. "And yes, we have been backtracking for about the last hour. When we slid down that cliff, I noticed a rock formation to the southwest that might offer us some refuge from the elements. We passed the area once, but now we're going back. I'm hoping the guys with the guns will think we continued on down the mountain. Most people don't turn around and look behind them when they're searching for someone."

"Smart move," she said with a tired smile. "Are we close?"

Derek nodded. "Another fifteen minutes or so ought to do it, but we'll still need to keep our voices down. I heard them say something about reinforcements, and I don't know how many others might be looking for us or how spread out they are. I do think those guys are going to be combing these woods until they find us, though. Like the guy said—we're a loose end. They can't allow us to get back to town. They know we'll report what happened and what we saw."

"I'm sorry I'm not much help," she said softly. "Hiking in the outdoors has never been my thing."

"I remember," he said so softly she wasn't even sure she'd actually heard the words. For a moment he seemed lost in memories, but then he suddenly looked up, his expression clear. "Stay close. It won't be much farther." He turned away and, without another sound, started walking again.

Flynn watched him for a moment or two, not quite sure what to make of him, then made eye contact with Kevin and gave him a soft smile. His nose was red and his shoulders slouched. "We're almost done for the day. I know you're tired, but can you make it another fifteen minutes?"

"I guess," he responded, his tone weary. "I just want to get away from those guys."

"We're going to make it," she affirmed, her tone confident. "You're doing great, Kevin. Just a little bit farther and we'll stop for the night and get some rest." She motioned toward Derek's retreating figure. "He's good. Really good. You don't need to worry. He'll make sure we make it down this mountain."

"Seems like you guys are friends, or used to be," Kevin said as he slowly pulled himself up and they started to follow Derek again. He kept his voice down, but there was genuine interest in his tone. "How do you know him?"

"Derek was actually my boyfriend back in college, if you can believe it. Remember how

I told you I went to school at Florida State in Tallahassee? Well, so did he. I haven't talked to him in years, though, and I was surprised to see him at the airport. I didn't even know he lived out here in Colorado. But I do know he was always good at getting out of a jam. You can trust him."

"Uh-huh," Kevin answered, apparently not convinced.

Flynn didn't respond. She wanted to reassure her nephew but didn't want to continue the conversation when danger could very well be around every corner. She gave him a gentle nudge, hoping to help him find his second wind. "We're going to make it," she said softly. "Don't give up."

Derek glanced behind him, verifying that Flynn and Kevin were only about twenty feet back. The snow was patchy here around the trees, and the walking was a bit easier than it had been when they had been more out in the open and farther east. Considering the boy's condition, he was grateful for the change, even though he knew the easier conditions wouldn't last. Most of the mountain was already covered with snow, and the forecast called for another storm to hit in the next few hours. The night would be difficult, especially if they couldn't have a fire.

His thoughts strayed back to Flynn again. His assistant had taken the reservation, and all he'd known before the flight was that a woman and boy wanted to scout out some coordinates on the mountain. He hadn't looked at the names of the passengers before arriving to perform his preflight checks. He had been floored to see Flynn standing by his helicopter on the flight line, her smile lighting up the tarmac like a warm sunny day, even though it was November, with a chill in the air.

Why was this kid with her on the flight? She'd introduced him as her nephew but hadn't given any other explanation or details about her life. He remembered that she had a sister but hadn't interacted with Erin much back in college while he'd dated Flynn and hardly recalled anything about her. Flynn had probably mentioned Kevin during college, but he just didn't remember.

Why was she even in Colorado? Questions plagued his mind as he walked.

Was Flynn married? He hadn't seen a ring, but that didn't mean much these days. Plenty of married folks in the military didn't wear jewelry to protect their hands from getting caught in machinery or weaponry. And she had mentioned that she was a new detective, which meant she must have been working in law enforcement for a few years. Earning the rank of detective was no small feat, especially at her young age. Perhaps her job had something to do with the reason why she kept her hands free of ornamentation. Or maybe she was still single...

But why did he care?

He shouldn't. *He didn't.* Flynn's marital status was none of his business. He forced his thoughts away from her. Unbidden, his mind turned to Jax, as it often did. Jax smiling as he played a practical joke on him. Jax playing the drums in their garage band as his own fingers strummed his bass guitar. Jax lying dead in the tangled heap of metal than had once been a helicopter before the bird had been shot from the sky...

Derek and Jax had joined the army together, but instead of making a career out of the service, Derek had gotten out as soon as he could after Jax was killed. Derek's guilt was crippling, even though he was exonerated of any wrongdoing by a military tribunal. Nowadays, Derek struggled to maintain a meaningful relationship with anyone. He couldn't be responsible for losing someone else close to him. Yet here he was, leading his old girlfriend and her young nephew on foot down the mountain with gunmen hot on their tails—after his helicopter was shot out of the sky again, no less! And his companion wasn't just any ex-girlfriend. It was Flynn Denning—the one he had loved with all his heart. She was the only woman who had actually made him consider settling down and having a family, even though the idea of marriage scared him right down to his toes. No one else he'd dated had come close to Flynn's feisty personality, sweet smile or caring heart. Whenever he daydreamed of a future, it was Flynn's face that appeared in his mind's eye.

But living life with Flynn by his side was a silly dream—one that could never happen.

How did he get here? Just by catching her eye before their flight, his chest had grown tight as the emotions of loss and love had nearly overwhelmed him. He'd had no choice but to bury his feelings beneath a veneer of indifference, knowing that he had lost her forever after he had signed on the dotted line and joined the army. Derek hadn't even discussed his decision with her after he'd met with the recruiter.

When she'd started talking about having a family, he'd been so scared that he would turn into his father that he'd run as fast as he could in the opposite direction. Derek knew he'd handled the whole situation badly. Communication had never been one of his strong suits. But even so, his actions had never erased the love he still held for her in his heart.

Derek shook his head and gritted his teeth. Once again, he found himself trying to push the thoughts of Flynn and their past into the dark recesses of his mind. Somehow, he had to lead these two down off this mountain without getting caught by the gunmen or the elements. He didn't have time for reminiscing, daydreaming or ruminating on his prior mistakes. The past was over and done. There was no going back.

He led them to the rock formation, then motioned for them to stay covered under the trees while he explored the area. Kevin sank down to sit in the snow, and Flynn stood protectively in front of him, her sharp eyes keeping watch for any signs of danger.

Derek pushed aside some brush, careful not to break the branches and leave signs of his presence, and pulled out a small flashlight attached to his key chain. He'd revealed a narrow opening, and he ducked and twisted to squeeze between the stones. The fissure formed an awkward entrance, but after several feet, the space opened up into an oval-shaped room about ten feet wide and seven feet long. The cave had a low ceiling—he couldn't stand up all the way—but it would suit his purposes and keep them safe from the elements during the night. There didn't seem to be a back entrance beyond some small crevices in the rocks, but he did see some daylight between the stones, so at least they would have some ventilation. The only negative he could see was that if they were discovered, they would be sitting ducks. There would be no escape.

He said a silent prayer as doubts assailed him. What if he failed? What if the gun-toting drug dealers killed Flynn and her nephew on his watch? How would he ever survive that?

"Derek!"

Derek turned and pointed his flashlight at the rock opening at Flynn's urgently whispered exclamation. Kevin was on his hands and knees and entering the small space, and Flynn was right behind him in a similar position. The beam caught her eyes, which were troubled yet filled with fire.

"They're right outside…"

Chapter Five

Derek quickly flipped the flashlight off and pocketed it, then hurried over to help move Kevin deeper into the cave while Flynn scurried in behind him as quietly as possible. Once inside, she pulled herself into a sitting position, leaned against the rock wall, and took a moment to collect herself and gain control over the adrenaline that was pulsing through her chest. Kevin seemed to be shivering, and even though she couldn't tell if his reaction was from fear or the cold, she pulled him wordlessly into an embrace, then listened carefully. At first, all she could hear was her own breathing and the roaring in her ears, but that gradually faded away and she could hear their pursuers' voices outside the cave. Even though they were slightly muffled, they were getting louder by the second, as if the men were walking right up to their hiding place. Her muscles tensed.

"We're not going to find them way up here," the first man said. There was a definite whine in his tone.

"Yeah, well, I'm not the boss, and until the boss says stop, we keep looking, and we go to the area he tells us to search." The second man's voice was firmer. Flynn imagined he was older than the first or at least knew the boss better and the way the drug cartel worked. "Those people saw the meth lab and the three dealers the boss executed. They know too much and have to be eliminated before they ruin all our future plans. You know that. The boss made it clear that these people can't make it down the mountain alive. If they report what they saw, their statements could destroy our whole organization. I don't know about you, but I don't want to go to prison."

"It's freezing up here!" the whiner complained. "Even if we don't find them, there's no way they'll survive the night. We'll find them tomorrow when the buzzards are circling overhead. This is a waste of time."

"Maybe, but again, we can't stop looking."

"I think they've already gone farther down the mountain. They'd be crazy to still be up this high," the complainer said, his voice raised an octave. There were some shuffling noises, and Flynn could feel Kevin tense. Were the two hunters right outside the entrance having this discussion? She listened a bit more, straining to understand what was happening and the level of danger their presence posed to the three of them. The noises sounded like more than a conversation was occurring on the other side of these rocks. Flynn wouldn't be surprised if a fistfight had broken out, or at least some serious shoving. She hugged Kevin even closer. When the second man spoke again, his voice had taken on a deadly edge.

"You're probably right, but there must be twenty of us out here looking, and only three of them, and one of them is a kid. They couldn't have gotten too far away, and we've got to come across them sooner or later, understand? So shut your mouth and do what you're told. I don't want to be the one that has to tell the boss that they escaped, and I don't think you want to be that guy, either."

"Fine. Okay. I get it." The younger man had resignation in his voice, and the two must have started walking away from the cave entrance, because their voices slowly became muffled again. Shortly thereafter, Flynn couldn't even hear them anymore. She blew out a breath of relief and gave Kevin a squeeze, then realized that he had fallen asleep in her arms. She moved her left shoulder a bit to relieve the cramp but otherwise did her best not to wake him. They'd had an exhausting day, and the stress had to be affecting him, on top of all the physical exertion. His mom was in the hospital fighting for her life, and now he was out here being shot at with a cartel hot on their trail. What had she been thinking taking Kevin along to investigate her sister's notes?

She heard Derek shuffle and stretch, then he settled down a few feet away from her. If he was half as tired as she was, his muscles must be aching, too.

"What's your plan?" she asked softly.

"I thought I'd rest for a few minutes and give those guys time to clear out. Then I'll go scout the area and make sure they're gone." He shifted. "How's Kevin?"

"Dog tired. He's out for the count. He was dealing with a stressful situation anyway, and being chased by these criminals has really rocked his world. I'm amazed he's doing as well as he is."

"He's a trouper. So are you." He paused. "So,

what's going on here? Why did we just stumble across some kind of drug operation?"

Flynn swallowed. "My sister, Erin, is a detective down in Frisco. She got shot a couple of days ago and is still fighting for her life in the hospital, so I flew in from Florida to be with her and help out with Kevin."

"I'm sorry," Derek said softly. "I didn't even know she lived in Colorado."

"Thanks," she replied. "She hasn't been here very long. Her husband left her and Kevin about a year ago, and she moved here, hoping to start fresh." She sniffed, trying to keep her nose from running in the cold. "Anyway, I'm trying to figure out who shot her and why, but the local folks aren't being very helpful. I found some of her notes on her desk. It looks like she was involved with a drug bust a few days before she was shot, and she was trying to get one of the dealers to flip. He mentioned this place up here on the mountain but didn't give a lot of details, and she was going to go check it out but didn't get the chance. Kevin and I were both going a little stir-crazy in the hospital, so I hoped the diversion would do us both some good. I had no idea we were going to come across a murder scene."

Flynn was tired and her emotions were on overdrive, but she still thought it was time to discuss the elephant in the room that had been plaguing her ever since she had recognized Derek this afternoon on the flight line. One of her big regrets in life was that she hadn't pushed for answers back when Derek had broken up with her, and she had always wished that she'd fought harder for their relationship. They had both said a lot of angry things, but ultimately, she had never really understood what had happened between them. All she could imagine was that she had done or said something that had driven him away. It was too late now to restore the camaraderie and love that had existed between them, but it wasn't too late to ask questions so she could finally get some closure.

"So, after graduation, I could never really figure out why you picked the army over a life with me. I know we weren't officially engaged, but I thought we were heading in that direction and planning a life together—you know, marriage, two-point-five kids, a home, a dog—the whole enchilada. Then, the next thing I know, you're ending our relationship, pretty abruptly, I might add, and heading to the Middle East to fly helicopters. Our American dream just went up in smoke with no explanation, no fanfare and not even much of a goodbye. Do you think you could enlighten me?"

Tension suddenly filled the air. It was so thick, she could feel it. Still, although she regretted the timing of her questions, she couldn't regret asking them. She'd been carrying them around for the last eight years. She held her breath, almost afraid to hear him say the words. Her feelings of self-worth had taken quite a beating during her life, but maybe if she could understand what drove men away from her, she could work on fixing the problem.

Finally, Derek spoke. "You really want to discuss this now?"

"Well, I agree the timing isn't ideal, but we may never get another chance to hash this out. If I've learned anything lately, it's that you don't always get a second chance to ask questions or tell someone what you're feeling." Her thoughts fluttered to her sister in the hospital, then returned to the situation before her. "I'd really like to know what happened. You committed to the military without even discussing it with me." She paused and swallowed. "We said a lot of angry words after that, but I still don't understand your decision. Then you left without even really saying goodbye."

He was quiet for a long time before answering. "Why does it matter now? That was over eight years ago."

"It matters," Flynn insisted. "I was in love with you, and then from one day to the next, our relationship was over and you were going down an entirely different path—one that we hadn't even discussed. I was shocked and hurt by your actions." She chewed her bottom lip, unsure. "What did I do or say that made you run in the opposite direction? I know the problem had to be my fault. Something's wrong with me. I get it. But I don't know what I did, and I really want to understand."

Again, Derek didn't answer, and the silence seemed to swell between them. Flynn had already gone this far. She pushed ahead. "Well, whatever it was, I'd like to apologize right here and now. I never meant to push you away." She closed her eyes for a moment, glad that Derek couldn't see the tears in her eyes. She hadn't meant to cry. She hadn't even planned to discuss this. Why did Derek have to be the helicopter pilot she'd encountered on the tarmac? Still, it felt good to finally confront the pain that she still carried from their separation. It was clear she was a social disaster. But what was it about her that drove men away? She really wanted to know. Maybe, just maybe, now that so much time had passed, Derek would be able to explain what had happened. If she told him a little more, would he answer her questions? It was worth a try.

"Until about two months ago, I was seriously dating a man back in Florida named Ted. I actually thought he might be the one, you know? We were together over two years. And then I discovered he was cheating on me and had another woman on the side." She swallowed. "I guess I have some serious flaws that sent you away, just like Ted, so again, for whatever I did, I'm sorry." She blew out a breath, for a moment reliving the pain of finding out about Ted's treachery. As a result, Flynn had decided she no longer needed a man in her life and was determined to shun any and all dating relationships. It just wasn't worth the heartache that inevitably followed. The breakup with Ted had been ugly and painful, much like the breakup with Derek, albeit for different reasons. Why did the men she cared about run in the opposite direction whenever the relationships got serious? What was wrong with her?

Flynn knew she was a good detective. She had one of the best case-closure rates in her entire law enforcement organization, and her career was blossoming. So why was her personal life such a mess? Maybe, just maybe, enough time had passed that Derek could be honest with her and tell her the truth so she could uncover her problems and grow. She waited, tense, but his silence was deafening, and she wondered if her flaws were so big that he was hesitant to even talk to her about them.

Derek froze at her questions and admissions, carefully sorting through everything Flynn had just revealed. Men with guns had shot them out of the sky and were hunting them down like animals. They were running for their lives and finally had a moment to sit and regroup—and now, of all times, Flynn wanted to discuss their old relationship that had ended years ago.

Could he really blame her? He was stunned that she was shouldering the guilt for his own mistakes and actions. Derek didn't want to rip off the scabs and watch them bleed again, but he knew he hadn't been fair to her eight years ago. It had been his fault, not hers, that their relationship had ended so abruptly. He didn't like her feeling responsible, or the fact that his actions had trampled Flynn's feelings of self-worth. Besides, if they didn't talk now, when would they talk? Kevin was still asleep—he could hear the boy softly snoring. Who knew if or when they would get another private opportunity to share their thoughts?

Derek took a moment and thought back over everything that had happened back then. Flynn was right about one thing—they had really never discussed his decision to leave the relationship. And it had definitely been Derek that had left. It was no surprise that she'd been shocked and hurt by his actions. He'd known his decision would devastate her, but he'd been powerless to choose another path regardless of the pain he caused. At least he'd felt that way at the time.

He tried to look at her and make out her features so he could see what she was thinking, but it was just too dark. He could see an outline of where she was sitting with the boy but couldn't make out her expression. Maybe that was a good thing. If he could see on her face the pain that was so evident in her voice, it would probably be his undoing. Flynn had been the love of his life. He'd never had that type of relationship with anyone else and expected he never would. Flynn was one of a kind. But that level of closeness had also scared him.

Derek's own family had been dysfunctional and traumatizing, and as soon as they had started talking about marriage, he had run as fast as he could in the other direction. He was terrified that he would turn into his father the moment he said, "I do," and that would have been unthinkable. His father had been a monster, and growing up, he'd seen his mother slowly become a lonely, miserable shell of a woman. He'd learned from watching his parents' relationship that it was better to keep everyone at arm's length and avoid marriage completely. The decision resulted in a lonely existence, but that was the only way to keep from getting hurt. Even friendships caused problems. Look what his bond with Jax had cost—if he and Jax hadn't joined up together, Jax would probably still be alive.

His thoughts returned to Flynn and their time together back in Tallahassee at Florida State University. They had been so in love back then. How could he explain his fear of com-

mitment that had basically immobilized him—
and his constant dread that he would turn out
to be a colossal failure as a husband and father?

He couldn't. He wouldn't. But he could help
her relieve some of her own angst if she was
blaming herself for their breakup. The truth was
small consolation after eight years but hopefully
enough to pour some salve on her wounded
spirit.

"There's no need for you to apologize, Flynn.
The fault was entirely mine. You didn't say or
do anything that pushed me away. I just decided
that I wanted something different. Marriage
wasn't the right choice for me. I wasn't ready
to settle down and have a family with you—or
anyone else—and I guess I didn't realize it until
it was too late."

Okay, that was part of the truth. He fisted
his hands. He owed her the whole story. "My
dad was a horrible nightmare, Flynn, and my
mother wasn't much better. There's a reason
why I never introduced you to them. I didn't
have a great upbringing, and the idea of starting a family terrified me. I just wasn't ready. I
didn't want to turn into my father."

She let those words hang for a minute or two
before responding. "I always wondered why you

never talked about your parents much. Even at holidays, you seemed to avoid the subject, and I didn't want to push," she said softly.

He sighed. "I had enough to eat, and they met my physical needs. I should be thankful for that. Plenty of people have it worse. But there was no love in the house, and my dad was a bully who used his fists to make sure he got his way. My mom was never strong enough to stand up to him, and she ended up drinking more often than not—probably just to escape him and the realities of her life."

He ran his tongue over his teeth, then pushed on. "I've always been embarrassed about my family, and when you started talking about starting one of our own, well, I admit, I didn't handle it well. I wasn't honest with you about my feelings and never even gave you an explanation or a chance to tell me what you were thinking. I'm sorry about that. I was truly in love with you, Flynn. I just couldn't be a husband or a father, and when I realized we were actually getting serious about tying the knot, I ran. I got scared that I would turn out to be just like my own father. I hope you can forgive me."

He really wished he could see her better. He could hear her breathing, but she was very still and probably digesting everything he'd just said. He silently willed her to speak—to say anything to ease his conscience. He silently hoped she would also offer the forgiveness that he had been craving without even realizing it.

"I forgave you long ago." Her voice was still soft and now filled with compassion that he didn't deserve. He wondered if she would continue the discussion, and he almost wanted her to so she would answer his own questions. Was she happy? Did she miss him as much as he missed her? Yet he heard a level of resignation in her voice, as if she still wasn't completely satisfied with his answer but wasn't prepared to make herself even more vulnerable in front of him. He didn't deserve more.

He silently wondered about this man named Ted who had cheated on her. Was the man a complete idiot? Yet how could he cast stones? He certainly had been so wrapped up in his own fears and failings that he'd let this beautiful woman slip through his fingers, and he'd regretted his decision ever since.

A moment passed, then another. Flynn must have decided to let the discussion go, because she changed the subject. "So, tell me about you. What's been going on in your life for the last eight years? How'd you end up in Frisco, Colorado? I had no idea you were the King behind King Helicopter Tours. I thought you were still in the army. In fact, I thought you'd make a career out of the military."

He shrugged, even though he knew she couldn't see him very well. "I was going to, but then I was in a horrible helicopter crash, and Jax Thomas died. Did you hear about that?"

"I heard he had died, but didn't know the circumstances. The college sends out this alumni magazine twice a year, and somebody did a story about him when it happened, but they didn't give the details about his death." She paused a moment. "What happened?"

"Jax died when the helicopter I was flying got shot down during a mission in Iraq. He was my copilot."

"Oh, Derek. I'm so sorry."

Derek didn't comment. He pushed on. "Anyway, after that, I just didn't want to stay in the military any longer. I finished my time and then came out here for a fresh start—kind of like Erin, I guess. A guy I met at the local airport was selling his helicopter touring business, and the opportunity seemed like a smart investment. Next thing I know, King Helicopter

Tours was up and running, and I started flying tourists around the mountains."

Flynn was quiet again, probably still processing everything he had just revealed. Jax had been in their college friend group. He and Flynn hadn't been buddies, but she had known him and spent time with him during their outings. Several times, they had all gone out to dinners, movies, hiking and even a couple of beach trips.

Once again, he found himself holding his breath, waiting to find out what she was thinking.

Would she blame him for Jax's death the way he blamed himself?

Chapter Six

"That must have been terrible," Flynn said softly. "I had no idea. When they shot down your helicopter today, that must have brought all those memories back, and here I am opening up even more old wounds. This whole day must just be a living nightmare for you. I should have just stayed quiet. I'm so sorry."

Derek was stunned at her words. How could she not judge him? *Hate* him? And again, why was she the one apologizing? To be forgiven so easily was beyond his understanding. His voice rose as he spoke, and he instantly dropped the volume, but couldn't help the intensity. "Didn't you hear me? I just told you I killed Jax. He's dead because of me."

"I heard you. But I'm also sure that's not true."

"What?" Now he couldn't keep the incredulousness from his tone. "How can you say that?"

"Because I know you, Derek. You're not perfect. None of us are. But you cared about Jax, and there is no way you would have ever hurt him intentionally or let him get hurt if you were able to stop it from happening. You're just not capable of that type of behavior. I know that for a fact. I don't need to see an incident report or read about the details of the crash to know that. But I am sorry that he's gone, and sorry for your loss. He was a good man, too—decent and caring. I'm sure his death left a large hole in your life. I know you were close friends." She sighed. "Our country has lost way too many good soldiers and first responders, especially over the last few years. But we have to keep fighting against the drugs and other problems sweeping over the world to keep the people we love safe. We can't give up."

Derek leaned back, surprise sweeping over him from head to toe. Flynn was a cop. She probably saw a lot of the same types of ugliness on the streets that he'd seen during the war, but she seemed to think that hope still existed. Flynn continued to see the good in people. A lightness he didn't expect started to slowly seep into his chest, as if part of the burden he had been carrying had suddenly been lifted.

He pulled himself to his feet, unable to sit still any longer as the thoughts swirled within him. He needed time alone to think about everything they'd just discussed. She was right about one thing—being shot out of the sky had brought back all sorts of memories that he'd hoped he had buried forever. "I'm going out to do some surveillance. Are you okay staying here with the boy?"

"We're good, unless you need help. I can wake him up if you want me to, so I can help you..."

"No, it's better if you stay with him. I don't want him to wake up and be scared." He really did need some time alone to chew on her words and soak them in, and scouting the area to make sure the perpetrators were really gone was vital to their survival. The killers had been right about one thing—it was going to get cold tonight, and they needed to make the best of the few supplies they had with them.

Derek quietly left the cave, making sure his sidearm was easily accessible in his coat pocket. He glanced at the sky. Thankfully, it was already dusk, and the sun was slowly sinking behind the mountain. He brushed away his boot prints from the entrance to the cave, then started walking away as carefully and quietly as possible, his mind lost in memories. He glanced up again, suddenly pulling his thoughts back to the here and now and trying to remember if the moon had been full recently. He said a short prayer of thanks that the moon was new and wouldn't be shining during the evening hours. A fire to keep warm would make this night safer, but telltale smoke was out of the question. If the moon came out, there was no way they could risk one.

He paused for a moment and listened to the sounds around him. The wind whispered through the trees, and he could hear dry branches scratching against each other. Occasionally a puff of snow would fall from a tree branch and a few birds could be heard in the distance.

But what interested him was the sound of voices, not far off to his left. He froze, making sure the trees were camouflaging him as best as he could hope, and perked up his ears, hoping for any news that he could use to protect Flynn and Kevin and see them all safely down the mountain.

"Cary won't let them live. You know that."

"Of course I know that. But we have to find

them first and see what they know and who they've told. I knew shooting that woman cop was going to be a problem. Once we kill these three, the police will be all over this mountain."

Cary? Could they be talking about Adam Cary? The name was unusual, and one that Derek hadn't heard in a while. Adam Cary was the man who had sold him his helicopter tourist company that he had renamed King Helicopter Tours. Cary was also the owner of Bear Creek Vacation Rentals, or at least he had been. Derek thought the man had sold everything and moved back to Denver, but maybe he was wrong. Derek advertised his services with some of the local vacation companies, but Bear Creek wasn't one of them. There were dozens of different vacation rental companies, and Bear Creek, like the others, owned several homes throughout the Breckenridge and Frisco areas. They made a killing every time the slopes were open as skiers flocked in to enjoy the mountains. Bear Creek properties were some of the nicest—and the most expensive and exclusive. Skiers from all over the world booked into the local hotels and Airbnbs, but Derek's customers were mostly upper middle class—not the superrich that Bear Creek catered to. Derek and

Cary had never really been friends or run in the same circles, but Frisco was a small town, and wealthy men like Cary got noticed.

And was Erin the "woman cop" they were referring to?

The men moved farther away from Derek, and he could no longer hear their voices clearly. He considered following them but decided against it. Job number one right now was keeping Flynn and Kevin safe. If they were talking about Adam Cary, then they had a very powerful adversary. Cary was a formidable and decisive man with abundant resources. He never did anything halfway, and if he was the one chasing them, then the mountain would be crawling with Cary's minions until they were discovered. They would have to get to safety first and then worry about stopping Cary's criminal activities. Surviving this trip, or even the night, now seemed even more improbable.

Flynn awoke with a start, Kevin's weight still heavy in her arms. How long had she been asleep? She glanced around, but all she saw was darkness. Kevin moaned and moved slightly in her arms.

"Mama?"

"No, it's Aunt Flynn."

Kevin sat up some but didn't pull away. "Where are we?"

"Still in the cave."

"Where's Mr. King?"

"He went out to do surveillance and make sure we were safe. He should be back soon." She kept her voice soft.

"I'm cold."

"I know. Me, too. Hopefully, once he gets back, we can figure out our next move. I'm hoping that involves a fire, but we'll see."

"What if the bad guys got him? What then?"

Flynn squeezed her arms around the young boy. "We just have to pray that he's safe."

Kevin made a disgusted sound with his mouth. "I don't believe in God. Praying won't work."

Flynn was surprised by this piece of news. "Why do you say that?"

Kevin leaned back against her. "I used to pray that God would bring my daddy back, but he didn't. And now my mom is hurt and might die. Then I'll be all alone. If God was real, none of that bad stuff would have happened."

Flynn had to think about how to respond to all that, and on a level an eleven-year-old would

understand. He'd hit on some of the critical issues that all Christians seemed to wrestle with
at some time during their walk with God—why
do bad things happen to good people?

"Kevin, I am sure there is a God. I have no
doubt. But sometimes we don't get what we
want when we pray. The first thing you need
to know is that God created all of us with free
will. Do you know what that means?"

Kevin shook his head, and Flynn continued. "Well, it means we have to make our
own choices. God didn't want a bunch of ro-
bots walking around on the earth. He wanted
to have a relationship with each of us and to
give us each the opportunity to choose whether
or not we wanted to have a relationship with
Him. He gave your dad the same choices." She
squeezed him even tighter in a bear hug. "I
know your dad left you and your mom a year
ago, but that was his choice, too. He made a
mistake, but sometimes we all make mistakes.
See, we all get to choose how we live our lives,
but we also have to deal with the consequences
of our actions. And sometimes the choices we
make hurt other people."

"He left because of me!"

Flynn shook her head. "That's not true,

Kevin. Your mom and I talked about the situation a lot when it happened. He left for a lot of grown-up reasons that you might not understand right now, and I know he hurt you when he moved away, but it wasn't your fault. I promise you that."

Kevin was silent a long time while he digested this information. She knew her sister had talked about all this with Kevin before, but sometimes it helped to hear it again from someone else who wasn't so directly involved. Erin had shared that Kevin was swamped with self-doubt and had been exhibiting a host of behavior problems lately, especially when Erin had tried dating again. Hopefully, her words could give him a bit of reassurance.

"Do you think my mom is going to be okay?" Kevin asked, breaking into her thoughts.

"I don't know. I sure hope so. I've been praying for her ever since I heard what happened. I know it's hard not to worry about her. That's why I brought you up on this trip today. I was hoping the flight would be something fun to do to keep our minds off her medical condition." She swallowed. "I'm sorry this day turned out the way it did."

"You didn't know they would shoot at us,"

Kevin allowed. He reached over and patted her arm, trying in his own way to give her a bit of comfort. His actions were sweet, and she acknowledged them with a rueful smile.

"No, I sure didn't. But I want you to know that no matter what happens, you're not going to be alone. I want my sister to get better, but if she doesn't, I'll take care of you. You won't be by yourself. Okay?" Flynn felt the little boy relax against her.

"Okay," Kevin whispered.

"But I also want you to know that God is real and I'm praying for your mom every day."

"Do I have to pray, too?"

"That's your choice. But I do know that God wants to get to know you better, and the best way for that to happen is for you to pray and read about Him in the Bible."

"Is that what you do?"

"Yep, but I have to admit, I haven't been going to church or reading the Bible as much as I should have been."

"Well, why is it important to go to church?"

"Church is where you learn even more about God," Flynn replied. "And it's like a big family. When you're with people who believe the same way you do, it makes your own faith stronger, and you get to learn together and grow at the same time." She sighed. "I need to reconnect with God myself. I let the busyness of my life get in the way, and I haven't been going to church or praying like I should have been. But ever since I got that call and came to Colorado, I've been praying a lot. This whole thing has reminded me that God and my relationship with Him need to come first in my life."

Kevin took a moment to let that sink in. Finally he spoke up. "Can we pray together?"

His voice was fragile, as if he was afraid she would refuse him, and she squeezed him again. "Of course." She said a prayer in a soft voice, asking God to keep them all safe, and to be with Erin and help the doctors know how to help her. Then she prayed for Kevin, that he would feel God's presence and that God would draw him close.

Just as she finished, she heard a noise outside. "Quiet," she whispered. "Someone's here."

Chapter Seven

"Flynn?"

Flynn breathed out a sigh of relief when she recognized Derek's voice. "We're here," she whispered, keeping her voice low in case any perps were still around. "Are you okay?"

"Yeah," he responded. She heard some scraping noises and moved Kevin closer to the cave wall, putting his hand out toward the rocks until he could touch the roughness to know where he was in the darkness. A dim light flickered near the entrance, and she recognized the small flashlight Derek had been using earlier. "Can you grab this wood?"

She pulled through the wood and pieces of dried leaves and bark that Derek had brought, then reached into the path and grabbed the larger logs that Derek was trying to get to her. A few minutes later, Derek pulled himself in behind the last of the wood.

"I love the idea of a fire, but is it safe?" Flynn asked.

Derek put the flashlight on the ground, then rubbed his hands together and blew into them, obviously trying to warm himself up. Their gloves helped but didn't completely keep out the cold. "I think so. The drug dealers are pretty far away from us now, and there isn't much of a moon, so I don't think they'll see the smoke. What I don't know is whether or not there's enough air moving around in here. I don't want us to die from carbon monoxide poisoning." He pulled a blue bandanna from his pocket, unfolded it and held the fabric loosely in different places around the cave, watching it move slightly in the different locations with the light from the flashlight. "Looks like there is some wind blowing through here, and it's moving from the back of the cave toward the entrance. See these crevices? That's where the air seems to be coming from. This cave probably opens up even more a little farther back." He pocketed the bandanna again. "That's good. We can build our fire back here near the rear. This is a small room, so we don't need much of a blaze to heat the space. I didn't want to block our way out anyway, and if we keep our heads pointed toward the opening while we're sleeping, we should have plenty of oxygen."

She watched in amazement as he pulled a small baggie of dryer lint from his backpack, then arranged the wood and dry leaves in a pile that resembled a rat's nest. The next thing she knew, he had used a match and the dryer lint to get the small fire going.

Kevin was quick to move closer once the fire was burning. "How come there isn't much smoke?" he asked as he held out his hands above the small flame.

"Because this is ash wood. I found a tree nearby that had lost a couple of branches. Ash wood is really dense and burns hot and longer than a lot of other woods. After a short time, these flames will disappear and the fire will be a smoldering bed of embers that should keep us warm throughout the night with hardly any smoke at all."

"That's so cool! How did you learn that?"

"Boy Scouts. We got to go camping sometimes, and I seemed to pull fire duty a lot. Apparently, the other guys thought it was a good idea to make sure I wasn't the one cooking the food." He leaned closer to Kevin and whispered, "I tend to burn things when I cook."

"I'd take burned food over nothing," Flynn said dryly as she also moved closer to the fire. "But we are not without resources. Although steaks and s'mores aren't on the menu, looks like tonight we're having oatmeal cream pies and Gatorade, thanks to Kevin here, who had the good sense to bring some food with him on our excursion." She gave him a smile. "We should probably save these granola bars for breakfast."

"That works," Derek agreed.

There were four of the soft oatmeal cookies, each individually wrapped in plastic. She passed them each one, then took the fourth and divided it into three equal pieces. "Okay, you two get to choose which parts of the cookie you want first. With Erin and me, the rule was always one person divides the food and the other gets to choose."

"Hey, that's a good rule!" Kevin agreed.

Flynn rubbed her hands together and put them even closer to the flames. She was still amazed that Derek carried dryer lint with him as a fire starter. Derek had saved some in a small Ziploc bag that he'd retrieved from the helicopter before they'd made their escape, and she was now starting to feel warm for the first time since the helicopter had been shot down.

After they finished their cookies and had passed around the Gatorade, the three of them went through the rest of their meager supplies in whispered tones. Kevin had managed to drop his bag of Gatorade and treats into the snow before climbing down the cliff, and miraculously, the bag was still intact and he'd remembered to retrieve it before they'd escaped into the woods. Derek and Flynn also had their cell phones, but of course, there was no service in this remote area of Colorado. They powered them down for now, hoping to save the battery power for a later date when they had a better chance of being able to reach someone.

Derek's navy backpack also contained a small survival kit with a thirteen-ounce pouch of peanut butter, a first aid kit, a small box of waterproof matches with the dryer lint, fishing line and hooks, and a Swiss Army knife. The kit also held an emergency blanket made out of Mylar polyester that Kevin had wrapped around his shoulders. The blanket was great for retaining body heat, even though the lightweight, waterproof material seemed like a flimsy piece of silver plastic wrap. Thankfully, Derek also had a small roll of toilet paper.

Flynn left the cave to use the bathroom,

moving quietly to make sure they were still alone. There wasn't much light to see by, but she had enough to maneuver. She filled the empty Gatorade bottle with snow while she was out and brought it back in the cave with her when she returned, being careful to brush away any evidence that she had walked in the area. Hopefully, the snow would melt and keep them from getting dehydrated. She knew that in cold weather it was hard to know how much water her body was losing, especially when she was being active. On top of that, she didn't feel thirsty, which was often the case during the winter, even though she knew from her law enforcement training that after so much strenuous movement, her body fluids needed to be replenished. She might be a Florida girl, but she knew that eating snow was a bad idea and could really do more harm than good—the body had to use a lot of extra energy to warm up the cold snow. But she hoped that by melting the snow first and drinking the water, it would help.

Besides, at this point, they didn't have many alternatives.

When she pulled herself back into the cave, she noticed that Kevin had curled into a ball near the fire and was once again asleep. She dropped down wearily beside him, then looked over at Derek, who had rested his arms on his knees. His eyes were closed, but she doubted he was sleeping. "Did you learn anything when you were out and about?" she asked softly.

Derek slowly raised his head, then watched the firelight dance in Flynn's eyes. Despite the danger they were in, he couldn't help being thankful that she was back in his life. Several of her curls had gotten free from her blue head-band, and while he watched, she pulled it loose, rearranged her hair and replaced the band, securing the strands away from her face.

The effect was mesmerizing. She was so beautiful, especially in the firelight. He couldn't believe he had pushed her away and slammed the door on their relationship so many years ago. Her skin was like creamy white porcelain, and the small brown freckles scattered across her nose gave her a youthful appearance that would never fade. She was cute and sweet like the girl next door, and her innocent appearance made her approachable and appealing.

Her inner beauty was just as hypnotic. Flynn was the most caring person he had ever met, and her forgiveness of his past actions was just more proof that she was a diamond that he should have treasured, not tossed aside. Yet even as the ice started to thaw from around his heart, he couldn't imagine that a relationship with her would ever be possible again, even though they were both single and unattached. That ship had sailed. But maybe, just maybe, now that they had cleared the air a bit between them, they could be friends as they worked together to survive this ordeal.

"I got close enough to hear some of them talking. They mentioned a man's name, and they might have been talking about Adam Cary. He's the one that I bought the helicopter business from when I got out of the army. I don't know him well, but he's wealthy and powerful and moved in important circles down in Breckenridge. I thought he moved to Denver, but I must be wrong. Or maybe he just told people that so he could operate more under the radar. In any case, he used to own a vacation rental company called Bear Creek. I don't know if he still does or not, but that might explain how he's able to keep his drug operation under wraps. Maybe he uses that company to launder his money or as a front for his illegal activities."

Flynn leaned forward, her expression animated. "Bear Creek was written on some of Erin's notes that I found in her apartment. I didn't know what it meant at the time. This is great information! If you're right and he's our drug lord, we may have just put a name and face to our enemy."

"There's more," Derek said quietly. "They mentioned a woman cop."

Flynn narrowed her eyes. "Did they say they shot her?"

Derek nodded. "Somebody from their organization did. I wouldn't be surprised if your sister found out about the drug trafficking and they shot her to take her out. It seems like they are hot to kill anyone that might stand in the way of their profits." He shifted. "I have to admit, they've done an admirable job of keeping their operation under wraps. Adam Cary is a powerful man who appears to be a wealthy and successful businessman—nothing more. He's well-liked and has an excellent reputation. If he is behind all this, the news is going to shock a lot of people."

Flynn ruminated on the information. "I'm not even sure Erin knew what she had discovered, but it could have been one of those cases where she was just starting to put the pieces together. Sometimes you don't know what you know or how it fits into the bigger picture until the evidence comes together. Her notes weren't that clear. She didn't mention Adam Cary, but maybe she hadn't gotten that far along in her investigation yet, and until she wakes up, I won't be able to ask her."

Derek nodded. "Well, she was certainly on the right track, and her digging must have scared Cary enough to want to put an end to her investigation. Without her pointing us in Cary's direction, who knows how long he would have continued getting away with his crimes? Now, once we get back into town, we have a real chance of stopping them." He poked at the fire with a small stick. There was basically just a bed of embers now, but they did a wonderful job of heating the small space.

He reached over and tucked the silver blanket closer to Kevin's sleeping body.

"You're good with him," Flynn whispered.

Derek laughed. He couldn't help himself. "I am not."

Flynn raised an eyebrow. "I'm not kidding. You'll make a great dad someday."

The thought terrified him. He thought back to images of his father and the pain he had endured at his father's hand. "I'm horrible with children. I don't have the patience."

"Says who?"

"Says me."

Flynn tilted her head, a look of surprise on her face. "I hope you change your mind someday. Just because your dad was a nightmare doesn't mean you don't have the heart and ability to take care of children. I know you, remember? And I know you'll make a good dad whenever the time comes. If it comes." She nodded toward the cave entrance before he had a chance to argue with her. "I'll take first watch. Why don't you get some sleep?"

He smiled at her. That was the second time she'd reminded him that she knew him to be a good person. He let that thought wash over him. It felt good. "I'm too tired to argue with you. Wake me up in a couple of hours and I'll relieve you."

"Deal."

He stretched out by the fire and pillowed his head on his arm, and another piece of ice melted from around his heart.

Chapter Eight

The buzzing seemed to get louder.

Flynn shook her head, but the pulsating mechanical sound didn't go away. She rubbed the sleep out of her eyes and looked across in the dim light at Kevin, who was swirling the Gatorade bottle over the fire embers, melting more snow into drinkable water. He smiled at her, and the peace she saw in his eyes warmed her heart. The sleep must have really rejuvenated him, and she said a silent prayer of thanks. She hadn't seen Kevin smile at all since she had arrived in Colorado, which hadn't surprised her, given the circumstances. Still, she welcomed the sight. The coals glowed softly, and the cave still held a wonderful warmth that made her feel rested and peaceful herself. She'd only had a few hours of sleep since she and Derek had traded off keeping watch during the night, but the rest had been enough to help her feel refreshed and ready to take on the new day.

The buzzing still didn't stop. Her brain clicked, and she finally recognized the sound. "Do you hear that?" she asked as she pulled herself up into a sitting position and then moved toward the entrance.

Kevin shrugged, not understanding. He took a drink from the bottle, then spun it some more. "Yeah. So?" She didn't take the time to explain but instead glanced around quickly in the dim light and noticed Derek's absence. On hands and knees she pulled herself outside, looking for enemies as she did so. Derek was standing outside in the early morning light, squinting at the sky.

"Can you see it?" he asked, keeping his voice low.

"Nope, but I can hear the engine," Flynn said with a grin. "Search and rescue plane?"

Derek nodded, but he looked anything but happy. "That's my guess. I didn't file a flight plan because the FAA doesn't require it when we fly with visual instead of instrument flight rules, but my staff knows we never came home last night, and they knew we were going to check out those coordinates you found in your sister's apartment. I'm sure they called our dis-appearance in to law enforcement."

"You don't look too pleased."

"I'm not," Derek replied, still keeping his tone soft. "The dealers are going to be looking for us even harder now and wanting to make sure they catch us before the rescuers find us. And the odds of us safely signaling the folks in that plane up there are pretty low." He ran his hands through his hair. "So, we have more danger, not less. That search party is going to make getting down this mountain even harder."

She nodded. "I hadn't thought of it that way." She pulled her headband off, ran her fingers through her own hair and then replaced it, try-ing to tame her unruly curls. What she wouldn't give for a hairbrush! She grimaced and ran her tongue over her teeth. And a toothbrush. She sighed. Oh, well. There was no use wishing for the impossible. "What's our next move?"

Derek quirked an eyebrow. "You're the big detective. I'll let you decide." His expression showed that he was joking, but she recognized a bit of truth in his words. She liked being in control of her own investigations and usually enjoyed taking the lead if the opportunity pre-sented itself or she was offered the chance. In this situation, however, she was happy to let Derek be in charge. She was definitely a city girl at heart, and not an outdoorswoman. "I'm a Florida girl, Derek. I can get you to the beach and back in a hundred-degree weather when the bridges are closed and show you were to find the spiny lobster in season, but these mountains and snowy conditions are your specialty, not mine." She gave him a wink and was happy that he was relaxing enough to tease her. In that small expression, she saw a piece of the Derek she had known back in college, when he had been happy and much more carefree.

She stretched a little, then stopped herself, hoping that their enemies were nowhere close by. Sound traveled farther than she thought, so she was purposefully keeping her voice low, but movement was also visible from a great distance, and the last thing she wanted to do was give away their position. Maybe she wasn't as awake as she thought.

She met Derek's eye, and her heart jumped. His beard and strong jaw made him look roguish and even more attractive in the morning light, and his dark blue eyes were watching her closely and shooting electricity across the small space that separated them. Memories flooded her of the many good times when they'd been dating back in the old days. She remembered talking for hours, walking hand in hand, and the softness of his lips. She recalled laughing at his jokes and cheering for him when he pitched softball in the church league. He had been her best friend. She missed the closeness they had shared.

What was wrong with her? They were fighting for their lives, and here she was reliving romantic thoughts from the past. She ruthlessly pushed the memories away. She was not getting back together with Derek, and recalling the past, even the good parts, was pointless. They'd had their chance to make it as a couple, and the relationship had crashed and burned before it had truly matured. Besides, she did not need or want a man in her life anymore. Hadn't she made that resolution after Ted had slammed the door on their relationship? What she did need was to focus on the here and now and keeping Kevin safe. That was all that mattered. Once they were back in civilization, then she could move on to solving her sister's shooting. There was no room for anything or anyone else in her life. "I'll take care of the fire," she said a little awkwardly and hurried back into the cave.

Flynn doused the embers with sand and packed up their meager supplies, then she and Kevin went outside with Derek, divided up the granola bars and passed around the Gatorade bottle. A grimness settled over the group, and the lighthearted atmosphere that had enveloped them only moments before dissipated like a fine mist. Survival and the trek ahead of them took precedence over all else. One way or another, they had to get down this mountain and to the police station with the evidence Flynn carried in her glove. Proving what they'd seen was the only way they could stop Adam Cary from continuing to manufacture and peddle his drugs.

After they drank all the water, Derek filled the bottle with snow again, then secured it in the backpack with the other items. He wasn't sure if the snow would melt during the trek, but it was worth the chance and didn't add much weight to his backpack.

Wordlessly, he set off with Kevin close behind him and Flynn in the rear. The sun's rays struggled to pierce the thick clouds and tree branches, but Derek was thankful for the overcast conditions. A storm had come during the night and dropped more snow on the mountain, and he predicted it would snow again later in the day. Hopefully the bad weather would send the search team home and would ultimately also make it harder on their pursuers. Of course, it would make it harder on them, too, but if it started snowing, the powder would cover their tracks and make it even tougher for the men with guns to discover their location.

They paused and rested twice before noon, and since the snow did indeed melt in the Gatorade bottle as they traveled, they were able to stop at times and take a drink and then refill the bottle with more snow. Even so, Derek wasn't sure they were getting enough hydration, even though the night before they had melted a copious amount of snow over the fire and drunk plentifully over and over again.

A little after lunchtime, the sky darkened and the heavy clouds began dropping fat white snowflakes. The three found a low-lying bush and huddled beneath the branches, and Derek pulled out the peanut butter. He was thankful the three of them were all mindful, including Kevin, of the need to share and make sure everyone got some of their precious food supplies. The peanut butter was the end of their rations, but he was grateful he'd kept the packet in his survival kit.

"Sure wish we had some crusty bread to go with that," Flynn said as she watched Derek squeeze some into his mouth.

"And some strawberry jam!" Kevin added as he took the silver pouch. Just as he was about to pinch some of the gooey butter into his mouth, they heard voices not far away.

"I saw movement over here. I'm sure of it!"

The man's voice instantly sent adrenaline throughout Derek's body, and he reached for his weapon and pulled the gun slowly out of his pocket. Flynn and Kevin both froze like statues, their eyes on him, looking for guidance.

About thirty feet away, a man in a dark green jacket came into view. He was wearing a black skull cap and carried a high-powered rifle in his gloved hands. He was struggling through the snow but heading right for them.

Derek had been in charge of his helicopter crew in the military and had been in a leadership role in several situations during his time in the service, but for some reason, the weight of responsibility he felt now with Flynn and Kevin at his side seemed almost tripled. Both Flynn and her nephew looked at him with such trust in their eyes that fear tightened a knot in his stomach. He *had* to keep them safe. There was no other option. He motioned for them to get down, and the three huddled behind the bushes and brush. Then he said a silent prayer, asking for God to protect them and hide them from the eyes of their pursuers.

"Wait for me," another man yelled, suddenly appearing behind the first. He was wearing a red parka, and while he also had a rifle, his was slung on his back. In his gloved hand, he carried a small set of binoculars. "Are you sure you really saw something?"

Even as the man's words drifted across the wooded area, the snow swirled and seemed to come down even harder than before, and a brisk wind suddenly buffeted them with a chilling yet obfuscating blast of snow, dried leaves and cold air.

The first man stopped about ten feet away from them, but it was obvious from his disoriented expression that he had lost sight of whatever he had thought he'd seen. "Who knows. This storm is picking up. I don't even care if we find them now. I just want a hot mug of coffee and a warm blanket. This is crazy!"

Derek had pulled his weapon, and he kept his

finger near the trigger, just in case. He could hear his heart pounding in his ears. He never wanted to fire his gun at a human target, especially not with a child nearby to witness the carnage, but he would do so if forced. He prayed fervently that the two men wouldn't discover their hiding place and would leave them unscathed.

The second man stopped by the first, pocketed the binoculars and rubbed his gloved hands together. He glanced around the area but didn't look down or even in the general direction of where the three were huddled under the bush. Then he worked a glove off his hand with his teeth, pulled out his phone and punched some buttons. "Good grief. No service. There's no service anywhere up here on this mountain! How are we supposed to communicate when these stupid things hardly ever work!"

"How should I know? Let's head back to the rendezvous site." The man in the green coat started heading west, not waiting to see if the other man followed. The man with the phone shrugged, then stored his phone, put his glove back on and followed him away from the area.

Flynn let out a breath, and the moist air left a cloud around her mouth. Derek noticed and then looked away, his own breath slowly returning to normal. Against his own volition, his eyes returned to her lips, then rose to the pink flush in her cheeks. A warmth filled him that he didn't expect, and another surge of protectiveness swept over him.

"That was a close one," he whispered. She nodded and pulled Kevin close, then actually leaned against him. Derek held his breath, surprised yet enjoying the contact. It was the first time she'd touched him of her own volition since he'd seen her walking toward his helicopter on the tarmac. The weight of her felt good against his shoulder and made him feel special and trusted.

He thought about that for a minute. Flynn had always been someone who craved human touch. It was one of her primary love languages. She had always enjoyed snuggling on the couch and watching a movie or walking hand in hand around a duck pond. When he had tried to date after he'd left Flynn behind, that was one of the biggest things he missed about her presence. Now she avoided touch and seemed to stiffen whenever he was close. His mind returned to some of the other things he missed as well, like her laugh and her easy smile. He'd never en-

joyed the company of other women the way
he had felt totally at ease with Flynn. She had
been his best friend...and had stolen his heart.

And he had walked away from her.

No, he had run away. And why? Because
he was afraid of commitment. Because he was
afraid he wasn't cut out to be a husband and a
dad. And he had left horrible scars...on both
of them.

But had anything really changed in his life
since he'd made that decision? He was still afraid
of having a family. He didn't want to imitate
his father—a man who had always selfishly put
his own needs above the wants and needs of his
wife and son. Everything had revolved around
him. No one else's opinion had ever mattered
or even factored into the equation. His mother
had slowly turned into an unhappy shell of a
woman right before his eyes, and he couldn't
stand it if he did the same thing to Flynn.

But would he have followed in his father's
footsteps?

Flynn didn't think so.

Flynn thought he was a good person. She
thought he would make a good dad. And the
more time they spent together, the more her
opinion of him mattered and bolstered his con-

fidence in his personal failings. Maybe he could make different decisions...

They waited a full ten minutes in the same location as he ruminated on the past. Finally, Flynn squeezed his arm and he pulled himself out of the thoughts and memories that had overtaken him. "Should we go?"

"We should." He nodded. They pulled themselves out of the small enclave where they had been hiding and continued their trek down the mountain, but after only a few minutes, Flynn came up next to him and gently grabbed his arm.

"This snow is getting thicker, and the wind is really blowing. I don't think we can go much farther today. What do you think?"

He stopped and then glanced around them. Kevin looked like he was about to collapse, and Flynn had lines of exhaustion around her mouth and eyes. The snow was pretty deep here, and they were making very little progress. The only good news was that the snow was covering their tracks almost as quickly as they made them.

"Okay, let's go just a little farther and see if we can find some sort of shelter." He shielded his eyes from the wind and looked hard at his surroundings. There wasn't much beyond trees and small boulders, and he suddenly realized just how blessed they had been to find the cave the night before. Today, he didn't see anything similar that would protect them from freezing to death. It was time to get creative, and he immediately started working on a plan and sorting through different options.

Flynn nodded and fell back behind Kevin again, and they walked for another half an hour or so without finding any place that Derek felt would adequately protect them during the night from the cold and the building storm.

Had they survived the helicopter crash and being chased by gunmen only to freeze to death out here in the swirling snow?

Chapter Nine

Derek watched as Kevin took another step, then sank to his knees, unable to go any farther. He'd been dragging the last part of the hour anyway, but it was now obvious he just couldn't go on. They needed a solution, and they needed one fast. Derek studied the surrounding area, then came up with an idea. People used igloos as winter decorations, but they had been a real housing option for the Eskimos, or Inuit people, who had once used the shelters to survive the brutal Canadian winters. Americans had been using something similar for years—a snow cave. He'd heard about them but never constructed one. Could he make a cave out of snow that would have the same basic thermal properties as an igloo? After all, igloos were particularly effective at providing protection from freezing temperatures and high winds, so he assumed a snow cave would be about the same.

He glanced around the area once again. There weren't any other options. He'd never made a snow cave before, but it was time to do some fast out-of-the-box thinking if they were going to survive the night.

He motioned to Flynn, who had helped Kevin get back on his feet, then waited for her to come up by his side before broaching the idea. "I think we're done walking, but I don't see any sort of shelter out here from this storm, and the weather is only going to get worse."

"Yeah, I noticed the same thing," Flynn agreed. "Got any ideas?"

Derek nodded. "Actually, I do. I think we can make a snow cave. Building a shelter like that may be our only shot at surviving until morning. The temperature is dropping fast. I think we need to start building one now."

Flynn shrugged. "Sounds like a plan to me, but I've never made a snow cave. The only thing I've ever done is make a snowman, and that was when I was a kid. I don't have the first clue how to start. How do we do it?"

"First we find the right spot. Let's keep walking, and I'll let you know when I see what I'm looking for."

After about another fifteen minutes, Derek

finally spotted an area that he thought might work for what he envisioned. Near the edge of a crop of rocks, there was a steep slope with a large buildup of snow already piled up against it. That mound of snow would be an excellent start and would save them valuable time since it was already several feet thick. The area was also heavily wooded, which would help eliminate some of the wind that was picking up.

"This will do," he said to Flynn, motioning with his hand. He glanced over at Kevin. "Kevin, just hang on for a little bit more. Your aunt and I are going to build you a really cool cave. Just wait. You're going to have an amazing story to tell your friends."

"Like Batman?" he asked hopefully, his teeth chattering. His eyes were red-rimmed and his lips were chapping, but the idea of living like a superhero sparked at least a bit of excitement and his brown eyes sparkled despite his weariness.

"Not exactly, but I'll see what I can do," Derek quipped.

He glanced around him and found a large piece of wood that resembled the head of a garden shovel, then got down on his hands and knees and started digging into the snow. "The entrance will be here, but it has to be below the main space where we're going to stay so the warm air will rise and stay in the cave with us. We can dig slightly upward here, see? Then we'll go more horizontally into this slope of snow when we get a couple of feet up. It looks like the snow is about six or seven feet deep here, so this ought to work perfectly."

Flynn raised her eyebrow but didn't comment. Instead, she found a similarly shaped piece of wood and started digging beside him. "Whatever you say, Balto."

"Balto?"

"Wasn't he a famous sled dog from way back when?"

Derek laughed. "I have absolutely no idea."

"Yeah, okay. Well, I'm a little short on jokes about famous creatures that have survived in the snowy wilderness. I'll try to come up with a few while we see if this snow cave idea of yours works." She smiled, and once again, her expression warmed him.

The snow was perfect for what he had envisioned, and thankfully, they didn't come across any large rocks or ice that would prevent the construction as they worked. The entrance was protected from the wind, and the angle allowed them to kick the displaced snow out behind them as they created the cave. The entrance tunnel was quickly complete and ended up being only a little wider than the space they need to crawl on their hands and knees. By the time they started working on the main chamber that would hold the three of them and give them a place to sleep, Kevin was a tad revived and was able to help with removing the snow they were shifting from the inside.

"Sure wish I had a real shovel," Flynn said under her breath as they pushed another load of snow behind them for Kevin to pull out. She leaned back for a moment and took a moment to catch her breath.

"What fun would that be?" Derek jibed. He winked at her, noticing her pink cheeks and vibrant red lips that were flushed from exertion. She sure was beautiful, even with the lines of strain and stress that painted her features. In fact, in his eyes, she was the most gorgeous woman on the planet. Who else would be working so diligently by his side, never giving up? He had to admit, they made a formidable team. He turned back to the snowy cave wall and continued digging.

Two and a half hours later, they were still excavating and tunneling in the cave, and Flynn and Derek started taking turns with one doing the digging and one removing the excess snow so they could each have a bit of time to rest. Kevin had taken refuge under a log and passed out, but before sleeping he had packed the snow tightly around the edges of their new home, giving their walls more stability.

Finally, Derek declared their new domicile complete. The walls and roof were a little over a foot thick, and they had constructed a pit of sorts that ran the length of the front of the cave that was deeper than the cave floor. This would allow a place for the colder air to go as the warmer air rose. The room wasn't large, but it was big enough for the three of them to sit up, lie down and stretch out a bit without being cramped. They also smoothed the inside roof and walls of the cave as much as possible with their gloves to prevent dripping. As an extra precaution, Derek, used a stick to carve grooves in the walls for the water to run down, just in case dripping did occur if their body heat managed to melt some of the interior.

Flynn woke Kevin with a gentle shake. "We're done. Want to come take a look?"

Kevin sat up and rubbed the sleep out of his

eyes. "Can we close the cave all up and start a fire?"

"No," Derek replied, still keeping his voice low in case the perpetrators were anywhere close. "But we really won't need one. Our body heat will keep the small space nice and cozy while we're in there." He brushed some snow off his shoulder. "We couldn't use a fire anyway. Fires take up a lot of oxygen, and we want to be able to breathe without a problem. We have to leave at least part of the entrance open, too, to make sure we get enough air circulation." He motioned toward the forest. "Can you find me a stick about an inch thick and about three feet long out there?"

"Sure," Kevin said, apparently glad to feel useful. He pulled himself up and quickly disappeared into the nearby stand of trees, apparently rejuvenated by his nap. Despite the wind and snow, he came back shortly with a stick just a bit smaller than a baseball bat. "How about this?"

"I think it will work," Derek replied with a small smile. He broke off the extra branches, then used the long stick to create a slanted hole in the roof of the structure, right through the snow.

"Why'd you just put a hole in the ceiling?"

Kevin asked. "Isn't that going to let out all of our warm air?"

"Like I was saying, we need to make sure we have enough air to breathe. This ventilation hole will let air in from the top. We will lose a little bit of the warm air, but it will also help make sure we don't suffocate during the night, and that is really important." He glanced around at the surrounding snow that was already piling up around them and doing a fairly adequate job of camouflaging their new cave, and all the footprints they'd made. Still, he wanted a bit more, just in case someone happened upon them. As far as they knew, the drug dealers were still out canvassing the area, despite the worsening weather. He didn't want to be sloppy and give away any clues about their whereabouts.

"Let's all use the bathroom one last time, and when you come back, bring some extra pine straw with you and throw it around the area so this place looks more natural, okay?"

They complied, and once Derek was satisfied with the result, they crawled inside the structure. The inside room was much smaller than the rock cave where they'd spent the previous evening. In fact, the entire area was only about as big as a Jacuzzi, but the space was sufficient for their needs, and Derek was extremely thankful he'd even heard about snow caves and knew the basics of building one. He was no expert, but the result of their labor would probably save their lives.

"Are you sure we don't need a fire?" Kevin asked as soon as they were settled. "I'm still really cold." They had brought in quite a bit of pine straw to keep themselves from having to lie directly on the snow, and Kevin was quick to pull out the thermal Mylar blanket again from the backpack and lay the fabric over the pine straw. It wasn't a fancy billet, but the makeshift bed would do for the night.

"I promise we won't need one, and the flames would only melt the cave anyway," Derek responded. He pushed the backpack over near the entrance but left plenty of room for air to pass by and was careful not to block the trench that the cooler air needed to escape. He also pulled out the Gatorade bottle, drank his fill after offering a drink to the others and then refilled the container with snow from the lower wall near the entrance. He didn't know how warm it would actually get inside their homemade cave and if the temperature would be sufficient to melt the snow in the bottle, but so far, they had been able to consume adequate water without suffering dehydration.

By the time he leaned back, Flynn was already lying supine and had placed Kevin between them. To his own surprise, the room was already getting warm. He felt a small breeze coming in through the hole he'd put in the ceiling but didn't put anything over the opening to block it. He wanted that air coming in to make sure they had good ventilation throughout the night.

"Got any more of that peanut butter left, champ?"

Kevin shook his head. "Nope. But I'm so tired, I'm having a hard time even thinking about food right now." The boy snuggled up to Derek, and although Derek stiffened at the contact, after a few minutes, he finally started to relax and allowed the closeness. Children had always made him uncomfortable, but with everything else they had been dealing with lately, it was hard to stress about his hang-ups, and he didn't want to push the boy away. After a few more minutes, Kevin's breathing evened out and he was once again asleep. To Derek's own surprise, after he was past his initial trepidation, he realized he was actually starting to enjoy having the boy near him. The kid needed guidance, and he found himself wanting to protect Kevin and help him, almost as much as he wanted to take care of Flynn. The feeling was odd and unexpected, yet he found the emotion strangely satisfying.

"Is he out?" Derek finally asked, wanting to make sure so he didn't move the wrong way and wake him up unnecessarily.

"Seems so," Flynn replied quietly. "You did a great job with him today. He'll remember building this snow cave with you for the rest of his life."

Derek let that idea sit for a minute or two before commenting. "It was a fun project, but more importantly, it will probably save us from freezing." He sighed. "I have a lot more respect for the Eskimos now. Who knew a snow cave took so long to build, though? Putting it together was a lot more work than I expected, too, but well worth it if it means we'll make it till tomorrow."

Flynn laughed softly. "You mean they didn't mention the time and effort requirements in the article you read in some outdoor explorer magazine?"

Derek had initially been lying on his back,

but he slowly rolled to his side so he could face Flynn and see her expressions. He was careful not to wake Kevin, who stayed sandwiched between them. With a click, Derek turned on his small flashlight and made the light reflect off the back of the cave so he could see Flynn's face better. Her visage was still steeped in shadows, but he had enough light to make out her beautiful blue eyes and the peaceful expression painted across her features, which made her even more beautiful than she'd seemed before. She had to be exhausted, and armed men were trying to track her down and kill her, but she hadn't complained once. She just kept going, like the Energizer Bunny, and managed to keep a positive attitude no matter what the circumstances. She was an inspiration. "Nope. I have no idea if I constructed this cave properly. I haven't read any articles about it. Let's hope our attempt works out as well as I planned."

"You're amazing, you know that? I never would have even thought of such an idea."

He didn't reply, and for a few minutes, he just looked at her and let those words soak in for a moment. Amazing? Really? She was serious—he could see admiration in her expression—but he didn't want to accept the compliment.

She was the amazing one. He didn't think he was amazing at all. In fact, his years on Earth seemed to be a series of horrible, life-changing mistakes, one right after another. Finally, he had to respond and deny her words. "There's nothing amazing about me. Anyone can build a snow cave. Even a Florida girl."

Flynn laughed again, then reached across Kevin and gave Derek a playful nudge. "Not this one. I don't have the first clue about how to build a snow cave, and I certainly wouldn't have known to make the entrance at an angle like that and build a trench in the front so the cold air can have a place to go. That's pure genius."

She paused for a moment and scrutinized his face. For some reason, she felt a desire to touch his cheek and encourage him, and she started to reach for him, but at the last second, she let her hand fall without doing so. She was afraid to touch him—afraid that if she did, her heart would get engaged and she would once again open herself up to hurt when he walked away after this was over. And he *would* walk away. It was a guarantee. He'd done it before, and he would do it again. Still, she could encourage him without opening herself up. It was the least she could do after everything he had done for them. "If you hadn't been our pilot, who knows what would have happened to us? And by the way, you were excellent with Kevin tonight. The poor kid was exhausted, but you gave him time to rest and then let him help with the building once he got his second wind. It really made him feel like he was contributing."

Derek paused a moment, apparently considering her words. "He's doing incredibly well."

"He's only eleven years old."

"He's pretty smart for a kid that age." Derek propped his head up on his hand. "I mean, I don't know many kids, but he seems to be a fast thinker."

"Yeah, Erin is really proud of him. She says a lot of times, Kevin is the one that comes up with the best ideas, and she forgets he's only eleven." Her thoughts turned to everything they had been through today. She was exhausted, both mentally and physically, yet she also felt an inner peace. Despite all that had happened, they had survived another day. "You know, I think God really protected us earlier when those shooters walked up on us. I mean, we were right there, only a few feet away from them, and they never saw us. And then that wind and snow started really coming down and camouflaged us even better—and just in the nick of time. It was great."

Derek nodded slightly. "I agree."

"Back in college, we used to go to church every Sunday together, but I have to admit, I haven't been attending like I used to. Unfortunately, I have to work a lot of weekends, but I need to make more of an effort and find something that will fit into my schedule regardless." She motioned with her hand. "Do you still go?"

"Not as much as I should," Derek admitted quietly.

Flynn grimaced. "I regret falling away. This trip is proof of how much I need God in my life." She paused a moment, thinking through old conversations she'd had with her sister. "You know, Erin's husband wouldn't let her go to church, or take Kevin, and I think even though he left them about a year ago, she struggled with going back, even though her ex is not in their lives anymore controlling their every move. I hope I can talk to her about her faith when she's healed up a bit and help them get plugged in somewhere in Frisco. Kevin and I have only talked about his beliefs a little so far, but I want to make sure I introduce him to Jesus really well before I go back to Florida."

Derek nodded. "That's a good idea. Maybe I'll go, too. I want to get reconnected, and sometimes it's easier to go with a friend. I don't know Erin very well, but it might be nice to see Kevin again after this is all over. It's obvious that God has been looking out for us this entire time. Without His help, we'd be dead by now for sure."

Flynn was shocked. She knew Derek struggled around children, even though they'd really never discussed why. He'd never wanted to talk much about his past and had quickly shut down the conversation any time she'd asked. Even so, here he was, considering helping her nephew out once they got back to the real world and out of this surreal life-or-death experience. "If you think about it, will you pray for Erin and Kevin?"

"You bet," Derek answered. "Finding a church home is important. I was already thinking about a few places that I'd like to visit."

Flynn let a moment pass, then another. She had so much to be thankful for in her life. She sighed, then murmured softly, "Have I told you how thankful I am that you're here with us? Although I am sorry to have involved you and put you in danger." She looked into his eyes and saw deep emotions there that surprised her. She quickly looked away.

"You didn't cause the danger we're in," Derek replied.

"Maybe not, but—"

"No buts," he interrupted. "There's no place I'd rather be than right here with you, right now."

Again, Flynn felt the desire to reach across and touch him, but she stopped herself a second time, even as electricity seemed to sizzle and crackle in the air. What was the point? They were renewing their friendship, and that was good. And there was definitely an attraction still bubbling between them. But that was it. Physical attraction. They'd already tried to have a meaningful relationship, and it just hadn't worked. When they reached civilization again, Derek would go his way and she would go hers.

So why did that idea make her feel even colder inside?

Chapter Ten

Flynn verified that the flash was turned off, then snapped a quick picture of the outside of their snow cave with her small camera. She'd taken a few shots of their expedition so far and hoped to share them with her sister to show off how well Kevin had done during the trip. Taking photos seemed kind of silly on some level, but she knew in her heart that they were going to make it, and someday, she'd want these pictures to prove how they had survived in such difficult circumstances.

Photography had been a hobby since she'd gotten her first digital camera when she was ten. Taking photos made her feel like herself, as if killers weren't actually chasing her, Kevin and Derek down the mountain.

She pocketed the camera, verified her pistol was still in her other pocket and the safety was engaged, and that the SD card with the photos of the crime scene was secured in her boot. All was well. With a quick last look around, she turned and followed Kevin and Derek, who were already moving slowly down the mountain.

She had no idea how much longer they were going to be walking through the snow, but the hunger was starting to catch up to her. They were now completely out of food and were burning tons of calories with their trek down the mountain. At least they had each managed to drink a fair amount of water before leaving the cave. Thankfully, they'd also all gotten a good night's sleep, and the rest and fluids had done quite a bit to revive all three of them. Derek and she had decided no one needed to stay up to keep watch, because the storm would probably keep their pursuers away during the night. Even if it didn't, the snow cave was hard to recognize as anything beyond an icy mound, and they both felt confident that they were safe—at least for the night.

Today, the weather had changed. Gone were the blistering cold wind and falling snow. This morning, the sun was shining and reflecting off the blanket of white that covered everything, and the brightness made everything look clean and fresh, despite their predicament. Snow covered the trees and fields, and the scene looked like a Christmas card. The landscape would have been a beautiful sight if she'd been on vacation. And she'd even seen a bright red fox in the distance, playing and jumping in the air. She was thankful that the wind had died down and the gray clouds had disappeared and been replaced by fluffy white puffs that dotted the blue sky. Hopefully, today they would make it back to civilization. They had to be getting close. Of course, if the weather made it easier for them, the clear skies also made it easier for their adversaries, and she was still very cognizant of the danger they faced. Still, what she wouldn't give for a good pair of sunglasses!

Sunglasses and a cheeseburger, she amended. And maybe a chocolate shake.

Flynn pulled out her cell phone and quickly checked the screen. Still no service. The lack of a cell tower nearby didn't surprise her, but it did frustrate her. Every time she'd checked she'd had zero bars, and she was using up precious battery power with her constant checking.

She turned and looked carefully around her, then followed Kevin and Derek. She hadn't seen anyone following them, but she kept her eyes peeled as well. She was sure their pursuers would be doubling their efforts to find them today since the weather had cleared. She didn't want anyone sneaking up on her six, and keeping watch was the least she could do since Derek was tasked with leading them down the mountainside. He had enough to worry about, and if she could put her law enforcement skills to good use to keep them safe, then all the better.

The three of them continued through the snowy pass, keeping to the tree line as much as possible so their footprints wouldn't be so easy to see or follow. There were no new flakes coming down that would help disguise their path, and the snow was still thick from yesterday's storm, making the going difficult and slow, despite the sunshine that made it easier to see. Hunger gnawed at her stomach, but she pushed the pain away and kept going. She would eat well once she made it to a restaurant...the biggest carb-filled plate she could find. But first they would all have to make it to the buffet unscathed.

Derek suddenly stopped and pointed up ahead, then motioned for them to stay quiet.

She went forward a few more steps, then saw what he had made him stop. Off in the distance, still a mile or so away, she could just make out a mountain pond that had apparently frozen over.

But that wasn't the interesting part.

The best part was that on the other side of the pond, there was a small cabin, and smoke was swirling out of the chimney, almost as if the wisps were welcoming them home. Long icicles decorated the edges of the roof, and snow covered the roof in gentle piles and was even hanging off the edges in places. Talk about a picturesque image for a Christmas card!

Excitement surged through her. They were saved! Surely someone was in the cabin. She didn't see any vehicles parked outside, nor did she see any movement around the building. But even so, the smoke testified to the occupancy, and whoever was living there probably had food, water, a way to communicate with the rest of the world and even warmth to share. Her hunger and worry seemed to suddenly disappear, and all three of them started forward with new vigor and excitement in their steps.

Eventually they reached the edge of the frozen water, although they were still trying to be mindful of their surroundings. Derek motioned for them to stop as he surveyed the scene. The pond was rather large, about the size of a baseball diamond, and the way around seemed long and difficult through a lot of underbrush and woods.

"What are we waiting for? I'm starving! Somebody's got to have food in there," Kevin cried, and before either adult could stop him, he ran out onto the ice.

Flynn's heart was in her throat as she heard the boy's words and watched him run as if he was in slow motion. He had thrown caution to the wind, not only by the volume of his words, but also by the rash behavior that now had him slipping across the ice as his feet tried to gain purchase on the slippery surface.

Suddenly, a loud crack sounded across the pond, and the ice started to splinter like a giant crack in a windshield. The sound was so loud that some of the nearby trees shook, and snow fell from the heavily laden branches in puffs around the edge. Kevin suddenly stopped and looked back at his aunt, fear painted across his face as he realized his mistake. Their eyes locked, and he mouthed one solitary word.

"Sorry."

Flynn didn't hesitate. She ran after him, right across the ice, and dived for him just as the primary fracture reached his feet. Her hands pushed him back, hard, and the momentum sent him flying across the ice, landing on his rear end and sliding to safety well away from the crack that was opening beneath them.

Flynn didn't make out as well. The ice splintered under her feet, and the next thing she knew, she had fallen into the frigid pond and she was flailing, completely underwater. The temperature shocked her, and for a moment she couldn't move as the darkness and quiet muted her senses. Then the lack of air started to cause a searing pain in her chest, and she began desperately trying to swim back to the surface. Air bubbles swirled around her head, making it hard to see, and chunks of ice hampered her progress. Flynn could tell the surface was close above her, though, and she kicked madly with her legs, desperate for air in her lungs. Her arms started to feel heavy, as if she could barely move them, but quitting was not an option. With her last ounce of strength, Flynn pushed her head through to the air outside and gulped madly, her arms finally obeying her and moving to grab on to something, anything, that would keep her from going under again. Chunks of ice of all sizes surrounded her. Her lungs burned, and a mixture of air and water entered her mouth, chilling her insides even more.

Bits of her life suddenly flashed before her eyes like a slideshow. She saw her parents, her first dog, her sister and herself riding bikes down the street, and later, the two of them celebrating her college graduation. Then she saw Derek walking away from her without looking back, followed by her own promotion to the rank of detective...then everything went black.

Derek's heart tripled its beat as he watched in horror. This couldn't be happening. They couldn't have gone through everything that they had survived the last two days to die here in a frozen lake in the Colorado mountains. He had lost Jax. He couldn't— *He wouldn't lose Flynn!* His heart told him to run after her on the ice, but his head stopped him and made him take a few moments to design a plan. He gingerly put one foot on the ice, then another, and came from an angle to the hole in the ice, rather than following the same path Flynn and Kevin had taken. Despite the fear and anxiety flowing through his veins, he forced himself to move carefully, making sure the ice was firm underneath him before taking another step to-

ward the shocking scene that was playing out
in front of him. He couldn't help Flynn if he
was also lost in the lake.

He took another step...then one more. He
made steady progress and moved as quickly as
he dared, even though everything inside him
was telling him to run toward the hole in the
ice where Flynn had fallen through. Would he
be able to even see her, or would she be locked
underneath the ice, unable to find the surface
again in a watery grave?

When he got close to the opening in the ice,
he quickly dropped to his knees on the sturdi-
est section he could find and bent over as far
as he dared. Flynn's body was right below the
water's surface, and her head kept popping up,
searching for air. Her arms were reaching upward, and she was grasping at the ice around
the edge of the hole, trying to pull herself out
but unable to find something sturdy to hold on
to or pull against. He reached for her under the
chunks of ice and tried to grab her thrashing
arms. It was tough at his angle, but he readjusted his body so he could reach even farther
under the ledge of ice. Finally, he was able to
secure one of her wrists, and he held it tightly,
grasping her with every ounce of strength he

possessed. Adrenaline and fear made him even stronger than normal, and he pulled as hard as he could, bringing her out from under the layers of ice and farther into the hole. Then he grabbed her other wrist so he had a firm grip on both of them. He tugged as hard as he could and as quickly as possible to get her out of the icy hole. She was incredibly heavy due to the water that had soaked her clothing, and he felt and heard the ice cracking under his own feet as he stood, picked her up off the ice and started making for the edge.

At the sound of another crack, he broke into a run, diving the last few feet and landing with Flynn in his arms on the bank of the lake in a pile of frozen snow and ice. He caught his breath, then quickly sat up and moved to her side. She was unresponsive. Her skin was pale, and her lips were blue. She had quit moving completely, and her eyes were closed and lifeless.

"Flynn!" He shook her but got no response. Panic and dread fought for supremacy as he rolled her to her side. Water and mucus dribbled out of her mouth and nose. He was about to roll her over on her back and start CPR when she suddenly started choking.

Relief, hot and heavy, swept over him from head to toe. "Oh God, thank You!" He pulled her into his arms and held her close for just a moment, then moved her quickly to her side so she could clear the remaining water from her system. "Flynn, I thought I'd lost you!" She continued to sputter and choke, but eventually, the spasms slowed and her breathing gradually improved. She raised up her gloved hand and touched his jaw, and they held each other for several minutes as she struggled to recover from the episode. Her body started shaking, and her teeth chattered.

Kevin stood a few steps away, his skin ashen. He was crying softly and shaking, and at one point, he covered his eyes with his sleeve. Derek noticed and reached out to him, beckoning with his hand. "Come here, Kevin." At first the boy stood frozen, as hard and unyielding as the ice that surrounded them, but after a moment he moved to Derek's side, each step filled with trepidation. Derek pulled the boy close as soon as he was within reach. "It's okay, Kevin. She's going to be okay."

"But she could have died..." he choked out.

"But she didn't. She's breathing now, and see? Her color is coming back," Derek reassured him. "After a while, she's going to be talking and laughing just like her old self."

The three of them stayed like that for a few minutes, but Derek knew they couldn't stay here much longer. Flynn *would* die from hypothermia if they couldn't get her warmed up immediately. Thankfully, they were across the pond now, and the cabin was only a short distance away. "Okay. I need your help, okay? We've got to get her into that house and close to a fire." He slowly disengaged himself, then stood and lifted Flynn into his arms. With Kevin following closely behind him, he made his way to the cabin.

Despite his words of assurance to Kevin and Flynn's physical improvement, Derek was still scared that Flynn was going to die, just like Jax. Even though his brain told him he had reached her in time and she would be good as new once they got her warmed up, his heart was still fluttering with fear. The anxiety was almost incapacitating. Even so, he couldn't stop—he had to do everything in his power to help her survive. He carefully carried her up the stairs and asked Kevin to knock on the door. He wanted to shout out but dared not take a chance since he still didn't know if their enemies were near or not. For that matter, he didn't know if the person living in the cabin was friend or foe, but either way, he was about to find out.

Without that person's help and the warmth the fire offered, Flynn would surely die.

Chapter Eleven

The door opened slowly, and a man in his early seventies or so raised his bushy eyebrows when he saw the sight on his porch. Flynn didn't get a good look at him but didn't really care what he looked like as long as he let them inside. She was colder than she'd ever been in her life, and her entire body was racked with shivers that she couldn't control or stop. It was hard for her to think or even concentrate on anything beside the tremendous cold that seemed to permeate every cell of her body.

"She fell in the lake," Derek said simply. "Can we borrow your fire?"

"Of course! Bring her in, bring her in," the older man said quickly as he stepped out of the way. Derek turned so he could carry her through the doorway and carefully stepped over the threshold. Kevin followed them in, gripping the navy backpack that held their small stash of supplies tightly in his gloved hands. Once they were all inside, the older man shut the door behind them.

The living room space wasn't large, but had an open feel with a cathedral ceiling. The walls were made of logs, and it was rustically decorated with deer and moose prints and a theme of dark green accents. A large fireplace with a roaring fire was in the corner, and Derek hurried over and laid Flynn in front of the fire. He took off his own gloves and coat, then turned to Flynn and removed her coat, gloves and boots. The older man was quickly at his side and offering a stack of blankets, a T-shirt and sweatpants. All were clean and smelled sweetly of cedar chips. Derek covered Flynn up to protect her modesty, and while she huddled under a blanket, he helped her pull off her wet jeans and flannel shirt and put on the dry shirt and pants. The pants were a bit big, but they had a drawstring, and she tied up the waist tightly, then lay on the floor, exhausted. That small bit of effort was all she could manage. She didn't even think she could sit up by herself. All she wanted to do was fall asleep and not wake up until next week sometime.

She turned slightly as she watched Derek

remove his boots. He left on the rest of his clothes, which had to be a bit damp in places, but he didn't seem to mind. Her eyes locked with his, and she could see the worry and fear still consuming him. He couldn't keep his eyes off her.

"Thank you," she said softly. "You saved my life."

"You're welcome," he said as he moved to kneel beside her. "I keep telling myself that you survived and you're going to be fine, but I don't think I've really accepted it yet." He gently pulled her hairband off and then pushed the wet hair back from her face. "Everything happened so fast. I don't think I've ever been more scared in my entire life. When I saw you go in that icy water..." He touched her cheek gently and then cupped her chin with his hand, even though she tensed. "I thought I had lost you."

He sat on the floor and leaned back against a nearby couch, then pulled her into his arms so she was facing the fire with her back to his chest. She stiffened, but he didn't let go. He pulled the blankets with her and rearranged them around her. With gentle fingers, he massaged her arms and neck, bringing a warm tingling to her skin as the circulation returned.

He took several deep breaths, and she could tell he was trying to slow his heartbeat and the panic that she could still feel beating strongly behind his ribs.

"I hope those clothes fit you okay," the older man said as he ambled up to the couch. "Are you doing better now?"

Flynn smiled and nodded, and Derek cleared his throat that was clogged with emotion. "You're a lifesaver, mister. I don't think she would have made it if you hadn't been here with your fire going. We owe you our lives."

The man tilted his head and looked embarrassed at the praise. "Anyone would do the same. But I'm happy to help."

Derek motioned with his head toward Kevin, who was still standing by the edge of the couch, looking a bit lost. "That's Kevin, my name is Derek and this is Flynn."

"I'm Lee Clark," the man responded. "Would you like some hot chocolate?"

"That would be wonderful," Derek said. "We haven't eaten today, so if you have any food, we would be very grateful if you could share some."

Lee raised his eyebrows but stood and didn't press for answers to the questions no doubt swirling in his head. "I'm sure there's a story there, but let's get you warm and fed before we do anything else." He looked toward Kevin. "Young man, why don't you take off your coat and stay awhile? I have those dining room chairs by the table over there. See them? How about you bring them over closer to the fire and spread out these wet clothes on them. That will probably help them dry faster."

Kevin nodded quickly and went to work, apparently happy to have something to do. While Lee rumbled around in the kitchen, Kevin took off his jacket and gloves and then brought over all the chairs and hung up the coats and wet clothing. Then he organized the boots so they were also closer to the flames.

A few minutes later, Lee came back over near the fire with a folded sheet tucked under his arm and a small serving tray laden with mugs and spoons. "I know you don't want to leave that fire, Ms. Flynn, so I think a picnic is in order."

He handed her a mug of steaming hot chocolate, and she wrapped her hands around the mug, letting the warmth seep into her skin. It was pure joy. She took a small sip, then another, letting the warm liquid slowly heat her from the inside out. Lee handed a second mug to Derek and a third to Kevin and then took his tray back into the kitchen. A few minutes later, he returned a second time with plates and silverware, and finally he came back again with mounds of food on two different platters. He laid out a spread that would have made a bed-and-breakfast jealous. There were stacks of pancakes, butter on a dish and a small pitcher of syrup, a plateful of scrambled eggs, and large slices of ham and crispy brown bacon.

Flynn let Derek make her a plate, and then she continued to lean against him as she started eating, having no shame as she dug hungrily into the plate of heaping food. She tried to move away to give him room to eat, too, but he held her gently in place. "Stay put. You need my body heat. It will help you warm up."

She wasn't sure about that, but she didn't want to argue. Being held by Derek helped her feel safe and secure for the first time since she had landed in Colorado. Yet the closeness they were sharing brought back memories of when they'd been a couple so many years ago, memories that were better off forgotten and were now a catalyst to making her feel lost and alone. There was something wrong with her—something that made men run in the opposite direction whenever they got too close. She didn't want to go through that heartache again. It was too painful. Derek's touch now made her feel vulnerable and unsure, even as the air seemed to sizzle with electricity that popped between them.

Did she want a man in her life? No, she did not. She had forsworn all relationships after her last one had ended so poorly. Derek and Ted had both said they loved her, and both had left her with deep emotional scars. She was fine on her own. She didn't need a man in her life. But she had to admit, she missed the closeness of having someone to share things with—both the good times and bad. She missed laughing together, the camaraderie, the knowledge that no matter how bad things got, someone had her back.

She missed Derek.

He had been the love of her life. No one else she had dated had even come close, not even Ted. She missed his kisses. She missed holding hands and snuggling during a movie.

But Derek had made it clear that he didn't want to be with her. Sure, he was being nice and helping her. But he was doing these things because he was a good person, not because he had any romantic feelings for her. She was the one projecting and hoping for feelings that just didn't exist and apparently never would.

She sighed inwardly. The past was over and done. For now, she would enjoy the companionship he offered. It was enough. It would have to be.

Derek reached over to the platters and filled a plate for himself, then set it on the floor within arm's reach and fed himself with his right arm while holding her with his left. She glanced over at Kevin, who was also eating a large stack of pancakes and tucking into some eggs and ham as well. A feeling of utter contentment settled over her despite their dire circumstances, and once she had eaten, she gave up the battle and fell asleep right there in Derek's arms.

Lee noticed and motioned with his hands toward Flynn as he sipped meditatively on a mug of hot chocolate. "She's out. Falling in that water took a lot out of her." He stood and started clearing the dishes away. "Boy, you weren't kidding when you said you were hungry!"

"I'm sorry we put you to so much trouble..." Derek started, but Lee waved his words away.

"I think it's great! Reminds me of my younger days. I always loved cooking for the family. Makes me feel useful."

Derek started to move Flynn a bit so he could stand. "I'll help you out with the dishes..."

This time, Lee put up his hands in a motion to stop him. "You will not. What you will do, young man, is sit right there with that pretty woman and take care of her and let her rest. I can take care of these dishes myself. I've been doing dishes for years, and I'm an expert. No, the three of you need rest, and rest is what you're going to get."

Derek watched Lee go, then turned his attention to Flynn. He shifted a bit and adjusted her against him so that his muscles wouldn't cramp. She felt so warm and perfect in his arms, he felt like he could sit like this forever. He didn't have the words to really express all that he was feeling, but he could show her with his actions. He would make sure she was safe, no matter the cost.

He glanced over at Kevin. The boy was still sitting at the edge of the fireplace, his expression dejected and unhappy. He'd finally removed his boots and added them to the rest by the fire and periodically held up his hands so they were closer to the flames. His skin was red from sun and windburn and his lips were chapped, but otherwise, the boy looked healthy and had done amazingly well during their quest for survival. Still, Derek realized the episode at the lake would probably bother him for some time. Maybe he could help with that. He wasn't good with kids, but he had to at least try to smooth things over.

"Kevin, why don't you come closer and wrap up in that blanket?" He motioned toward a navy throw that lay in a heap by the fire.

The boy looked wary at first but slowly complied. Then he sat and wrapped the blanket around his thin shoulders and stared into the fire.

"How are you doing?" Derek asked.

"Okay," he responded, his voice low.

"Hmm. Well, we should probably talk about what happened at the lake, don't you think?"

Kevin shrugged. "I guess." He was quiet for a moment, and then Derek could hear his quiet sobs.

"Well, you made a mistake today, but I want you to know that I forgive you, and I'm sure Flynn does, too."

The boy stopped crying in surprise and made

a hiccupping sound. "What? Really? I thought you'd be really mad at me. Don't you hate me now? I feel so guilty. Aunt Flynn got hurt and it's all my fault." He sniffled, found a stray napkin and blew his nose.

"No, Kevin. I'm not mad, and I don't hate you. Everyone makes mistakes."

"Not you," Kevin said, his eyes large. "I bet you never make mistakes."

Derek laughed. If this kid only knew… "I've made plenty, believe me. Some mistakes I've even made more than once." He shifted slightly. "In fact, all people make mistakes, but let me tell you a little secret. It's how we fix those mistakes that matters, and how we learn from them." He looked the boy in the eye. "You start by apologizing to the people who were hurt by your actions, and really mean it. And then you do your best to fix the mistake and try not to make the same mistake twice."

Kevin's eyes widened. "But you said you've made the same mistake more than once before."

"That's very true. And you know what? That's because none of us are perfect. We're all going to get it wrong sometimes, no matter how hard we try to get it right. And that's okay. It's our attitude and our hearts that matter. As long as you're doing your best, that's all we can ask of you. Just be sure to always do the best you can, and apologize if you get it wrong, and take responsibility for your mistakes. Then forgive yourself and move on. Sound like a good plan?"

"Yes, sir," the boy responded, a hopeful tone to his voice.

Derek reached over and pulled Kevin close with his right hand, letting the boy rest against him. Once again, he actually felt comfortable with the closeness, and he didn't shy away from the contact. The irony of his words wasn't lost on him. Here he was teaching this kid an important life lesson—a lesson he still hadn't learned himself.

Even though the military tribunal had cleared him of all wrongdoing, Derek had never really forgiven himself for being the pilot in the crash that had killed his friend. Had he done his best to save him? Yes, he had. He would never have intentionally hurt Jax, and he had done all in his power to do his job and protect the people who flew with him. Yet tragedy had still occurred, and he had been powerless to stop it. He needed to forgive himself and move on, just as he was trying to teach this young boy.

He hugged Kevin and Flynn, and felt another big piece of ice chip off his frozen heart. Maybe there was hope for him after all.

Chapter Twelve

Flynn woke up a few hours later on the floor by the fire, still lying against Derek's chest with Kevin also huddled next to them. Heat still radiated from the flames, and the bone-deep chill that had invaded her body when she'd gone under the ice had finally subsided. She was beginning to feel like herself again, and even her stomach had quit complaining because she had eaten her fill of their host's wonderful breakfast.

She stretched slightly, and Derek must have felt it, because he woke as well. She'd hoped to slip away before he realized how long they'd been sitting together. She didn't want to make him feel awkward or uncomfortable by their closeness. "You make a pretty good pillow," she quipped as she sat up and quickly moved away from him. She scooted closer to the fire and stretched out her hands, soaking up the warmth. Why did she feel so chilled all of a sudden?

Derek glanced at Kevin, who was still sleeping against him, and gently shifted him so he was lying completely on the floor on a dark green braided rug. The boy didn't stir, even when Derek tucked the blanket around him. Derek stretched out his arm and rubbed his shoulder. "Kid weighs a ton," he said lightly, but Flynn was sure she heard a pleased tone to his voice. She was glad he wasn't annoyed. Derek had always been good around children, even though he seemed to have a hard time realizing it. They'd rarely talked about it, and whenever she'd asked him about kids in the past, he'd changed the subject and refused to discuss his feelings. There was something there, some issue, but she had no right to press him if he didn't want to share—especially now, since they were only friends and nothing more.

They *were* friends, right? She glanced back over at Derek. Maybe this entire trip was a way to heal those old scars and finally get that closure she'd been seeking so she could move on with her life. She still wasn't interested in dating anyone, but it was nice to finally close the door on some of the feelings of inadequacy and hurt their relationship had caused. "I think it's time to ask our host to call for help. What do you think?"

"Agreed," Derek said. He stood, then saw Lee out of the corner of his eye working in the kitchen and motioned with a friendly gesture for the man to join them. Lee came over carrying a cup of coffee and settled himself in a brown recliner while Derek and Flynn sat together across from him on the chocolate-colored couch they had been leaning against moments before.

"Y'all feel better after that nap?" Lee asked.

"And the food," Derek added. "Your food was a real lifesaver."

Lee smiled at the compliment. "I used to be a cook at a diner down in Frisco. Nothing fancy, but fast and tasty usually fit the bill."

"Ah! No wonder your food was so good!" Flynn smiled. "We didn't really get a chance to talk earlier." Her voice was still a bit scratchy from swallowing that lake water, but she cleared her throat and went on. "I want to thank you for allowing us in your home and feeding us so well."

"You're very welcome. Now, y'all want to tell me what you're doing walking around out there and swimming in my lake? I don't get many visitors up here, especially ones that look like they've been lost in the wilderness with a kid in tow." He said it with a smile, but there was both a curiosity and a hard tone to his voice that didn't seem to match his friendly, grandfatherly demeanor up until now. Or maybe she was just now picking up on the nuances of his behavior and speech because she had been so out of sorts after the episode at the lake. Either way, Flynn's radar immediately went up. The situation seemed innocuous enough, but being a cop, she had learned quite a bit about watching body language and listening to people when they talked to gather hints about their veracity. The man seemed stiff and oddly anxious. Something just wasn't right. Maybe Lee just didn't like unannounced visitors? Or was there more to it? Up until now, he'd been the perfect host, but had he just been putting on a show?

Before Flynn could even answer, Derek jumped in. "We had some trouble with our vehicle and ended up walking. It has been a rather harrowing experience, and we'd like to get back to town as soon as we can. Actually, if you have a phone, we can call for help and be on our way. And I insist you let us pay you for the food we ate."

Vehicle? Not helicopter? Still, Flynn bit her tongue and let Derek's comment go. He must have sensed the same red flags that she was seeing with Lee's deportment and was being careful with his language.

Lee shook his head. "No payment is necessary." He sat back a little in his chair. "Unfortunately, I can't let you borrow a phone."

Derek raised his eyebrows, but before he could comment, Lee raised his hands. "I don't have a phone. Can't let you use something I don't have. I'm pretty remote and can't get a landline, and cell service is also almost nonexistent in this neck of the woods, so I just never bothered. I do have a ham radio, though. If you tell me who to call, I can probably get a message out for you."

Derek nodded, but his features were still alert. "That would be great. My assistant's name is Candice O'Rourke. She lives down in Frisco. If you could get a message to her and give her this address, she could send her brother up in his truck to get us. He's got chains and four-wheel drive and can probably make it through. He's also a pretty good mechanic and might even be able to fix our vehicle if it's not too complicated and he has the parts."

"Well, we can give it a try," Lee said with a smile. He gave Derek a notepad and pen, and Derek wrote down the name and phone number. Lee gave Derek a smile, then headed down the hallway.

"Why didn't you tell him about the helicopter and the drug dealers?" Flynn asked.

Derek shrugged. "I don't know. I was getting a strange vibe from him. I just thought caution seemed more prudent. He doesn't need to know our business."

"I agree. I'm not sure what it is, but something is off about the way he's acting now. Maybe we should just start walking again? I feel like we're on borrowed time here. We've already been here longer than I'd hoped. What if he somehow has a connection with the drug dealers?"

"Anything is possible," Derek agreed. "But I'm not sure walking is the best option, either. I'm worried about you."

"I can make it," Flynn said fiercely. "My chest hurts a little, but otherwise I'm good to go. That food and rest did wonders for me."

"What about Kevin?"

Flynn glanced over at the boy, who was still sleeping soundly. "The rest and food have been good for him, too. We can both make it. We'll do whatever it takes."

Derek tilted his head. "I wonder if he really does have a ham radio or if he's been lying this whole time." He ran his hands through his hair. "Do you still have that pistol?"

Flynn frowned. "It should be in my coat pocket. The lake water probably ruined my phone, but I bet that gun will still fire, and the small camera I had in there is waterproof, so it should be fine, too." She stood and went over to where her coat was still hanging on the back of the chair where Kevin had put it. The coat was mostly dry, and the pistol and camera both seemed in good shape. Her phone, as predicted, was waterlogged.

"Guess I'll need a new one of these once we get back into town. I don't think a bucketful of rice would help. The case said it was waterproof, but I bet that didn't mean it could take a dunking in a frozen Colorado lake at these temperatures." She smiled to herself, determined to find the good even in a bad situation. She was alive and hopefully they would be rescued soon. She checked her boot as well and breathed a sigh of relief once she saw that the SD card with the photos from the crime scene was still tucked safely inside the lining. Water wouldn't hurt the card, but she had wondered if it had fallen out and gotten lost when she'd gone in the lake. Thankfully, it was right where she'd left it. She really did have a lot to be thankful for.

"Keep your gun handy," Derek advised. "I'm hoping we won't need it, but anything is possible."

Flynn nodded, her good mood slipping away as these new perils started to weigh down on her shoulders. They weren't saved yet, and they couldn't relax their vigilance until they were sitting in the police station downtown, telling their story to the local law enforcement team. "I think I'll change back into my own clothes while I have a chance." She gathered her things from the around the fireplace and easily found a bathroom down the hall. She could hear voices from behind a closed door but couldn't make out the words. It certainly sounded like Lee was using his ham radio, but had he actually called Candice as he promised he would do?

She returned shortly with the handgun stowed in her waistband and covered by her flannel shirt. Everything was dry except for her coat, which only had a few damp spots.

She adjusted the sleeves and moved it closer to the fire, hoping the remaining sections would dry quickly. As soon as she finished, Lee came back into the room.

"Well, that's done," he said mildly.

"Did you have any trouble reaching your friend with the radio?" she asked.

"None at all. He keeps his ham radio on most days and just listens to the chatter. He lives down in Frisco, and he was happy to call Ms. O'Rourke right then while I waited on the radio. He had her on Speaker, and I could hear her talking in the background. She said she'd been really worried about you three, and she'd send someone up to give you a ride down right away. We're a fair distance away from Frisco, though, so it might take some time for them to get here, and the roads are bad due to yesterday's storm. I hope you don't mind waiting a little longer."

Flynn sat back on the couch. "No problem for us, as long as you aren't too terribly inconvenienced. We sure appreciate your help, but I imagine you probably had other plans for the day that didn't include helping out a group of strangers." She leaned back, making sure her shirt covered the bulge from the weapon. Was she right to be wary of this man? He'd done nothing but help so far, but she was still getting an uncomfortable feeling that something wasn't just right. She watched his eyes, which seemed to dart around the room, and he kept playing with the hair at his nape, as if he was uncomfortable and his shirt collar was just a bit too tight.

"I didn't have any real plans beyond reading the latest Lee Child novel. I can always pick that up later." Lee returned to the recliner where he'd previously been sitting and began chitchatting about the storm that had hit the previous day and all the commotion it had caused. "I was listening to the radio most of the day yesterday. That snow and wind caused quite a bit of hardship. I'm really sorry you folks got caught up in it, too." The topic seemed innocuous enough, but Flynn still got the feeling that the older man was on edge and was no longer the kind and benevolent host he had pretended to be.

Suddenly the doorbell rang and sent an alert down Flynn's spine that interrupted her musings. They had a visitor? Here? Now?

"Hmm. I wonder who that could be," Lee said in a deceptively friendly tone.

Flynn's head snapped toward the front door.

They hadn't heard a vehicle, and although she didn't know the area well, it seemed way too soon for anyone from Frisco to have arrived at the cabin, especially based on Lee's own comments that it would take some time for anyone to reach them. As Lee rose to go to the door, Flynn reached over and gave Kevin a little shake. "Kevin? Wake up and get your boots on." She didn't know what to expect, but she did want to be ready if things suddenly went south in a hurry.

The boy stirred and then started slowly putting on his boots. He crinkled his brow but said nothing as he obeyed her request. His eyes met hers, and she tried to telegraph a need for caution without scaring him.

Derek tensed on the couch and turned slightly so he had Lee in his line of vision as the older man went to answer the door. In an abundance of caution, he pulled his weapon but kept his gun hand down and hidden from anyone by the front door. He heard Lee release the lock, and a tingle of adrenaline shot down his arms.

Suddenly, the door crashed open and two young men wearing blue coats and skull caps burst into the living room brandishing pistols.

Derek instantly raised his weapon, and his first shot caught the first man through the door in the chest. He went down with a grunt as a circle of red instantly spread around his upper body. The second man reacted quickly. He pulled Lee in front of him, grasping him around the neck and using him as a shield while also pointed a .45 pistol at Lee's head.

Derek had no time for a second shot that wouldn't also endanger their elderly host. He quickly glanced over at Flynn, who had dropped behind the couch on the floor, pushing Kevin with her. He leaned down on the couch himself, trying to make a smaller target of his body.

"Unless you want me to shoot this old man, you'd better put that gun down," the aggressor stated in a deep, nasty tone.

"Unless you want me to shoot you, you should put your gun down," Derek responded in a calm voice, instantly thankful for the military training that had honed his firearm skills. He was an excellent shot, yet he didn't want to put Lee at risk if it wasn't absolutely necessary.

"That's not going to happen," came the dark response.

Derek saw a gleam in the man's eye and

thought he recognized the voice as the more mature of the two men who had been chasing them when they had spent the first night in the mountain cave. Nervous men often made mistakes, but this man seemed in complete control and a formidable adversary. He remembered the man's fortitude and commitment to the cause when he and his partner been out searching for them in the bitter cold. If it was the same guy, he would not give up easily, if at all.

Derek adjusted his aim slightly, but despite his skills, there was no way to get off a shot without also putting Lee in danger. Although Derek had some doubts about Lee, he wasn't ready to take a chance on shooting him or getting into a gun battle with Flynn and Kevin so close behind him. His mind raced. "I guess we've reached a draw, because I'm not putting down my weapon. Maybe you should just go back out that door and take your dead friend with you."

The perpetrator gave an evil smile and pushed his pistol into Lee's temple. "I'm not inclined to leave just yet. But I will shoot this guy right here and now if you don't surrender your weapon."

"And as soon as you do, I'm going to shoot you," Derek said, his voice cool.

"And then I'll kill this pretty little lady of yours."

That raspy, deadly voice was new—and totally unexpected.

Derek's head snapped around as he quickly looked back to where Flynn had been crouching only moments before. Two other killers had apparently come in from the back of the cabin and silently approached as he'd been occupied with the drama at the front door. The first man was tall and wearing a red coat. He had dark hair and eyes that seemed cold and unmoving, just like the other perpetrators, and he pointed a 9mm Glock right at Flynn's head. His other arm was around her neck, holding her motionless. A second man in a green coat was holding Kevin tightly against his chest. He had a hand over the kid's mouth, and a gun in his other hand was pointed at Derek. Kevin's eyes rounded, and his face had paled. As Derek watched, the boy started to tremble.

"Your move, friend," the man at the front door said calmly. "What's it going to be?"

Derek's breath seemed frozen in his throat. His kept his gun trained on the man holding

Lee, but his eyes darted to Flynn's and held. He saw anger there in those blue depths, but also vulnerability and fear. Would she try to fight her captive's hold? Would he have enough time to save them all? He couldn't lose Flynn. Intrinsically, he knew keeping a cool head was important in dire circumstances like this, but he couldn't stop the fear from invading his heart.

And what if he was wrong about Lee? He probably could only take one shot before one of the three aggressors also fired, killing at least one of the innocent people in the room. Sweat beaded on his forehead, and a knot twisted in his chest.

Could he sacrifice Lee for a chance to save Flynn and Kevin? Was saving both Flynn and Kevin even possible?

Chapter Thirteen

"I'm going to give you to the count of three to put that gun down, and if you don't, I'm going to shoot this woman." Red Coat pulled her even tighter against him, and Flynn gave an involuntary yelp as the man's rough handling pulled her neck into an unnatural position. The perpetrator's voice was deadly and still calm, as if they were discussing the weather on a hot summer day.

Derek had no doubt he would do exactly what he threatened.

"One."

Derek's hand started shaking imperceptibly, and the weapon suddenly felt heavy and cold in his hand. Would they all die if he surrendered his weapon? Could he live with himself if Flynn was shot dead in front of him and he could have prevented it?

"Two."

"You win," Derek said with resignation in his voice. He pointed his weapon toward the ceiling, making it clear he was no longer a threat, and put his other hand up in mock surrender. There was no time to consider it further. Flynn and Kevin might survive if he waited for a better opportunity to escape. If he tried to fight back now, someone would probably get shot.

Green Coat reached over and took his gun, then secured it in his waistband as he pushed Kevin into the chair where Flynn's coat was drying. At the same time, Red Coat frisked Flynn, found the sidearm and took it away from her. He pocketed it, then forced her to sit in the other chair next to Kevin.

Derek's eyes returned to the front door. The blue-coated man released Lee and pushed him aside, causing the older man to stumble and fall to his knees. The gunman stepped over his fallen colleague, who lay dead on the floor, then turned and shut the front door firmly behind him. With a click, he engaged the dead bolt.

"We don't want to be interrupted, do we?" he said with a smirk.

Lee pulled himself back up to his feet. "You sure took your time getting here," he complained with a nasal tone. "I've been watching over them for hours."

So Lee Clark was the enemy after all. Derek clenched his teeth. The man should get an Oscar for his acting ability. He'd put on quite a show.

"We weren't in a rush once we knew where they were," Blue Coat replied. "Believe it or not, we've actually got a lot going on today. This was high priority, but not as high as making sure our out-of-town guests were properly greeted."

"Harrumph," Lee said acerbically. Right before Derek's eyes, the old man's countenance changed from one of a benevolent grandfatherly type to a look of greed and fury. "You're going to have to pay me more if you want me to babysit for you. I agreed to be a courier, nothing more, and you already don't pay me enough for the risks I take."

Blue Coat turned, raised his weapon and fired at Lee's chest before the man could say another word or even realize the danger he was in. A dark red circle started to slowly spread across his shirt as he gasped and sputtered. "Consider yourself paid."

Lee sank slowly to his knees, then fell forward, his face now registering surprise before his eyes went completely blank. Behind him, Derek could hear Flynn groan as Lee's body hit the floor. Kevin whimpered, but to his credit, he didn't cry out.

Some static sounded from a radio in Blue Coat's pocket, and he pulled out the transmitter and pushed a button. "We're ready for our ride."

The answer was quick in coming. "We're still about five minutes out. We'll be there shortly."

"Ride?" Derek asked, keeping his eye on both the man's eyes and his gun hand.

"Our boss wants to ask you a few questions before he kills you and disposes of your bodies. Don't worry, nobody will ever find them."

"Who's your boss?" Flynn asked.

Blue Coat laughed. "You'll find out soon enough. And really, of all the things you should be worried about right now, his name is definitely at the bottom of the list."

So, they weren't going to kill them right away. That was important news, but the man's tone was so nasty that his words still sent a chill down Derek's spine.

Red Coat pulled some zip ties out of his pocket. "Put on your coats," he ordered all three of them with a sneer.

The three of them stood and put on their coats and gloves, and then Red Coat quickly zip-tied Flynn's and Kevin's hands in front of them. Green Coat started to do the same with Derek, and for a moment, Derek considered trying to fight him off. He glanced around the room, trying to think of any feasible way to escape, and ended up locking eyes with Flynn. She gave an almost imperceptible shake of her head, and the look she gave him made him decide not to chance it—at least not right now. After all, despite whatever orders the man had from the boss, in the blink of an eye, he'd had no trouble at all ending Lee's life. He decided to wait and hope for a better opportunity.

Each of the invaders grabbed one of the captives by the arm and led them around the fallen bodies and out onto the front porch. Years of working as an aviator helped Derek identify the sound of the rotors before the helicopter was even visible, and a short time later, a chopper bearing the logo of Bear Creek Vacation Rentals approached and landed in the snow-covered area between the cabin and the lake.

A sinking feeling settled in Derek's gut. They were planning to kill them for sure. Otherwise, there was no way they'd let them all see the

connection between the drugs, murders and
Bear Creek. Still, a new resolve also formed.
They weren't beaten yet. He prayed for God
to give him an opportunity, any opportunity,
to help the three of them escape without getting hurt.

The helicopter ride was short, less than half
an hour, and Flynn immediately recognized
the clearing as they started to land near the
place where they had first seen the dead bodies
in the field. There was no sign of the murders
now, and it appeared that the snowstorm had
completely covered up whatever crime-scene
cleanup had been accomplished. Smoke rose
from the chimney on the large log cabin—style
house, but the building still looked rather dilapidated, although it was clear that it was in
use. As they landed, they could see several new
tarps covering some large, bulky items under
the pole barn that hadn't been there before. She
didn't have a clue what was under those tarps,
but it was interesting that the area that had previously looked abandoned now had so much life
teeming around it and had a cleaner and neater
appearance overall.

They landed on the helicopter pad near the

house in the middle of the field and were met by four new men, who came out of the house garbed in dark heavy winter clothes, as if they were soldiers from a winter clime in some remote country. Each was carrying a high-powered rifle, and they all looked very adept at using them. Were they mercenaries? They sure fit the part. A couple of snowmobiles were parked near the house's front door, and it was obvious that the helicopter pad had been blown and cleaned, as had a path through the snow to the main house and the outbuildings.

"Where do you want them? Inside the cabin?" Red Coat asked the leader of the new group of men as he dragged the captives, none too gently, out of the helicopter one by one onto the concrete pad. He grabbed Kevin's arm and started to walk the boy toward the big main house before he got an answer, but the man in charge of the military-looking group raised his hands and stopped him. "Hold on. There's a meeting going on inside. No one else goes in."

Red Coat shrugged. "Fine. Where to, then?"

Another man approached from the vicinity of the pole barn, wiping his hands on an oily rag as he walked. He had a scruffy beard and long dark hair that he'd pulled back in a ponytail and was wearing a black skull cap. Flynn noticed his teeth were damaged, as if he was or had been a heavy methamphetamine user. Still, he was large and muscular and had the look of someone who had no problem hurting other people. Once he arrived, the others that had tied them up and guarded them on the helicopter gave him a measure of deference, so Flynn guessed he had some measure of power on the compound.

"They don't need to see any more than they've already seen. The workroom behind the barn will serve just fine. Go ahead and take them over there," the scruffy man responded. He pocketed the rag and put his hands on his hips as he surveyed the captives. Flynn noticed he was wearing dark green snow overalls and heavy black boots, both covered with grime. She wondered if he was some sort of mechanic, or if he had some other role. Even though his appearance was unkempt and that of a mountain man who hadn't seen civilization in a long time, he carried himself as if he was in charge, and the other men definitely gave him respect and looked to him for direction. Even the soldiers seemed to be waiting for his orders.

"Well, you gave us quite the chase," Mountain Man said with a smile as he eyed each of the captives. "I'd love to hear how you survived the night during that storm."

Flynn shrugged. "I'm not a storyteller. You'll have to wait for the movie."

He smiled and raised a gloved hand to roughly grab her chin, but she pulled away. His smile instantly disappeared, and a hard, flint-eyed expression took its place. "You'll tell me what I want you to tell me. Understand? You don't have a choice."

"It's pretty cold in there," Red Coat said. "You sure you want them in that room?" He never quite looked the newcomer in the eye, and Flynn wasn't sure if he was worried about them freezing—or himself if he was unfortunate enough to pull guard duty. She was glad they'd at least allowed them to put on their coats before taking them from Lee Clark's house.

"It won't matter," the man responded gruffly. "They aren't going to be there that long. We'll have ourselves a conversation, and then you'll be free to dispose of them however the boss wants it done."

Flynn met Derek's eyes and saw frustration and simmering anger. She turned to look at Kevin, hoping to instill new confidence and hope into the boy's sullen expression. He had to be scared. She was scared herself, and probably even Derek was a bit insecure about their current situation—it was obvious he didn't like the mountain man touching her.

But she would not give up. The God they served was a big God. Nothing was impossible, and she refused to give up, just because things were looking pretty bad. The small flame of hope still burned inside her. Somehow, they would find a way out of this mess. They just had to.

Their captors left the militia-looking group behind and pulled them past the pole barn and toward a small shed attached to the back right corner of the structure. Flynn still couldn't tell what was underneath all the tarps, but some of the items looked like big barrels of chemicals. Were the barrels full of substances and supplies used to cook meth? She didn't know the entire recipe but wouldn't be surprised if they were stocking up. Twice, the perps had mentioned visitors and it being a big day today. Were they trying to woo and impress a new buyer or supplier? Anything was possible, and she made mental notes of what she was seeing, just in case it would help with the prosecution once they got to tell their story to law enforcement.

Apparently, while their small party had been trying to escape down the mountain, the people here had been working hard to clean the place up. The old truck and other trash had been removed. A large fire pit was behind the pole barn, and sizable hunks of burned wood and other unidentifiable items were strewn about in the center and looked like the remains of a bonfire. As the small group approached, a man on a bulldozer was busy covering up the pit by pushing dirt and snow over the contents. There were other implements under the pole barn that weren't covered, including a snowplow attachment and a large box blade that were probably used for road repairs. Near the back of the barn, she saw two faded metal signs that advertised Bear Creek Vacation Rentals. She also noticed a few more snowmobiles on the right, and a couple of them looked like they were being worked on. Tools and rags littered a short workbench and the surrounding area.

When they reached the small room, Red Coat pulled out a set of keys and unlocked the door, then flipped up the light switch on the left-hand wall. Two shelving units covered the back wall and were filled with boxes of gadgets, dust and outdoor yard supplies. Another wall had racks of snow supplies, including snow-shoes, fishing equipment and skis. In the mid-dle of the room, a long table was surrounded by several wooden chairs. Flynn wasn't sure, but if she had to guess, she could imagine a group of dealers sitting around that table, dividing up packets of meth for distribution. There was a small heater in the corner, but the room was drafty, and even though Blue Coat turned the heater on as soon as he entered the room, it did little to combat the cold that permeated the air and seemed to soak into her bones.

"Tie them to the chairs," Blue Coat ordered. He searched through the boxes on the shelf but only found a couple of rolls of duct tape. "Use this," he ordered, and threw one to Green Coat, who forced them to sit and then started secur-ing them to the chairs. He cut the zip ties with a pocketknife and then taped each arm to the arm of the chair and each ankle to a chair leg. Finally, he taped each captive to the back of the chair as tightly as he could around the chest.

Flynn flexed her muscles and tried to puff out her chest and shoulders, just in case that little bit would help if they were ever given the chance to escape, but she doubted it made any difference. She could barely move.

"They were armed," Green Coat offered once he was done. He put on the table the gun he'd taken from Flynn and also the small camera she'd been carrying and her ruined cell phone. Red Coat followed suit and put the pistol he'd taken from Derek beside it. The navy backpack they'd been using was nowhere around, and Flynn figured it had gotten left behind at Lee Clark's house, along with Derek's phone.

"Okay, go secure the area," Mountain Man ordered. He pulled back a chair and seated himself as close to the heater as possible, picking up the guns and inspecting them as he did so. He picked up the camera, too, powered it on and then scanned through the photos. Seeing nothing that caught his eye, he flipped it back on the table.

"From those photos, it looks like you're having a great vacation," Mountain Man said in a conversational tone.

"We were until your men shot at us," Flynn replied caustically.

He smiled in response, but it was an evil smile.

"Want me to stay?" Blue Coat asked.

"Yeah, stick around and guard that door, just

in case they start thinking escape is even possible." He turned and studied the three captives as the other men filed out, leaving Blue Coat by the door with a rifle someone handed him on their way out. "Escape isn't possible, you know, but I'd sure like for you to try. We could use some excitement to break up the day."

"We didn't give you enough of a thrill by making you spend two days chasing us down the mountain?" Derek replied, his tone derisive.

Mountain Man grinned, his entire countenance changing back to the good ole boy persona, as if he was an old buddy and they were just sitting around talking about the weather. "Well, that was a bit of fun, up until our friend Lee had to go and get greedy. He wanted quite a sum for finding you three, but we decided not to pay his price." He pulled off his gloves and held his hands out toward the heater. "Apparently, you also gave the boys some target practice with your helicopter." He raised an eyebrow. "Iraq?"

Derek looked away, apparently unwilling to give the man any information about his service to the country or anything else.

As a law enforcement officer, Flynn was familiar with a variety of interrogation techniques and wasn't surprised by Derek's response—or lack of one. His military training had probably been similar to her own, so he likely knew all the tricks. This man's first attempt seemed to be feigning friendship, but she wasn't fooled by his suddenly sociable demeanor, and they'd already seen his true personality come out once. She glanced at Kevin, knowing that with him in the mix, it would ultimately be impossible to keep secrets, regardless of what method Mountain Man used. She would do anything to protect the boy—anything—and any decent interrogator would know that. Still, if there was any way to drag this out, it might allow that much more time for planning and executing an escape attempt.

"So let's start with introductions," Mountain Man said. "You can call me Sam." He glanced at Derek. "According to the registration from the downed whirlybird, you're Derek King."

"Guilty," Derek said through gritted teeth. "No how about you let me take these nice people home? They've already been through more than they bargained for."

"Well, that's not going to happen," Sam said as he made a clicking sound with his tongue.

He motioned toward Flynn. "This your wife and kid?"

"Nope. I'm not married," Derek replied, his tone now taking on a bored, disinterested tone. "They're just customers, plain and simple."

Sam narrowed his eyes as if he didn't quite believe him, then turned to Flynn. "That true?"

Flynn instantly understood Derek's strategy. "Of course. Why would he lie? We hired Mr. King to give us a sightseeing tour. You probably even found my expensive camera by the helicopter. It was too heavy for me to carry, but maybe you can give it back to me now?" She prayed they didn't know anything about photography and hadn't noticed the missing SD card. She rambled on, trying to bolster her story. "I hope the cold weather didn't damage it. I'm visiting from Florida, and the mountains here are beautiful and very different from what I'm used to. Y'all don't have a beach in sight." If she distanced herself from Derek in this man's eyes, hopefully he wouldn't use them as leverage to get Derek to comply with whatever he had planned. She wanted to do the same with Kevin so he also had a chance to survive, but it was harder to explain the child's presence. She hoped she could just avoid describing their relationship, but realized the attempt would probably be futile.

"Really? So, you're telling me you're just a tourist?" Sam leaned over and brushed his hand suggestively over Flynn's cheek. She forced herself not to react but saw Derek tense out of the corner of her eye. She didn't think she was in any real danger of being molested. The man was just trying to get a rise out of her or Derek to test the veracity of their words.

"Why don't you just tell us what you want?" Flynn said quickly, trying to keep the man's attention on herself instead of on Derek. "We don't even know why you shot us down in the first place. Are you and your men in the habit of shooting tourists out of the sky?"

"I don't believe that tourist story for a minute," Sam said as he leaned back, his smile once again disappearing. He furrowed his brow, and his features hardened. "I want to know who you are and why you're up here on this mountain." He locked eyes with Flynn. "And unless I like your answers, I'm going to kill this boy slowly and painfully right here in front of you."

Chapter Fourteen

Flynn watched Sam carefully. His eyes were dark, and there was a coldness there that had quickly erased any hint of friendliness. She heard Kevin whimper, but she kept her attention on the evil man in front of her. They'd gotten to the threats faster than she'd thought, but obviously, this guy wasn't playing games.

"Okay, fine. The boy has nothing to do with this, and neither does the pilot, so leave them out of it. In fact, you should let them both go right now so the two of us can settle this. I'm the one you want. My name is Flynn Denning, and you or someone in your organization shot my sister a few days ago in Frisco. I'm here to find out why."

Sam digested her words, then nodded. "So, you're that cop's sister."

"That cop has a name. It is Erin. Erin Denning. And she's still in the hospital, fighting for her life, because of you or someone here on your payroll."

He shrugged. "Now we're getting somewhere." He glanced from Derek to Kevin. "But no one is leaving here today, whether they're related to that cop or not."

"Then there's no reason why you shouldn't tell me why Erin was shot. She's my only sibling. Her life matters, and somebody tried to take that away from her. If you're going to kill me anyway, you might as well satisfy my curiosity." She tilted her head. "And I'm very curious." She felt Derek tense again at the challenge in her words but couldn't regret her tone. This man seemed proud of his crimes and his voice and body language were begging for an audience. He wanted others to think he was smart and organized.

The man laughed outright. "You have a point." He ran his fingers over her pistol, which was still in his grip but pointed away from their group, as if he was considering his words. He didn't speak, though, so Flynn prompted him.

"Bear Creek Vacation Rentals is a front, right?" Flynn said, pushing the envelope. She heard Derek make a noise, but didn't back down. "You're just using that company to launder the money you make selling meth up and down the Rockies. Am I right?" She narrowed her eyes. "My sister found out about your business and started investigating, so you had her shot to get her out of the way. You hoped that if you killed her before she got any farther, then the investigation would die with her."

Sam drew his lips into a thin, unrepentant line. "You are remarkably well informed." Suddenly, he stood and motioned to Blue Coat. "Stay here and keep an eye on them. I'll be back." He pocketed the camera and one of the pistols, then handed the other pistol to Blue Coat as he left the room and closed the door firmly behind him. Blue Coat zipped the pistol into his coat pocket, then moved over by the door and took up a sentry pose, his rifle on his back and his arms crossed.

Derek looked over at Flynn and lowered his voice for her ears only. "Well, you were right. At least now we know why your sister was hurt. I don't even think that they care that we saw the murders, although that's one more strike against us. We know about the drugs, we know they shot Erin and we saw them murder Lee Clark. To their way of thinking, they have to get rid of us."

"Something tells me they're in a hurry to

do so, too. What did that one guy say back at Lee's house? That something else big was happening today?"

Blue Coat stood up straighter by the door. "Shut up, the two of you."

They complied, but Flynn's mind was turning. There was no sign of the murdered drug dealers outside, but that wasn't the only change. The buildings and surrounding area had been spiffed up since they'd seen the bodies two days ago. Why were they cleaning up?

She rapidly considered several possibilities but discarded them all. Before she could dig even further, there was a noise at the door, and Blue Coat moved aside as another man came in. He was tall, broad shouldered and wearing a very expensive-looking gray woolen double-breasted suit with a burgundy power tie and a black topcoat. His designer leather shoes had to be custom-made, and his black leather gloves appeared luxurious and sleek, completing the ensemble. Once he entered, he pulled off his gloves and then smoothed down his windblown hair with manicured fingers. He was obviously wealthy and very concerned about his appearance, even in this drafty, dilapidated structure out in the middle of the wilderness.

"So, you've destroyed my helicopter." The man's voice was calm, yet almost teasing.

Derek shook his head. "No, *you* destroyed *my* helicopter. I think I'm entitled to a refund. You sold it to me and then had your men shoot me out of the sky. That wasn't part of our deal."

The suited man shrugged as Flynn's eyes flew back and forth between the two men. Suddenly, the pieces clicked together as Flynn listened to the conversation. Adam Cary stood before them—the man who had sold Derek his company. He was also the owner and CEO of Bear Creek Vacation Rentals.

Adam took the empty seat across from the three captives and took a moment to look each one up and down. He was totally unaffected by the fact that they were taped securely to the chairs or that one of the three was indeed a child. Despite his friendly demeanor, under the surface, there was a calculating coldness to his persona, and the air suddenly felt thick and malevolent. "You should have stayed in your lane, Derek," he finally said, turning his attention back to the pilot. "There was no reason to come flying up this high. We picked this location for a reason. I simply can't afford to have you know about us and what we're doing up here. You understand, right?"

"I understand that you're nothing but a drug dealer, dressed up in a fancy suit." Flynn bit out the words. "And you had someone try to kill my sister."

Adam slowly turned his head toward Flynn and appraised her flippantly with his eyes, as if she had no value and was beneath his notice. "Ah yes, Erin Denning. I'm afraid she stuck her nose where it didn't belong."

"So, you tried to murder her? Is that how you treat anyone that crosses you?"

Adam shrugged. "It's the cost of doing business. A few pawns have to be sacrificed for the good of the organization. Collateral damage is unavoidable."

"Lee Clark was a pawn. He was on your team and he got in your way, so your man killed him. But Erin is a detective. She wasn't one of your game pieces that you can just dismiss and take off the board. She plays for the other team. She's going to get better, and then she's going to arrest you and shut you down. This is the beginning of the end for you. I hope you like wearing the color orange, Mr. Cary. I hear it's all the rage in prisons these days."

Adam laughed. "Quite a feisty friend you have here, Derek," he said with a smile.

Cary's reaction made it clear he didn't think much of her threat, but Flynn just couldn't keep her mouth shut. She had finally found the man responsible for trying to kill her sister. Her enemy now had a face and a name. Anger and disgust bubbled inside her, and she wanted nothing more than to slap the handcuffs on his manicured hands and drag him to jail. She pulled at her bonds in frustration, but the tape held fast. "I might not be able to stop you, but my sister will. You've failed. You're going to be sorry you ever set up shop in Colorado."

Adam's face contorted and became a mask of prideful maliciousness right in front of them. He stood and fisted his hands, as if he was about to strike. "No one is going to stop me. I'm the most powerful man in the valley, and I'm about to become the most powerful man in the state—maybe even the whole Southwest region."

"And how do you plan on becoming that?" Flynn sneered.

"I'm about to make a deal with a new distributor, and his network doubles what I already own." He leaned closer, his lip curled. "You think one small-town cop is going to change that? Or the three of you?"

"So how did Erin discover your involvement?" Derek asked, apparently trying to divert Adam's anger from Flynn before he struck her or did something worse.

Cary paused a moment, leaned back and glanced back at Derek. His mask of indifference slowly returned. "She came across my stash house in Frisco—and got some of my dealers to talk more than they should have about my mountain lab and our distribution process. I believe you discovered what I do to people who defy me. You saw their bodies, or what was left of them, after I found out about their treachery." He lifted his chin and brushed a fleck of dirt off his coat. "I don't believe in second chances—for anyone. You've all seen too much, which is a pity. I just came by to tell you that you're going to die today. And then I'm going to sit down, have a good meal, and I'm going to kill your sister, too."

His words made the blood in Flynn's veins turn to ice. Apparently, this man killed anyone he perceived as a threat. She watched him go, and Blue Coat followed him out and closed the door behind them, leaving them alone for the first time since they'd arrived. She could hear the two men talking outside the door but could only make out some of the words.

"...in about an hour or so. Just stay here and watch them, then take them...up in the helicopter...dump their bodies..."

Kevin started crying, and Flynn turned to him. "Don't worry, Kevin. We're going to get out of here, and we're going to save your mom."

"How?" he said through the tears. "That man is a monster! He's the one that hurt my mom, and he said he's going to kill her." He swallowed hard, obviously trying to gain control of his rolling emotions. "How can we stop him?"

"Pray," Derek said softly. "We all need to start by praying." He bowed his head. "Lord, we are stuck, and this situation looks really scary, but You are a big God, and nothing is too hard for You. Please show us a way out of this mess and make us strong so we can do whatever it takes to escape and save Kevin's mom. Amen." He leaned forward and kept his voice low. "Okay, in the army, we actually used to play around with how to get free from duct tape, and it's not as hard as it looks." He gave Kevin a wink to bolster his confidence. "So here goes. Just watch what I do. You're actually re-creating the angle where duct tape normally tears. Step one—bring your arms in as hard and fast as you can, as if you're trying to hit yourself in the chest. Got it? Ready? Go!"

Both Flynn and Kevin looked at him dubiously, but he demonstrated, and in one quick motion, the tape tore as he pulled hard against the bonds around his arms. They glanced at each other, then shrugged and copied Derek's actions. A few moments later, they successfully freed their arms as well.

Even though his hands were free, Derek's chest was still taped to the back of the chair. "Okay, now we move to step two. We could try to use our hands to pull off all this tape, but that takes too long. Instead, you have to lean forward really quickly, as if you're going to throw up on the floor between your legs. Ready? Go!" He demonstrated again, and the duct tape that held his chest tore with a satisfying rip. He quickly pulled the tape away, then reached down and freed his feet.

Flynn followed Derek's example and was also able to get her chest free, but Kevin didn't manage it since he was so upset and didn't quite understand how to make the tape tear. Flynn quickly freed her legs and then reached over, freed Kevin and pulled him into a giant bear hug. Derek hid behind the door, waiting for Blue Coat to come back in.

He didn't have to wait long. Blue Coat opened the door only a few minutes later, and his face immediately mirrored his surprise when he noticed the prisoners were all free. He tried to shout, but Derek was quick to pull him into the room, shut the door firmly before anyone could be alerted to what was happening and grab his rifle from him at the same time.

Blue Coat started to fumble with his pocket but wasn't able to pull out anything before Derek gave him a quick punch to the cheek, which sent him reeling backward against the table, unconscious. Flynn grabbed Blue Coat and moved his body to the floor, and once he was down, Derek handed her the man's rifle, then bent down and frisked him and found his pistol in the man's coat. He took the handgun and secured it in his own jacket pocket but didn't find anything else of value. Then he motioned to Kevin. He wanted to make sure the boy had a role in their escape, and this was the perfect way to include him.

"Help me duct-tape him, okay, Kevin?"

Derek said softly. The boy nodded and brought him the remains of the roll of tape, and with Kevin's help, the two secured the man so he couldn't stop their escape.

"Won't he be able to escape like we just did?" Flynn asked as she guarded the door.

"No, we had the advantage of having our hands in front of us, and the angle of the chairs where we were sitting made it easy to tear the tape. This guy is going to be taped with his hands behind him and with his mouth covered. We'll also leave him on the floor. He'll be trussed up just like a Christmas turkey and won't be able to get free—at least not right away. He might eventually manage to escape, but hopefully by that time we'll already be down the mountain."

Derek finished taping up their captor, then leaned Blue Coat's body against the back wall so he was out of the way. Then he joined Flynn, who had swung the rifle onto her back and was quickly going through the boxes on the shelves. "Find anything interesting?"

"Not so far," she replied as she pulled out yet another box and examined the contents. "No weapons or anything else that would help us get out of here." She put that box back and pulled out another. "I don't even really know what I'm looking for. Just something—anything—that will help." She closed up another box and slid it back on the shelf. "I wish we had a way to communicate with the folks down in Frisco so we could warn them and get them to put a guard on Erin before the cartel gets someone down there."

Derek ran his hand through his hair. "Yeah, me, too. I guess the only thing we can hope for is that Adam was telling us the truth—he wants to kill Erin himself, and he's in no hurry to go to Frisco and commit the crime. If that's the case, we might have a fighting chance of beating him to the hospital."

"How?" Kevin asked with renewed hope in his voice. "How can we beat him?"

Chapter Fifteen

Flynn felt in her boot, once again verifying that the SD card with the photos of the murdered victims was still safely hidden away. She had seen with her own eyes how the crime scenes had been cleaned up, and by now, any evidence of those heinous acts was probably tainted or destroyed completely. Lee Clark's house had probably also been sanitized, with no evidence of murder left behind. Adam Cary was obviously a very wealthy and powerful man. Flynn was sure he would be a difficult adversary in any venue, but especially in court, where he could afford to hire the best and brightest legal minds to defend him. The photos might not even be enough to do the job of convicting him, but hopefully, with the photos and their own eyewitness testimony, it would be enough. Regardless, they had to try. With renewed energy, she vowed not only to survive and save her sister, but to also see Cary punished for selling poison throughout the state of Colorado.

Unfortunately, they were still stuck in a very remote area, once again without transportation, and in a very snowy and frigidly cold environment. They'd already spent two days trying to get down the mountain and were now back where they'd started, and this time they had no food and were already exhausted from the past two days' exertion. How could they ever make it to the hospital in time to save Erin? "Well, we don't have time to walk down this mountain, and flying seems out of the question. Maybe we can find a car or truck out there somewhere?" She met Derek's eyes. "Do you have any idea how to hot-wire one if we can find one?"

Derek blew out a breath and shrugged his shoulders. "Maybe. If it's an older model. These newer cars and trucks are really hard to start without keys. Most modern cars have ignition immobilizers that make hot-wiring them almost impossible."

"I'm not even sure I saw any cars or trucks out there anyway. It seems like most of them fly in and out..." She snapped her fingers as an idea hit her. "Or use the snowmobiles."

Derek smiled, obviously following her line

of thought. "Now those, I might actually be able to hot-wire. They're not nearly as complicated as the new cars out on the road." He moved over to the shelves again and quickly sifted through the boxes, this time pulling out some small hand tools and wires and pocketing them.

"I saw a lot of tarps covering something under the pole barn. Maybe we should start by looking there." She glanced around. "I don't see any cameras in here. Hopefully, there aren't any covering the pole barn, either. Even if there aren't any, though, we need to stay out of sight and hurry to beat Cary to the hospital."

"Agreed," Derek said with a nod. "Even if there aren't any cameras, motion will usually catch someone's eye if they happen to be looking in our direction, so stay down and move slowly so we don't attract attention."

"Sounds like a plan," Flynn said softly. She could tell Derek's words were mostly for Kevin, and she really liked how Derek was including him as an important member of the group. She turned to her nephew, who had calmed down considerably and actually had a look of hope in his eyes. "You can do this, okay? We're going to do everything we can to escape and get down this mountain so we can save your mom. Are you ready?"

He put on a fierce expression. "I'm ready, Aunt Flynn."

"Great! Let's do this!" She spoke quietly but with encouragement and got a nod from the boy in return.

They quietly sneaked out the door, staying low and quiet as they went from tarp to tarp, surreptitiously lifting them up and checking underneath them for a snowmobile or other way to get down the mountain. The first few tarps covered barrels of chemicals, presumably the ingredients needed for manufacturing the methamphetamines in the main cabin. They were labeled, and Flynn made mental notes of the chemicals so she could include them in her report to law enforcement. Two other tarps covered split wood for the fireplace, and they passed two snowmobiles that looked like they were being worked on. The hoods were off both, and tools were strewn around the small workbench. They passed them both, but then hit pay dirt under a musty-smelling gray tarp near the back right corner of the barn. Two snowmobiles, one a red 2015 Yamaha Viper and the other an older 1997 blue Polaris Wedge snowmobile, were both clean and complete and seemed ready to go.

"I hope these are here because they're in working order," she said softly. "Let's hope Sam did a great job repairing them and they'll take us down the mountain without any hiccups."

Derek nodded as he did a quick inspection. They both looked like they were ridden regularly, but looks could be deceiving. Flynn said a quick prayer that they were both still functional.

Derek took off the cover of the red Yamaha and unscrewed the ignition button. Underneath there was a small white square with two large wires coming out. He hit the power switch and let out a sigh of relief as the lights came on, showing that the machine was indeed getting power. Then he pulled out a small length of wire about the size of a large paper clip and bent it into a U. Carefully, he put it in the small white box and touched it to the wire. The engine sputtered but then sprang to life.

He smiled to himself, then motioned for Flynn and Kevin to get on. Flynn slung the rifle onto her back and took the front of the seat, and Kevin quickly got on behind her, both with anxious faces but ready to go. Flynn made herself familiar with the dials and gauges on the snowmobile, then continually surveyed the surrounding area, making sure none of Cary's men were approaching.

Derek turned to the Polaris and did a quick inspection of the machine, then raised the hood. "Where is that key switch..." he muttered under his breath. "Ah, here it is." He unplugged it, then pulled the cord, and the motor sprang to life. He quickly moved the tarp out of the way and jumped on the seat, then revved the motor with his gloved hand. "Let's get out of here!"

Suddenly, they heard a shot, and the wood behind Derek's head splintered. Another shot quickly followed.

They quickly sped out from under the barn and headed south, away from the buildings and the shooters. Derek could just hear shouting above the noise of his engine, but he ignored it and focused on staying low on the machine and getting out of there as quickly but safely as possible. His front right ski hit some ice and puddled water, but he shifted his weight, turned with the skid and managed to stay in complete control of the powerful machine.

They moved quickly through the clearing

and around the helicopter pad, passing through the area where they'd first discovered the murder victims. Flynn was doing a great job of keeping up—instead of following him, she was driving just slightly back and to his left. That was smart of her, Derek acknowledged. Neither one of them had the proper headgear or goggles to keep the snow out of their faces, and by staying to his side, she avoided the snow spray and water that was flying up behind his snowmobile. He squinted and leaned lower, trying to use the small windshield to block some of the wind that was slapping him in the face. Thankfully, it wasn't snowing right now. The air was cold, but at least it wasn't also wet.

He chanced a look behind him and saw three snowmobiles beginning to pursue them. A few seconds later, he checked again and saw that two of them were still there, but the third had peeled off and was trying to take a shortcut through the trees to cut them off.

They went over a large bump, and Derek once again glanced over at Flynn and Kevin to see how she was managing to drive the unfamiliar machine. So far, they were both handling everything well, and a measure of relief swept over him. Kevin's small body had flown a few inches off the seat as they'd gone airborne for a second or two, but he still had a good grasp on Flynn's waist as they continued down the mountainside, and Flynn wore a look of grim determination that made him proud of her efforts as she piloted the machine.

A sudden realization made him gasp.

He was still in love her.

It hit him with such ferocity that he almost faltered driving his own snowmobile. He gave himself a mental shake and tried to stay focused, yet he couldn't stop the wave of warmth that swept over him as his admission took root. He loved Flynn Denning. Here. Now. He wanted to marry her and spend the rest of his life in her arms. He just had to survive long enough to tell her.

The white snowmobile pursuing them that had separated from the others suddenly broke through the trees and came up on Derek's left. Within moments, it came directly even with Derek's machine, and the driver was pushing it so close that the skis bumped. Derek kicked out at the pursuer two times, then a third, but the driver veered to avoid the blows, and he didn't manage to make contact. A group of trees was not too far ahead of them, and Derek was afraid he would be forced into the trees if he couldn't get the man to back off. Their skis bumped again, and he shifted and pushed at the driver with his hand, trying to force him to turn. The man fought back, and Derek's machine actually went up on one ski as he tried to avoid the pursuer's snowmobile and stay safely away from him, but the man's onslaught didn't stop and he rammed Derek's ride with even more viciousness.

Derek kicked out again and managed to hit the man this time, but still the man attacked, using his own snowmobile to ram Derek's. Derek grimaced at the copse of trees, only yards away now, and pulled hard on the handlebars, hoping he could avoid them at the very last minute without destroying his machine. He leaned low, then put everything he had into one final kick. His boot hit the other man's snowmobile near the front of the hood, and this time it was strong enough that the machine veered left and drove straight into the trees. The perpetrator saw his mistake but couldn't correct his trajectory fast enough, and his snowmobile plowed into the edge of tree line. A branch knocked the driver to the ground, while the snowmobile kept going forward for several yards before crashing into a different tree. Smoke immediately emitted from the hood of the damaged snowmobile, and a loud blast ensued. Derek chanced a look behind him and saw the man moving, albeit slowly, to a crouching position. He was glad he wasn't dead. He wasn't trying to kill anyone. He just wanted to get Flynn and Kevin to safety and save Erin's life too.

One down, two to go.

Derek's face felt like it was freezing, and ice particles were forming on his beard. He slowed enough to bring up his free hand to blow some warm breath on his face, then continued his trek with Flynn and Kevin close behind him. The other two snowmobiles were still back there, too, and gaining fast. Derek considered motioning for Flynn to split up, but he couldn't take a chance that they would follow her and not him, and he desperately wanted to protect her to the best of his ability.

One of their pursuers had a faster, more powerful snowmobile, and after a few more minutes, he was able to pull up alongside Flynn. He bumped her machine, and she cried out but kept control. Derek pulled up alongside him and bumped him from the other side, sandwiching the attacker between them. The trees whizzed by as their speed increased, and Derek leaned closer to the engine, then kicked out as their pursuer bumped Flynn again. Derek met Flynn's eye, and she motioned with her head. He wasn't sure he understood her message, but he hoped he did. She suddenly slowed her snowmobile considerably, and Derek and the drug dealer shot forward, leaving her behind. With one final kick, Derek reached out and made contact, and the other man's snowmobile veered hard to the right and ran right into the trunk of a large tree. An explosion ensued, and flames shot to the sky. The driver lay prone on the ground, away from the explosion but definitely down.

Flynn sped around the disaster and came up next to Derek again. The wind whipped at her hair and skin, but Derek was able to see a look of grim satisfaction on her face as they continued.

Only one pursuer left. This one was apparently not as well versed at driving the snowmobile, but he did start curving to the right in an effort to cut them off as they crested a hill. He probably could have matched or exceeded their speed, but he didn't try. Instead, he suddenly slowed, pulled out a pistol, aimed and fired a shot. The bullet went high, but the loud report shocked both Derek and Flynn, and they flinched at the sound and veered, trying to make harder targets of themselves.

Derek watched helplessly as the man slowed, then steadied himself and once again aimed his pistol at Flynn and Kevin...

Chapter Sixteen

With a swift flick of his wrist, Derek slowed his ride just enough, then fell back and jolted up beside Flynn and Kevin, effectively blocking them from the shooter's view and using his own body as a shield. The bullet sounded, and with a wave of relief, Derek heard and saw the side of his snowmobile's hood take the hit. The engine sputtered and died, but still he flinched, surprised but exhilarated that the bullet hadn't hit his body. He'd been prepared to give his life for theirs, but it appeared that God had other plans. His snowmobile went forward a few more feet, then stopped once the momentum had given way, leaving a dark trail of engine oil behind him in the snow. Derek quickly jumped off, using the snowmobile as a shield, and pulled out his own pistol. Although Flynn and Kevin were safe, at least for the moment, the man was still coming straight for them and was steadying himself for yet another round.

The shooter didn't get a chance.

Derek's first bullet caught him high in the shoulder, and the man lost his grip and the gun went flying. Derek's second shot rang out in quick procession, and a circle of red instantly began to spread across the man's chest as his snowmobile slowed, then stopped completely. The engine continued running, much like a lawn mower, but the driver slumped over, dead.

Derek pocketed his pistol, said a quick prayer of thanks, counted his remaining bullets and then stood and started walking over to the dead man's machine. He reached it at the same time that Flynn circled back and drove up next to him. She left the motor running, jumped off her snowmobile and flung herself into Derek's arms. Her inhibitions that he'd witnessed up until now seemed to have dissipated, and for several minutes, they just stayed like that, holding each other. He grasped her tightly, so thankful that she was still alive. Death had been knocking at her door, but he hadn't lost her. He reveled in her strength, which buoyed his own. For the first time since Jax's death in the Middle East, he felt whole and hopeful about the future. In fact, the love that pulsed through him was so overwhelming that he had no words, and he felt like he could hold her like this for hours, just relishing her closeness. He bent and kissed her, gently at first, then fuller when her hesitance started to wane and she actually kissed him back.

Finally, the kiss broke. "I can't believe you did that," Flynn exclaimed, her cheeks flushed. "You put yourself right in the line of fire! You saved our lives—again." She reached up, and her gloved hand cupped his bearded chin, brushing away some of the ice and snow that had accumulated there as they'd driven across the snowy tundra. Their breath mingled in puffs of moist air in the cold, crisp weather. "Thank you!"

Before she spoke, he wasn't even sure that she had seen or understood what he had done, but her tone was fierce as she locked eyes with him. She knew. He saw admiration, thankfulness and a whole host of other emotions there that he was afraid to name or even speculate about. Could she still have any feelings at all for him? A part of him wanted to hope—that maybe, just maybe, she did, and if they ever survived this mess, they could fan that flame into a conflagration. She had kissed him back, hadn't she? She had been hesitant at first, but then fire had erupted between them. But what if he was wrong? What if she was just grateful for his sacrifice?

Or what if he was right?

He hadn't dared hope, but if a relationship was a possibility, was he ready for that? He was suddenly swamped with feelings and emotions that surprised him, and even though they were uncomfortable at first, he felt alive and vibrant for the first time in years. She motioned to Kevin to join them, and a moment later, all three of them were huddled together, hugging each other like a tight little family. It didn't bother Derek one little bit. In fact, he gloried in the contact. He pushed all other thoughts aside, including his worry, hope and speculation about the future. For now, he just enjoyed the moment. They were all still alive, and they had a mode of transportation to help get them down the mountain.

Okay, well, he couldn't *completely* push all the other feelings aside. "I would do anything for you," he whispered for her ears alone. "I hope you know that."

She smiled at him. Her eyes were luminous.

Was that love shining back at him in those blue depths?

Her expression melted his heart and removed another brick of the prison he had made for himself after Jax's death.

He finally broke the hug, then moved over to the man he had shot. He took off his glove, then reached the man's neck and verified that he was indeed dead. There was no pulse. He pulled his body off the still running snowmobile and laid him under a nearby tree. There wasn't time to bury him. They were still in a race to save Erin, and any moment their adversary could appear and start shooting at them. They had to get back to civilization as soon as possible.

He checked the newly acquired snowmobile's gas gauge and was pleasantly surprised to see that the machine had nearly a full tank and was slightly larger than the model he had been driving. Getting shot at and having to kill a man were horrible ways to acquire a new machine, but at least with the upgrade, they had a fighting chance of making it down the mountain, as long as they didn't encounter any other obstacles.

Just as the thought entered his mind, he heard

the familiar sound of rotor blades in the background. As he turned and watched, the Bear Creek helicopter rose ominously above the skyline.

It was headed straight for them.

They weren't safe yet after all.

Flynn heard the noise but didn't recognize it as quickly as Derek. She watched his head snap toward the sound and then saw the worry reflected in his face as the helicopter appeared. It wasn't a military-grade helicopter armed with rocket launchers, but she could easily make out the shapes of two gunmen, one on each side, who each held a high-powered rifle in his hands.

She motioned for Kevin to join her and jumped back on her snowmobile. Kevin scrambled aboard, and they followed Derek, who had commandeered the dead man's machine and was waving for her to head toward the trees. The forest would slow them down, but it would also slow down the helicopter and give them some much-needed cover. Fear and adrenaline pumped through her veins as she pushed the snowmobile's engine as fast as it could go toward the safety zone.

She made it to the tree line, then followed Derek as he made a hard left down and around a group of aspens. The snowmobile sank quite a bit in the powdery snow but finally gained purchase and surged forward. She felt Kevin shift behind her, but to his credit, he managed to stay on with a tight grip on her waist. She was suddenly grateful for the times she had driven a motorcycle back in college. It had only been a small Honda 250, but it had been quite a lot of fun and gave her at least a basic idea of how to drive the snow machine. Thankfully, she didn't need to shift gears, but the throttle and brakes worked much like her old Honda, and if they didn't have gunmen chasing them and taking shots at them through the canopy of leaves and needles, she would probably be really enjoying the ride.

They continued down through the trees. At one point, Derek had to get off his machine and walk beside it, still directing the big snowmobile by using the grips, throttle and brakes as he pushed it through the deep, powdery mounds of snow. The motor strained and protested, but his actions left a clear path for her to follow. Snow and ice stuck to his black cargo pants and covered him from the chest down, but he got back

on the snowmobile and continued, occasionally looking up as he went, making sure that
the trees were still providing the cover they
needed from the gunmen in the helicopter. He
slowed their speed and ducked under branches,
and she followed suit, using her legs as well to
steady her own Yamaha as it struggled through
the snow. Finally, they made it through the
thicker areas, and with a little more gas, they
were finally able to reach an area where the
snow wasn't quite as deep.

They were able to pick up the speed a little
but still were forced to stay under the trees. The
helicopter's rotors sounded relentlessly above
them. They crested a hill, and Derek's snowmobile suddenly went airborne for a few seconds as he drove over a small ledge. He landed
without incident and continued, but Flynn took
some extra time to go around the ledge instead
of over it. Kevin was doing a good job of holding on, but she didn't want to take any more
chances than she had to. She caught up to Derek
again but continued to drive several feet behind
him to stay out of the snow cloud he was kicking up. Her cheeks and lips already felt frozen,
and she didn't want to get plastered with any
more of the ice or powder that were filling the

air. At one point, his snowmobile went up another mound, and he released it so it wouldn't fall backward on him, but it continued running and landed at a good angle, and he jumped back on and bolted forward.

A shot rang out and Flynn recoiled, but neither she, Kevin nor Derek were hit. The gunmen fired some more, but the shots seemed random, meant to scare them since they were well hidden from the helicopter. They could still hear the rotors and got glimpses of the helicopter through the tree branches, but Flynn doubted they could be seen, even through binoculars, in their current location.

Derek slowed as they entered another section of the woods that had a lot of underbrush, and he stood on the running boards, trying to get a better view of where he was going as he drove.

Another shot rang out, but this time, it hit a tree only a few feet away from Flynn, and she cried out involuntarily as the wood splintered in a cloud. Apparently, they were no longer as hidden as they had been only a few minutes before. Were they going to escape from this newest threat? Her muscles tightened as her eyes met Derek's. Then she cried out as the next shot hit Derek with such force that it threw him off his snowmobile and into a large mound of snow.

Chapter Seventeen

"No!" Flynn cried out as anguish filled her. "Derek!" She stopped her snowmobile and left it running under some trees but jumped off and rushed over to Derek's side. Another shot rang out that hit an aspen near them, and she screamed in frustration. She couldn't lose him now. There was a look of anguish on his face, and he was breathing hard, but he was still alive. He was lying in the snow, caked with the powder. But now, a bright red splash of blood covered his left shoulder. Hundreds of memories, fears and thoughts flitted through Flynn's mind as she considered the ramifications of his wound.

She couldn't play the what-if game. She had to move Derek, now, and do what she could to save his life. "Can you help me get you out of the line of fire?" she said tightly as Kevin appeared by her right arm, his expression also one of worry and fear. "I don't think I can lift you by myself."

"I'll try," Derek said as he held his left arm as tightly as possible against his body. He'd obviously lost the ability to do much with that arm and was trying to immobilize it the best he could to ease the pain that had to be racing clear to his fingertips. He was such a big man that Flynn was sure they wouldn't have been able to move him if he hadn't helped, but between the three of them, they were able to get him back behind the trees. A large outcrop of rocks about the size of a set of bunk beds also provided some additional cover, and they huddled behind it, trying to keep the rocks between them and the gunmen. Flynn and Kevin moved Derek as carefully as possible until he was propped up in a sitting position against the rocks. She pulled off the rifle she had been carrying and handed it to Kevin, then she gently peeled back Derek's jacket to look at the wound, hoping that she was also staying beyond the snipers' line of sight.

"It's a serious injury—they must be using a .223 rifle," she muttered under her breath. He cried out as she moved him a little to see his back, and she winced in response. "I'm so sorry! I don't mean to hurt you, but I have to see what we're dealing with." She pulled back the coat a bit more, being as mindful as possible of her movements and how they were affecting Derek's pain level. "Looks like the bullet went straight through." She pulled off her jacket and gloves, removed her flannel shirt, and then put her coat back on before pulling tightly on the fabric so she could rip it into pieces to help stop the bleeding.

Derek shook his head. When he spoke his voice was raspy and laced with pain. "Stop. You need that shirt to keep warm."

"And you need it to live. I'll be okay."

Derek swallowed hard, evidently trying to keep the agony under control. "Okay, but first, take my pistol."

She felt his coat pocket, unzipped it and pulled out the gun.

"Are you a good shot?" he asked. "We only have a few bullets left."

She smiled, hoping to reassure him.

"I ranked sharpshooter the last time I qualified."

"That'll do." Derek nodded. "Use the rifle if you can, but if you run out of bullets, use the pistol. Aim at the helicopter when it gets close enough, and fire at the tail rotor. That will knock them out of the sky. Then we need to get out of here as fast as we can in case any of them survive the landing."

The rotors of the helicopter sounded even louder, and suddenly more shots hit the rocks and ricocheted away from them, while another barrage decimated the tree branches near their hiding place. Then another bullet hit the snowmobile that Flynn and Kevin had been riding moments before. The engine stopped, and suddenly the pungent smell of gasoline filled the air. A moment later, flames shot out of the sides behind the hood, and with a loud crack, the entire machine exploded. A wave of heat hit the three of them, despite the rocks, and knocked both Flynn and Kevin off their feet and into the snow. Bits of engine and other parts flew through the air and landed in all directions, some still on fire as they flew through the sky.

"Flynn! Kevin!"

Derek's voice rang out, but Flynn barely heard it over the roaring in her ears. Still, somewhere in her brain, it registered that they had just lost one of their rides, and they desperately needed to secure the other one if they were going to beat Cary in this race down the mountain to save her sister. She pulled herself up to a sitting position, trying to get her bearings. Kevin moved slightly at her side, and she touched his arm, then met his eyes to make sure he was okay. He nodded at her wordlessly, then started crawling over to Derek's side. Once she knew he was safe, she grabbed the gun she had dropped, as well as the rifle Kevin had been holding, and pulled herself up to her feet and leaned heavily on a tree. There was a bit of dizziness, but it gradually subsided, and sounds from the helicopter seemed to drown out everything else in her head.

She had to stop that helicopter.

She steeled her spine and, using the trees for cover, moved away from the rocks so she could get a clear shot. The shooters noticed she had moved, and moments later, the helicopter was clearly visible as it followed her. It was a fair distance away from her, but she said a silent prayer, hoping that the bird was still within the range of her rifle and her shooting skills hadn't been adversely affected by the explosion and the ringing in her ears.

Dear God, please let my bullets hit the right spot.

She closed her eyes for a moment as she held the weapon, gathering her strength. Then she quickly peeked around the tree trunk, raised the rifle and fired three quick shots at the tail rotor. Answering fire forced her back behind the tree again as her bullets hit metal, but then she heard sputtering noises from the helicopter, and it jerked and tilted strangely, then started spinning in midair. A minute or two later, the helicopter smashed into a stand of trees, and another loud explosion sounded as the entire machine burst into flames. Fire licked at the larger pieces of metal, and a heavy cloud of black smoke filled the air above the crash site.

Thank You, Lord.

She couldn't imagine anyone had lived after that conflagration, but she didn't stick around to find out. Her head was still pounding, but she was gaining more control over the dizziness. She made her way back over to the outcrop of rocks where Kevin and Derek were huddled together.

"Did you get them, Aunt Flynn?"

"I did," Flynn confirmed as she handed him the rifle. "They won't be bothering us anymore, but they could be sending reinforcements. We need to move on as soon as we can. Can you hold on to this?"

Kevin took the rifle again, his expression solemn yet determined. "Yes, I can. Mom taught me how to be careful around guns."

"Excellent," she replied with a nod. She could still hear the faint puttering of Derek's snow-mobile in the background, along with crackling sounds from the fire at the helicopter's crash site. She was thankful that her hearing was returning to normal, albeit slowly.

She stored Derek's pistol in her own coat pocket, then picked up her shirt that she had dropped earlier and tore it into several strips. Her rush of adrenaline made her stronger than normal, and the fabric tore easily under her fingers. When she was finished, she balled up two sections of cloth and put them on the entrance and exit wounds, using the folds as makeshift bandages. Then she wrapped more strips as tightly as she dared around his torso and neck so the bandages would be held in place and the bleeding would slow. Finally, she used the last of the fabric to create a sling of sorts to hold his left arm. She could feel the cold starting to penetrate her coat, since she only had on a T-shirt underneath, but the sacrifice was worth it. Derek had saved her life over and over again during the last few days. Bandaging him up after he had taken a bullet on her behalf was the least she could do.

She leaned back on her heels and remembered the words he had spoken softly in her ear, right after he had used his own body to protect her and her nephew from the gunmen. *I would do anything for you...*

What did that mean, exactly?

Did he have feelings for her again? Were they growing inside him like they were in her? She had to admit, she was falling in love with him all over again, and that kiss they'd shared had been something special. She hadn't been looking for love. In fact, she had been dead set against it, ready to push it away with both hands if someone even tried to offer her their heart.

But this was Derek. She had never really stopped loving him. Sure, she had moved on with her life after he had joined the military and left her behind, but if she was being completely honest, she had to admit that her feelings were still very much engaged—especially now, when he was doing everything in his power to keep her and Kevin alive. Would her feelings change when they were back in civilization and Bear Creek Vacation Rentals was closed down for good? Would his? Would he walk away once life returned to normal? Would he break her heart all over again?

She didn't know the answer to that and was almost afraid to speculate. Hope could be a dangerous thing...and could end up crushing her if she misinterpreted his angst and protectiveness during a moment of danger as true love. A large part of her was truly tempted to throw herself into his arms and declare her love, but she would not. If this relationship had any hope of surviving once they got back to Frisco, then Derek would have to make the first move. He would have to share his feelings first.

Enough guessing.

They needed to move. She stopped ruminating, and she and Kevin helped Derek get to his feet then head back over to his snowmobile. She pulled it back from the tree trunk where it had gently landed, then pointed it where they needed to go and got on board. Derek got behind her, and Kevin sandwiched himself in between them, being extra careful not to jostle Derek's arm as he did so, securing the rifle across his lap.

Flynn was worried about how the bumps they were sure to hit would affect Derek's injuries, but they had no choice at all. They had to get down the mountain, and the snowmobile was the only mode of transportation available if they wanted to get to the hospital before Adam Cary. Still, she resolved to drive a bit slower than they had been moving before and be extra careful about both of her passengers. She pulled on her gloves, then revved the engine and started back into the snow, her heart hopeful for the first time in days.

Derek gripped the seat the best he could with his knees, his one good arm still holding tightly to Flynn as she drove. The pain in his shoulder was still very intense, and he was a bit lightheaded from losing so much blood. He let his mind wander as Flynn drove, trying not to focus on his injury, but instead on the job ahead of them. Had Adam Cary already reached the hospital ahead of them? Was Erin Denning already dead? He thought of Kevin, who was snugly between them and probably warmer than he had been since their original crash. The boy already didn't have a father in his life. How would he survive the lost of his one remaining parent? He was just entering the formative years, when he really needed the guidance and help of a father figure in his life.

If Erin was dead, Flynn would need support, too. Yet she didn't even live in Colorado. How could he help her if she returned home right away? He pulled her a tad closer with his good arm and felt a wave of elation sweep over him, despite the circumstances. He had missed her more than he had realized, and now that she was back and he had finally acknowledged his true feelings, he couldn't imagine going back to the empty days he'd trudged through before she had walked out on that tarmac to his helicopter. The fierceness of his protective emotions surprised him, but he didn't dismiss them. Whether Erin was okay or not, he wanted Flynn in his life, and somehow, he was determined to make that happen once this horrible situation with Bear Creek was resolved. He didn't know what that looked like. They lived in different states and had gone down totally different paths. But that was okay. He didn't have to have all the answers right now. He was in love, and everything else was just details that could be figured out once Cary was behind bars.

They drove for a steady half an hour, sticking mostly to the tree line as best they could, just in case an adversary once again appeared. Eventually, they came out of the woods and saw a road up ahead. Pure jubilation soared through Flynn, and was so pronounced that Derek could actually feel it radiate from her, despite the cold. They didn't see any traffic on the road, but it had been recently plowed and the snow was packed and allowed for higher speeds than they'd been able to maintain before. Derek used his good hand to point in the direction they needed to go, and Flynn turned, following his lead. They continued on for several more minutes and finally reached the outskirts of town and some slow, lumbering traffic. They didn't have time to wait, and Flynn sped around the cars on the roadside when necessary, almost as if she was driving a motorcycle around them. Thankfully, the storm from the day before had dumped a heap of snow on the roads and shoulders and made maneuvering relatively easy. A few minutes later, the hospital was in sight. It was a three-story, southwestern-style building with large wooden beams that formed an impressive covered doorway and lobby for the main building, with an emergency room entrance on the side.

Flynn pulled up toward the side of the building, just as Derek noticed a large SUV that was parked near the covered entrance. His heart im-

mediately sank. On the door was a large adver-
tisement for Bear Creek Vacation Rentals, with
a huge logo and phone number.

And he could just make out Adam Cary entering the building through the main hospital doors.
He felt Flynn stiffen and was pretty sure she had
seen both the vehicle and Cary as well. Somehow, they had to stop that man before he could
wreak any more havoc on the Denning family.

Chapter Eighteen

Flynn jumped off the snowmobile and motioned to Kevin as she pulled off her gloves. "Stay with Derek," she ordered.

"Hold on..." Derek protested as he dismounted. He was a bit awkward with his motion since his arm was still in the makeshift sling, so she helped him briefly, then stepped back.

"I don't have time to argue with you," she responded forcefully. "I need to know that both of you are safe while I do this, and you need to go to the emergency room for that gunshot wound."

Kevin slowly got off the machine, his eyes darting back and forth between the two adults. He was still holding the rifle. "Do you want this?" he asked, his eyes big.

Flynn shook her head. "No, I have the pistol. You keep that with you and keep it safe."

The boy nodded solemnly, slung the rifle on

his shoulder and moved toward Derek's side, where he grabbed ahold of Derek's jacket near the hem. "I'll take good care of him, Aunt Flynn."

"You need my help," Derek protested. He took a step in her direction, but Kevin pulled him back and Flynn held up her hands in a motion to stop him.

"Please, do what I'm asking," she said softly. She quickly pulled off her gloves and tossed them aside, then gently caressed Derek's cheek. His skin was pale from blood loss and pain, and she hated to rush off and leave him behind, but she had no choice. She had to stop Adam Cary, and she also had to make sure Kevin was protected. "Please. You're injured. Stay with Kevin and keep him safe. You're the only one I can trust. And while you're at it, get some medical help for that shoulder." She dropped her hand and took a step back toward the front hospital door, then turned and ran, unzipping her pocket as she went so she would have easy access to the pistol.

She could feel Derek's eyes on her and knew he wasn't happy about being left behind, but it had to be done. Derek and Kevin were the two most important men in her life right now, and she needed them both out of harm's way while she confronted Adam Cary.

She quickly made it to the front entrance and passed the lobby kiosk, her eyes surveying the room, looking for any signs of Cary or his minions. She saw neither and ignored the stares and questions from the staff at the help desk. Finally, the lit sign for the stairwell caught her eye, and she ran to the entryway and rushed up the steps. The last time she had visited Erin, her sister had been on the third floor in the ICU department. Adam Cary had undoubtedly taken the elevator. She didn't have a moment to lose.

Her breath caught in her chest as she reached the top floor. She pulled her pistol, verified the safety was off and a bullet was in the chamber, and pointed the weapon toward the floor. She took a moment to get her bearings, then rushed to the nurses' station. She didn't see Cary, or anyone moving around in the halls, for that matter, but he had to be close. There was a nurse leaning over a computer keyboard at the desk, and she quickly tried to get her attention. "I'm here to see Erin Denning. She's in danger..."

Something wasn't right. The nurse was actually lying on the keyboard and wasn't moving.

Flynn reached over the counter, touched her shoulder and tried to shake her, and in response, the woman's body leaned to the left and then slowly fell out of the chair. Blood covered the front of her scrubs where a bullet had recently ended her life, and a pool of blood had formed on and under the keyboard and was dripping silently onto the floor. The poor woman's face still showed her surprise.

Panic swamped over Flynn. Assuming a law enforcement stance, she continued to point her pistol at the floor and moved as quietly as possible toward the room where her sister had been the last time she visited. Was Erin already dead?

Dread and fear tightened a knot in her stomach as she cautiously approached the room. She inched past the door and peeked quickly through the glass wall that separated the room from the hallway.

There was no one in the bed. In fact, the bare mattress was sitting on the bedframe without sheets or pillows, as if the room had been unoccupied for some time. There were no machines, no tubes or monitors, and no notes on the dry-erase board that previously listed the patient's name, medical condition and when she had last received her medication.

A dread she hadn't prepared for physically made her stomach twist even tighter, and the pain hurt so badly that she almost sank to the floor. Grief and heartache melted together and nearly incapacitated her. Had Erin died while they'd been fighting their way down the mountain today, or had it been while they'd been sleeping in the snow cave? Had she been alone at the final hour, or had someone been with her to hold her hand? Regret mixed in with the other emotions and began to take precedence. Flynn had never had a chance to say goodbye or tell her sister how much she loved her. Now, she would never get that chance. She couldn't believe her sister had died, and yet the bed was definitely empty, and her sister's body was nowhere around.

A scream behind her surprised her, and she turned quickly and aimed at the newcomer, her hands amazingly steady despite the sentiments running rampant in her body.

A young female health-care assistant carrying a stack of clean sheets and towels had just come across the dead woman at the nurses' station, and her shrieks grew louder as Flynn approached. When she saw the gun in Flynn's hand, she dropped the linens and took several steps back, obviously terrified and thinking Flynn was the shooter. She held up her hands in a motion of surrender. "Don't kill me, too! Please!"

"I didn't shoot her," Flynn said, keeping her tone as calm as possible. She lowered the weapon. "But I'm a cop and I'm looking for the man who did. He's tall, has dark hair and eyes, and is wearing a black overcoat. Have you seen him? I'm pretty sure he was just here."

The woman stopped whimpering but shook her head. She took another step back, as if she wasn't quite sure whether she should believe Flynn or not.

"He wants to hurt my sister, Erin Denning, who was in room 342 a couple of days ago. Do you know what happened to her?"

The orderly's breath was coming fast, but she pulled herself together and moved over to the desk behind the counter, trying her best not to look at the dead woman's body as she grabbed a clipboard off the wall. Flynn didn't have a badge to show her, but the orderly was either too scared to ask or unconcerned about her lack of credentials. Or maybe she remembered Flynn visiting Erin for several days and seeing her around the hospital. Regardless, Flynn was happy that the young woman was ready and willing to help her out, especially when every second mattered. "Erin Denning got better and they moved her to a different room." She flipped through a couple of pages. "Here she is—room 267."

"Thanks," Flynn said, already heading toward the stairs. She leaped down them two at a time and burst through the door onto the second floor, then eyed the directory and took the hallway to the right.

Chaos reigned. She slowed as she passed the nursing station and stopped completely as she took in the scene. Hospital personnel were huddled behind furniture and computer carts and peeking around at the showdown that was happening in the hallway.

About thirty feet away, Adam Cary was standing in the hallway. He was still dressed the same as he'd been up on the mountain with his fancy suit and topcoat, and he looked oddly out of place in the hospital, as if he'd just come from a board meeting or a face-to-face appointment with an attorney.

He also had Erin Denning by the neck and held a 9mm handgun with a silencer pressed against her temple. Erin was very much alive but still weak and pale. Despite her current circumstance, however, Erin's eyes locked with Flynn's, and Flynn could see her sister's fighting spirit was still very much alive and well.

Flynn's emotions were already near a breaking point, but when she saw the danger her sister was in, a new wave of both relief and fear swamped her as she quickly stepped to the left and took cover behind a cart holding several trays of food. Her sister was alive! Not only that, but she was conscious. Flynn's heart squeezed, and she felt her stomach twist even tighter, like she was on a roller coaster. She remembered quite vividly how her sister had been in a coma when she'd left the hospital a few days ago. Erin's eyes were vibrant now, but it was also painfully obvious that she was still very ill. She was definitely not well enough to be dragged out into the hall by a madman and was struggling to stand, yet she also didn't have much choice. Cary's grip was firm, and he had a ghost of a smile on his face, as if he was pleased with the control he wielded, despite the circumstances. Flynn had missed the drama that had preceded this event and wasn't exactly sure what all had happened, but in the grand scheme of things, all that really mattered was her sister's life.

"Mr. Cary, you don't need to hurt her," Flynn called out. "Just tell us what you want and we'll help you get out of here."

"Nice try," he replied, his voice all business as if he was discussing his company's quarterly earning reports. "This woman is my get-out-of-jail-free card."

Flynn was an excellent shot. She'd made a name for herself in her agency as one of the best sharpshooters ever seen in her department. But shooting at a target and shooting at a madman who was holding her only sister hostage were two entirely different things. She loved her sister with all her heart. What if she missed? What if Adam Cary moved at the last second and Erin became the target? What if she hit Erin by mistake? She looked at the pistol in her grip and noticed that her hands were shaking. It was impossible to be accurate with any weapon if she couldn't steady herself and carefully squeeze the trigger. This was her sister's life! How could she live with herself if she killed or injured her?

Yet how could she let this drug dealer drag Erin out of the hospital? If Adam Cary managed to get her out the door and into a vehicle of any kind, he would definitely kill her sister as soon as he no longer needed her. Also, if

Flynn didn't stop Cary here and now, the man would grow his drug enterprise and continue to leave a path of destruction in his wake as the poison he sold desecrated the lives of everyone around him. He had enough money to buy the best and brightest attorneys, who could probably even manage to somehow get him off for the poor murdered nurse whose body was still warm on the floor above them.

She locked eyes with her sister, whose expression was one of fear and trepidation, yet she could also see hope in those brown depths.

What should she do?

Derek couldn't handle letting Flynn confront Adam Cary by himself. Even injured and unsure if he could help or not, it just was not in him to stay behind. He had no clear plan in mind besides protecting Flynn and keeping her safe. That was his one and only goal. He left Kevin and the rifle with the security guard at the emergency room entrance with little explanation, but promised to return shortly and ran out to the front of the hospital and raced through the automatic glass doors. He headed straight to the stairwell, and just as he entered, he heard her coming back down the stairs in a rush. He stepped back against the wall on the level below her to avoid the confrontation, and she didn't notice him as she charged down to the second floor. Mere seconds behind her, he surreptitiously entered the floor and took in the scene. Instantly he analyzed the situation, and the angst in Flynn's body language and expression as she noticed him from her refuge behind the tray cart and acknowledged him with a nod.

He didn't have two good arms, but he did have something she didn't have—an idea of the general setup of the hospital. He'd been here several times before while visiting an old friend who was getting cancer treatments on this very floor. It had been a year or so since he'd been here, but it was a small hospital, and he felt confident there had been little change, if any, to the general layout. He made a motion to Flynn to wait, then turned and took the stairs back down to the first floor, ignored the guard who was yelling at him to return to the emergency room and get the boy, and headed for the second set of stairs that would come out behind where Adam Cary was holding Erin. He reached the stairway door and stopped, surprised to see a lit keypad by the door lock. He knew the stairs were used by doctors and hospital staff and were not meant for the general public, but they hadn't been locked before. He pulled on the door, just in case, but verified that the red light did indeed mean the door was firmly locked. He looked around desperately and saw the security guard approaching with Kevin in tow.

"Look, fella," he said testily. "I ain't no baby-sitting service. You've got to take the kid with you. And you should know better than to leave a weapon like this in the hands of a kid." He shook the rifle. "Hospitals are no place for guns, buddy. I can't do my job with you just leaving him—"

"I need your key card for the stairs," Derek demanded. "There's a man on the second floor holding a gun on a patient. I need to get up there to help."

The guard's eyebrows lifted. "Are you serious?"

"Is that my mom?" Kevin asked at the same time.

"Yes," Derek answered both questions at the same time.

"Well, I can't just give you—" the guard started.

He didn't get a chance to finish. The guard had the credit card–size badge attached to a re-tractable holder that snapped on his belt, and

Kevin noticed, yanked it off and thrust it into Derek's good right hand. "Save my mom!" Kevin pleaded.

The guard made a grab for the key card, but Kevin swiftly blocked the man and pushed him back. Once Derek had the card, he quickly used it to open the door, then pocketed it in case he needed it again.

The guard continued to protest, but Derek gave him a withering look, and the smaller man backed up and held up his hands. "I'm calling the police," the guard threatened with narrowed eyes.

"You do that, but keep an eye on the boy in the meantime," Derek said fiercely. "If anything happens to him, I'm coming after you next." He paused on the stairs. "And tell them to bring a body bag for the bad guy." He took one last moment to lock eyes with Kevin, and he gave the boy a reassuring smile. "Stay here. I promise I'll do everything I can to save her." He turned back to the stairs, letting the door close softly behind him.

Could he make it to the scene and do something—anything—to help Flynn before it was too late? His injured shoulder and arm were a problem. He couldn't shoot a rifle with one arm, and he didn't have any other weapon. Still, he had to try.

With his heart beating like a bass drum, he ran up the stairs.

Chapter Nineteen

Four bullets. Flynn checked the clip again, just to verify her ammunition. Yep. That's all she had left. Three in the magazine and one in the chamber. It would have to be enough.

"Let Erin go," she demanded, her tone firm as she called out to Cary. "Nobody's going to stop you if you try to walk out of here. She'll just slow you down."

"You're right nobody is going to stop me. This woman is my insurance plan. Now, everybody back up or I'll shoot her right here and now." Cary's voice was vicious and confident and held the air of authority that came from running a criminal enterprise and never having his orders questioned. He probably believed he would escape unscathed and his army of lawyers could fix any mess he left behind. His arrogance was irritating.

She heard Erin whimper and glanced around

the cart. Cary had pulled Erin even tighter against him and was moving toward her. Her mind reeled. How could she stop him without putting her sister's life in jeopardy?

Flynn knew one thing—Adam Cary was not leaving this hospital with Erin in tow. She made that decision, even though she still had no idea how she was going to stop him. If Cary managed to get Erin alone somewhere, her sister was as good as dead. He would surely kill her once she was no longer necessary for his escape. Flynn said a silent prayer, then took a deep, calming breath once she finished. God was with her. She could feel a peace invade her chest that hadn't been there moments before. *I will never leave thee nor forsake thee.* The Bible verse came instantly to mind and gave her another measure of peace. Unbidden, another verse also floated into her heart. *I can do all things through Christ which stregtheneth me.* She stepped out from behind the cart and pointed the gun at Adam Cary's head—at least the part of it she could see.

"I changed my mind. I am going to stop you. You're under arrest, Adam Cary, and you're not taking my sister anywhere." Her voice held all the steel she could muster.

She heard murmurs behind her from hospital staff, but she tuned everything out—everything except the eyes of the man holding her sister at gunpoint.

He smiled at her audacity. "I'm holding the life of your sister in my hand. Are you really going to challenge me?" His voice was filled with derision, as if he considered her threat completely inconsequential. He probably had good reason. He was a powerful man, with not only wealth at his disposal but also an arsenal of armed men that constituted his own private army. For all she knew, he had people just waiting to shoot her the moment she left the building. She thought back to the many men who had been chasing them over the last few days and the fate of Lee Clark. Yes, Adam Cary was undoubtedly very formidable and rarely got challenged. But this was her sister. Flynn would sacrifice whatever it took to free her from the man's grasp—even her own life.

Suddenly, several things happened in the blink of an eye. A loud bang sounded behind Cary and her sister, as if an entire computer cart had been upended and thrown across the floor. Within seconds of hearing the sound, Erin elbowed Cary hard when he took a distracted moment to turn and see what was going on behind him. As a result, he relaxed his hold on her neck, and she pulled against his arm, throwing him off balance.

That moment was all Flynn needed. She aimed, steadied her breathing and squeezed the trigger.

Time suddenly seemed to go into slow motion.

The bullet caught Adam Cary in the forehead, and his body was pushed back by the force of the blow. His arms fell away from his captive, and he crumpled to the floor, his gun landing on the ground and skittering away. Erin pushed away from him and took several steps away before leaning heavily on a small linen cart that was a few feet away. Her hospital gown was twisted around her legs, but she didn't seem to care as relief painted her features.

As Cary fell and Erin moved, Flynn could plainly see Derek standing behind them but to the side, safely out of the trajectory of her bullet.

Derek was in pain and injured and only had one arm he could use, but he had used what he could to cause the distraction she needed to gain the upper hand. He gave her a nod, then turned and disappeared back into the stairwell as she rushed forward and enveloped Erin in a bear hug.

"Oh, thank God!" Flynn said vehemently. "I'm so glad you're alive!"

"Ouch." Derek flinched a short time later as he sat on the edge of the bed in the emergency room where they'd taken him after the chaos had started to settle down. He'd immediately returned to the first floor and found Kevin, then brought the boy back up to his mother in her hospital room on the second floor. Flynn, Erin and Kevin had had a tearful reunion, and he had unobtrusively stepped back out, leaving the family to celebrate their survival. It had only taken Flynn a few minutes, though, to realize he had gone and to search and find him in the seats down by the nurses' station. She had enveloped him in the warmest hug he'd ever received and then walked him back to the emergency room for his exam. He would have made it there himself eventually, but exhaustion and relief had caught up to him first and he had taken a few minutes to just sit and regroup.

They had survived. Their journey was finally over. A prayer of thankfulness was in order, and he had done just that, right there by the elevators with Flynn in his arms.

It hadn't taken the police long to arrive, and in between medical exams, he and Flynn had explained the entire story, starting with the coordinates that Erin had discovered during her initial investigation and how they had flown up to see the site. Flynn had produced the SD card from her boot, and the detectives had taken it quickly, excited to see the photos that documented the murdered dealers and would undoubtedly bolster their case. They assured her that if the photos showed what she promised, they would have no problem using them to investigate the drug cartel and dismantle it piece by piece.

The doctor raised an eyebrow at Derek's complaint but made a slight adjustment. "You've had the local anesthesia. It should have numbed the area so I can stitch you up."

"I feel like a giant pincushion."

The doctor laughed. "You should be glad that we didn't have to surgically repair that shoulder."

"I'll take your word for it," Derek said as he winced again. "I hate hospitals."

"He's a big baby," Flynn laughed, and her

smile grew as Derek furrowed his brow, then winked at her.

"Let him stick a needle in you and see how you like it," Derek muttered, although his tone was playful and contradicted his stormy words. After X-rays and a thorough examination, the emergency room doctor had pulled out a suture kit and begun the work of closing the wound. Although Derek would need some physical therapy after the wound healed, the doctor was confident his patient would regain full use of his arm.

Flynn grabbed his good hand and gave it a squeeze, and then to Derek's surprise, she didn't let it go. She was touching him and not pulling away. "Thank you for causing that distraction in the hallway. I was worried about my aim. You gave me the extra help I needed." She pulled his hand up to her lips and brushed his knuckles against her lips, and he reveled at their softness. Had her feelings for him returned? He saw a glow in her eyes and hoped it was the same love that was slowly spreading and warming his chest. The doctor finished up, picked up his tray and let them know a nurse would be by soon to start the discharge process. Once they were alone, Derek took a chance, laying all his cards face up on the table. He met Flynn's eye and gave her a tender smile.

"You know, we've been through a lot the last couple of days. It's amazing how much a person can learn in just a short time."

She raised an eyebrow and quirked her lips. "Oh, really? And what have you learned?"

He tilted his head. "I've learned to put the past behind me, and that I need God in my life." He reached for her hand, squeezed her fingers, then released her. "I also need you." He took his good hand and gently cupped the back of her head and drew her near for a kiss. She came closer willingly, her hesitance slowly receding, and the kiss was soft and sweet and full of promise. When they finally drew apart, he pulled her close again into a bear hug embrace with his good arm. This time she didn't stiffen in his arms but instead molded against him. Holding her felt so right. He didn't want to ever let her go.

"I was so wrong to leave you after graduation—really, really wrong." He pulled back a bit, but only so he could see into her eyes. "Marry me, Flynn Denning? I love you with all my heart. I can't go on without you. Please say you'll be my wife."

Flynn took her hand and drew it slowly down his cheek, then kissed him again. It was even better than the first, and full of promise. "Yes, I'll marry you, Derek. I never stopped loving you. Never."

Epilogue

"And now, ladies and gentlemen, we'd like to award our three heroes a key to our wonderful town of Frisco, Colorado. As you know, the key to the city is a beloved symbol of civic recognition and gratitude, which is reserved for individuals whose service to the public and the common good rises to the highest level of achievement. Derek and Flynn King, and Kevin Wallace, are being awarded this key because of their outstanding work in putting the largest drug cartel in Colorado's history out of business. Not only is Frisco, Colorado, a safer city to live in today because of their efforts, but indeed, the entire state of Colorado has benefited from their work, and we thank them from the bottom of our hearts."

The mayor gave an award box to each of them, and they opened them together. Each had a golden key inscribed with their names and the date with *Frisco, Colorado*, embroidered into the box lining. They were beautiful awards but made Flynn a little uncomfortable. After all, they would have done their best to stop the drug dealers regardless and didn't need an award for their efforts. Still, the mayor and town council had been quite insistent, and she and Derek had finally acquiesced.

Flynn looked over at her sister, Erin, who was standing a few feet away, almost completely healed from her ordeal almost six months ago. During that time, she had shared everything she had discovered about Bear Creek Vacation Rentals with her team at the local police department. Due to her diligence and efforts, the photos that Flynn had managed to salvage, the driver's license of the other murder victim that Derek had saved and all their eyewitness testimony, the Frisco police had been able to cripple the drug cartel and make dozens of arrests. The mayor had wanted to give Erin a key to the city as well, but she had refused in no uncertain terms. She was a police officer, and weeding out crime was her duty. Besides, she claimed Flynn, Derek and Kevin had done the heavy lifting by actually finding the meth lab and escaping down the mountain to bring the drug dealers to justice.

Flynn smiled over at Derek and then slipped into his arms as the crowd slowly dispersed. He gave her a gentle squeeze, then took her hand. They had been married about two months ago and she couldn't be happier. It had been hard for her to learn to trust again, but after all the difficulties they'd faced together on the mountain, she had realized that being together with Derek was just where she wanted and needed to be. They had both welcomed God back into their lives, and over the past few months, they had grown closer and loved each other more than she ever thought possible.

She turned and smiled at Kevin, who had rushed over to his mom and was showing her his award. He was very proud of the golden key, as well he should be. He had lived with Flynn for about two months before the wedding, and she had been able to get him in with a Christian counselor, who had really been helping him sort through his feelings. Derek had also played a large role in the boy's healing as well and been spending quite a bit of quality time with him. The time Derek had spent had been cathartic for Derek as well, and she had been amazed to see the change in him around Kevin. Their relationship was exciting to witness as they helped each other grow.

She glanced over at her sister. Erin had been able to come home with the help of a home health aide, whose services had eventually become unnecessary as she had regained her strength. She was now almost back to one hundred percent and had returned to desk duty on the police force. She claimed she was ready to hit the streets again as soon as the doctors gave her a release, which she expected any day, but Flynn was glad Erin's superiors were taking it slowly. She knew Erin could handle herself, but she wanted her sister to be as strong as possible before going back onto regular duty.

"Pretty exciting day," Derek said softly as they walked hand in hand back toward their vehicle. "It sure is great the way you've been welcomed here in Frisco." He stopped for a minute so he could read her expression better. "What did you decide to do about the mayor's job offer?"

Flynn had given up her job in Florida when she'd moved to Colorado and married him, and although he was delighted and excited to have her sharing his life, he knew she had sacrificed a lot by leaving her job and friends behind. Thankfully, the governor had pulled some strings and gotten her a job offer from the local

Border Patrol office, but she hadn't officially accepted yet. Derek hadn't even realized the Border Patrol had a representative in the area, but if that's what Flynn wanted to do, then he would support her choice.

"I'm not sure yet," she murmured. "I'll probably end up taking it in nine months or so." She smiled and changed the subject. "I love the way you and Kevin have been doing so much together. Erin and I have both seen a huge improvement in his behavior, and it's largely due to your efforts. Thank you."

Derek shrugged. "He's a great kid. You know, I was always scared of being a father. That's the whole reason why I ran away to the army in the first place. But after getting to know Kevin, I've realized I don't have to be like my father. I think I would be a good dad someday."

Flynn leaned forward and kissed him. There was a sweet smile on her face that told him there was more to come, and he laughed. "What?"

"I'm just really glad to hear you say that," she said with a mischievous look in her eye. "I'm pregnant."

★ ★ ★ ★ ★